ABSOLUTE
SURRENDER

A FALLEN GUARDIAN NOVEL

GEORGIA LYN HUNTER

GENRE: PARANORMAL ROMANCE

This book is a work of fiction. Names, places, characters and incidents are either the product of the author's imagination or are used fictitiously. Any resemblance to actual people, living or dead, businesses, organizations, events or locales is entirely coincidental.

GLOSSARY

Absolute Laws: Forbids the mating between mortal and immortal. If broken, the couple is executed. These laws do not apply to demons.

Ancients: The mystical forces that watches over all realms.

Archangel: Michael: Leader of the Fallen Guardians (also referred to as "Arc." A term coined by Týr, and used by the others)

Ater: A place like Hell for dead, evil Empyreans.

Celestial Realm: Home to the divine angels.

Dark Realm: Where the species with dark souls dwell, along with other amorphous entities.

1. **Blood Demons:** A genus of demons that live on blood, but like the high of human blood.
2. **Demonii:** Demons who have consumed human souls, and in turn lose their natural dark souls. However, human souls fade within them, and they need to constantly replenish it with another. Human blood temporarily extends the life of the soul.
3. **Demons:** Supernatural beings with dark souls who resides in the Dark Realm.
4. **Otiums:** A species of demons, more docile in nature. Many of who escaped the tyranny of their realm to dwell on the human world. They usually live below the radar not keen to draw attention to themselves.
5. **Wyverns:** Seven-foot or taller lizard/dragon-like creatures.

Empyreans: They were created in the image of the divine angels but enjoy a more carnal life.

Elysium: Like the mortal Heaven, but where the dead Empyrean go to for eternity.

Fallen: Angels who fall and give up their wings and stronger abilities when they leave the Celestial Realm.

Fallen Guardians: A formidable group of fallen immortal warriors banished from their realm for past misdeeds. They swore their fealty to Gaia to protect humans from supernatural evil, and now reside on Earth. Some of whom are referred to by their pantheon's name.

Gaia: A powerful mystical Being who watches over Earth and mankind.

Nephilim: Half angel offspring born from human females and divine angels mating.

Others: A collective term for other supernatural beings, eg: gods, faes, vampires, etc.

Pantheons: Where the gods of various religions dwell.

Psionics: The human descendants of the Watchers. (All females)

Seraphim: The highest-level angels who oversees all things.

Sins: The Seven Deadly Sins, counterparts to the Ancients.

Tartarus: Where immortals are incarcerated.

Throne: Third level divine angels, created for war.

Urias: Spawned from Chaos, Creator of the Empyreans.

Watchers: Higher-level angels who were tasked to watch over fledgling mankind, but fell in love with mortal women.

Whitefire: A heavenly immortal flame that can

cause untold destruction. Used to destroy the wings and abilities of angels who fall.

***

Name pronunciation:
Aethan: A-thin
Týr: Tier
Blaéz: Blaze
Dagan: Day-gun
A'Damiel: Adam-iel (Damon)

***

Empyrean Wordlist:

Me'morae: my love
Me'seya: sweetheart

DEDICATION

To my wonderful parents, George and Ann.
You always believed in me and let me live my dream.

"One word frees us of all the weight and pain of life: that word is love."

~Sophocles

ABSOLUTE SURRENDER

Chapter 1

Death.

It was inevitable.

None could evade it.

The two scourges Aethan had been tracking had a few more moments to enjoy life. But their faint odor of sulfur was fast dissipating in the frigid night air.

In a burst of inhuman speed, Aethan left the crowded streets and cut through a dingy alley on the Lower East Side and pulled up short. Despite the stench of decay from the trash bags piled high on the side, the acrid reek of sulfur stung his heightened senses.

Eyes narrowing, he scanned the alley. There, in the shadows of the looming buildings, he found the two hauling a whimpering female along with them.

Demoniis were a damn menace, always drawn to a mortal's life force with a constant fix needed to sustain their decaying bodies.

Anticipation stirred. With edginess riding him, he

needed the fight.

Aethan strolled closer. "Let her go."

The pair swung around. Shades covered their eyes. The two men whipped off their sunglasses and their eerie red irises glowed in the dark.

Like that would frighten him.

The female took one look at them, then at Aethan and an ear-splitting shriek filled the alley. He couldn't blame her if she thought him one of those deadbeats. Dressed all in black, and with his intimidating height, he probably looked more like the killer he was than those two who had no doubt seduced her into leaving with their pretty-boy faces. Too bad for her, she'd chosen wrong.

The blond demonii punched her in the jaw, silencing her. Smirking, he grazed the unconscious female's neck with his fangs. "Back off, or I'll kill her."

They thought to threaten him? Not only did the fuckers gorge on souls, but also blood, judging by the length of their fangs.

"By the time you reach us, I'll have torn out her jugular," blond dickhead said. "There's little you can do, Guardian."

"Pity. How long would her soul sustain you?" Aethan asked. "Mine's better. Lasts longer, too." He held out his hands to show he was unharmed.

The demoniis' eyes slitted. He could see the wheels turning as they contemplated how fast they could kill him for the coveted prize. Dumb shits.

The dark-haired demonii's gaze lowered to Aethan's belt. "The dagger, throw it here. And anything else you have in your pockets."

With a shrug, Aethan tossed his obsidian dagger

Georgia Lyn Hunter

onto the dirt-encrusted asphalt near the demonii's feet. Then he emptied his pocket of a few sticks of gum.

The blond laughed, kicking the obsidian away. He flung the female aside, and they came at him like unleashed bullets. Dodging the attack, he lashed out, his fist connecting with a jaw. A roundhouse kick, and one of them crashed into a wall.

A fiery missile zinged past his face. He jumped back. Shit, too close. A hit by a demonii-bolt, and he might as well lie down and let them have his soul.

"Not so brave now, are you?" The dark-haired one advanced, sporting a macabre grin at how easily they'd cornered a Guardian. The scourge's hand moved in a wave, pilfering the earth of its natural energies and turning them into deadly bolts. The fuckers may have lost their abilities at their true death, but they still found a way to compensate.

Damn scourges. Too bad they didn't fight fair. He'd been quite prepared to extend their lives by a few more minutes. He willed his obsidian back to him, and in a move so fast, he nailed the dark-haired demonii in the chest. A raucous snarl filled the backstreet.

Aethan summoned the mystical weapon tattooed on his biceps. The thing shifted, a tingle running down his arm. He lunged after the blond as a six-foot-long obsidian sword took form in his hand. He spun around, the blade hissing in a deadly arc, and decapitated the demonii set on fleeing. The scourge disintegrated within moments. Just a thick, black, glutinous mess remained for a second before it, too, disappeared. He didn't bother looking for the wounded demonii, knowing he'd flashed out of the alley.

Aethan let his sword shimmer and settle back on his biceps. He picked up his dagger, and walked over to the brown-haired female lying on the ground. Crouching beside her, he examined her for injuries. She appeared to be fine, except for the light bruise on her jaw.

He scanned her for a psychic vibe. Nope. Nothing. Not even a hint of a spark. She didn't possess the *pyre and rime* abilities he'd been searching for the past few weeks. He'd hoped she was it and he could be done with this damn job. Scrubbing her memories of the last hour, he woke her and willed her on her way.

Brief flashes of lightning brightened the dismal alley, revealing the grimy walls. He rose and sheathed his dagger on his belt, and his shoulder twinged from the injury he'd sustained last night in another demonii fight.

He headed out of the alley and up the street. In the distance, opposite Club Anarchy, he spotted the familiar figure of his fellow Guardian. Týr's pale hair gleamed beneath the streetlight. The warrior might be easy on the eyes, but he was as lethal as the blade tattooed on his biceps.

Once a god from the Norse pantheon, Týr's virulent rage towards demons and their altered brethren, the demoniis, was all that kept his jets going. One couldn't blame him when he'd once been at their mercy, imprisoned in the deepest pits of Tartarus, for centuries. But judging by the way the females obstructed his path and the easy grin on his face, the warrior had found a way to ease his nightmares.

Unlike him. No matter how many demoniis Aethan took out in the name of protecting mortals, his nightmares never ceased. Just the thought of them and his shields fractured.

'A'than!' The childish whisper tore into his heart.

Georgia Lyn Hunter

He staggered to a halt, images flashing through his mind. The ground drenched with blood...*so much blood.*

Urias. He struggled to shut down the memories. But he could do little about the ache that bled through him, even centuries later. There was no off switch for that.

Inhaling a harsh breath, he pinched the bridge of his nose.

"You okay, man?"

Shit. No one should be able to creep up on him like that. He dropped his hand to find Týr beside him. "Yeah, fine." He ignored the hard stare Týr pinned him, and continued up the street. "Anything on the psychic female Michael wants found?"

At the mention of their latest job, Týr shoved his hands into the pockets of his leathers. "Enticing as they are, scanning all the females in this city for abilities of *pyre and rime* is not my idea of a good time."

"Yeah. Flat on their backs is more your thing."

"Not just that. Up against a wall, bent over...I'm flexible. Or they usually are." A smirk rode Týr's face. He stepped around a suspicious-looking puddle. "What's so important about a female possessing powers of fire and ice, anyway?"

"Can't say. Maybe he just wants to stop her from burning down the city."

"Michael's too tight-lipped when it comes to shit like this. Who the fuck are we gonna tell? The demons?"

Aethan shrugged. He really didn't care for the latest job dumped on them. Being among mortal females was not at the top of his to-do list. "He's probably trying to stop a prophecy or some such disaster. It's the first time he's thrown a job at us—"

"—without the ritual meet and greet," Týr finished, his eyes narrowing thoughtfully. "A prophecy? Damn! It would make sense, wouldn't it?"

Noisy laughter drew Aethan's attention to the line forming alongside the faded, graffiti-covered walls of Club Anarchy. This early in the night, the popular nightspot for mortals and demons teemed with revelers. Beneath the stench of garbage, the faint trace of sulfur drifted to him. He could easily follow the smell to its source, but since it led to the Otium demons waiting to get into the club, he didn't bother. Several of them chose to live among the humans now, preferring a quiet life—unlike their turned brethren, demoniis, who trawled clubs like these looking for their next prey.

"Humans," he muttered. "Can't understand their fascination with danger."

"Never understood them myself," Týr agreed. "But the females sure are one helluva temptation." He shot Aethan a shit-eating grin that didn't reach his eyes. "You called one to slake off that edge, yet? Just say the word, and I'll cover your patrol."

"I'm fine."

"Yeah, *rrright*."

Aethan bit back a retort. He didn't need a reminder of how close to the edge he was and, worse, that Týr noticed. While he now had total control over his powers, the same couldn't be said of the restlessness pushing at him. The damn feeling had plagued him for days. He had no idea what the hell it was.

Reaching into his coat pockets, he realized he'd thrown his gum away. *Damn.* He rolled his taut shoulders, the ache flaring up again. The fight earlier

Georgia Lyn Hunter

had done little to ease the power roiling beneath his skin. A constant reminder of why he could never escape what he was. A crack in his psychic shields, and he'd not only flatten the entire island of Manhattan but take every single life with it. Not something he cared to think of.

"I don't get you, Empyrean." Týr pulled a pack of M&M's from his jacket pocket and poured several into his palm. He sorted through the colors. "What's wrong with being with a human? Find a female. Get that power level down to green. It's a helluva lot more fun than running your feet to stumps."

Perhaps. But another faceless person? Another bout of empty sex? His belly churned at the thought. He'd rather have stumps.

A limousine cruised to a halt in front of the club. The doors opened to a dissonance of voices, music, and laughter. Males and females stumbled from the car, and the sharp whiff of illegal dust floated to him.

Týr popped several of the yellow candies into his mouth, his attention on the noisy humans. "They make it so easy for trawling demoniis to hunt them."

Aethan turned away, only to find a female obstructing his path.

His gaze skimmed over her. She was an incitement for dark pleasures, all right. Big breasts covered in a leather Band-Aid were teamed with a crotch-short skirt beneath her long coat. Long red hair fell around her face in wanton disarray. A seductive smile tilted her mouth. Heavy on the cosmetics, her hot blue eyes swept over him with avid interest.

"Can't hide that angelic shit, after all." Týr's annoying murmur rang in his ear. The bastard was enjoying this.

Being an Empyrean, Aethan could do nothing about the way he looked. But if any of the angelic allure his race was born with leaked out, the humans would be unable to resist the pull—the very thought had him tightening his psychic shields. He was the farthest thing from the humans' concept of an angel. Hell, he didn't even have wings, so why was he cursed with this crap?

"I'll tell you a secret." The female raised her sultry peepers at him. "I can see the future. It's your lucky night, handsome." Her husky voice dropped an octave. She stepped closer and slowly ran her hand down his chest. Her gaze wandered to the grinning son of a bitch next to him, and her smile grew. "Or we could *all* go someplace else..."

Aethan ignored her scent of lust, his jaw hard. Still, he scanned her for a psychic vibe, and found nothing.

"Trust me, you don't want me." *Not unless you have a death wish.*

He peeled her hand off his coat and stepped around her. Her gasp of disbelief that he'd turned her down followed him as he headed up the street. These females had no idea how dangerous he was. They might as well stick their finger in a live socket if they thought *he* could give them what they desired.

"You're one stubborn bastard." Týr's laughter drifted to him. "Me, I'll take the pleasurable way out." He cast a quick look back at the redhead. "Would've been something, nailing her. She was game to be tag-teamed, too. Hell, shield in that cursed power of yours if you're afraid of hurting her, and we'll all be good to go. But you're just too selfish to share."

Afraid of hurting her? Týr had no idea what he

Georgia Lyn Hunter

was capable of—why he could never take a human as a lover. And his possessive nature was his own damn business.

Aethan rolled his injured shoulder again, easing the tightness, and paused. A group of teen thugs with pierced lips stepped into their path, aggression oozing from their pores.

Eyes cool, he returned their stares.

"Sure you want to take us on?" Týr calmly exchanged the M&M's for his obsidian dagger. At the sight of the wicked looking blade, the teens' heads dropped and they scurried away like rats. "Annoying little punks," Týr muttered, re-sheathing his dagger. "So, you gonna go see Lila?"

"Why would I?"

"Stop messin' around, man. Go see Lila and get that damn shoulder fixed. You can't leave something that dangerous untreated—"

"I'm good."

"Well, then... Good to know." Týr slapped him on the shoulder. Hard.

"*Godsdammit*!" Aethan expelled a harsh breath at the pain blazing through him. "I should incinerate your damn ass!"

Despite their quick healing abilities, lesions caused by demonii-bolts weren't so easy to cure. Lila, an Oracle from the Village, was the only one who could treat those wounds with her potions that drained the evil taint out of them.

Týr laughed and shook his head. Taking a black beanie out of his jacket pocket, he pulled it over his pale hair. "Go see Lila, man, or you're gonna be a direct fucking GPS for the demonii shitheads—" He broke off, his eyes narrowing. "We have company."

With his heightened senses, Aethan felt the brush of ice against his skin. He could smell the familiar strain of rotting evil that surrounded the wounded demonii who'd escaped him earlier.

Time to end this. "This one's mine. Later."

He headed for a recessed doorway and dematerialized.

***

Echo Carter wrapped her arms around her waist and paced along the top step in front of the well-lit cathedral, trying to keep warm while she waited for Kira. The chilly sea breeze stung her nostrils as she debated going back to her car and cranking up the heater to full blast. But being trapped in the vehicle for a half hour? Ugh. She far preferred the cold. It helped ease the dull ache in her temples.

Her head still felt heavy and fuzzy from her restless night. Dreams she didn't want to remember throbbed in her mind, so she concentrated on a tugboat gliding over the ominous waters of the East River. A streak of lightning raced across the dark skies, briefly enveloping everything in a portentous silver light.

The night wind stole under her denim jacket and beneath her sweater like an icy caress. She buttoned up the front and slid her hands into her pockets. Her fingers wrapped around the two stones she carried around like talismans, their warmth seeping into her. But it wasn't enough. She seriously needed a distraction to clear her head and rid her body of the chill.

Her cell beeped. Eagerly, she retrieved the phone from her pocket and sat on her backpack, avoiding the cold cement step, only to find it was a text from Damon.

Away on business. Get Kira to stay with you. You know why. Call if you need me.

P.S. Don't do anything stupid.

She snorted. Everyone had bad dreams. It didn't mean she needed a babysitter. Damon's postscripts, however, never changed, even if his messages did. The way her guardian hovered, you'd think she was thirteen instead of twenty-three and living on her own.

But she couldn't blame him. All that mattered to her was finding Tamsyn's killer and ending the son of a bitch. That had to be the *stupid* thing Damon worried about. She rolled her eyes.

A man, rushing past her, snagged her attention. Echo watched him skid to a halt. Above average height, this one embodied the perfect male, with bronzed skin, dark, wavy hair, and a sculptured jaw. Black shades covered his eyes.

He made a U-turn, giving her a closed mouthed smile. Well now, she *had* asked for a distraction. Sliding the phone back into her pocket, she rose to her feet. She'd deal with this before Kira got back, and she knew the perfect spot for this little rendezvous. With a casual, seductive sway of her hips, she tossed him a sultry look over her shoulder and glided toward the back of the cathedral.

He followed.

Of course he'd follow. They always did.

She popped her jacket buttons free as she rounded the rear of the building and headed for the alcove where the statue of an angel with massive wings stood. He grabbed her from behind and slammed her against the cathedral wall. She sucked in a breath, pain jarring up her arm to her shoulder. She twisted around. The acrid stink of sulfur flooded her nostrils. Bile rushed to her throat, telling her exactly what this thing was.

"Ah, little mortal. So good of you to choose this place—" He stopped, confusion flickering across his face, frowned, and leaned in to sniff her.

Oh, yeah, her cursed pheromones always worked in her favor. They threw them off track and gave her the crucial edge she needed. But the black sludge that coated her hands as she held him off warned her this one had been wounded.

"You smell different. Must taste." His tone slurred. Something wet and rough slithered along her neck. *Crap!* The slimy saliva on her skin sent a shudder of revulsion through her. But she didn't let that distract her. Once his foul-breathed mouth claimed hers, life as she knew it would be over.

Nope, not happening. She had no plans to die at the hands of this fiend.

"Pity I have to cut our fun short." His face cracked into a menacing smile to reveal pointy canines. "Your light's mine."

That's what he thought.

"If you want it, come and claim it." The familiar words rolled out of her mouth. Darn, she had to stop watching *The Lord of the Rings*. But Aragorn was so—

Argh, kill first, then think about the sexy Aragorn—she kneed the demonii hard in the crotch, breaking his hold. Spinning around, she kicked out her leg in a fast sweep, knocking his feet out from under him. He stumbled to the ground. About to go in for what would have been a routine kill, the demonii sprang up. He flung his shades aside. Eerily red eyes flamed with fury.

"I'll drain every drop of your blood before I rip out your soul!"

"Promises—promises," she taunted.

He came at her. Echo palmed her dagger and met him head-on. She went in low and rammed the blade into his sternum. The demonii fell to his knees, eyes widening in surprise.

"Didn't see that one coming, did ya?" Vengeance burned in her as she grabbed him by the hair and slashed his exposed throat, severing the carotid artery. Blood, black and thick, gushed out.

Her breathing harsh, she let the body fall to the ground. Disappointment burned through her. This fiend hadn't killed Tamsyn. The stink of the sulfur now coating her skin lacked the coppery, sweet odor of vanilla she was after. No matter. It meant one less evil fiend roaming the streets and robbing the innocents of their souls.

The body decomposed and vanished within seconds. No sign remained that the demonii had ever existed. The oily ooze on her dagger had disappeared, too, when a frisson shot through her. The tiny hairs on the back of her neck rose in warning. *Oh, hell. More of them.*

Survival mode on high alert, Echo whipped around in a defensive strike and met steel with steel. The metallic sound reverberated through the cathedral's garden. The sheer power of the blow vibrated up her hand to her injured shoulder. Pain streaked through her but didn't slow her down.

She attacked. He countered.

This one was too strong, too canny. She lunged at him, but he grabbed her in a move that made her head spin and imprisoned her in an ironclad grip against a wall of muscles. It took her a second to realize the stranger had no intention of disarming or hurting her. He merely shielded himself from *her* attack.

Irritated, she glared up. The impact of the man facing her over their crossed daggers hit her like a blow to the stomach. She stumbled back, dragging in lungfuls of air. Wild as rainstorms and earthy as sin, his scent crowded her. She blinked, sure the vision before her was a fantasy induced by her sleep-starved brain.

He was so tall, he had to be at least six-seven or more. His long, black coat parted to reveal muscular, leather-covered legs. All that black he wore was the perfect backdrop for a wickedly handsome face. The hard, sensual curve of his lips and that focused way he studied her told her he would know every carnal pleasure there was.

A tiny shiver of awareness darted up her spine, but she brutally clamped it down.

The chilly breeze tossed back strands of his long hair to reveal the glitter of small silver hoops in his ears. But his hair—she'd never seen anything like it. It was as if nature had stroked it with every shade of the blue spectrum then laid a careless dash of ebony between those strands.

The air around him shifted. Power rolled off him in aggressive waves. But his eyes held her spellbound—gunmetal gray irises took on streaks of white—a caveat, a warning not to attack him again.

Echo tightened her grip on the dagger, her gaze fixed on the stranger who radiated menace, her stance ready for a fight.

Oh, Mr. Goth-man could send out all the signals he liked. She wasn't easy to intimidate.

Georgia Lyn Hunter

"Who the hell are you?" she snapped.

Chapter 2

"I'm not going to hurt you."

The cadence of his voice startled Echo. Like a low rumble of thunder, it caressed her senses. A flash of heat zipped through her veins. Was he trying to seduce her into giving him whatever it was he wanted? It sure as hell was close to working.

She stared pointedly at the obsidian dagger he held. "Yeah, right."

An odd stillness seemed to come over him at her words. Then he relaxed and sheathed the blade in his belt.

Was she supposed to do the same? Too bad for him. She waved him off with her dagger. "Good. Now, get out of my way."

There was a slight shift in those cool gray depths. Irritation? Amusement? She couldn't be sure, not when his expression had all the flexibility of granite.

He nodded to the spot where she'd killed the demonii. "We need to talk about that."

Echo arched a brow. Seriously? She didn't care

how sexy that lightly accented voice of his was. If he thought for a second she was going to tell him how she saw demoniis, or how she killed the fiends, he was doomed for disappointment. People already thought her strange. And for some insane reason she didn't want him to think so, too.

"Not happening." She stepped around him, passed a stone bench, and was sheathing her dagger when he grasped her denim-clad arm. His touch sent a jolt to her system, unsettling her.

"That wasn't a request."

"I don't care. Now unhand me."

Ignoring her demands, his dark eyes skimmed over her face. "It must be a mortal trait, to delve into things best left alone."

"Mortal trait?" Indignation surging through her, she shoved away from him and knocked into something hard. Too late, she recalled the bench. Only her agile reflexes kept her from tipping over and landing on her backside. And the fact that he grabbed her arm. She yanked free and drew in a steadying breath, only to breathe in his wild, cool scent again.

Her eyes rushed to his. He was too close. She couldn't move, not unless she wanted to crawl up him. Tempting as that was, it wasn't a good idea. Not when her hormones were shooting down her common sense and waving a white flag in surrender.

In a move born out of pure self-preservation, she leaped onto the stone bench to put some distance between them. Only to find herself trapped on the seat with trees around her and him in the front.

"And you have a temper to match."

That's it! Her fist clenched. She took a swing.

Faster than a freaking rattlesnake, he grasped her

wrist, his grip gentle despite the unbreakable hold. "I wouldn't if I were you. Hitting me will gain you more than you bargained for. Trust me, you don't want that."

Echo counted to ten, but that relaxing crap never worked with her. It took a moment longer before she could force herself to unclench her fist.

"Good."

At his murmured approval, she tugged her arm free; his touch increasing her uneasiness. But his words disturbed her on an inherent level. As did his dark stare.

Hitting me will gain you more than you bargained for.

What the hell did that even mean? He had her thinking of rumpled sheets, the slide of his gorgeous tawny skin against hers—

She'd finally lost her mind.

This was not good. Not good at all.

Uneasy, Echo stuck her hands in her jacket pockets. The moment she touched the stones, calmness seeped through her, as did the futility of her actions.

Why did she hop up onto this dumb bench? Now she was stuck on the thing, eye-to-eye with this maddening, beautiful man who was making her act like an idiot.

***

Aethan was struck stupid.

It had to be the damn lightning bolts zipping overhead that short-circuited his brain, he decided, studying the female in front of him.

Short, choppy hair, black as a raven's wing, stood out in all directions. Long wisps fell into her annoyed brown eyes. It was the worst haircut he'd ever seen on a female, yet it suited her angular, honey-gold features—her tan skin tone indicative of her mixed-race heritage.

At his perusal, her lush mouth compressed in annoyance.

For a brief second, he experienced an extraordinary urge to taste her. Instead, he brushed his knuckles across the shallow dent in her chin. Her eyes widened in shock.

Gods. He reeled back in unexpected desire and dropped his hand. Not many caught him unawares, especially not a prickly human. She had to be the one who'd ended the demonii. He must've been only a few minutes behind the bastard, and *she'd* taken him down—killed him. What the hell was she thinking? One misstep and the demonii could've ended her.

He ran his eyes over her jeans covered legs, ending at scuffed leather boots. The deep red sweater she wore beneath her denim jacket did little to hide her feminine curves. She was too fragile to be involved in this dangerous pastime. Someone needed to point out the risks of her reckless activity. And he was more than willing.

Aethan closed the space between them, and her subtle scent of sun-ripened berries invaded his nose, intoxicating him. Hurriedly, she stepped back, but trapped on the stone bench with the shrubs behind her, she had nowhere to run. She settled for slaying him with her eyes.

Like that would work.

"Your little hobby will only land you in trouble."

"I have no idea what you're talking about." With an impatient hand, she brushed the hair out of her eyes to reveal a star-shaped scar above her left brow.

So she didn't want to talk?

"Okay, we'll do this your way. Whenever you're ready." He folded his arms and waited, ignoring the pull of the wound on his shoulder. He could read nothing off her mind. Her thoughts were walled up behind pure steel. It didn't matter because none could play the waiting game like he could. Besides, he usually got what he wanted.

"You can't keep me here against my will."

"I'm not. You chose to stand up there. I just want answers."

A low, frustrated growl left her.

She made him want to smile.

Nothing in his long life had prepared him for the sensations crowding him. Blood buzzed in his veins and rushed to his head as he faced a female who affected him like no other ever had. He knew he was on a headlong collision with disaster, and yet he remained. Intrigued. Challenged by her.

The wind picked up, rustling the fallen leaves around them, and whipped at her hair. Brown eyes glittered in irritation. Something about her eyes caught his attention, but before he could determine what it was, she turned away.

"You killed someone," he told her.

"Yeah? Prove it. Besides, what are you, the Goth Cop?" She leaped off the bench and brushed past him, leaving behind a trail of her heady scent.

Goth Cop? That stumped him for a second. Then reality surged through him. *Urias.* What the hell was he doing, playing her game? If she was the female they searched for, he'd have to find out what her abilities were. With her snippy attitude, he'd have as much luck

Georgia Lyn Hunter

getting her to admit to that as he'd had getting her to reveal how she killed the demonii. Not many humans could take down those fuckers, especially not a fragile female.

His mind back on the job, he went after her and deliberately brushed up against her back. She wheeled around, glared at him in exasperation, then stalked off, mumbling something about wretched pheromones being the bane of her life.

Aethan offered no apology for his actions. He got what he wanted; his fingers tightened around her weapon. If this was the only way to get her to talk, so be it.

"Answer a few questions and I won't bother you again."

"Yeah, yeah. We all have dreams, doesn't mean we get what we want—"

He flipped her dagger into the air. Her mouth dropped open. The shock on her face made his day. He spun the blade again. "Tell me about this."

Her belligerent attitude skyrocketed. "You—you stole that!"

"Semantics. I'm waiting."

That seductive mouth flattened, her gaze pinned on the blade. He knew better than to get too close and give her a chance to nab the thing from him.

"This is New York. I'm not stupid enough to schlep around unprotected," she retorted. Her hand shot out, and she snapped her fingers. "I want my dagger back."

"This is sharp. You could hurt yourself." He deliberately ran a finger over the blade's edge and had the pleasure of witnessing her irritation increase. A furious glower flayed him, before she stomped off to the front of the cathedral.

He followed, amusement riding him. Slipping her blade into his coat pocket, he watched as she chased off a tabby cat pawing through her bag. Then, just to see those eyes spark again, he moved closer. Hastily, she straightened and collided with him. A muffled gasp of pain escaped her.

Two things registered as he caught her: she was hurt and he had a damn hard-on.

Him and his dumbass ideas.

***

Echo struggled to breathe. The discomfort in her shoulder barely registered as a wave of pure need awakened her body. Every inch of his rock-hard physique was aligned against hers.

The man was like coiled steel beneath her hands. An invitation she couldn't resist. She stroked his broad chest. His fault entirely, she decided, for being so damn hot and tempting.

He shifted, and her lungs seized at the hardness pressing against her stomach.

Uh-oh! Her eyes flew to his.

"Are you hurt?" Concern crossed his face. He didn't seem in the least bit bothered by his body's reaction to her. Or the fact that she was aware of it.

"I'm fine." It surprised her that she was still capable of speech. The molten intensity in his white-flecked gray eyes disturbed her. Need twisted her insides, but reality smacked her upside the head. How could she be this stupid? Men followed her for one reason only.

Stupid, cursed pheromones.

Georgia Lyn Hunter

She pushed away from him. His hard-on was just a reaction to her pheromones. Disappointment slid into her tummy like a lead ball. She'd drunk the foul-tasting suppressant potion Gran made for her without fail, so why the hell couldn't she ever get an honest response from a guy?

"Look," she said, "I don't know who you are. Just be glad there's one less of those things in the world."

The heat in his gaze flickered out. Something dark and lethal slid into those gray depths. "What things?"

"Demoniis, all right? Now give me back my blade."

His expression changed to one full of menace. It made her wary. "You are *not* to hunt them."

"Fine." Whatever. She held out her hand for her weapon.

At her easy capitulation, he continued to stare at her, making no move to return her blade. Okay, so she'd lied. She simply didn't care to get into an argument over a decision she'd made years ago. She'd find the fiend who killed her friend, and no one would stop her. No matter how good-looking he was.

"How did you kill the demonii? They're not easy to take down."

"What are you?" she asked instead, searching his face as if she could find her answers there.

"The Goth Cop."

"Ha, ha." Damn man thought he was so funny. Mr. Invincible had to be a demonii hunter. They certainly were an arrogant lot. It was the only thing that made sense, considering his interest in how she killed the fiends.

"How did you kill the demonii?" he repeated.

She smirked. "What can I say? I'm that good."

***

Gods, but she had a mouth on her. One he desperately wanted to taste.

Aethan shoved his hands in his pockets and encountered her blade.

Hauling himself out of his lust-filled haze, he opened his mind to hers, which he should have done from the get-go. He waited a heartbeat. *There.* He picked up the slight vibrations of her psychic powers just as an odd sensation hummed through him. A light, sparkling touch of her essence brushed up against his. Stunned, he slammed his shields shut. His heart pounding hard against his ribs, he tried to forget the intimate, iridescent caress of her energy.

She wasn't the female they searched for. Definitely no *pyre and rime* in her. An unexpected rush of relief flooded him. "You're psychic, though not a strong one."

"Jeez, thanks for the newsflash." She rolled her eyes, picked up her backpack, and tried to walk around him.

"I'm not done." He stepped in her path. "You need to start explaining."

"Oh, bite me!"

A hell of a provocation that set him off. He yanked her forward, ignoring her gasp of outrage, and bit her. Coherent thoughts flew out of his head the moment his mouth clamped down on her neck. Her enticing warmth and the fragrant taste of her skin coated his tongue and scattered his senses.

For a moment, she remained utterly still, most likely from the shock, before she started struggling. He

Georgia Lyn Hunter

tightened his grip on her waist, and a delicious friction built between them. Her heart pounded against his chest like a drum roll. He licked her slowly over the bruised skin.

She shoved at him, a flush streaking her cheekbones. "Are you crazy?"

Probably. "No. Just gave you what you asked for. Prepared to talk, or do we go for round two? I'm game. Are you?" He dropped his hands to her hips, keeping their lower bodies connected.

"All right." She scowled. "I see them."

He let her go, stepped back, and shoved his hands into his pockets, away from the temptation of her. As ideas went, this was a really bad one, because he was so damn hard, his leathers chafed against his arousal.

"I can see auras. Demons are red—a pulsing red for the soul-eating fiends! It's how I know." Then she snatched her fallen backpack and sped off for the cathedral entrance as if hellhounds were after her.

Aethan watched her go.

Dammit! He rubbed his jaw. Had he completely lost his fucking mind? Indulgence in a fantasy wasn't something he could afford, especially not with a human. Gritting down on whatever the hell had gotten hold of him, he crushed the compelling need to go after her. And took off for the far side of the cathedral and dematerialized.

***

Echo stepped inside the cathedral for the first time since she'd been in foster care. She leaned against the stone wall in the dim entrance, a hand pressed to the side of her neck.

This should've been a run-of-the-mill kill. Instead, she'd gotten entangled with a man unlike any she'd ever met.

She could still feel the glide of his lips, the sharp sting of his teeth, and the lick of his tongue on her skin. Desire flared awake. Crap. Exhaling roughly, she slipped her hand into her jacket pocket and pulled out *his* obsidian dagger. Satisfaction spilled through her.

He'd soon find out that what he'd stolen from her, she'd now replaced. Taking his dagger had been too easy. When she fell against him, even distracted as she'd been by his hot body, she'd made sure to nip the weapon off him. A quick sleight of hand and she'd slipped it into her pocket.

The smooth black metal of the hilt fitted her palm as if made for her. The etching on the guard formed a swirling pattern. She traced a finger over the design, and the obsidian blade began to glow, a deep amber taking over the black. Warmth invaded her palm before the light faded.

How odd.

She examined the blade up close. No light. Nothing. Just the dull glint of cool obsidian. At the sound of light footsteps hitting the tiled surface, she slipped the dagger into her backpack and smiled at the tall, curvy redhead hurrying toward her.

Kira Smith was one of the few people she called a friend. They'd been an unlikely pair ever since they'd met over ten years ago. Kira was vivacious and outgoing, while Echo had been a withdrawn street kid. But their relationship worked and had strengthened over the years.

"Echo, you're inside?" Kira's shock gave way to a relieved grin, displaying two perfect dimples in her face, her skin the color of a rich latte. "I don't care what made you change your mind, I'm just glad you did." She gave Echo a quick hug.

"I thought about what you said, about letting go. Tamsyn's gone." The excuse came out of nowhere as she pushed aside her strange encounter with the sexy Goth.

"You're gonna come to church now?"

Echo exhaled in resignation, guilt flooding her. The only reason she'd even entered a church again was because she ran from a man. Now, she was trapped by her friend's happy expression in a place she'd avoided for over a decade. "Yeah, okay. But not to service, Ki. Only when you do the candle thing on Sundays."

"Guess it's better than nothing." Kira's smile turned sad. "Echo, Tamsyn was my friend, too, and I miss her just as much."

"She shouldn't have died. I should never have left her alone in that alley." Pain filled her at the memory.

"Then you would have died, too," Kira said quietly. "You couldn't predict those demoniis stalking you both. It was fate."

"Fate? If you believe in that crap, it'll mess with your head. We pave our own path in life. *We* fight for what we want, and that's not fate."

"You're far too melancholy." Kira sighed. "Come on, let's get out of here. What shall we watch tonight? A *LOTR* marathon? You like Aragorn," she teased.

"Oh, God!" Echo choked back a wry laugh, thinking of the demonii she killed earlier. And for some reason the Goth took up space in her mind again. "Let's try something else. I'm quoting lines now."

Chapter 3

Twilight crept over the Guardian's island estate off Manhasset Bay on Long Island Sound. Mist floated around the tall, dark trees and drifted into the clearing. The wet scent of brine and green woodland surrounded Aethan as he scanned the area for his target. Sweat dripped down his face, the chilly air doing little to cool him.

He studied the swirling miasma, tracking the shadowy movement within. The figure drew closer. Aethan knew better than to lose eye contact with the crafty warrior.

Short, black hair plastered to his skull, Blaéz watched him like a rabid wolf. The Celtic ex-god made no move to get back in the game but persisted in skirting around him. With his precog ability, the bastard probably knew Aethan's moves.

Dragging in a deep breath, Aethan balled his fingers, his knuckles bruised to the bone. Weapon-free combat was a pain in the ass, but it eased some of his edginess. Good thing Blaéz preferred hands-on fighting.

Through the haze, Aethan saw the shimmer on the warrior's thick biceps. *Fuck!* Blaéz just had to go and do that. Use the one weapon none of the Guardians would summon without cause. The Sword of Gaia always remained in the form of a tattoo, unless they were on the hunt for demoniis.

Aethan summoned his own. No way would he let the Celt crow over this.

Instead of smoothly gliding off his flesh to shimmer and take form in his hand like usual, the weapon tore out of his skin. Aethan gritted his teeth. The pain just about brought him to his knees.

Blaéz came flying through the air, attacking with the deadly mystical sword.

Shit! Aethan leaped back and blocked. The power of the blow reverberating up his arm, he swung around and struck. Blaéz easily countered. The sound of the clanging swords echoed in the forest as they dueled.

Hours later, Aethan wiped the sweat off his brow with the back of his hand. Dammit, he needed a break. His straining muscles started to knot in protest. He'd worked up a thirst, too, and could drink the freakin' Nile dry, if only the clueless bastard would call it quits.

Blaéz didn't know the meaning of the word *rest*. He could go on for days, if Aethan would let him. The hardhead couldn't feel tired or any emotion for that matter. Never had since he lost his soul. Except for pain—the reason why he summoned the sword.

But Aethan had had enough. The Celt could go fight the damn trees for all he cared. He willed his sword back onto his biceps and dematerialized to the castle, taking form inside the huge, underground gymnasium in a shimmer of bright sparks. Here, away from humans, he didn't bother to tone down his true color.

The enormous facility was nearly bare and protected by arcane magic against the Guardians' powers. Concealed lights were embedded in the high ceiling. White walls flowed around him and light gray tiles ran the length of the floor. On the far end, an array of swords was displayed in a stand next to a fridge. As Aethan headed over, Blaéz flashed in front of him.

"Hell, man, Blaéz—time out."

"Scared?"

Aethan grabbed a katana from the reserves. No fucking way was he summoning his sword again. He came in hard, his sudden thrust sending Blaéz tripping and sliding on his ass some distance away. The Celt's tattered tee hung by its seams, and blood welled from the new wound on his chest, dripping down his abs. His eyes narrowed as he sprang up. Grabbing the neckline of his shirt, he ripped it apart and threw it aside. "That was my favorite."

Aethan shrugged. "It's black, like everything else you—"

A shift in the air caught his attention. Power of unparalleled force surrounded the castle. The brief distraction cost Aethan. His sword, snatched from his hand, went sailing through the air. Blaéz caught the katana and attacked.

Aethan evaded a swing guaranteed to detach his head from his body.

Godsdammit! Didn't the crazy bastard ever give up?

"What do you know—he *can* get excited," Týr drawled, strolling into the gymnasium. "Empyrean, think it's you who's got the Celt hot under the collar?"

Aethan stilled. It was time Blaéz found a new target. And the Norse's irritating yapping made the choice so easy. He changed direction and charged at Týr, catching the katana Blaéz tossed back at him.

Týr flashed and snatched a sword from the backups, and deflected their powered strikes. Grinning, he disappeared out of the gym and into the weight room. They followed.

"Now, now," Týr chastised. "You both have to stop chasing after me. I don't swing that way—"

Aethan struck from the front. Blaéz came in from the side. The meeting of steel reverberated off the walls.

Týr grunted, skidding back as his sword fell. He didn't seem to care that two deadly blades were pressed against his throat. Aethan stepped away, his objective achieved. He headed for the fridge and snagged a bottle of water.

"Cheating now, Celt? Well then." A flame burst out of Týr's palm. He rolled the fire in his hand as one would a tennis ball. "I think you need a tan. You look like the Ghost of Christmas Past."

Chest heaving, Blaéz didn't respond. His winter-blue eyes were placid lakes of ice and all the more dangerous for it. "You owe me a fight."

Týr snorted.

"My lords?" A low voice rumbled through the gym.

Aethan turned and saw Hedori standing in the doorway. His steel-colored hair pulled into a single braid lay down his back, his expression in its usual impassive lines. The male who'd followed him from Empyrea eons ago had once been his bodyguard and now acted as butler.

"Yes, Hedori?"

"The Archangel's here."

They didn't need the warning, having already sensed their leader, but Hedori insisted on announcing his arrival.

The flame Týr had been rolling in his palm snapped back into his body at the news. "I'd hoped that shift in the air was Armageddon happening or something equally delightful. Shit's about to fly. Time to haul out the heavy-duty shovels."

Týr was right. It was never a good thing when Michael showed up. It just meant more crappy jobs were about to be heaped on them.

Aethan twisted the cap and took a deep swallow of his water.

The sharp glacial scent flooded the room. Cursing, Aethan clamped down his shields against the draw. Couldn't Michael just tone down the angelic allure?

"Thanks, Hedori, for announcing my arrival. Hearing delightful words of welcome makes my day," Michael drawled as he strode into the weight room.

Hedori bowed and left the room.

Taller than most immortals, with thick muscular arms, Michael let his black hair hang wild and free around massive shoulders. Dark shades covered his eyes, his tanned face set in foreboding lines. At six-foot-nine, the Archangel was a helluva sight, even without wings.

"Cut it out, Michael," Aethan muttered. "If the humans get a whiff of that stuff… Unless you want the chaos?"

Instantly, the fragrance disappeared, and Aethan snorted.

Michael glanced around the place. "It's been a

while. Good to see all's in one piece and the castle still stands."

Týr smirked. "So, what's doing, Arc?"

Michael turned to them. "There's been a spike of activity on the psychic planes, which is of concern to the Celestial Realm. It correlates to another smaller one that occurred several years ago."

And there it was, the reason for Michael's sudden arrival. The last contact, several weeks ago, with orders to find the psychic female, had been through a phone call. And it meant this one couldn't be put on hold. Restlessness started to creep back into Aethan, despite the punishing training hours earlier. Now, he itched to head out and find a real fight. But that wasn't happening until this meeting was over.

Setting the water bottle aside, Aethan took a soft cloth from the supplies stored near the lockers, sat astride an exercise bench, and began to wipe his sword. As long as the psychic spike didn't concern this realm, he cared less about it happening in others.

"Why should we care?" Týr asked. He opened his locker and pulled out a change of clothes. "Celestial problems are the angels' deal."

"Not this one," Michael said, his expression grim. "A prophecy has come to pass. A mortal of Zarias's bloodline has awakened and is the reason for the increase in demonii activity."

Aethan paused in cleaning his blade. "Demoniis look for the same female we search for—the psychic one?"

"Yes. Did you find any with even a spark of *pyre and rime*?"

"Nothing," Týr said. Stripping off his clothes, he pulled on sweats and a tee.

"Same," Blaéz added.

The image of honey-kissed skin, annoyed brown eyes, and a lush mouth compressed in irritation flashed through Aethan's mind. Dammit. He shut off the vision and met the Archangel's stare. Shrugged. "No."

He wasn't about to confess crap to anyone at how a mortal affected him. The taste of her was like a drug to his senses. He shifted on the bench, rattled by how easily that damn part of him he had no control over hardened at the mere thought of her.

"Not what I was hoping to hear," Michael said. "We have to find her fast. The demons may not have the actual prophecy, but they are aware of its existence. They will use anyone, do anything to get to her."

"How can you be sure that particular prophecy has begun?" Blaéz asked. He finally let his sword shimmer and settle back on his biceps. "This could be another foolish attempt by them to seek world dominion."

"Gaia summoned me. She wants the mortal found."

Aethan stilled at the name.

Gaia. That mystical force of nature, the creator of all they stood on, who saw to the protection of mortals. She was the Being they'd sworn allegiance to. The fact that she chose to task them with this proved they had no choice but to wade into ancient crap. And clean it up.

"Talk about heading into shitsville," Týr muttered, winding his way between the benches as he joined them. "Who was Zarias, for this to happen?"

"An immortal. The first to disregard a fundamental law and be executed—long before your time."

Aethan tossed the terry cloth on the bench and

glanced back at Michael. "Why did the Celestial Realm take this to Gaia?"

"They cannot ask us to deal with such prophecies without her approval. Our allegiance lies with her now. But Zarias's descendant is mortal. So either way—"

"We're still drawn into the cesspit," Blaéz said.

Michael nodded, bracing his arm on a treadmill. "More importantly, hers is a bloodline far more powerful than you can imagine. It's imperative she is found and brought here, to the castle. Before you say anything, I get that it's going to be difficult to have a human female underfoot—"

"You don't hear me complaining," Týr drawled, sitting on a bench. He picked up a free weight and began to work his right biceps. "Having one of the forbidden, fairer sex living under our roof should liven things up a bit."

Aethan got up and put away his sword. The Norse might want to rile Michael, but he understood far too well the temptation mortal females presented. Thoughts of *her* had his restlessness growing in spades. He should've let her punch him yesterday—maybe her tiny fist would've knocked some sense into him.

In this realm, darkness shadowed the immortals in the form of the Absolute Law, which forbade a mating between mortal and immortal. If caught, it meant a death sentence for both. The same law it seems Zarias had broken and had been executed for.

These males who now guarded Earth as warriors were once gods who'd been stripped off their godhood and banished from their pantheons for all eternity for failing to protect an important goddess. She'd been abducted, causing a civil war to break out in the Realm of the Gods several millennia ago. And yet they were still bound by the archaic ruling.

The Absolute Law didn't apply to him anyway, since he came from the Empyrean Realm, because his cursed powers were a surefire way not to break those decrees.

He should know.

There'd been a female once, eons ago. A human female. Hannah. The moment he'd seen her, he'd wanted her. Hell, he hadn't known better. When his powers filled her at the height of passion, her writhing beneath him hadn't been one of ecstasy, but of death. He'd broken away so fast and tried to save her, but her mortal heart gave out, unable to survive the electrical surge of his powers flowing through her.

He regretted her death. Something he would never allow to happen again. And no amount of taunting from Týr would make him forget that. He stuck to summoning immortal females from the pantheons the rare times he'd given in to his sexual demands...but here he was, back to threading dangerous grounds. He couldn't stop thinking about *her*. But he had no desire for those empty liaisons from before, he wanted more. He wanted—*hell*! What he needed was a damn fight to get his head screwed on right again.

Týr's voice dragged him back. "Arc, you plan on bringing the others in on this?"

Michael drew off his shades, pinched the bridge of his nose, then glanced at them with eyes resembling fractured sapphires. The strange silver light glowing between the fissures in his wild blue irises made them all the more eerie. "Just one. The demoniis are gathering in forces searching for the female. I asked Dagan to assist."

Týr became motionless. For an infinitesimal

second, Aethan thought he saw regret flicker in Týr's dark eyes.

Whatever had happened between them, Aethan knew that, in the three thousand years he'd been on this realm, Týr and Dagan hadn't spoken a word to each other. With the violent lives they led, most males would beat the tar out of the other, but not these two. Which made the silent war all the more deadly.

Aethan picked up his water bottle and drained it, then said, "Why don't you give him this job? It's his kind of thing, sensing power of any sort. And he doesn't have to scan anyone. Makes life easier for us."

"No." Michael shook his head. "Dagan cannot be in every place at once. I want us all working on this."

"What's the real reason the Celestial Realm wants her?" Blaéz asked, raking a hand through his short, sweat-slicked hair. "Sure, a human with godlike or angelic powers would be a catastrophe in the making. But why *pyre and rime*? What is it about her powers?"

"It would make life easier if I had that answer, wouldn't it?" Michael responded.

"How is it, Arc?" Týr drawled. "You have access to all the realms and still can't tell us anything?"

"Nothing is that simple. It's bloody hard work schlepping the realms, trying to find the remains of a prophecy that came into being long before any of you were born. I'd gladly exchange places with one of you."

Týr snorted. "We just want answers, man, not your lifestyle. Celibacy is not for me."

Michael ignored him. "I will search the ancient archives for anything relating to this prophecy. In the meantime, whatever catches your attention, check it out. If you find her before I get back, inform me immediately. The spiking on the psychic planes means her powers are awakening. Before they escalate and she catches the public's attention, we need her contained." He put on his shades. "The psychic vibration remains within this city, so concentrate your search here."

"Gotcha." Týr grinned and set down the weight. "Find the girl. Call you. No playing with her."

"Exactly," Michael agreed with a cool look. "Now, what about the rift in Demon Alley?"

"Had a few incidents," Aethan told him. A fracture in the mystical veils between the realms had opened in a backstreet off Times Square several days ago. The rift allowed demoniis to enter at will, giving the warriors no choice but to guard it at all times. "But we've managed to keep them at bay." Aethan rose, unable to sit still any longer. He had to get out of here.

"Good. Find the girl, fast. I'll be in touch." The air shifted. Michael shimmered and vanished in a scatter of silvery-white sparks.

***

Cursing, Aethan stepped into the shower. He hoped the icy needles of water pelting him would set him back on track. But no such luck.

How the hell could he look for the prophesied female when every molecule in him demanded he go after another? One he shouldn't even look at, let alone touch.

And talks of Gaia had brought back black memories scored deep in his soul. He braced his fists against the tiled wall, head bent, as the water sluiced down his body. Pain, fresh as if it had happened yesterday, bled into him.

They hadn't allowed him near his sister when she died. Instead, he'd been banished from Empyrea. He'd roamed this world, wreaking havoc in his pain and anger, and destroying all he came across. For the first century, he hadn't been able to think past the agony of Ariana's death.

Not until Gaia, a Being unlike any he'd ever seen, rose from the very grounds he destroyed, in all her furious beauty. With hair like the sun, her skin bronzed like the earth, and the green markings swirling around her brows, she resembled the very things she protected.

Gaia had demanded propitiation for his *senseless* damage to her realm. Doubtless, she'd wanted to kick his ass into oblivion. Instead, she'd taken his allegiance and then thrown his worthless hide into a horde of demoniis coming out of a portal. When a sword appeared in his hand, he hadn't cared how it came to be. He fought to rid himself of the pain.

Much later, the truth of the blade hit him.

He'd never forget the first time the sword shimmered and settled onto his arm in the form of a tattoo. He'd been horrified by Gaia's gift. He'd tried to get it off him and damn near lost his mind in the pain. That was a lesson learned in agony; never summon the blade without cause.

Aethan shut off the shower and rubbed his biceps where the blade remained silent for now. Naked, he made his way to his dressing room and changed into leather pants and a t-shirt, and made quick work of pulling on his socks and his boots. Then he raked a hand through his damp hair and secured the flowing mass with a leather tie before he crossed to the back of the room.

He pressed a concealed button on the wall and the wooden paneling slid open to reveal an arsenal of weapons. His gaze settled on the iron dagger he'd nipped from *her*. He'd known the minute she nicked his and had been amused, because the obsidian dagger could not be stolen, taken, or given away. Ever.

Then why the hell hadn't it returned to him when he willed it back? Did she chain the blade to her side?

Frowning, Aethan picked up her dagger and ran a finger down the lethal edge. A thin line of red appeared on his skin. He stared as the wound knitted together, his mind lost in the taste of her warm silky skin beneath his tongue—

Dammit. He set the blade back on the shelf then grabbed a few throwing stars and dropped them into his pockets. Picking up a pewter dagger, he sheathed it on his belt and strode out of his room.

A day ago, his life had been simple. Find demoniis and eradicate them. Find prophesied female with powers of fire and ice and hand her over to Michael.

Now, his life was knocked off its axis, all because he'd followed a damn demonii to church.

***

Later that night, as Aethan headed toward the Bowery, on his way to recon with Týr and Blaéz, his cell vibrated. He pulled the phone from his pocket and answered. "Yeah?"

"We need to talk," his contact said.

"Meet me at the usual place."

A quick scan of the alley revealed no signs of life around him. Aethan dematerialized. A moment later, he took form again in a gloomy backstreet on the

Lower East Side. Beneath the stench of stale piss and overflowing dumpsters, the faint smell of wood smoke drifted to him. His informant was already here.

Riley had taken a chance, meeting Aethan out in the open. It meant certain death for the demon if he was seen with a Guardian. So he kept to the shadows cast by the buildings flanking the alley.

Theirs was an unusual relationship. He'd saved the demon's ass from being annihilated by his own kind a millennium ago. He had no idea why he'd done so. Maybe his own nightmares, his guilt, made him save the life of one that most wouldn't give a damn about.

"What's so urgent?" he asked the demon.

The male, like the rest of his species, was good-looking, with brown hair and sharp green eyes.

"There's rumbling in the Dark Realm." Riley got straight to the point. "Seems a demon from the upper hierarchy's gotten hold of a scroll—a prophecy. He searches for an oracle who can translate the cryptic writings."

Aethan narrowed his eyes. Most demoniis were a damn nuisance, a pest to the human world. But demons, on the other hand, were a whole other curse, especially those who dwelled in the Dark Realm and had their hands on a prophecy.

"He's an old one and dangerous from what I've heard," Riley said, his gaze growing wary as he glanced around the decrepit alley. "I don't have his name as yet. There's more—"

The air near them shifted, and Týr materialized.

Aethan cursed. He'd hoped to do this meeting without Týr coming across them. No surprise Riley had been edgy. The moment Týr's gaze fastened on Riley, residual rage spilled out of him like lava. He attacked.

For fuck's sake!

Aethan grabbed the warrior's arm a second too late. The coppery scent of blood invaded his nose. "Dammit, Norse! Back the hell off."

"Just being honest about my feelings, man." Týr jerked free of Aethan's grip. "A demon's still a fucking demon. You can't trust these bastards." Cold amusement laced his words. He stepped back, wiping the bloody blade on his black t-shirt.

"I'll meet up with you later," Aethan said. A warning that meant; *Get the fuck outta here.*

"You want to listen to his shit, it's on your head." Týr dematerialized.

Aethan turned, surprised the demon hadn't hightailed it out of there. Riley didn't bother wiping off the blood dripping down his neck. But his green eyes were a blaze of color in the darkness.

The demon stared at him, his expression unreadable. Cold. "The prophecy is about the angels," he said, and then he flashed out of the alley.

Chapter 4

The jarring sound of the alarm going crazy on the bedside table jolted Echo awake. She fought to free her limbs from the tangle of covers as a remnant of her dream held her in its grip, her heart hammering against her ribs.

Faint rays of early morning light crept between the gaps in the parted curtain, casting eerie shadows in her room. Reaching out, she slammed her hand down on the alarm, and welcomed silence filled her small apartment.

"It's only a dream," she whispered. Dragging in a shuddering breath, she sat up and switched on the bedside lamp. Soft light illuminated the room. The images of her nightmare faded, but Tamsyn's voice still rang in her head. *'It's your fault—your fault I'm dead!'*

Echo dropped her head into her hands and squeezed her burning lids closed. It wasn't the first time she'd dreamed of Tamsyn. And her friend's voice always haunted her long after the dreams ended.

Sighing, she lay back on her bed, covered her eyes with her arm, and tried to push away her nightmare...only to have it replaced by images of another kind. Images she couldn't forget, no matter how much she tried. The glide of his mouth on her nape had desire flowing through her blood like molasses. Groaning, Echo rolled onto her stomach and buried her face in her pillow. *Argh!* She shouldn't feel this way about a man she didn't even know.

A heavy weight landed on her butt, distracting her, and a rumbling purr filled the air.

She glanced over her shoulder. "Bob, get off me—owww!"

Claws pierced her t-shirt, and dug into her skin for purchase, as Bob shimmied his way up her back to her head. Ignoring her grunts of pain, he let out a loud, plaintive meow near her ear. His tail, gray as the smoke from an old chimney, flicked her face.

"I got you the first time," Echo grumbled, pushing him off her head. She might as well get an early start to her day. She rolled off the bed and stretched her arms above her head, only to find Bob glaring at her.

"What? I can't even loosen up?" She arched a brow at her pet. "Come on, let's go get you fed."

The cat streaked in front of her, heading to the kitchen.

A half hour later, after a hot shower, Echo slicked back her wet hair and stepped into her small bedroom. Walk too fast, and you'd probably crash into the opposite wall. But her bed pushed up against one wall gave her the illusion of space. Bright curtains fell from the single window in an explosion of yellow and blue flowers and cheered up drab beige walls.

The scent of brewing coffee, drifting to her from

the kitchen, made her hurry. Good thing her job as a fitness instructor didn't require much thought when it came to dressing for work. She pulled on black sweats, a turquoise tank top, and a gray hoodie, then grabbed her stones off the dresser, dropped them in her pocket, and made for the stamp-sized kitchen.

She poured a mug of the steaming brew, took a sip, and hummed in pleasure as the life-saving beverage slid down her throat. The caffeine buzzing through her system powered her up and eased her frayed nerves.

The doorbell rang, ruining her moment of bliss. Bob stirred from where he was napping on the couch and opened one eye.

"It would help if you could answer that, since you've already had *your* breakfast," Echo told the ball of gray fur. Setting her mug on the counter, she crossed to the door and peered through the peep-hole before she opened it. "Damon?"

"Expecting someone else?" he drawled, amusement lighting his eyes.

"Yeah, right. No one in their right mind would disturb me at ten past six in the morning, 'cept you."

He laughed.

But her mind rushed back to the sexy, blue-haired stranger like a heat-seeking missile. Ugh, she must have lost her ever-loving mind. The man was far too dangerous, and she wanted normal. *Normal, Echo,* she reminded herself. Stepping aside, she let her guardian in. As usual, he was impeccably dressed in black dress pants, a white shirt, and a long, rough leather coat.

She frowned. Damon being here this early wasn't a good thing. She shut the door behind him. "I thought you were in San Francisco?"

He glanced around her apartment then turned to her. Inky black hair fell from a widow's peak and framed his striking but serious face.

"I was, but business brought me back, and I wanted to see you before I leave for Romania in a couple of hours. Here." He handed her a brown paper bag. A light touch on her shoulder was his version of a greeting. Damon wasn't a demonstrative person, but then neither was she.

She stared at the package. "What is this?"

His brow shot up as he removed his outer garment and dropped it over the armchair. "Coffee. What? You stop drinking the stuff?"

Her panic eased. She carried no scars or bruises from her nighttime activities. And he didn't seem annoyed about anything, so all was cool. She hoped.

Relaxing a bit, she inhaled the contents. It was her one weakness, the rich, dark coffee Damon always indulged her with. A definite change from the cocoa he used to make for her when she was younger. No surprise his favorite brand had become hers.

"Thanks, Damon. There's food. Kira cooked...er...something, if you're hungry. It's in the fridge."

A pained grimace crossed his face. "Tell Kira to take up another hobby."

"It's edible this time," she protested, defending her friend.

"I'll pass, thanks." He picked up the remote from the coffee table and switched on the flat screen TV. Turning to the couch, he shoved Bob aside and sat down. An annoyed hiss left her cat before he hopped off the sofa and took up space on the armchair.

"So? Anything occur since I've been away?"

"You've been gone two days. What could possibly happen in that short amount of time?" Echo reached down, scratched Bob's belly, and was rewarded with a euphoric rumble.

"You don't want me to answer that, do you?" Damon's eyes narrowed when he saw her stroking the cat. "For chrissakes, don't scratch that lazy creature's belly."

Her fluff-ball purred even louder. Echo smiled. It was as if he understood what was going on. "Really, Damon, you're so temperamental with Bob. I don't understand why you can't get along with him. You gave him to me."

"My mistake." Damon gave Bob another black look. "I should have given you a dog."

"Do you want coffee?" she asked, heading for the kitchen.

"No." He switched off the flat screen and tossed the remote aside.

Retrieving her coffee, Echo took a sip and studied him. Something was off. Her unease started to rise again. "Damon, what is it?"

He turned. She was taken aback at the dark expression on his face. A nerve ticked in his jaw. His mouth was drawn into a thin line. "I don't want you out on the streets. These are dangerous times."

"I can look after myself, Damon," she said. Despite their constant disagreement about her hunting, Damon wasn't usually one for dramas or ordering her about. "After all, you were the one who taught me how to fight."

"So you could protect yourself, not so you could go hunting those bastards!"

She watched him warily. He never got angry.

"Bloody hell. I'm sorry, Echo, but I'm worried."

"Then why don't you help me?" she asked softly. "You were once a hunter. Together, we could find the fiend sooner and get rid of him. That's the only reason I go out, and you know it."

Damon pushed to his feet and roamed the small room like a caged animal. Impatiently, he raked back his hair, which just fell forward again. "Echo, I gave that up when I adopted you because I want you safe."

"I know, Damon, but I can't. I have to find the demonii who killed Tamsyn. I owe her that for keeping me safe when I lived on the streets—"

"I know exactly what she's done for you," Damon cut in, his violet eyes dark with anger.

Oh, hell, this can't be good.

"I still have contacts out on the streets. Demoniis are searching for you. You go out there, killing the bastards, and now they're coming after you."

She opened her mouth to speak, but what could she say without further riling him? She shut it again. Finally, she understood why Damon had cut his trip short and rushed home.

So, the soul-sucking fiends wanted her dead? Well, they could try.

Chapter 5

Aethan headed down East Houston Street as bleak afternoon sun filtered through the thin layer of smog hovering around the tops of the skyscrapers. He'd concluded his business in Midtown earlier in the day but too edgy to go back to the castle, he'd taken to the streets.

He hoped Michael got back soon from wherever he'd disappeared to. If they were going to stop some prophecy from unfolding, he wanted to know if the female they searched for was tied into this prophecy about the angels Riley had spoken of.

Stopping under a leafless tree, he sent out his senses and performed a wide scan of the humans in his immediate vicinity. Hands in his pockets, he waited for anything resembling a psychic spike...

Nothing.

Not one godsdamn glitch. Just a shitload of stray thoughts...

Oh, yeah, he's a big one. Hot damn! He can ride me anyway he likes—

Aethan's gaze zoomed in on the hefty Hell's Angel astride a Harley eyeing him from across the street. The human's leather vest strained over a beer gut, and tattoos spread like a virus over his chunky arms, his expression sporting an *I'm all yours* look.

Urias. Aethan turned away. Not even if he was inclined in that direction.

His mood dropped another notch as he continued down the street. He needed to head back to the castle since he had a training session scheduled with Týr. Reaching Sunshine Cinema, he crossed the road and staggered to a halt.

Children scampered around the playground like colorful little rainbows, dressed in warm clothes against the crisp bite in the air. Some climbed the jungle gym, while others swooshed down the slides, letting out whooping shrieks of laughter.

The sounds of their joy took Aethan back hard, cracking open dark, painful memories that rendered him helpless. Ones he had no way of shutting off.

'A'than!'

The childish voice filled his head.

'Here, for you.' A few wilted stems of wildflowers dangled from her fist as she came careening toward him.

'Aria, no—get back!' They were frantic words she didn't understand as his lethal sword went flying through the air.

Blood, so much blood.

His lungs seized as if a tanker had landed on his chest. His mind scrambled around like a blind man, found the off switch, and shut down. He inhaled a harsh breath, pushed up his shades and pinched the bridge of his nose.

He had to get the hell out of here.

In a fast stride, he left the playground behind, looking around for a place to dematerialize, when a tantalizing spark brushed against his psyche. He faltered mid-step. That touch unforgettable.

Focusing on the taunting flicker, Aethan tracked the psychic tug. He dashed across the road to the corner of Norfolk Street and stopped, zeroing in on the basement gymnasium there. Wilde's Health & Fitness Center.

He took the few stairs down and pushed open the glass door. A female receptionist sat at the front desk popping gum, the phone pressed to her ear. She looked up and her mouth dropped open. The phone slipped from her grasp.

Her expression changed, became sultry. "Hello. Can I help you?"

The words were a subtle invitation he ignored. Removing his shades, Aethan slipped them into his jacket pocket, then held the blonde's gaze and willed her mind to his. Her pupils dilated and took over her blue irises.

"I'm looking for a female. This tall." His hand stopped at chest level. "Short, spiky black hair, brown eyes—"

"You mean Echo?"

Echo. The name wrapped around him and seeped into his soul. "Yes."

"She has a class at the moment, should be done in five. Please have a seat."

Before releasing his hold on her mind, Aethan planted the suggestion that he was waiting for Echo and to ignore him. Leaning against the wall, he scanned the massive place.

White walls displayed photos of humans engaged in various types of exercise. His acute hearing picked up on the sounds of an intense workout session of some kind taking place farther down the corridor. Grunts and curses, along with the hiss of a steam room, added to the cacophony, but through it all, he kept track of her provocative psychic sparkle.

Arms folded over his chest, he waited, ignoring the flow of human traffic that stopped to gape at him. It reminded him of why he preferred the night—way easier to disappear into the shadows.

***

Echo rubbed the goosebumps on her arms, still far too restless to settle. Damon had only left that morning after she'd promised to be careful. She realized hunting for Tamsyn's killer was dangerous, just like he understood it was something she had to do. And Damon didn't need to know she used her pheromones to lure and then kill the fiends. He'd have a coronary or lock her up forever. With him, probably both.

A quick glance at the wall clock revealed time was nearly up. "All right, people, cool down phase—five minutes, and no dodging this part. It's as important as the actual training."

As usual, this group of teens didn't care about easing off. They bolted for the door like a tornado of human bodies.

Who knew a self-defense class could be this much fun?

Echo picked up her hoodie from the floor and made her way to the staff lounge. The room was a white box broken up by several bright prints of New

York's skyline. Vivid sofas and two armchairs, in greens and blues, surrounded three low, glass-topped coffee tables. Two small basement windows, at street level, revealed the assortment of feet that ambled, walked, or jogged by. A small kitchenette was set back off the lounge.

She went in and helped herself to a shot of caffeine. Drinking her coffee, Echo strolled out of the kitchen as the door to the lounge opened. She glanced up with a ready smile, expecting another staff member or her boss, Jimar. And froze. Only her excellent reflexes kept her mug from crashing to the floor.

The man who'd persisted in haunting her ever since she'd seen him at the cathedral stood in the threshold. Every moody inch of him.

Her gaze slid over him, because, really, with a man like him there wasn't any other alternative. And drooling wasn't an option. He wore leathers again, a dress shirt and coat. His long, striking hair, he'd tied into a ponytail. The small silver earrings he favored gleamed in his ears.

Her gaze collided with his and she found him watching her with a dark, intense stare that took her straight back to when he'd bitten her. She had to restrain herself from touching the spot on her neck. He hadn't left a mark, but the sensation still lingered.

She tried to get her mind to function again. "What are you doing here?"

He strolled in, the door swinging shut behind him. Those mercurial eyes took in everything with one sweep before settling back on her. "It's a gym—open to all, I believe."

No way. He couldn't have. "Did you join?"

"Yes, and you're my personal trainer."

She speared him with a glare. "Dream on, pal. I may be a trainer, but I don't get personal."

"Really?" His dark voice told her that if he was of a mind, she'd hand her best friend over to the demoniis for a tumble with him. Lord. She scrambled to find her balance, because truth was, she'd probably gift-wrap Kira, too.

"My name's Aethan."

"And here I thought it was Sarcasm." She headed for an armchair. Far safer, she decided, than to tackle him to the floor and take a bite of his scrumptious mouth.

"I see your temper hasn't improved."

She heard the smile in his voice. And knew he followed her, because every inch of her felt too warm. "I don't have a temper," she grumbled and sat down, only to realize too late that she was at a horrible disadvantage. He towered over her. "I am—*was* a calm, rational person. Until you showed up."

Amusement brightened his gaze. His brief smile floored her. Oh, why couldn't her stupid heart settle? Give her time to build up her defenses again.

"If you want to see my boss," she said airily, "you missed his office by a mile. It's at the front. Can't miss him. Big guy, good-looking, and really buff. Lots of tatts."

The amusement faded from his eyes, leaving behind gray diamonds. Echo wondered at her stupidity in taunting him. The last time she did, he bit her.

"He means something to you?"

Wariness settled in her at the ice in his tone. "Sure. He's the guy who pays my salary. If you came to see me, you caught me at a bad time. I have another session in ten."

The tension visibly eased out of his big body. His expression relaxed, as much as a stone could.

He planted a hand on the armrest of her chair, and she drew back warily. A swathe of silky blue hair, escaping its confines of a leather tie, swung forward as he leaned toward her. His seductive scent of warm male and leather surrounded her. It was like fighting a riptide, one determined to suck her in.

Aethan cupped her chin and tilted her face to his. "Breathe," he said softly.

How could she, when a vacuum had sucked all the air out of the room?

The door opened.

"Hey, Echo," someone called. Her barely functioning brain recognized the voice, but hers had deserted her. "I'll come back later." Laughter followed Chris as he left again.

Try as she might, she couldn't break the hypnotic allure of Aethan's gaze.

Aethan.

God, even his name sounded hot. There was just something so compellingly seductive about him... Argh! This wasn't helping her situation. She was grateful he had no idea how her body responded to him, short of sliding his hand between her thighs—

Dammit. She bit the inside of her lip and squeezed down on her inner muscles.

His gray eyes searched hers. "You wear contacts?"

As if someone had dumped icy water over her, her lust fizzled out, and she got herself back in hand again. "Damn, you caught me." She wrenched her face free of his grip. "And here I thought I could get away with it."

He just had to bring *that* up. As if nature hadn't been cruel enough in *blessing* her with cursed pheromones, she got mismatched eyes along with it. She wasn't some Aussie Shepherd, for chrissakes. Brown contacts were simple, safe.

"It must be really heavy."

The low cadence of his voice tugged her attention back to him. "What?"

"That chip you carry around like armor, keeping everyone at a distance," he murmured, brushing a thumb across her chin.

She desperately wanted to push him away, needed the breathing space, but didn't dare. Even if she could command her limbs to move, she didn't want to touch him, not with the way she felt. Besides, a man like him wouldn't budge unless he wanted to. She'd learned *that* two days ago.

Echo dropped her gaze to his swaying ribbon of hair and gave in to temptation. Like silk, the strands slid between her fingers. "Is this real, the color?"

"There's only one way to find out."

Of course he'd say *that*, but his mesmerizing voice filled her with sensual suggestions. Echo swore she could feel his hands on her skin, the slide of his naked body between her legs, his mouth devouring hers—

Laughter in the corridor jerked her out of her moment of madness. She dropped her hand. Leveling him with the same cool look she used on her disruptive students, she said, "That's my cue."

He straightened, amusement flashing again in his dark eyes.

Damn, she should have known her attempt to intimidate would amuse him. Pushing to her feet, she hurried past him, her fingers clenching the handle of the mug she still held. Oh, for goodness sake! The man had the ability to make her forget where she was.

She pivoted, set the cup on the table, and headed for the door. She wanted to be gone from this erotic web he'd spun around her.

"Echo, wait."

That magnetic pull of his voice had her stopping. She turned and faced eyes gone impossibly cold. How the heck had he turned himself off so easily when desire still blazed a trail through her body? *Wait.* He knew her name? Of course he did, he must have asked Becky. One look from him and the blabbermouth receptionist probably spewed out everything he wanted to know.

She scowled. "What?"

"I want you to stay off the streets at night."

Damn! Not again. "Why would I do that?"

***

Why?

She would ask him that, the stubborn female. "Because demoniis are on the hunt for those with any kind of psychic abilities. I don't want you in their sights."

He didn't need to be clairvoyant to know exactly how she spent her nights. Her next words confirmed it. "Look, I've been killing those fiends for a few years, I'm used to this. Why do you care what happens to me, anyway?"

Aethan closed the distance between them and grasped her arms. "Killing *one* demonii is a helluva lot different than battling a horde of them. They get you, you *will* die. Do you hear me?"

"I am aware of the risks." She tried to shrug off his hold. "Getting hurt is part of the job—collateral damage and all that."

His ire shot up at her careless words, the utter disregard for her life.

"You think this is some thrill-seeking adventure?" He yanked her close. The delicate, musky scent of her arousal wasn't helping matters, and all he could think about was laying her on the table and tasting her right between—

"I know exactly what *I'm* doing." She shoved at him.

"And what exactly is that?" he snapped, tightening his grip. "Being on top of the fuckers' menu list?"

Scowling, she leaned back. "I'm willing to risk that to keep this place safe. How about you?" she challenged, each word punctuated with a poke to his chest.

His blood buzzed in fury. He was seconds from kissing the hotheaded female into submission. Instead, he grabbed that annoying finger and bit it.

She froze.

Deliberately, he licked her finger, slowly sucking on it, and saw confusion tingeing the desire in her eyes. A strangled breath escaped her. She tugged her hand free and fisted her fingers.

"This isn't about me," he said, edgy now. The taste of her on his tongue made him all too aware of how easily she was getting past his rigid control.

"Fine, don't answer me," she countered, keeping her balled hands at her side. "But until you're willing to do so, you don't have the right to tell me what to do." Then she tipped her chin at him, stubbornness written all over her tempting face. "How did you find me?"

Protective urges he thought long dead burst free.

He didn't want anything to happen to her. But from her mulish expression he was fast losing ground.

"How did I find you?" he repeated. "You'll have to stay alive to find out, because I sure as hell am not getting into that right now."

She glared at him. "What is wrong with you?"

"Your unbelievable recklessness is what's wrong! Demoniis are cruel, vicious, and cause death wherever they go. They're nothing like the demons who live—"

"I'm well aware of what demoniis do. I've seen it."

"If you know the risks, then stay off the damn streets!"

"Oh, cut the crap. You want me to stay off the streets? Then come up with a better explanation than the one you gave me."

"You're one pig-headed female," he bit out in frustration. He had to clamp down on the urge to shake some sense into her. "You want a reason?" His voice hardened, filling with menace. "Hunting demoniis is my job. The gods help you, I find you on the streets again. I *will* lock you up some place if it means keeping you safe." His eyes bored into hers. "Go ahead, test me."

She whirled away, outrage sparking off her. "It's *God*—singular! And you'd have to catch me first!"

The door banged shut on her words.

Scowling, Aethan stormed out of the gym. Echo had no clue how far he'd go to keep her delectable ass safe.

Chapter 6

Echo still seethed with irritation as she walked out into the chilly air later that evening. The icy touch of early winter felt good on her heated face.

Lock her up, will he?

She'd see about that. And that infuriating man had bitten her again! Okay, maybe it was her fault for stabbing him with her finger. Dammit, it was just her finger, not like she used a dagger.

Scowling, she pulled on her coat and took the few stairs up to street level. Her backpack hitched over one shoulder, she hotfooted it toward the warmth and comfort of the Peacock Lounge on East First Street.

As she pushed open the door to the bar, the odor of beer and fried food greeted her. A flat screen TV suspended in the corner of the bar replayed highlights from a recent hockey game.

She found Kira taking orders at a table. There was a bounce in her friend's step, as if she moved to some inner rhythm—music only she heard. Echo waved and headed for the bar. She squeezed in between a heavyset man and a woman whose overpowering perfume made her head swim. Her breathing shallow, she rummaged in her coat pockets for change to buy a drink.

"Your usual." A misty glass of Pepsi appeared in front of her. Echo looked up and met Jon's warm gaze. Tall and lanky with short blond hair, he worked at the bar part-time.

"Thank you." She set the money on the counter and tried not to think about the crush he had on her. "How's university?"

"It's good, but not the shit—" A sheepish grin spread across his face as he took the money. "I mean, the *stack* of assignments I have holed up in my dorm."

Someone at the end of the bar called out his name. He glanced away, nodded, then gave her a wry smile when she said nothing, and went to serve the customer.

Echo picked up her drink and took a sip. At least Jon didn't chase after her or make a nuisance of himself... A shiver skated over her. She glanced up and encountered the malevolent green stare of the other bartender. Neal.

Oh, yeah, evil came in all forms. This one was human and wore his auburn hair in a buzz-cut. A sneer she was all too familiar with marred his face. She could kick herself for ever getting involved with him. She should have trusted her instincts and stayed away. But Neal had been charming and attentive when they first met. And he pursued her until she said yes.

As it turned out, the weasel just wanted to get her into bed. "No" was not a word he understood. His pawing had only riled her. She'd ended the date, furious, leaving Neal with an imprint of her hand on his face.

Echo couldn't even blame it on pheromones. Neal

Casey was a smarmy snake, interested only in how many notches he scored on his bedpost. With his ego battered, he now lived to make her life hell every chance he got. The fact Kira worked here made him unavoidable.

"Don't waste your time on Jon," he hissed, stopping opposite her. He snatched a couple of empty glasses from the counter. "He has more taste than to want a frigid bitch like you."

The slap still stung several months later, it appeared. Being called a bitch so many times was growing old. Echo pasted on a sweet smile. "Two words, Neal. *New. Thesaurus.*"

"Bitch."

"Point proven." She swung away from him. A dull throb started right behind the scar on her forehead. She rubbed it, trying to soothe her headache.

"Hey." Kira grinned, easing between Echo and another customer. "Thought you weren't coming over this evening."

"Last client rescheduled. I had some time."

"Come on, I need to go to the toilet." Kira turned to speak with another waitress, before she headed down the hallway at the back of the bar. Echo followed.

"What happened with Jon? He looks like someone dropped a bus on him."

"Not sure," Echo dodged the question. She didn't want to get into the usual debate about her non-existent love life. Staring at her friend's hair, she realized the color genius was back and gratefully changed the subject. "Brunette? What's next—no, wait, what's your real color anyway?"

Kira laughed. "This useless talent I'm *blessed* with might as well have some use. So, it's brown for now."

Georgia Lyn Hunter

Kira had the ability to change the color of any object, which she did with great dedication to herself, especially her hair. "Hey, you ever considered going platinum? With the emo look you have going for you, it'll be perfect. A touch and you're blond, no dark roots to worry about."

Echo grimaced. "Thanks, but I'll pass."

Kira entered the staff restroom and disappeared into a stall. "You know Jon likes you, right?" she called out. "One date with him won't hurt."

Echo sighed and leaned against the sink. "Ki, please, you have to stop fixing me up with every available guy we come across."

"Like that ever works." Her hazel eyes sparked in annoyance as she came out of the stall moments later. "You can't still be hankering after Philip. It's been over three years." She pumped liquid soap into her hands and washed them.

Not in the mood to talk about her ex, Echo shifted her backpack to her other shoulder. "I'm fine. It's not Philip." At Kira's skeptical look, she added, "Really."

"Good. Because there is someone amazing out there for you."

"You can't seriously believe that nonsense? What am I saying? Of course you do when you change your boyfriend as frequently as you do your hair color, looking for Mr. Right."

"Why not? I don't see the point in staying in a relationship if there's no magic. Anyway, this isn't about me." Kira tore paper towels from the dispenser. "Something's troubling you."

Yeah, there was. But what could she tell her about Aethan? The man wanted to haul her butt off the street and place her under house arrest. He had this ridiculous idea that she'd get hurt going after demoniis. He had no clue as to how fast she was, or of her unusual strength.

What was it with men? First Damon going hard-ass on her this morning, then the original hard-ass reappeared to dish out more orders.

She shook her head. "Just tired. I'm heading home. You're still coming over later?"

"Yes." Then Kira pinned Echo with her gimlet stare. "You're gonna be there, right?"

"Where else would I be?"

"Oh, I don't know. The alleys, filthy backstreets, anywhere rundown, trolling streets and nightclubs, searching for trouble?"

Echo blinked innocently. "I'm hurt. My best friend thinks I like street rats."

With a snort, Kira left the restroom. Smiling, Echo followed her into the narrow hallway, where Jon and Neal stood farther down, talking.

"You can't be serious," Neal protested. "There's Jessie, she's a looker. Even Kira, but not the weirdo. Thought you had better taste, man."

Echo stopped, rooted to the spot.

"What's wrong, Neal? Echo turn you down?" Jon's amused voice floated to her, and the knot in her stomach unraveled a little. Obviously, the slimy rat hadn't told Jon about their fiasco of a date.

"Please." Neal sneered. "I like them hot and with some shape, not plain and scrawny."

Jon shook his head. "I like her. If she ever shows an interest, I'll ask her out." He disappeared into the bar. Scowling, Neal stomped after him.

Her hand tightened around her stones in her coat pocket, she struggled to push away the hurt.

"The bastard," Kira muttered.

Echo's mouth tightened briefly as old wounds reopened and bled from the salt of Neal's words. "See? That's why I don't want to date. It's a pain in the ass. Half the time I don't know if it's my pheromones responsible or if I just bring out the jerks in them."

"No," Kira growled angrily. "It's his dick that's twisted his brain. I'd like to strangle him with—"

Echo sputtered in laughter at the sudden vision in her head.

"What?" Kira asked, then she shuddered in disgust. "Eww. I was going to say 'his nasty tongue,' silly. Not touching *that* thing."

"I know, but the image just popped into my head. I'll see you later." Echo headed for the exit, her smile vanishing. Outside, she dragged in a lungful of cold air, hoping it would calm her. She knew better than to let Neal get to her, but it was hard to turn old wounds into wisdom when they continued to blindside her.

And Jon? He would come to her defense, because he was an all-round Mr. Nice Guy. Why couldn't she give him a chance when she did so with a slime ball?

Because Jon *was* a decent man, and she couldn't hurt him, not when her heart insisted on tugging her in another direction.

***

Aethan hunkered on the formation of rocks jutting out into the ocean on the northern side of the estate, and gazed into the distance, his mood piss low. The brackish scent of the sea swirled around him. Moonlight illuminated the cold night, reflecting in a pale line on the calm, dark waters of the Atlantic.

He should have met up with Týr for his training

session hours ago, but all he wanted was a quiet place to think.

Echo. The female was hell-bent on scaring the shit out of him going after demoniis. The way things ended between them left him irritated and confused. Lust rode him hard, but deeper, a need to claim her took hold. He'd never reacted this way with any female before. She tempted him beyond the levels he was prepared for. There was fierceness in her, a fire he longed to burn in.

Gods. He dragged a hand down his face. His way of thinking wasn't good for either of them. She was human, and he had to get rid of this deadly obsession riding him. He blew out a frustrated breath and tried to calm the war going on inside him.

The air around him displaced as a figure took form next to him.

"So, you hide out here?" Týr drawled, glancing around. "Nice night to contemplate the mysteries of the universe."

Aethan grunted. Ignoring the thick-skinned male wasn't working. He settled for flat-out aggression. "I want a little solitude—do you mind?"

"Dude," Týr said, his teasing tone taking on an edge, "in case you've forgotten, our lives *are* solitude."

Like he needed a reminder.

The bleakness of their reality swallowed the tranquil atmosphere. Aethan dematerialized back to the castle and headed for the gym. Yanking open his gray locker, he grabbed his workout clothes, changed, then made his way to one of the several punching bags.

A few brutal kicks and the enormous bag shattered. An avalanche of sand flowed to the floor. He moved to the next one. A rapid succession of heavy

Georgia Lyn Hunter

thuds filled the gym. Just when he'd worked up enough pain, using his bare fists to numb the battle in his heart, the door swung open. Týr strolled in. He shrugged off his black hoodie and tossed it on the treadmill. "Want to explain something to me?"

"What?" Aethan had to force the words out through clenched teeth.

"Why is it every time I've scheduled a training session with you in the last two days, you've been busy?"

What the hell was wrong with Týr? Did he really look the type to open up his heart and bare all? Aethan struck the punching bag, hard. Pain tore through his bruised knuckles. Not enough. He hit harder, and his skin ruptured.

He would forget her, put her out of his mind.

Hell, he'd lived alone for three thousand years. Two days would not change him—

"Catch."

At the sound of a metallic hiss, Aethan swung around, just as a sword came flying toward him. His heart racing, he grabbed the weapon. Images flashed in his mind.

Another sword, blazing with white light, winging through the air. Ariana running to him—

Snarling, Aethan attacked, his sword swinging.

Týr jumped back, the blade whistling past his carotid a deadly inch away. "What the hell is your problem? I thought you'd appreciate fighting me, instead of beating up the damn equipment."

"Stay outta my way."

"You have issues, man. Serious ones. You know what I speak off. Grounding in the mountains is not cutting it. Call one of the females from the pantheons."

Týr shot him a hard look. "If you won't see to it, I will."

"Stay out of my damn business, Norse." Aethan tossed the sword aside and ripped into the punching bag once more.

"That's a real polite request. Sorry I can't comply. Have you taken a look at yourself recently?"

"I don't need a fucking keeper, or your advice!"

"You're hearing it anyway."

"I didn't know you cared."

"I don't." Anger flowed. The air around them shifted, crackled. "You don't settle those powers, you're gonna go nuclear on this place—and be responsible for taking a lot more innocent lives. The Dark Ages would be nothing compared to this carnage. Is that what you want?"

The reminder of how his lethal powers had eliminated not only towns and villages, but mortals, too, caught Aethan off guard.

He wheeled around, shoved Týr back. "You think you're any better? At least I don't look for the easy way out of this life."

"Unlike you, *I* won't murder thousands. It's only my life that will end. What's the matter? Some female left you all bent-up, so you—" Týr's eyes narrowed as understanding dawned. "Must suck not to be bound by our fucked-up laws and still not have what you want."

Týr struck too close to the truth. Knowing he could never touch Echo the way he wanted spiked Aethan's temper to dangerous levels. The pit in his gut grew. He lashed out, wanting to maim. "Guess five centuries in Tartarus wasn't enough?"

Týr stiffened. Red-hot fury and utter betrayal thickened the air. He shoved Aethan back hard. "Fuck you, asshole!"

His sword falling to the floor with an ominous clang, Týr stalked out of the gym.

Aethan swung around and smashed his fist into the wall. Bones shattered, skin split, and blood dripped onto the floor. Mentioning Týr's imprisonment in the deepest part of the Dark Realm was a low blow, even for him.

His gaze settled on the fallen sword. He'd drawn blood without the need of a weapon.

When the layers of his soul were peeled away, he wondered if he had any heart left. Or did he just not care who he hurt anymore? Self-loathing could do that to a person. Too many deaths, too many *innocent* deaths, had stained his soul. He could still hear their screams from centuries ago, as he took out demonii-infested villages and towns, leaving nothing behind but ash.

The door to the gymnasium opened, and Blaéz strolled in.

"What happened? Týr left in a blaze, like he couldn't get out of here fast enough." Blaéz glanced at the spots of blood on the floor then at Aethan's ruined hand.

Ignoring him, Aethan strode to the fridge, grabbed a bottle of water. *Why not tell Blaéz the truth?* the darkness creeping inside his head prodded him. He tried to shut out the destructive whispers and took a sip, but the cold water sliding down his throat did little to dull his anger. Remorse slithered into his chest and settled like an old friend.

He wouldn't sink lower than he already had. How could he tell Blaéz anything without bringing back horrifying memories of a past best forgotten?

In the Realms of the Gods, Blaéz and Týr, along with Dagan and the other Guardians, had once been protectors of the Goddess of Life, until evil intruded and she'd disappeared, never to be seen again. As punishment, they'd been stripped of their powers and incarcerated in the deepest, darkest level of the Dark Realm.

Tartarus.

A place where Blaéz lost all emotions after his soul had been ripped from him, leaving him a husk.

Icy water splashing on his hand, jerked him back to the room.

"Your mood's been off lately," Blaéz said, his empty stare revealing the void he lived in. No emotions. No feelings. Inflicted pain was all Blaéz felt.

"Leave it alone, Celt." Aethan refused to talk about Echo with anyone. Ever.

He tossed the water bottle into the recycle bin and turned to the stack of towels on a shelf near the lockers. He picked one, threw it over his face, and squeezed his eyes shut. Then he inhaled slowly. Gods, he needed to calm down.

Which was damn hard to do when self-hatred raged in him. His fists tightened. The scabs crusting over on his knuckles cracked, split, and started oozing again. The pain in his busted hands reminded him he'd finally taken the prize for Asshole of the Year.

He'd find Týr and...yeah. The thought of apologizing stuck in his craw. He should have shut his damn mouth and left well enough alone—like he always did when dealing with Týr.

He strode past Blaéz.

"Wait."

Teeth gritted, Aethan turned slowly. He didn't

trust himself to speak. The intense look Blaéz was giving him did nothing for his mood.

Then it hit him, a blow to the gut, and he struggled for breath. The Celt would already know without a word being spoken. He wouldn't just see *Echo*—he'd have seen them *both*.

Abso-fuckin-lutely great.

"Let it go, man. I don't care what you've seen in your visions. I'm not in the mood for this." Then he slammed out of the gym.

Chapter 7

The following night, Aethan materialized in the alley on the Lower East Side. He scanned the area. No sign of Týr.

Not surprising. Calls to his cell phone went unanswered. Every time Aethan tried to connect through their telepathic link, he hit a wall. The warrior had cut himself off from contact—too damn bad for him. He would find Týr and do the necessary evil.

At the stiffness in his jaw, Aethan released his clenched teeth. Apologies bit ass big time.

Aethan headed for Club Anarchy. He knew the male well enough to know how he'd vent his rage. And since he wasn't out on the streets, what better place to find willing partners than the club?

Heavy-metal music rocked through the worn building like an earthquake. Strobe lights bopped blue and green neon dots over a sea of frenzied, near-naked bodies on the lower level. Laser beams flashed in rhythm to the music, heating up their feverish movements.

Georgia Lyn Hunter

Aethan stepped around the rowdy, lurching drunks and headed upstairs to the VIP lounge. Beneath the awful cocktail of heavily perfumed air, stale liquor, and the sharp odor of illegal dust, he found the scent he wanted. The citrusy smell was infused with cold rage.

Avoiding several of the females who made a stumbling beeline toward him, he tracked the chilly anger down a short corridor. The club's owner, a tall black male, waited outside a door, dressed in tailored cream-colored pants and jacket. On the other side of the door, flanking him, stood a big bouncer clad in black leather. They turned as Aethan approached. The glazed look in their eyes confirmed he was in the right place.

"You're not allowed here—"

The bouncer didn't get a chance to say more. Aethan shoved into the mortals' minds and took control, instilling the message to ignore him.

Both men went back to staring at the wall opposite. Aethan willed the door open and stepped into the darkened office, the door closing behind him.

Loud feminine moans and the sound of flesh slapping against flesh filled the room, drowning out the muffled music thumping in the club below. The musky scent of sex hit him. Týr had a female flat on her back on the desk, her legs wrapped around his waist, as he pounded into the human.

From the way she was writhing, Aethan doubted she cared much where she was.

Her unbuttoned top hung off her shoulders and displayed her ample assets, which jiggled with each thrust of Týr's plundering hips. He still wore his clothes, and his long coat hid most of the action from view, for which Aethan was grateful.

Týr didn't slow down. But a cool smile now rode his face as he ran a hand up the female's torso and squeezed her plump breast, eliciting a louder moan from her. Quick fingers worked her pink nipples. The woman's whimper grew nosier, but not a sound came from Týr. Still keeping perfect rhythm, he started in on her other mound.

Yeah, the bastard knew he was here and was shoving this in his face—paying him back, big time. Damn hard to swallow when the truth was shoved down your throat with a fist the size of Thor's hammer.

The carnal pleasures Aethan pretended not to have an interest in gained momentum. His body stirred awake and it had nothing to do with the erotic activities taking place on the desk. He'd been in a constant state of arousal since he'd met Echo. His blood pounded in his veins and heated his groin with a need he'd give anything to satiate—to sink deep into her silky heat, have those honey-toned limbs wrapped around his waist, until his hunger for her was sated. Then he saw Echo's face frozen in terror, her legs still around his hips, where she lay dead beneath him.

His blood ran cold.

Pivoting, Aethan stalked from the room. He joined the males outside the office and stared at the opposite wall, trying desperately to clear his head.

The door opened moments later, and Týr swung past him, his expression unyielding. Aethan joined him. They left the club and headed into the brisk night air, the wind snapping open their long coats.

Aethan stuck his hands in the pocket of his leathers. "Týr—"

"Not interested."

He was still pissed. Aethan couldn't blame him.

Hell, if he had to deal with someone like himself, he'd be worse.

"Too bad. You're going to hear it anyway." He threw Týr's sentiment from yesterday back at him but got no reaction. "I was out of line. What I said—"

"It matters little." Cold. Clipped. "I'm on duty at the rift."

Týr stepped into a darkened doorway. Before he could dematerialize, Aethan clamped a hand on his arm. "You want to take a shot at me, go ahead."

Týr shrugged him off. "I have work."

Training. Duty. That's what their lives amounted to. Aethan stepped back. "For what it's worth…I'm sorry."

Týr didn't respond. The air around him shifted. He dematerialized.

That went well. Aethan rubbed his face with a weary hand. Redemption wasn't for them. This was their life, the only one Gaia granted them—a damn cruel fate to walk amongst the freedom of others and never be able to touch it. Their existence was set in stone. Protect those whose lives were forever barred from them. A life they could never have.

In the distance, church bells rang. Drunken laughter echoed through the darkness. Aethan tensed, glanced around. A strange sensation rushed over him, unlike any he'd ever encountered.

What the hell?

His thoughts scattered as the air around him shifted and sucked him into a whirlpool of unimaginable power.

***

Echo stepped out of her apartment door. The flurry of footsteps resounding through the silent hallway had her biting back a groan.

"Darn it, Echo. Wait up." Kira rushed after her, tugging on her jacket. She hooked her arm through Echo's as they left the building and headed up the street. A thin layer of mist swirled around them, blurring the lampposts lining the road.

"Sane people stay inside their homes, where it's safe and warm," Kira grumbled, zipping up her jacket.

"I have to get out, need some air. Go back inside. I won't be long."

"No. I know you. You're still upset over what that jackass, Neal, said."

"Kira, I'm fine. I can't sleep, so I walk. It helps settle me."

"At night? Echo, that's like sticking a flashlight on your forehead and telling the demoniis a delicious human is available—no, wait, your pheromones do that well enough."

"I know." Echo smiled. "And I don't have to expend any energy looking for them."

Clearly not pleased by her smart-ass response, Kira's tone filled with irritation. "I'm afraid, one of these days, things will end badly for us."

"Us?" Echo asked, unable to keep the amusement from her voice.

"Yes. If you die, I'll be sad forever."

Echo lost her smile. "I'm not going to die, silly."

The incident with Neal had opened an old wound. If she were honest enough, a part of her would always hurt, a part that remained a child. Most of the time, she didn't let it bother her until she looked in the mirror...and saw her eyes.

Georgia Lyn Hunter

Weirdo. Freak. She'd heard it all before.

Memories nudged through the cracks in her mental armor.

'Stay here, you little freak.'

'No! Please, don't, please—I'm sorry.'

He loomed over her, tall, thin, with dark eyes and a sneer on his face. Her foster father didn't care for her pleas.

'You mention that aura shit again, I'll cut out your tongue and feed it to the dog. Auras? Only the devil's spawn sees those things!' He shoved her into the darkened basement and locked her in there.

A shudder filled her. Her parents had died in a mugging when she was four, leaving her to the tender mercies of the foster care system. She'd been young, barely six years old, when her foster father locked her in the basement, and she had no idea what she'd done wrong. But she'd learned one thing that day. She never again spoke about her abilities to just anyone.

You did with Aethan.

Yeah, well, Aethan didn't count. He just bulldozed his way into her life and demanded answers. They'd probably still be there, standing behind the cathedral in a deadlock, if she hadn't given him some kind of response.

"You okay?"

Echo nodded and squeezed Kira's hand. "I'm fine."

They'd been friends a long time, and Kira understood her too well. They continued on silently, turned left, and bypassed a homeless man sprawled on the sidewalk, soaked in alcoholic fumes.

"I don't like the nights. They give me the creeps," Kira whispered, glancing around the shadowy street and holding tighter onto Echo.

"That's only because you know what else is out there."

"True. Had I not met you, I would've never known. Gran certainly wouldn't have told me. You know how protective she is."

"She just wants to keep you safe."

"Any safer and I might as well be holed up in a convent."

"Now, there's an idea," Echo teased. "But would they let you change boyfriends every other week at a convent?"

Kira laughed.

As they passed the old Delancey subway station, an odd sound reached Echo. She frowned.

There it was again—a scuffle, followed by a...moan? She slowed down and listened, her attention drawn to the subway's barricaded entrance. "Did you hear that?"

Warily, Kira glanced up then down the empty street. "No."

"Wait here." Echo freed her arm from Kira's tight grip and jogged for the subway entrance.

Kira grabbed her arm. "No—no, don't go down there."

"Something's wrong. I feel it."

"But all kinds of people hang out in that place, even thugs."

"I grew up with *those* kinds of people. Most can't help what life's handed them. I'll be fine. Go back to the apartment." Echo climbed through a gap in the barricade.

"If you're gonna risk your limbs, well, someone's got to be there to haul your butt home," Kira retorted, following her.

They picked their way carefully down the broken steps and entered the darkened tunnel. The station, a casualty of a gas explosion several years ago, had been left to decay. Most of the lights were broken and probably didn't work anyway. But flickers of light from candles the homeless burned cast a wavery illumination on the faded graffiti and damp patches on the walls. Water dripped from pipes overhead and formed puddles on the deteriorating concrete floor.

"I'm never watching horror movies again," Kira muttered.

"So says the queen of horror-fests."

But the silence there was warning enough for Echo. The homeless had scattered and danger was close. Movement farther along the platform caught her attention. She opened her psychic sight and sighed when she saw several pulsing red lights hovering around a single warm yellow one.

"What? Demoniis?" Kira asked, staring at the men.

"Yeah. I can handle them. Sit this one out, Ki."

"Nuh-uh! If you think I'm leaving you to fight those things alone, you're nuts. Besides, what's the point of you teaching me how to fight and defend myself, huh?"

Echo exhaled roughly. She never wanted her friend caught in a situation like she'd been in so long ago. Helpless, while Tamsyn fought alone.

"Okay, okay. Fine." She relented. "Remember, we stay back to back and worry about what's in front. If it gets bad, we run. Got it?"

"Got it," Kira said, anxiety seeping off her.

Echo reached for a spare blade in her right boot,

but Kira pulled out her own from her jacket pocket. "Going anywhere with you, I need to be armed."

Snorting, she turned. "Hey, boys! Why don't ya come over here and play with us?"

"Jeez, Echo, no need to provoke them."

"But that's half the fun," she murmured, as the three gorgeous "men" turned.

The demoniis tossed the homeless man aside and rushed for her, hunger flickering in their auras. Stopping abruptly, the leader of the pack held the others back and sniffed the air.

Oh, yeah, her cursed pheromones weren't selective. Anything possessing a Y chromosome found its way to her.

"You. Woman. Come here," the demonii ordered, his voice like rusty nails.

"Are you some kind of stupid? Do I look like I'm coming anywhere near you?" Legs braced apart, she slid her hand to the sheath belted to her waist and palmed the obsidian dagger.

The leader slithered closer as the other two fanned out, eyes gleaming like red moons.

"Jesus! Don't you *things* ever take a bath?" she griped, edging backwards. She feinted right as the leader pounced. She moved left, dropped down, swung her booted foot out and connected with his knees. He stumbled backward. A quick glance over her shoulder confirmed Kira had her situation in hand.

"Hey, not to be prejudiced or anything, but blond, really?" Echo danced back then lashed out with a final kick to the crotch and knocked Blondie down. "It clashes with your eyes. And *so* not the look for your ugly-ass face." She plunged her dagger into his heart, then yanked it out and sliced his throat.

"You killed him!"

At the screech, Echo pivoted from the disintegrating fiend to face the other demonii circling her. "Stop whining. You'll see him soon enough."

She dodged the blade coming at her, went in low, her dagger flashing, and slashed through the tendons behind his legs. A guttural shriek filled the tunnel as he fell to his knees. About to go in for the kill, a dark shimmer in the air several feet in front of her, distracted her. Her stomach lurched.

Oh, crap! Portal.

"Kira, *run*!"

Chapter 8

The stench of sulfur hit Echo hard, making her choke. She swung around, her heart hammering in fear.

"Dammit, move, Kira!" She shoved her frozen friend in the direction of the exit.

"I-I'm not leaving you here a-alone," Kira sputtered, her fearful gaze fixed on the dark, flickering portal.

"Now, Kira! You know the rules. Move. I'll be right behind you!"

As Kira scurried off, Echo slashed the throat of the demonii struggling to get back on his feet.

"Well, well, that was most impressive," a lazy voice drawled.

Echo wheeled around. Several demoniis stood near the portal while it spewed out more of the fiends. Their creepy red eyes glowed like embers in the darkness.

A demonii unlike any she'd seen before stepped forward. He was so handsome, it left a sick feeling in her stomach. The air around him was dense, his aura

Georgia Lyn Hunter

dark, like coagulated blood.

His long, chocolate-colored hair had been meticulously dreaded and gathered into a ponytail. His skin was far paler than most demoniis she'd seen. And unlike the others, who dressed casually, he wore a tailored suit. He looked bored and completely out of place in the dank subway station.

"So, you're the one causing a ruckus *down under*," he said, strolling toward her. His gaze drifted down her body, then slowly back up again, making her cringe. "You're curious, aren't you? Wondering why I haven't killed you yet. Why I haven't taken your soul."

Echo stepped back, caution in her every move. The power surrounding him suffocated her the closer he got. The urge to run crowded her, but she wasn't stupid. She understood she could never hope to outrun him and his small army. "What do you want?"

His chuckle flayed her skin. "Ah, she shows courage—interesting. I want *you*."

"You can't have me." Echo slowly backed away. She didn't fear death. Hell, she'd long ago accepted that by hunting demoniis she'd die sooner. But not tonight. "Is this dance gonna take all night?" she demanded. A sleight of her hand and her dagger became hidden beneath her sleeve.

He laughed as if charmed. "You are delightful. Come, we waste time. We must leave this place." He cast a distasteful glance at the rundown station.

What? Hell is now a five-star resort?

"Do I look like I want to go anywhere with you?"

He glided closer. "You will," he promised. The words caused a chill to sweep over her.

He circled her, sniffing. Echo gritted her teeth against the urge to shut her eyes. She didn't like him being this close. Beneath the acrid reek of sulfur, the sweet scent of honeysuckle drifted to her.

"You want to kill me? Go ahead—I hope you choke on my soul."

"So dramatic." He stopped in front of her, cocked his head, and studied her face.

Echo gaped, taken aback. His tobacco-brown eyes were clear. Why weren't his eyes red? He consumed human souls, too, didn't he?

As if tuned in to her thoughts, images appeared in his eyes as orange flames leaped out of them and licked over his face.

Oh, dear God! Echo stumbled back. Her breath lodged in her chest. His eyes—she'd seen *Hell* in his eyes!

"It's easy to conceal, if one knows how." He smiled. Moving behind her, he sniffed again. "I am not demonii. I don't gorge myself on human blood or their frail souls. But I do keep them for my own amusement. Now, I will have a taste of you."

Before she could figure out what he meant, a wet trail slid across her nape. A shiver of revulsion raced over her. Why did every freakin' demon she came across have to lick her?

"You do taste delicious," he said, licking his lips. His gaze flattened. "Enough stalling. Time to leave."

Her heart knocked around so hard, she had no idea how it managed to remain in her chest. Demoniis surrounded her with only one clear path out, leading directly to the portal.

The demon flicked his hand. An invisible force took hold of her, pushing her along. Her legs sauntered forward with an ease that terrified her. Her mind screamed, she struggled for control, but her limbs

Georgia Lyn Hunter

refused to listen. Try as she might, she couldn't break free.

The portal drew closer. Gripped with terror, Echo couldn't take her eyes off it. Through the flickering opening, she saw the same images she'd seen in the leader's eyes; a dark chamber, and locked behind the walls, the damned. Humans, along with demons, were being mercilessly tortured. Skin was peeled away, bones broken, before being put together again. And the torment started all over again.

He whispered in her ear, "Don't be afraid. It's only my humble abode."

Echo struggled with her unresponsive limbs. It didn't matter that the bastard would undoubtedly win, but she refused to let him drag her into his hellhole without a damn fight. She willed herself to move, to twist free. Still, her body remained in lockdown. "I'm not going through there. You want to kill me, then do it, you bastard!"

"Names, little human," he drawled. "How unoriginal. I prefer Lazaar. You will want to remember it, because"—he ran one clawed finger along her jaw— "you are going to be mine. I have no intention of killing you. Well, not yet, anyway."

She yanked her head back. Inhaling more suffocating sulfur-drenched air, bile shot to her throat, and she hurled. Right there, on a pair of boots.

The boots' owner backhanded her across the face. Her lip split open, warm blood trailed down her chin. Pain spread from her jaw into her head.

"Annoy my commander and Girion will hurt you more," Lazaar warned. "As long as you live, I do not care what condition you are in."

Girion, unable to hold on to his human form,

became more beastlike, grotesque. His black eyes were filled with such malevolence, they sent involuntary shivers down her spine. His mouth pulled into a sneer, revealing sharp canines and blackened teeth. Echo turned her head, her heart wedged in her throat.

A demonii entered the portal and waited on the other side. Lazaar grabbed her arm, his talon-like nails digging into her flesh, and stepped through the gateway, dragging her behind him.

The searing pain in her arm overtook her fear when she slammed into a stretchy, invisible wall and stumbled back.

"That bloody hurts!" she yelled.

"Force her through," Lazaar ordered, confusion etching his features. Rough hands grabbed her by the hair and shoved her into the portal. She hit the invisible wall again, bounced back, and went flying to the ground, jarring every bone in her body. Her dagger flew out of her hand and landed several feet away. The black blade started to glow a deep, pulsing amber.

***

What the hell?

The whirlpool of power that had sucked Aethan from the street, where he'd stood with Týr moments ago, finally dumped him in…

It took him a second to recognize the old abandoned subway station.

His tattoo shifted, and his sword materialized in his hand. The portal flickering in the dark some distance away snagged his attention. Several demoniis surrounded it, watching while two forced someone through—a human.

His irritation fell away. Ice encased him. Cold, brutal ice. His sword gripped in one hand, he remained where he was and focused his mind. In seconds, he'd shielded the mortal and let loose his power. It connected with his sword.

The portal snapped closed. Pandemonium erupted as the demoniis realized what had happened. They scurried away, crashing into trashcans and tripping over broken pipes and metal debris, the sounds resonating through the gloomy tunnel. Ear-piercing screeches filled the air as they desperately tried to flee. As if he would ever let the fuckers escape.

Aethan swung his sword, and white light hissed, spreading out in a deadly wave and obliterating every demonii in the station. Only their ashes remained, scattering on the ground.

His blade retracting, Aethan hurried to the fallen human. When he saw the choppy fall of black hair, his breath seized.

"Echo!" He fell to his knees beside her. She lay there curled in a protective ball, bleeding and unmoving. He pressed two fingers to her neck. No pulse.

Terror swept through him. *Urias, please.* Not like his damn creator would answer him now.

"Come on, dammit!" He pressed harder on her neck…there, he found a faint beat.

Quickly, he checked her external injuries. Three deep slashes scored the arm of her jacket and bled copiously, and her shoulder was dislocated. A psychic scan revealed her internal injuries. His mouth tightened. A fractured rib and abdominal bleeding. Finally, he moved her bloodied hand from her face and saw the damage she'd suffered from the feet of stampeding demoniis. Her face was a mess—blood oozed from deep scrapes, a large bruise was forming on the right side of her jaw, and her lip was split open.

Keeping his rage in check, Aethan laid his hand over her wounds, letting the healing blue light leave him and enter her.

***

Echo slammed back into her body like a comet crashing to Earth. Mind-numbing pain tore through her, as if someone had bashed her against a wall then used her body to scrape up gravel. Through the pain she could feel hands probing her, but she hurt too much to protest and prayed death would come quickly.

Instead, gentle warmth swept through her. Her eyes cracked open, her blurry gaze fixed on the shimmering blue light coalescing into her.

*The light souls traveled to after death is white, not blue...*she thought fuzzily. *But there had been white light too...*

The heat made her body warm and tingly. If God was giving her a second chance at life, she wanted just one thing—

"Remember our bargain," she rasped. Her throat felt raw, like she'd swallowed a handful of razors. And her head hurt. She shut her eyes again.

"What bargain?"

The darkly sexy voice seeped into her, drawing her toward it. She tried to snuggle closer, but pain held her in its grip. "To...to make me normal."

He shifted and her body rose off the ground. Like a homing signal, she sought the wonderful, familiar scent. Rainstorms.

Georgia Lyn Hunter

Aethan? Did he come to save her? If she was leaving this mortal life, then she'd leave with one of her wishes granted. One she'd dreamed of. "Kiss me."

His entire body stilled. Then, lips brushed hers. As light as butterfly wings, they touched her mouth and pressed gently. She sighed.

Then a whimper of pain escaped her as the clamps around her head intensified. "I hurt all over."

"I'll make it all go away. I promise. As soon as I get you to the Oracle—"

"Don't tell Damon," she fretted. Gran would be upset, but Damon would blow a gasket. "He gets mad when I—" Pain blazed again, and she moaned. "You're hurting me."

Instantly, his arms relaxed, became gentle. A whisper of a breath brushed over her hair as if in apology. "Who is Damon?" The words were a low, hard rumble of displeasure.

Echo forced her eyes open and stared blurrily at her savior. His image wavered. She blinked, trying to bring him into focus. Reaching up, she touched a swathe of blue hair, but pain flared and spiked higher at the gesture. Her hand fell away.

"Damon…pretty…like you." She lost the fight to stay conscious and let blessed darkness take over.

***

Aethan dematerialized to the Oracle's brownstone in Greenwich Village. He pounded up the stairs, his booted footsteps disrupting the quiet night. The entrance to the house sported a jungle of shrubs and vines sprouting from old tubs and creeping over the trellis around the door. A person would need a machete to hack through it just to gain entry.

Aethan willed the hanging vines away from the doorway. Adjusting Echo's weight in his arms, he knocked.

The door swung open to reveal a female of indiscernible age. Her salt-and-pepper hair was held back in a braid, but her cocoa-colored skin appeared smooth and unlined. Lila Smith's black eyes widened in surprise when she saw him on her doorstep.

"Warrior—" She broke off and frowned, her attention dropping to his arms. Her surprised expression morphed into horror.

"*Echo*? Oh, dear heaven!" Worry aged her face instantly. "Bring her in—come." At a fast trot, she led the way into her home, which smelled of herbs and incense, and toward the stairs.

"Do you know Echo?" he asked, shock sliding through him. Hell, he couldn't have been more astonished if his old mage jumped out of the portal and told him his banishment was over.

"Yes, from the time she was a young girl," Lila explained. "She and my granddaughter, Kira, are close friends—Kira's supposed to be staying with her tonight—where's Kira?" she demanded.

"Echo was alone when I found her."

Her face tense, Lila nodded. She'd treated the Guardians for their demonii wounds and understood how bad their battles could get.

The wooden stairs creaked under Aethan's weight as he followed Lila upstairs. She barged through a door on the second floor and into a feminine room with twin beds. Gently, he laid Echo on the bed against the inner wall and forced himself to step back.

"What happened?" Lila asked as she removed

Echo's jacket.

He filled her in about the attack, what he knew of it anyway.

Lila nodded as she listened, making short work of removing Echo's sweater. She cut through it with a pair of shears, leaving her in a tank top. Moving aside when Lila turned to set the scissors on the bedside table, Aethan paced to the end of the bed and back again. But staring at Echo's damaged face made it hard for him to think rationally, so he walked to the end of the bed again. Then remembered he still had to go do recon at the subway station and check that the dark portal hadn't done any damage to the smooth flow of the psychic veils between the realms. *And* find his missing dagger—

"Warrior?"

His head jerked up. At Lila's pointed stare, he snapped himself out of his gloomy thoughts. Shit, he was in her way again. He had to get out of here, before she cast a binding spell on him.

"I'll be back." He left the room and hurried down the stairs. As he passed a mirror at the bottom landing, he halted. His anger grew when he saw the blood on his mouth and chin. He swiped it off with the back of his hand and dematerialized, taking form in the dank tunnel.

The subway station appeared as if all life force had been wiped out. The continuous drip of water hitting the floor cut through the deafening silence.

Aethan opened his psychic senses and studied the planes between the realms for a fracture. The smooth transcendent waves flowed into each other. They revealed glimpses of the mystical thread woven together into a veil that shimmered like millions of crystals. He found no tears, not even a snag, as the waves flowed over and hid the veil again.

He scanned the filthy concrete floor for his dagger. He found a shitload of roaches scuttling about, and rats, their beady black eyes staring holes into him for ruining their scavenging. But no dagger.

He'd seen his weapon glowing on the ground beside Echo. But the image of her lying in the same filth, battered and bleeding, rendered him helpless—and rage blazed once more. He would find the ones responsible and eliminate the bastards.

He willed his dagger back, but nothing happened. He summoned a light ball. The glowing white orb sailed alongside him, lighting his way as he combed every corner of the crap-infested dump.

Where the hell was his blade? The damn thing was nowhere to be found. When Echo dropped the dagger, it should have returned to him. The obsidian couldn't be stolen. So where—

The truth hit him like a sledgehammer rammed into his gut. Air whooshed from his lungs. He staggered back.

Urias—no! No, his soul pleaded. *It cannot be!*

Chapter 9

Stalking the narrow passages of the black cavern he called home, Andras banged open the door to his chambers. A flick of his hand and several torches lit, casting an orangey glow to reveal the Wall of Screams.

Flames leaped up to melt the skin of those trapped in the wall, while invisible hands tore off their limbs, piece by piece. The cries of those he trapped soothed his soul and fed his psyche.

He'd have to devise something a little more interesting for tomorrow's entertainment.

Passing a mirror, he growled. His fist shot out and he shattered it, despising the image it revealed. That gaunt male with sunken holes for eyes wasn't him. He was handsome and he would be so again. Tugging at his lank blond hair, he stomped away from the scattered pieces of mirror which lay sparkling like diamonds on the black floor.

Taking a mortal's life had bound him for a century. It had been a careless decision, he'd realized too late. But he'd been so sure he'd found the one he'd been searching for. The moment he got a whiff of her scent, a dark haze took over. He'd torn into her neck and fed voraciously on her blood, then sucked her soul into him.

Delicious as she was, the bitch wasn't *her*. She'd been *with* the one he sought—had to be why that bastard, A'Damiel, had him incarcerated.

It didn't matter. Being old and powerful, he would have it all once he got the next part of the scroll translated. It was damn annoying he couldn't decipher it himself.

At least he'd known what to look for; a puny human with angelic powers.

Oh, yes, it was only a matter of time before he found her. Next on the list: finding out what must be done with her.

Andras cringed as his chest constricted. Breathing became difficult as stinging pain caused other parts of his body to follow in a mind-numbing cramp.

His cravings were growing worse. He wanted, *needed* a human soul to ease his pain. He never understood why light filled that weak species, while demons, so strong and powerful, were plagued with darkness. And then there were those Otium demons trying to walk the line between both. They were a disgrace to his kind, preferring to live like mortals. But they would all fall, one by one, like the traitorous insects they were. Their dark souls would succumb to the temptation, eventually.

The door to his chamber opened. He snarled, barely managing to hold himself back from killing the unfortunate person. He hoped it was either Bael with a soul, or Lazaar with news.

He tempered his scowl when he saw who it was.

Georgia Lyn Hunter

His sire, the Sin of Greed, strolled inside, his expression calm, his eyes bland in a parchment-pale face. Long brown hair looped into a tail flowed past his hips.

The fact that the Sins weren't tempted to take a soul made him hate his sire more. Of course they weren't. Not when souls were sent to them in Hell to satisfy their depraved needs.

"This is a surprise." He forced a smile, concealing his contempt. "A visit from the Sin."

"Boy, you do not want to take that tone with me," Greed said coolly, ambling around the room.

Boy? Andras's jaw clenched at the word. He fisted his hands to keep from wrapping them around the decrepit fool's neck. But he didn't dare take on his sire. Greed would kill him without remorse.

Besides, he had bigger plans.

Greed turned off the Wall of Screams with a flick of his hand. His gaze fell on the broken shards of mirror on the floor. His tone implacable, he said, "I sent for you."

"I'm busy. I have work to do. An army to oversee."

"Would this *work* have anything to do with breaking the Ancients' laws that keep the balance in place?" Greed stopped strolling and fixed unflinching eyes on him.

Andras dismissed the comment with a wave of his hand. "I have no idea what you speak of. I'm merely preparing my army for war."

"Yes, the very war that will occur by the rift that opened into the mortal realm. You have no idea of what you meddle in, boy. Fix it. Get those demoniis back to the Dark Strata."

Andras stared at his father, flames licking across his skin as he fought to keep his temper in check. The old goat had repudiated him as heir to inherit the Sin of Greed, because he'd taken the soul of a protected mortal. And because of that one foolish mistake, Greed had chosen Andras's fuckhead-loser brother, Lazaar, to inherit.

No matter. He had better things to look forward to. His sire would regret his choice soon enough. The tension eased from his body at the thought, the flames dwindling.

Greed's demeanor didn't change. His black eyes pinned on Andras. "You show restraint. Good. A'Damiel bound you to this realm for your transgressions. You *had* to go after a protected mortal..." Greed shook his head. "I saved your life only as a favor to your dead mother. She was my favorite. But break out of here and you *will* die. There will be no rebirth for you. Nor will I intervene again." After delivering his warning, Greed flashed out of the chamber.

Bastard.

Like Andras cared about rebirth. The same damn cycle, over and over again. The only way to end it was by iron or if those flaming Guardians got hold of them. But once they turned demonii, then there was no rebirth. Just Purgatory.

Why had he given into impulse and taken that soul?

Andras's teeth snapped down hard, and a molar shattered. He cursed again at his fate. Grabbing the chair nearest him, he sent it crashing into the wall, the splintering sounds soothing to his ears.

His sire's threat meant nothing to him. He could

taste his success, the freedom of having it all. Elation flowed through him like a dam breaking its walls. He would find the right mortal psychic this time, and all would be his.

"Bael!"

The demon came in a few seconds later, his dark gaze wary. He wasn't a demonii, which made it easy for him to procure souls.

"Did you find me an oracle?" Andras demanded.

Bael shifted on his feet. "No, my lord. If there are any in the human city, they've covered their tracks—"

A blast from Andras's hand and Bael slammed into the wall behind him. The acrid smell of burning hair and bubbling skin filled the chambers. The blisters erupted. Slimy yellow pus trailed down Bael's face.

"See what you made me do," Andras reprimanded him. He stalked to his armchair and sprawled on it, his face tight in annoyance. "You're a bunch of incompetent fools. If I weren't bound here, I'd have found both the oracle and the psychic female already. Get me an oracle, now!"

Bael straightened from the wall, the sores on his face oozing faster.

"I need a damn soul first. Then find Lazaar." Andras eyed Bael's ruined face in distaste and waved him away. "Go, clean yourself. You're a mess."

Alone once more, Andras drummed his fingers on the arm of his chair in contemplation.

When he had dominion over all, the Ancients would bow to him. A'Damiel could go burn in Hellfire. And all the fuckers who guarded the mortal realm would cower in fear of him!

Chapter 10

Aethan materialized in front of the Oracle's house. His body may have taken form, but his mind was in complete chaos, struggling to accept the truth. The horror of the reality staggered him as he tried to fit in pieces of a conversation that had faded over three millennia.

After his violent initiation into a Guardian's life, Gaia had held out several obsidian daggers, each with a swirling pattern on the hilts. They could never be stolen, taken, or lost, she'd told him. They'd always return to their rightful owner. Then she'd asked him to choose one.

One look, and he'd hated them on sight. Something eerie had skated across his skin just looking at them.

He'd refused.

She'd insisted. *Your dagger is an embodiment of your one weakness and your ultimate strength. When it fails to return to you, you have found your salvation.*

He hadn't understood her meaning at the time, but

Gaia's last words haunted him now.

Only with Echo had he experienced fear, and he damn well knew she was his weakness.

His salvation.

His…mate.

The one person who mattered to him for the first time in over three thousand years and she could very well die by his hands.

Aethan broke free of his paralysis and paced down the sidewalk, pinching the bridge of his nose. He veered back again. Shit, he didn't do headaches.

Where are you?

At the mind-link connection, Aethan growled, *Can't talk—later.*

Make the time, Blaéz ordered.

Dammit. *I'm at the Oracle's.*

He shut down the connection and promptly dismissed Blaéz. Hands on his hips, he glared up at the brownstone.

What the hell was he supposed to do now?

He'd spent centuries searching for his mate. But after his banishment to Earth, he no longer bothered. Why would he? This fragile race of humans was the last species he would have thought to find her.

But to discover that his mate was the tempestuous female he desired—gods, he'd give his life to claim her. But the fact was, she'd be the one to pay the ultimate price.

Already, his power prowled inside him, a dark reminder of what he was. The females from the pantheons chased him for that very reason—the rush of power that surged through them when sex was involved. They were immortal, their bodies repairable. But Echo dying the way Hannah had—

His brain disconnected on the thought, unable to handle it.

Even if, by some miracle, there was a way to overcome his cursed affliction, he had so little to offer her: a dead heart and a soul stained black with his many sins. All those innocents he'd killed in the name of eliminating demonii infestation. What female in her right mind would want a mate like him?

He exhaled roughly. No, he'd do the right thing. Once he killed the demon responsible for hurting her, he'd walk away.

Like Týr pointed out, they were warriors and their lives solitary ones.

The breeze picked up and snagged at his unbound hair. Reaching into his pocket for another tie, he secured the strands back into a ponytail. And glanced around.

Where the hell was Blaéz?

He cast his mind out into the night, scanning. His senses alerted him that he wasn't alone. A few seconds later, the Celt materialized like a ghost several feet from him.

"What's going on?" he demanded. Right then, he didn't care if the entire city had been invaded by demoniis.

Blaéz didn't answer, his eyes cool but searching. If he'd had a vision or premonition or whatever, he gave no sign of it. But those winter-pale eyes, almost pearlescent in the night, trailed over him.

"You aren't hurt," Blaéz finally spoke.

No shit. Why else would he be pacing outside the Oracle's house?

"Makes sense now," Blaéz murmured. "I saw something. Demoniis—a concealed place. They will

Georgia Lyn Hunter

take a mortal, and you are a part of it. I called you, but you'd shut down your telepathic link and didn't answer your cell."

Aethan pulled his cell phone out of his coat pocket. He stared at the melted lump of plastic and metal in his hand. Another dark reminder of why it could never be. Phones, he could replace, but not Echo.

"Guess that explains it," Blaéz said.

"I eliminated the bastards." Aethan dropped the melted phone back into his pocket. "But she got hurt. I brought her here." He glanced up at the house. Lights shone from the brownstone's windows despite the late hour.

"She's strong. Must have incredible shields if they couldn't bend her mind to theirs and get her to enter the portal."

Aethan's eyes narrowed at Blaéz's comment. For the first time, he saw something other than apathy on the Celt's face: interest.

The expression wasn't one he cared for.

"What?" Aethan growled. He might as well have advertised on a billboard. He couldn't even control his own possessive responses.

"They will try again," Blaéz said, still staring at the house.

"Then they'll have to go through me."

"She confuses them with her resilient mind."

"Why are *you* concerned?"

Blaéz glanced at him. His eyes seemed to smirk in the moonlight. His voice, however, remained as cool as the wind snagging their coats. "She's different. Intriguing. Her destiny entwines with yours, but you've already made your decision."

"Meaning?"

"You weren't ready to listen yesterday," Blaéz reminded him. "This path you've chosen to travel? Be prepared for the consequences. Later." With that, Blaéz sauntered off down the street, disappearing like a damn apparition.

He should have known better than to ask the Celt anything. His obscure reference was a pain in the ass.

Aethan took the stairs up to the Oracle's house. At his knock, the door opened to reveal a tall, curvy brunette dressed in jeans and pale green sweater, her hair woven into multiple braids. She had to be the Oracle's granddaughter, Kira. And Echo's friend.

Her creamy, coffee-colored skin was blotchy from crying. Her red-rimmed hazel eyes widened in surprise when she saw him.

"Lila?" he asked.

"Gran's busy," she sniffed. "You're gonna have to wait a while." She brushed at her eyes and stepped aside, letting him into the herbal-smelling house.

"What's wrong—Echo?" His gut fisted in panic, and he anxiously scanned the upstairs for her. Finding the steady rhythm of her heartbeat, his fear eased.

Surprise flashed in the brunette's wet gaze. "You know Echo?"

"I brought her here. She got hurt at the subway station."

At his words, her hazel eyes flooded with more tears. "I was with her when the demoniis attacked. Then the portal opened. She made me leave. I shouldn't have—it's all my fault."

Aethan wasn't surprised she knew about demoniis, considering who her grandmother was, but he cut off her self-recriminations. "You did the right thing. Or there could have been two casualties."

"I didn't want her going down into the subway. It's a horrid, horrid place. But Echo, she won't leave when someone's in trouble..." She scrubbed her wet face with the sleeve of her sweater. "I-I have to go help Gran."

Halfway up the stairs, she stopped and spun back. "Who are you, anyway? And how do you know Echo?"

"I'm Aethan. I've known her for a while."

Suspicion flickered over her features. "How come she didn't mention you? I know all her guy friends. She tells me everything."

"You'll have to ask her that."

Why hadn't Echo mentioned him? Maybe she didn't care enough to bother. The thought pissed him off. The sound of footsteps on the stairs interrupted his spark of irritation.

Lila patted Kira's arm as she passed her. Her dark face appeared ashen, and faint lines marred her skin. She tucked a few loose strands of hair behind her ear and sat down in a green armchair, weariness seeping from her.

Aethan crossed the room to her. "What's wrong?"

She sighed heavily, her dark eyes meeting his. "The bruises, the internal injuries, you've healed them. It's the deep wounds on her arm that worry me. She's been hurt by an old and powerful demon. He left his mark on her."

There was only one reason for inflicting such a wound. So the bastard could track Echo while the lesions remained unhealed. Yeah, he'd see about that.

"Then heal her."

Lila shot him a surprised look. "I can't. It's unlike wounds from demonii-bolts. It will take time."

"What if they come after her again?" he asked, his

fear for Echo growing. He cared little that his behavior was at odds with the person Lila knew him to be. Echo's life was at risk, and that's all that mattered.

"Then she must be kept safe until those lesions heal," Lila said.

Safe. Aethan looked away to glower at a painting of a seascape on the wall. The demon had tried to take her through the portal. If he'd appeared even a second later—

Aethan's mouth tightened at the thought he could have lost her before he even recognized what she was to him.

"Warrior, you got there in time to save her," Lila said, drawing his attention back. A grateful smile lifted the exhaustion from her face. But it did little to reassure him.

"How long will it take for her arm to heal?"

"A few days. Don't worry, she'll be safe here."

Did she really think he would leave Echo behind, knowing the wound acted like a damn beacon? That would put not only Echo at risk, but Lila and Kira as well. Time to put an end to that speculation.

"I'm taking her with me. The safest place is the castle. The demoniis won't be able to track her there."

Though Lila appeared calm, her wariness swamped him like a thick cloud.

"You know I'm right. With her at the castle, she'll be safe, and you can continue to treat her wounds without putting yourself or your granddaughter at risk."

She stared at him, not showing any sign of relenting. It didn't matter. He wasn't going to be dissuaded from his course of action. Echo would go with him.

He would have done so right then but for the fact

112   Georgia Lyn Hunter

that it hurt like a bitch to dematerialize while wounded, and he wouldn't put Echo through more pain. With no choice but to cool his heels, he strolled over to the window and stared through the net curtains.

"Why would you take on this responsibility, warrior?"

He couldn't fault Lila for asking, since she was one of the few humans who knew they were immortal Guardians. Not like they could've hidden that from a strong oracle like her.

"Warrior, I don't know how long you've known Echo, but I must say this, since she is mine. You take her, it changes everything. Echo's past has shaped who she is. Her life hasn't been an easy one, and I ask you to think carefully before doing anything."

He turned slowly in disbelief. "You think I will hurt her?"

"No, not intentionally, but you know what I speak of."

Her blunt words had his defense mechanism locking into place. So what if he was an immortal? Or, for that matter, a Guardian? Even if she picked up on his chaotic thoughts about Echo, it made little difference to him.

"My duty is to keep her safe. Even more so now that I know she's one of yours. You know the rules."

Lila's black eyes seemed to see right through the bullshit he was spouting. He didn't care. He wanted Echo secure within the castle walls. It was Michael's order, after all, to safeguard the Oracle's family. And it suited his purpose.

"I understand your concern. However, I still think it's best to leave her with me. I will keep her here until Damon gets back."

"No." His voice hardened, became layered in steel. He didn't give a rat's ass who Damon was. And he sure as hell wasn't leaving Echo with him.

"What do I tell him?"

"The truth. She's in danger and is under my protection." If the bastard couldn't do a better job of protecting her, then he'd see to it.

Lila sighed. "He won't like this, but all right. Keep in mind, warrior, you cannot expect to keep her safe by caging her. She's human. Free will is her right."

Not if it came down to keeping her alive. Then free will could damn-well take a back seat. Hell, he lived without free will. Being who they were, immortal and born with immense power, their lives were always governed by laws.

But there was something else he wanted to know. One thought that gnawed at him, dug its claws into his mind, and insisted on being answered.

"Tell me what happened to her—about her past."

Lila looked into his eyes. Whatever she saw there, made her nod in agreement, which surprised him. He'd expected her to question his motives. Maybe she couldn't see through to his blackened soul, after all.

"Echo was young when her parents died. She ended up in foster care. It's not an easy life for any grieving child to adapt to, and worse when one has abilities like hers. It was the worst kind of persecution when the people chosen to look after her turned on her."

The anger in Lila's voice troubled him. Not once, in all the years he'd known her, had she shown this kind of emotion. She rose, appearing older, tired, and slowly made her way to the dining-room table, where a tea service waited.

"Tea?" she offered.

He declined, preferring his caffeine strong enough to burn a hole in his gut. He waited while Lila poured the golden liquid into a thin china cup then stirred in a teaspoon of honey.

"What happened?" Aethan prompted.

"She wouldn't talk about it. But I've seen it in her memories..." Lila's gaze took on the same eerie swirling thing Blaéz's did whenever a vision took hold of him.

"You need to see for yourself, warrior." She came over, and laid a hand on his temple. Her psychic sight took over his, drawing him back to the past...

Into a shadowy night.

A dark basement.

Echo, just a girl, cowered in a corner. She appeared to be about six years old. A wealth of long black hair covered her face. Her pain evident in her stiff movements, but her fear was downright tangible, thickening the dank, musty air.

'*Stay there, you little bitch. Open your nasty mouth about Clyde again—don't you look at me with those eyes.*'

'*I'm sor—*'

Her foster father backhanded her. The force of the blow sent her slamming into the wall. Pain crashed through her shoulder, her jaw. But she never cried in front of him. To do so meant more beatings. But Clyde, her foster brother, was bad. He always tried to put his hand up her dress. Her foster father wouldn't believe her, called her a liar.

'*You ever look at me again, I'll cut out those cursed eyes.*'

Echo squeezed her eyes shut. God, please make

him go away. Please don't let him take my eyes.

'Don't even think about crying to Social Services when they come over or you'll regret it, you little freak.' He slammed the basement door closed and locked it.

Echo huddled against the wall as the tears finally trickled down her face. Hopelessness filled her. She looked up at the small basement window, her only source of light, which came from a lamppost across the street.

'Please—please, Daddy, Mama, come back. Take me with you.' More tears dripped down her face...

Aethan tore away from the visions, his breathing harsh. The unanswered prayers of the child Echo had wrapped around his heart like barbed wire, dug in their claws, and slowly shredded it apart. He'd heard every thought she hadn't yet learned to shield.

The pain, hurt, and sheer terror of his mate put him in an icy, murderous rage. The air became heavy with the promise of retribution.

"Where are they?"

Chapter 11

Anger crawling through him, Aethan entered the darkened bedroom permeated with the strong smells of potions recently used. Lila had to point out it served no purpose to seek vengeance now. But her logic made him feel helpless, which only fueled his ire.

He struggled to calm down. But...*shit*. He'd have better luck stopping the next major earthquake. The images of Echo's childhood haunted him. Too worked up to sit still, he paced at the foot of her bed, the carpeted floor subduing his heavy footsteps.

The curtains, fluttering in the breeze coming through the half-opened window, caught his attention. Lila may have left it open to get rid of the overwhelming smells, but this obvious breach in security was exactly why he wanted Echo at the castle.

He walked over and shut the window, then willed the bedside lamp on. It cast a soft glow over the bed. He shrugged off his coat and tossed it on the chair.

A large gray cat with a ginger ruff lay near Echo's head, taking up most of her pillow. Unflinching amber eyes watched Aethan's every move. Its heavy tail draped on her shoulder, flicked in warning when he drew too close.

"Tough luck, pal. I'm not leaving." Aethan crossed his arms and eyed the feline, undaunted by the animal's threat. "I'm her mate, get used to it."

The animal stilled. The hair on its back rose.

Aethan narrowed his eyes. There was something about the feline that made his psychic senses twitch. He prowled closer.

A low rumble escaped the animal's throat before it went back to napping. Its tail swished along Echo's arm as if reassuring itself she was safe.

The standoff over, Aethan shook his head. "I know how you feel," he murmured.

After a soft rap, the door opened.

"I'm sorry," Kira whispered, poking her head into the room. "Bob got away from me." Her gaze shifted to the bed then back at Aethan. "Gran said you're taking Echo with you when you leave and I'm to stay out of it. Normally, I wouldn't question her. But for some reason she trusts you. However—" She gave him a gimlet stare. "I'm gonna say this: Don't let my friend anywhere near those horrible demoniis until Damon comes back. He'll keep her safe."

Damon. The name was starting to irritate the hell out of him. "You would trust this person with Echo's safety?"

The answer shouldn't matter to him. He'd made his decision to let her go as soon as he'd turned the demon fucker after her to ash. But, as if under a compulsion, he had to know.

"With my life," Kira said, her tone sharp. "He is her guardian, after all."

Relief flooded him, one he didn't know he sought.

"Come on, kitty-cat. You're sleeping with me tonight. Echo needs her rest." She scooped the growling, chubby animal off the bed and left the room, closing the door softly behind her.

Aethan turned back to Echo. He examined the bruises on her face, which appeared to be getting worse as they darkened. He'd have to wait another day before he could attempt more healing.

Her fragile body had already taken on more than it could handle for one night. Demoniis using her as a stomping ground, him healing the severe internal injuries, and mending her fractured ribs, and the added pain of dematerializing—

He shut off the thoughts, knowing he'd lose his mind if he continued down the path of how close he'd come to losing her.

However, through it all, he couldn't stop thinking of the child weeping in the basement. He'd only promised Lila not to seek vengeance. But if he ever came across that human, he'd kill him.

Aethan hunkered near the bed and skimmed Echo's uninjured cheek with a gentle finger. She didn't stir. Lila had taped gauze over the wounds on her arm. A loose t-shirt had replaced her ruined and bloodied clothes.

Why the hell had she been in that subway? Taking on demoniis by herself? He'd warned her. Well, no more. He'd make sure of her safety. Aethan rose to his feet. A glint on the bedside table caught his eyes. The obsidian blade had returned. Not to him, but back to its rightful owner.

**

Echo awoke, feeling like she was floating through molasses. She glanced around and tried to get her bearings. It took her several minutes to recognize the striped pink and green curtains and the pale green walls.

Gran's.

She sighed in relief then gasped as a sharp pain pierced her chest. She tried to move her arm, but her shoulder protested. Her throat was parched and achy, and felt as if she'd swallowed sand.

Water. She needed water.

Someone helped her sit up and held a glass to her lips. She gulped down the cool, soothing liquid and grabbed the hand when it tried to take away the glass.

"More."

"No. A little at a time or you'll be sick."

At the low masculine voice, Echo frowned and squinted, trying to focus on the man in the dim light. Her heart did a wild little flip when she saw him.

"Aethan?"

"Yes?"

She licked her painfully dry lips and winced when she touched the swelling there. Everything came rushing back to her—the subway, demoniis, the demon trying to take her through the portal—and fear flooded her, followed sharply by relief.

"Y-you saved me," she croaked. "Thank you."

"I don't scare easily, but you managed to do just that."

His tone was far too quiet. Nothing of the arrogance she was used to. She met his dark, concerned gaze. "I'm sorry."

He brushed a hand over her hair. "Are you up to

Georgia Lyn Hunter

talking?"

She closed her eyes, trying to shut out the memory. "You want to know what happened." Nothing much frightened her these days, due to all the crap she'd lived through, but what she'd seen through the dark portal, had her trembling in horror. "They–he, the demon–Lazaar. He tried to take me to Hell," she whispered.

"Lazaar?"

She nodded. "That's what he said his name was. I could see that awful place through the portal." The words were difficult to get out. "The torturing of humans, and demons, too—peeling off their skin, ripping their limbs—" Her breathing hitched.

The horror, the depravity, caused a violent shudder to wrack her body.

The bed dipped. Aethan sat down and lifted her onto his lap. He wrapped his arms around her, his warmth soothing her. She didn't want to think. She wanted to forget. Inhaling a shuddering breath, she rested her face against his chest and tried to calm down.

"As long as I have breath left in me, I will keep you safe. I will find this demon and end him."

She reared back, fear stealing her breath. "No–no, don't. Please don't. He'll take you, too."

"He can try."

***

Aethan gently rubbed her back, willing her to relax. She had no idea of what he was capable off—he'd probably scare her more than that demon had. Slowly, the stiffness in her spine eased, and she lay against his chest.

"He made me walk to the portal, like I was his puppet," she whispered, her fingers absently stroking his chest. "How could he do that?"

"I'd say mind control, but that wasn't quite the case. He only controlled your physical movements." Aethan tried hard to concentrate on what he was saying. No surprise his body reacted like a lit fuse to her light touch. "His dark magic had no effect on your mind. He didn't succeed in taking you through because you are strong. Stronger than he obviously gave you credit for."

Her brown eyes lifted to his in confusion. He brushed the overly long bangs away from her face, then gave in to the impulse and skimmed his thumb over the irresistible dimple in her chin.

"Strong?"

"Unbelievably so." Hell, she'd kept him out of her mind when he first tried to read her at the cathedral. Her expression became skeptical. "You have built shields like an armor around your mind—your thoughts," he explained. He reached to the bedside table, picked up the liquid potion Lila had left for her and held out the glass. "Here, drink this."

The moment she got a whiff of the thick brown liquid, she wrinkled her nose and turned her head away. "I'm not drinking that."

"Take it, Echo, or I'll be forced to feed it to you. Trust me, you won't like that."

She scowled. "Gran makes awful-tasting potions. I ought to know."

"It matters little. This will aid in easing the pain and speeding up your healing."

"I'll heal the natural way then."

"Echo," he said, hardening his tone.

Sighing, she took the glass from him and, with eyes squeezed shut, drank the brown sludge in one gulp. Then she clamped a hand to her mouth as if to prevent herself from gagging, her eyes reproachful.

Aethan set the glass down, drew her into his arms, and found, despite the seriousness of her condition, he wanted to smile. The pleasure of holding his mate, the solid feel of her warm body in his arms—gods, nothing compared to this. Ever.

He reveled in it for a bit longer then ran a hand down her back in a gentle caress. "Echo?"

"Hmmm?" She sounded sleepy.

"I'm taking you to my home."

Her head jerked up so fast, she bashed him on his chin—hard.

"No!" Her eyes went wild with panic as she rubbed the sore spot on her head. "I'm staying here with Gran."

"Easy." He settled her against him once more, laid his humming jaw against her hair and inhaled her subtle scent of berries, now combined with the faint stench of sulfur from the demoniis he'd turned to ash. "Want to tell me why?"

"I must keep an eye on Gran and Kira. Keep them safe."

Of course, she'd say that. Hell, she'd put her life at risk saving the dredge of humanity, the reason why she was in this situation in the first place.

"Echo, listen to me. Staying here is dangerous. Not only for you, but for Lila and Kira, too. The demon after you will hurt them to get to you."

Is that what you want? He didn't say it but the question hung in the air.

"God, no—I don't want those monsters hurting Gran and Kira."

The anguish in her voice made him regret his words. But he needed her to understand. He brushed his lips against her hair. "You'll be safe at my home. Demons cannot enter there, and you will be well protected. If you refuse, I'll be forced to live with you 'til this mess is over."

The silence stretched and tautened, and just when he thought he'd be packing to move in, a soft sigh escaped her. "Okay, I'll go with you."

***

The Range Rover's headlights brightened the dark roads, illuminating the woodlands they traveled through later that evening. Shifting in her seat, careful of the aches in her body, Echo glanced out through the window. She didn't recognize the place. Her gaze followed the tall trees to their pinnacle and was rewarded by the sight of skies painted with the golden-red streaks of sunset.

"How do you feel?"

Her heart kicked up at the sound of his voice. She cut him a quick look. "The cartwheels will have to wait a while. I'm achy and a little sore."

He nodded. "We'll be there in a few minutes. You can take more of the potion Lila sent and rest."

She scrunched her face in distaste, but the sounds of purring from the back seat drew her attention. Glancing over her shoulder to where Bob napped in his carrier, she saw him flick his tail, no doubt dreaming of chasing the neighbor's teacup poodle.

"Thanks for letting Bob come. He means a lot to

Georgia Lyn Hunter

me." She settled back in her seat.

"He gave me little choice, hopped into the vehicle first."

His dry tone made her smile.

Aethan drove past a park and turned left. Fog soon submerged the road. Echo didn't like the sensation of being enclosed in the miasma, of being trapped, unable to see anything. She gripped the edges of her seat. Moments later, she caught glimpses of steel railings, skimming close to the side of the vehicle, like they were driving across some sort of bridge.

Her worried gaze darted to him. "Where are we?"

"Long Island Sound." He reached for her hand still digging into her seat. His thumb stroked her palm, distracting her. "Once we're on the other side of the bridge, we'll be there in ten minutes."

Even though she couldn't see anything out of the window beyond the steel and fog, her gaze flew downward and stayed there. Only when the bridge met up with solid land was she able to breathe easier.

Soon enough they came to a tall, heavily designed wrought-iron gate, which automatically opened at their arrival. Tall maple trees rose majestically along the winding driveway, casting deeper shadows over the dark road. The fog thinned and disappeared. After a while, the trees gave way to rolling green lawns and elegantly landscaped gardens that defied the onset of winter. Echo simply stared at the view in front of her, her pain forgotten.

He lives in a castle on an island.

Dark and gothic, it rose, disappearing into the mist suspended over it.

Aethan let go of her hand and drove the vehicle up the circular driveway, stopping at the front portico. She peered through the windshield at the imposing towers, castellated battlement, and terraces. It was pure fantasy. One she never dreamed would exist in her world. And now she would live here, for a while, at least.

Her gaze slid from the magnificent castle covered in ivy to Aethan as he circled the hood of the black SUV and came to her side.

This place resembles its owner a lot, she thought. *Dark, forbidding, and gorgeous.*

He opened the door, unbuckled her seatbelt, and lifted her into his arms.

"I can walk," she protested, anchoring her arms around his neck.

"When you're better, you can do all the walking you like. But for now..." He carried her up the stairs to the colossal front door, and it swung open at their approach.

Wide-eyed, she looked back at him. "Did you do that?"

He nodded and stepped into the foyer. The questions she wanted to ask evaporated like smoke. Her mouth dropped open as she stared around her in awe.

A grand mahogany staircase flowed from the upper levels down to the huge light-gray marbled foyer. Fading sunlight seeped through stained-glass windows which ran parallel to the stairs, showering the place in a kaleidoscope of colors. Tall marble statues stood guard over lush green plants.

Echo sighed. "This is beautiful," she whispered, her gaze going back to the intricate windows. Scenes of angels, massive warrior knights, and women in flowing gowns were depicted on the glass. In a place like this, it was only right to have knights and ladies. The angels

Georgia Lyn Hunter

fitted, too.

"I'll show you the rest when you're better," Aethan said.

Movement drew her attention to a man who waited in the foyer, dressed in black pants and shirt.

"Hedori," Aethan said. "This is Echo Carter. Echo, my butler, Hedori."

He looked nothing like her image of a stodgy butler in a penguin suit. He appeared too hard, too tough. Older than Aethan, he had skin the color of teakwood. He wore his steel-toned hair in a long braid.

He bowed. "M'lady."

Aethan's arms tensed at the man's greeting, his muscles like coiled springs. Echo glanced at him, but his expression revealed nothing. He merely cocked a brow. Hurriedly, she looked away, heat staining her cheeks.

"Hello." Echo attempted to smile at Hedori, but her jaw hurt and weariness tugged at her. She gave up and rested her head against Aethan's chest, wondering at the tension she sensed in him.

"Echo will be staying with us."

"Of course, sire." Pleasure lit Hedori's odd, orange-green eyes. Then he addressed Aethan, his expression reverting to its impassive state once again. "Sire, the Arc—"

"I know."

Echo frowned and glanced at Aethan.

Why did he cut the butler off? And what was an *arc*?

***

Aethan headed downstairs after settling Echo in his

bed. For once, she hadn't argued with him and simply gave in to sleep at the demands of her healing body. He'd left Bob on guard duty, the cat curling into a protective cocoon around her head.

Scanning, he found Michael in the study. A blast of heat hit him when he pushed open the door to the small room. Flames sputtered in the fireplace, casting a soft glow on the black leather recliners facing the hearth.

Michael sat behind a sleek mahogany desk adjacent to the fireplace.

"One moment," he said, not looking up from whatever he was doing on the computer. But his hand reached for the open can of Coke beside him. He sucked down the soda like a life-sustaining liquid, draining the can dry, then tossed it into the wastepaper basket.

This had to be the smallest room in the entire castle, yet Michael chose to have his meetings here. The Archangel's idiosyncrasies never failed to astound him.

Aethan crossed over to the French doors and opened them, inhaling the biting air. Night had settled over the estate. The pale, cool moonlight cast ominous shadows over the trellised walkway. He missed the dissonance of nocturnal insects that fall had scared away. Everything was too damn quiet.

He moved away from the doors and dropped into the chair opposite the desk.

"What's going on?" Michael asked moments later.

Aethan lifted his eyes from the sputtering flames and met the Archangel's probing stare. He would have already sensed Echo's presence in the castle and know she was hurt.

Georgia Lyn Hunter

Aethan didn't want to talk about Echo. But no matter how he felt, he had a duty to perform, a job to do. He leaned back in his seat and reeled out the facts. "Her name's Echo Carter. I came across a demon with a demonii horde forcing her through a portal."

The pen Michael had been flipping through his fingers fell. The next second the wall sconces blazed brighter, highlighting the bookshelf behind him. "You stumbled upon demoniis forcing a mortal through a portal—how did this happen?"

"In the old Delancey subway. It's a known hunting ground. I cleaned house, but Echo got hurt." His tone flat, he told Michael what he'd witnessed and about the wound the demon left on her. "That's why I brought her here. It's the only place she'll be safe until this mess is dealt with and the demon after her is dead."

Michael rose and came around to lean against the side of the mahogany desk. Good thing the furniture in this place was made to take their weight. "This demon, did you get a look at him?"

Aethan shook his head. "There were too many of them. The portal slammed shut the moment I appeared. But she said the demon called himself Lazaar."

Michael frowned. "Not familiar with the name. I'll check it out. Does she fit into the parameters of the one we search for?"

"No. Her psychic abilities are slight. There's nothing of *pyre and rime* in her powers, I checked. She sees auras. It's how she recognizes demons and demoniis and how I first came across her."

He filled Michael in about the incident at the cathedral. "I arrived just as the demonii disintegrated, and she attacked me like I was one of them in a move so skilled, calculated. Someone's trained her to kill that way..." Aethan narrowed his eyes. It had to be that idiot guardian of hers. But then if he hadn't, Echo could have died—*gods!* He guessed he should be thankful.

Unable to sit still, Aethan jerked up from the chair, and paced back to the open door.

"What are you going to do?"

He wasn't surprised Michael knew the truth, knew what Echo was to him. The fact that he hadn't checked in for two days, still wore the same clothes, and was now prowling around like a riled beast—yeah, he didn't need to say a word.

"Nothing. As soon as this threat's over, she goes back to her life."

The damn Fates were probably laughing their asses off, giving him a mate who was mortal—one he couldn't even claim.

Gods! Aethan scrubbed a hand over his face. His nerves were on the verge of snapping. "What the hell am I supposed to do?" He pivoted to Michael. "You know why I can't be with her."

Michael's shattered blues stared right into him. "When it comes to mates, no one can interfere, you know this."

To claim one's chosen mate was a journey traveled alone. And Michael had no intention of getting involved. Not that Aethan expected the Archangel to know a way out of his mess. Besides, Michael was of the divine, warrior angels. They didn't take mates.

Heavy footfalls sounded in the corridor, ending their conversation. Blaéz strolled in, took the leather recliner close to the desk, and eyed him but said nothing.

Týr followed a few minutes later. Ignoring

Georgia Lyn Hunter

Aethan, he sprawled into the other chair adjacent to Blaéz.

Right, he still had the mess with Týr to deal with, too.

The warrior plucked an M&M's package out of his leather jacket and poured several into his palm. He made his selection, tossed the red candy-covered, chocolate pebbles into his mouth, then carefully poured the rest back into the bag. Before he could put the candy back into his pocket, Blaéz reached out and nabbed the bag, tipping the entire contents into his mouth.

"And that's how you eat candy." Crunching on the sweets, he balled up the empty packet and shot it into the crackling flames.

Týr merely stared at Blaéz, but a ghost of a smile flickered in his dark gaze.

"Right," Michael said, drawing their attention. "I've spoken with Gaia. She decrees when the female is found, one of us will be chosen as her protector. It's imperative."

"What do you mean?" Aethan asked. He didn't like the sound of that. Hell, he had enough shit to deal with. Echo was a magnet for trouble of the worse kind.

"It would be overwhelming for a mortal, who has no idea we exist and isn't aware of the powerful bloodline she carries, to come to terms with all this. She will need someone she can trust to ease her into the path her life will take and guide her to her destiny. More importantly, *she* will choose her protector. The rest of us will guard her until this is over. If I have to call the others in to help, I will."

"Same old, nothing new," Týr muttered and pushed to his feet.

"No, it isn't." Michael's eyes became slits of sapphire ice. "She is more. The female we search for will be the only one who can enter any realm at will. She'll have the ability to heal fractures in the psychic veils and strengthen them, keeping out entities that cannot be allowed to pass through. She will be The One. The long awaited Healer of the Veils."

Michael straightened from the desk, his expression somber. "If the demons get hold of her, this realm will be the first to fall. Should that occur, it would be a disaster of cataclysmic proportions. We must find her fast."

Chapter 12

The sound of clashing metal reverberated around the white cliffs. Echo strained forward, but the man holding her hand wouldn't let her go.

"I want to see."

The man shook his head. But the branches parted out of the way, and there she saw the men, fighting with deadly swords. Lightning flashed from them, bouncing off the cliff walls and sizzling around her. She pulled back in fear.

"It's all right," his soothing voice said. "You can handle us, little one. Remember that."

She glanced up and met the darkest eyes she'd ever seen. But the man's face dissipated like fog...

Echo awoke to the scent of rainstorms teasing her nose. She rubbed the scar on her forehead and a sense of déjà vu settled over her. She had the strangest feeling she'd dreamt of that man before. He seemed familiar, but try as she might, she couldn't remember anything.

Sighing, she looked around her and found herself

on an ocean-sized bed, undeniably warm. The source of that beautiful heat came from a huge fireplace at the far end of the enormous bedroom. Above the mantel, antique swords were displayed on the dark wall, and she recalled where she was.

Aethan's home.

She'd slept in a real castle. Even the inside walls were of gray stone. French doors opened to a balcony. The outer wall flowed into a spacious turret sitting room with deep brown leather loungers and a flat screen TV. And near the fireplace, an open door revealed a dressing room. It had to be the most amazing...room? Suite? She had no idea what to call it, but it was gorgeous. Despite its extravagance, what really drew her attention was the huge bank of windows. Heavy indigo curtains cascaded from the ceiling, flanking either end.

Echo eased out of the bed and pushed to her feet. She swayed and landed back on the mattress.

Darn! She hadn't realized how weak she was. Slowly, she rose again and made her way steadily across the room to the windows. Late afternoon sun cast a pinky-orange glow across the sky. The terrace below, edged with rambling vines and potted plants, led out to a lush garden. She could see miles of parkland leading to the edge of a forest. Leaning her head against the cool pane, she braced her hands on the glass to support her shaky limbs and let tranquility seep into her.

"What are you doing out of bed?"

Aethan's annoyed voice shattered the serenity. Before she could turn around, warm, calloused hands swept her off her feet. Breathless, she flung her arms around his neck as he carried her back.

Georgia Lyn Hunter

"I just got out of bed and you're putting me back in it," she protested as he laid her down and drew the covers over her. He didn't respond, just leaned over her and stacked more pillows behind her.

It was the first time she'd seen him without his coat. Instead of his usual all black, he wore jeans and a gray t-shirt with one of those three-button openings that hugged his big, hard body—the long sleeves pushed up, revealing strong forearms.

This close, she itched to touch him, to run her fingers through his untied stunning hair flowing down his shoulders. Instead, she closed her eyes and inhaled his scent of warm man and wild storms.

"Now, stay here. If you want anything, ring for Hedori or call me."

Her eyes snapped open. Just because she'd been compliant on the drive here, it didn't mean he could continue to tell her what to do. The fault lay with the potion. It made her soft, loopy, and annoyingly agreeable.

"I'm not staying in bed. Nothing hurts anymore."

He straightened, crossed his thick arms over his chest, his expression grim. "Two nights ago, I saw a horde of demoniis three times your weight trample you. And moments ago, I found you using the damn window as a prop—my decision stands."

He just had to point that out. She slumped against the pillows in resignation, exasperated at his dogged determination to make her an invalid.

Echo glared at the vaulted ceilings and considered her options, unable to stay in bed when she was awake. Usually, she was at work—

"Oh, crap!" She shoved the covers aside. "I didn't call work. Jim's gonna be furious with me."

"What do you plan on doing?" Aethan blocked her escape. "Walk back to the city?"

"Aethan," she began in what she hoped was a reasonable tone. She didn't feel up to fighting him right now. "I can't be away from work. I have clients who rely on me."

Gray eyes pinned hers, beautiful, intense, and about as welcoming as ice. "I saved your stubborn hide from being taken to a person's worst nightmare, so yeah, I don't give a damn about anything else."

At his cold fury, she drew back. "But I feel better."

A nerve ticked in his jaw. "Do you? Very well. Show me. Do one minute of any workout."

She scowled, knowing he was right. She'd fall flat on her face, then he'd keep her shackled to this bed even longer.

He didn't say a word when she didn't move but hunkered down beside the bed and removed the dressing from her arm. He examined the wound, his touch gentle as he pressed the reddened skin surrounding the gouges.

Owww! That hurt. Echo bit the inside of her lips as pain spread. So he'd proved his point.

He rewrapped the dressing, his gaze leveled with hers. This close, she could see the icy white fissures in his gray irises.

"Echo, this is important." He rested his forearms on the bed. "As long as those lacerations are unhealed, you cannot go out unescorted. A powerful demon caused those wounds. He can track you wherever you go while in this condition. And trust me on this, he's probably found a way to get you through the portal by now."

Georgia Lyn Hunter

She gave in to the impulse, reached out and stroked his lean cheek. The roughness of his unshaven jaw, the warmth of his skin beneath her fingers, pulled a sigh from her throat. Desire simmered in her stomach.

At his sharp look, she dropped her hand to her lap and lifted her shoulders in a little shrug. "You're beautiful—can't help myself."

He watched her for a second longer. "Echo, did you hear me?"

"Uh-huh."

He was probably used to women throwing themselves at him. She didn't care for the thought and tried to focus on their conversation. He'd said something about being careful. Well, she was always careful.

"Whatever happens, even after your arm heals, the nights are off limits. Don't ask me why again. This time heed my request." His words held a hard bite.

If her life was normal, she wouldn't have hesitated to follow his advice after nearly being dragged into Hell. But her life wasn't normal. She had a mission to accomplish, a demonii to kill, before she laid her dagger to rest. Since she couldn't agree to his latest suggestion, she changed the subject.

"What happened in the subway? I remember the demoniis, the portal, then feeling like someone used a baseball bat on me." She frowned, trying to grasp onto wispy images. "I felt warm, but...it gets a little hazy there. I thought I saw a white light—" She shook her head, wrinkling her nose. "Imagine, seeing lightning in the subway. Stupid, huh? Guess I must have taken a harder hit to the head than I thought."

Aethan shifted on his haunches. "You took more

than a blow to your head. The white light you saw…was me."

Echo stilled, her fingers squashing the bed linens as her heartbeat sped up. She'd read about people having really strong powers, but that was in books, fiction. In reality, she'd come across very few people who were like her. It had been hard, but she'd accepted her ability that had caused her so much pain. A small part of her still envied Kira with her simple gift of changing the color of anything. But it was the first time she'd met someone with this kind of ability. "You can control lightning?"

"In a way, yes."

"That's a powerful ability. People could get hurt...die. Have you—have you ever killed anyone with it?" she asked him.

***

Had he ever killed anyone?

Right. Like he was going to answer that question. Ever.

He moved to stand. "Rest now, leave the questions for later."

"Wait-wait." She laid her hand on his arm. And his body craved more. "How did you find me in the subway?"

"I didn't. My dagger summoned me. The one you stole at the cathedral."

"I don't know what you—hey-hey!" She glowered at him. "You stole mine first. You didn't think I would let you get away with it, did you?"

Amusement tugged the corners of his lips. Her gaze dropped to his mouth. He had to shut off the urge to lean in and kiss her.

"You should smile more," she said softly.

Aethan jerked to his feet and moved away. Gods, she was too close, too tempting. He found himself wanting her with an increasing desperation. Her scent, her honeyed skin made him want to lay her out on the bed and taste every inch of her. He stopped at the fireplace as if distance would rid him of her touch. His need.

"Aethan?"

"What?" Frustration igniting his temper, he pivoted to her. At her wary expression, he instantly regretted his brusque tone. He rubbed his face and tried for a softer one. "What is it?"

"You–what do you do? What are you?"

He stared at her for a heartbeat.

I'm your mate. The words hovered, demanding to be said. He choked them back. The decision not to claim her was the toughest he'd ever made, but he had no choice. Not when the alternative meant her death.

"For now, I'm the one who's going to keep you safe. You need help to the bathroom?"

***

Echo stepped out of the shower and plucked the bath towel from the rail. Her entire apartment could have easily fit inside this stunning bathroom with its dark green marble tiles and trio of elongated windows. But it didn't hold her attention for long as she thought about the man in the other room. She quickly dried herself, crossed to the counter, and pulled out clothes she had in her backpack. Changing into sweats and a tee, she headed back to the bedroom.

Disappointment slid to her stomach when she found it empty. She dropped her backpack on the armchair in the sitting room, and turned, hearing the door open. Aethan walked in, carrying a tray, which he set on the low coffee table. His gaze skimmed over her, no doubt checking to see if she could stand without falling face first to the floor.

But Echo could do nothing to stop the little tremors rushing through her at his potent scrutiny. Nervously, she scraped back her damp hair.

Jesus, she had no idea why he affected her like that. Granted, she was attracted to him. Heck, who wouldn't be? The man exuded such visceral sexuality. It seeped into her pores and hummed in her like another heartbeat.

His dark eyes skimmed over the sweats riding low on her hips then traveled up to linger over her form-fitting green tee. Her nipples tightened under his perusal. His gray eyes flared in response, but he merely said, "Take a sweatshirt from my closet if you're cold."

"I'll be fine," she murmured, aware that the goosebumps dotting her skin had little to do with being cold. And she had a feeling he knew, too.

Aethan closed the small distance between them and examined the wound on her arm, then headed for the bedside drawer. Retrieving the ointment, he came back and applied it on her lacerations.

Echo let her gaze trail over him to distract her. He'd changed, she realized. Leathers hugged his muscular legs, and a black crew-neck shirt molded his chest. He'd tied his hair into a ponytail.

"You're going out?" The words escaped before she could stop them.

He glanced at her. "Yes."

Dressed the way he was, it had to be one of those hard-core clubs—

She cut off the thought, dropped her eyes, and struggled to breathe through the constriction in her chest. He hunted demoniis. She understood that, but for the entire night? And dressed like that? Yeah, right.

He looked ready for a night of debauchery with some woman who wasn't her. A woman who'd touch him, kiss him and—

Echo bit the insides of her lip. The pain helped distract her while she waited impatiently for him to apply a fresh dressing, then she could put much-needed distance between them.

No such luck.

Tossing the ointment on the table, he ushered her to a seat with a hand on her lower back, like she couldn't find her own way.

"Eat." He indicated the tray. Sandwiches covered one plate and thick slices of chocolate cake another. The thought of eating anything made her want to heave.

"I'm not hungry." Ignoring his frown, she turned to her backpack. She'd missed taking her suppressant last night—no, make that two nights. Panicking, she took the fist-sized bottle from one of the pockets. And wondered why she bothered.

The pheromone suppressant helped keep men at bay, so they wouldn't go into a frenzy and jump her. But the one man she wanted didn't seem interested in her at all. Oh, he reacted all right, but only when she provoked him.

Well, she wasn't taking this potion in front of him. She had some pride.

Pivoting, she headed for the bathroom, only to

collide with his hard chest. She hastily pulled back, like she'd been burned. His gaze smoldered like a living flame, a hot silver, before blanking out to cool gray.

He took the bottle from her hand, uncapped it and sniffed. "What is this?"

The horrid aroma of moss and other vegetation Gran must have dug up from beneath a rotting copse of trees infused the air. Embarrassment heated her face.

"Nothing." She held out her hand. At his unyielding look, she glared at him. "My suppressant, okay?"

"For what?"

She ignored his question, just wiggled her fingers.

He didn't budge.

She made a grab for the bottle, but he pulled it out of her reach. Then cocked his brow and waited. Irritation fired her blood. "Suppressing my pheromones, all right? Gran makes it for me. It keeps anything with a Y chromosome at bay. Well, most of them, anyway. I missed two days. So don't be surprised if you find demoniis on your doorstep."

"Demoniis are drawn to you?"

"Yeah, I got the crappy end of the deal when abilities were handed out. Seeing demoniis and having them attracted to you, it doesn't get better than that."

His eyes narrowed at her caustic comment.

"I'm allowed to be annoyed," she muttered. "The suppressant keeps men away, but doesn't work on demon-kind."

"And you had no choice but to protect yourself," he said, as if realizing the truth of her problem.

"No. I use my pheromones to lure the fiends, then I kill them!"

"You what?" The words exploded in the quiet

Georgia Lyn Hunter

room. He hauled her to him. "You ever pull that stunt again"—his nose touched hers—"I will take you so far away, you won't see the light of day again. Understand?"

Shocked, it took Echo several seconds to react. The cool, calm man had become a seething mass of magma. Maybe it hadn't been such a good idea to reveal that.

She shoved at him, but found his grip on her arm unbreakable. "I don't see how it's any of your business."

"Everything about you is my business. But go ahead—try me." There was grim resolve in his gaze.

Echo snapped her mouth shut and dropped her eyes, hiding her irritation. Fine. She'd play the spineless damsel in distress, if it got him to back off.

He let her go.

Snatching the bottle from him, she tossed it in her backpack and dropped into the armchair, fuming. She hoped the demoniis came by the hordes and knocked him off his gorgeous ass.

"If demoniis follow you here, I'll take care of them," he said taking the seat opposite hers. The fragrant scent of coffee teased her nose as he poured the dark liquid into a mug. Handing it to her, he sat back, as if all was right in the world. As if he hadn't just behaved like a throwback to the Dark Ages, threatening to lock her up in some godforsaken place.

Gripping the mug's handle, she slowly counted to ten.

"Is that what you meant by wanting to be 'normal'?"

Her gaze shot to him, her counting forgotten. He nodded to the suppressant in her bag. His question tugged the rug out from under her. A feeling she was becoming uncomfortably familiar with around him. "Who told you that?"

"You did. In the subway."

And she'd thought it was all a dream. That meant… Crap! She asked him to kiss her, too.

What was the matter with her? Could she possibly humiliate herself any further with this man? Oh, yeah, already did that. She bit her lip, right on the wound, and winced.

"Let me see that," he said.

"It's nothing."

She might as well have spoken to the wall. He got up and parked himself on the coffee table, right in front of her. Trapping her between his spread knees, he took her mug and set it aside. Tilting her chin, he examined her lip then traced a finger over the bruise on her jaw.

"Stupid demonii punched me in the face for throwing up on him," she complained, struggling to clamp down on needs surging through her at his touch.

His dark expression worried her. Then he held his hand an inch from the bruise, and a blue light shimmered from his palm, startling her. She jerked away.

"Easy…" His thumb stroked the shallow dent in her chin. "I healed you the same way in the tunnel." His tone lowered. "I don't like seeing you hurt."

Healed her? If he had such strong abilities, then healing must be one of them.

Oh, damn. Being this close to him wasn't such a good idea. She shut her eyes in pure self-defense. The warmth condensing on the aching spot on her jaw soon eased. Her eyelids flickered open, and she found him watching her, his eyes dark. Brooding.

Unsettled, she reached up to touch her jaw. He shook his head and pushed her hand aside. "I haven't finished."

Then he leaned in and swept his tongue along her lower lip. Her breath seized, and her heart crashed against her ribs. Her shocked gaze flew to his. "Why did you do that?"

"Do you want the biology lesson now or shall I finish this first?" A heartbeat passed then he said, "My saliva heals, is what matters."

"Oh."

She deserved his sarcasm. Like he'd want to kiss her.

He ran his tongue across her mouth again in a warm, gentle caress. Arrows of heat shot straight to her dampening center. A fever took hold of her.

Oh, Jesus, let him be finished already. This is torture of the worst kind!

He licked her lip again. Her mouth parted, and a puff of air escaped. The temptation of him being so close, licking her mouth was too much to endure. She didn't think, just reacted, and touched his tongue with hers.

He went absolutely still.

She recoiled. Idiot. He wasn't kissing you!

Mortification flooded her. She tried to move away, but his parted thighs caged her in. Why couldn't a hole open up and suck her in?

With a hand on her nape, he pulled her back to him. His tongue glided between the seams of her lips. He teased and tormented her until she finally let him in, and captured her mouth in a kiss that knocked the breath right out of her. Hot. Carnal...

Drunk on the taste of him, she moaned in pleasure.

No one—no one had kissed her like this. Ever. The man was making love to her mouth.

Breaking the kiss, Aethan moved and sat down on the couch, he lifted her onto his lap.

Echo turned and straddled him. Hands on her hips, he pulled her closer, his leather-covered erection pressing against her core. With a small moan, she rubbed herself against his hardness as her desire skyrocketed.

Finally, after three long years, she'd found a man she wanted to be with.

***

For the first time in thousands of years, Aethan had found the one person who could fulfill him. Her kiss was magical. Her warmth, her very essence seeped into the depths of his dark soul. Desire surged, made him greedy to know, to taste every part of her.

His tongue tangled with hers in an erotic dance. He slid his hands under her t-shirt to caress her smooth, warm skin. The scent of her arousal fueled his own. He pressed harder into her heated center. Her gasp was like tinder to his flame.

He raised her body up and bit her nipple through her tee. Damn thing was in his way. She wriggled back into his lap and rubbed herself against his rigid cock, making his body ache with a need so primal, he was seconds from laying her on the couch, stripping her bare, and sliding into her silky heat.

Ever present, beneath his skin, power simmered, molten-hot, looking for release. The air around him shifted. Too close—gods, he was so close to disaster.

He had to get out. Slamming down his shields, he

broke off the kiss.

"No." Her soft protest cleaved him in half as her grip tightened on his shirt. He closed himself off to her plea, dumped her on the couch, and shot to his feet. Grabbing his coat from the foot of the bed, he strode for the door, frustration vibrating through him.

Then he stopped and faced her. A sword through his gut would have felt better than the hurt look in her eyes, the confusion. She wrapped her arms around her waist.

"I'm heading out on patrol—go to bed." He walked out of the room and closed the door quietly behind him.

Chapter 13

Her heart thudding painfully, Echo stared at the shut door. Confusion and embarrassment churned through her. She'd not only clung to him like some horny leech when he ended the kiss, she'd begged him not to stop.

The truth was she couldn't regret the kiss. Raw and powerful, need still pounded in her. She touched her swollen lips, tried to focus, to calm the desire flooding her veins, and failed.

He'd reduced her to this quivering mess with just a kiss. A groan escaped. She was in so much trouble. If she let this man get too close, she'd be the one left broken when he walked away. With shaky hands, she picked up her coffee and drank some of it. The strong brew slid down her throat, easing her, and taking away the taste of him.

Finally, she managed to rein in the madness that gripped her to chase after him and demand he finish what he started. She glanced at the big bed once more.

Go to bed?

Yeah, right. She wasn't a child to be ordered

Georgia Lyn Hunter

around. She set her mug on the low table then took her usual dose of the suppressant. Pushing the bottle back in her backpack, she got to her feet, straightened her tee, and left the bedroom.

Wall sconces illuminated the corridor, which was filled with paintings that belonged in museums, along with several marble statues. It led her to the grand stairway. Holding onto the balustrade, she slowly made her way down, her spellbound gaze on the stained-glass windows.

"Whoa, hold it right there, little lady," a laughing voice said.

Startled, she turned and found herself staring into seductive, toffee-brown eyes.

His beauty had to defy the laws of perfection, Echo decided. Hair the color of ripened wheat fell in wanton disarray around his wide shoulders. He wore black leathers and a t-shirt with a neon skeletal hand on it.

"Hello there." Masculine dimples dented his cheeks, adding more to his sexual allure. Like he needed the edge. "I'm Týr. And you are?"

"Leaving," she muttered, wariness filling her. She'd taken her pheromone suppressant, but still, it had been two days. Echo stepped away, but he moved with her as if they were dancing.

"Aw, don't be like that. It's not often one as fair as you graces this dull place. Tell me who it is you're with, and I'll challenge him for you."

She almost smiled. He sounded like someone from a nineteenth-century novel.

He angled his head closer to hers and sniffed. Her wariness turned to exasperation. "Do you mind?"

A sudden gleam warmed his wicked brown eyes

as he pulled back. He looked as if he'd discovered the eighth wonder of the world or whatever.

Yep, too handsome and, from the twinkle in his eyes, an undeniable flirt as well. For a fleeting second, Echo wondered why she felt...nothing.

But how could she? When *his* kiss was imprinted on her? Aethan had knocked her for a loop from the moment she first saw him. The man simply steamrolled her defenses, into her thoughts, and was busy chipping down the walls around her heart.

"So, where's the blue-haired ass—I mean, charmer?" the hunk drawled.

"Why would I know?" Did she have it tattooed on her forehead that she was here because of Aethan?

He grinned. "Good answer. A name then, gorgeous?" His gaze traveled over her face and down her body.

Lord, why me? She'd barely recovered from what had occurred with Aethan and now she had to deal with this.

That's what happens when you don't take your suppressant.

"I don't have time for this." She glared pointedly at him. "If you don't mind…?"

He didn't move.

She sighed in annoyance. "I'll hurt you."

His grin widened. Of course he'd laugh. Compared to him she was probably the size of a gnat.

"You've wounded my feelings. I'll have to take a kiss in compensation."

The moment he leaned in, Echo didn't think, she just pulled back her fist and rammed it into his face. Ducking past the laughing man, she hurried down the stairs, shaking her sore fingers, but stopped as the

Georgia Lyn Hunter

staircase swayed and dizziness engulfed her. She grabbed the banister. Inhaling deeply, she shook her head free of the lightheadedness and glanced over her shoulder, only to find the stairs empty. The blond had disappeared.

How did he move so fast?

***

Aethan stormed into the kitchen and flung his coat on a chair. He slammed his hands on the granite counter and stared out through the window. What the hell was he thinking? He should never have touched her, now he knew what she tasted like—

"You okay there?"

At the sound of Blaéz's voice, Aethan turned. He thought the warrior had already left on patrol. Pushing away from the counter, he headed for the coffee pot.

"She settled in then?"

Aethan poured the dark, aromatic liquid into a mug, unsurprised the Celt already knew Echo was here. He drank some of his coffee before he answered. "Yeah. She's good."

The chair scraped on the tiles as Blaéz rose, folding the newspaper he'd been reading. The kitchen door swung open and Týr sauntered in, a familiar smirk on his face. He looked like he was spoiling for a fight. Whatever.

"At your own peril," Blaéz warned. "Or there won't be anything left for a chalk tracing."

Týr ignored him. "Damn. She's cute—feisty. Can't belong to you," he told Blaéz. "So, who's the spitfire?"

"Stay for bloodshed or go hunt demoniis?" Blaéz

drawled. "Can't believe the demonii fuckers won. Later." He tossed the paper aside, picked his leather coat off a chair, and strolled out.

Aethan set his mug down on the counter, his teeth on edge. "Did you touch her?"

Primal instincts, like a dam giving way, surged to the surface. The thought of Týr making moves on his female wasn't something he'd tolerate.

Týr pinned him with cold eyes. "Why do you care? All *you* can do is look—"

Aethan struck, fist connecting with bone. Týr stumbled back then charged Aethan in an icy rage. Fists flew and punches landed as grunts filled the kitchen. Pain streaked through Aethan's face from a blow to the jaw.

"My lords!"

At Hedori's bellow, Aethan shoved away from Týr, who tripped and went crashing into a chair, landing on the floor.

"She isn't one of your damn whores!" Aethan snarled at the fallen male.

Týr wiped the blood trickling from his nose. He glanced at his hand then up at Aethan. A cool smile curled his lips. "*She* touched me first, if it makes you feel any—"

He lunged for Týr.

"Aethan!" Echo's appalled voice broke through the red haze enveloping his mind.

His gaze zeroed in on her. He hauled himself off Týr and took in her skimpy green top and low-riding sweats that revealed a handspan of tanned flesh. Unmitigated fury flared through him at the thought of her with Týr.

He stalked over to her. "Did you touch him?"

Georgia Lyn Hunter

Her eyes widened and her mouth dropped open. The scent of her outrage, her shock, hit him square in the chest. It was the worst fucking thing he could have said, but his brain had shut off reason.

Her lips tightening, she wheeled away and marched out of the kitchen.

His blood firing in his veins, Aethan went after her.

***

Stupid man! Was that what he thought?

First, he rushed out of the bedroom like she'd jumped him—okay, maybe she had. But that didn't mean she did that with everyone, nor did it give him the right to treat her as if she did.

She stomped up the stairs.

Aethan caught her arm and spun her to face him. "Don't walk away from me."

"Let go of me," she said, her voice tight with anger.

He dragged her closer. "That's not what you wanted me to do earlier in my room."

The jerk! Her face heated in mortification that he would mention how she'd clung to him. She slapped her palm against his chest, pushing away, but barely put an inch between them. Dredging up the remnants of her pride, she raised her chin. "So what if I touched him? I don't need your permission to do so—"

"Don't even go there," he growled. "And stay away from him!"

"Don't tell me what to do." She shot him a cold look, her chest constricting at his accusatory attitude. "I didn't want to come here, but you insisted. I'd rather take my chances out there with the demoniis." Yanking free of his hold, she headed up the stairs. A hollow pit formed in her stomach that he thought so little of her. He didn't trust her.

"*Hedori!*"

She didn't bother turning around at the roar that almost deafened her. What did she expect? That he would come chasing after her and beg her forgiveness? Yeah, right. Things like that didn't happen to her. She bit down on her pain, on her feelings of inadequacy. She didn't need to get her heart broken. Again.

Philip had left because he couldn't handle her strength, her strange abilities, or her nighttime activities. Aethan simply didn't want her. He couldn't have made it clearer when he walked away from her in his bedroom.

***

Aethan stopped on Canal Street, adjacent to the Buddhist temple, after hours of aimless trolling for demoniis. His grim expression had most people giving him a wide berth. The stink from the road grills and the over-flowing dumpsters made even his cast-iron stomach rebel.

He scrubbed a hand over his jaw. How could he have lost his temper with her? It was Týr's way of getting his licks in. Why the hell couldn't she have just told him the truth? Instinct made him want to apologize, to rectify the situation. But reality was a cold shower. If he put things right between them, then what? Give her false hope?

Something hurt inside him. He rubbed at his chest.

No, it was better this way.

She already thought him a bastard. At least now he'd be able to keep his distance, and she would live. He'd asked Hedori to keep an eye on her, so she wouldn't get it into her head and leave while he was gone.

The tattoo on his arm itched in warning. Finally. The bastards were on the prowl. He shoved his troubles aside and forced himself to focus.

Blaéz approached from down the street seconds later. Together, they followed the demonii vibration. The trail led them to a dingy alley off Canal Street and a Taekwondo studio's back entrance. Icy, insidious sensations crept over him as they drew closer.

Glass from a broken light fixture near the door crunched under their feet as they stepped into the building. The large, open room, with one mirrored wall, was empty. The odor of death permeated the air, and beneath it clung the stench of demoniis.

Adrenalin flowed in Aethan. The tattoo on his biceps shifted. But he didn't summon his sword. On silent feet, he approached a closed door and opened it. Four hulking humans lounged about in the empty hallway that connected the large studio to other workout rooms. The humans leaped to their feet the moment Aethan stepped out with Blaéz, and thudded forward. The glazed look in their eyes made it clear the males, better suited to WWE, had been reduced to demon minions.

Itching for a good fight, Aethan charged. A taller male, with yellow hair and a broken nose, rushed him. Aethan evaded the ham-sized fist, but the human came at him again like a tanker. He dodged. The tanker dove and landed a solid blow to Aethan's stomach. A thick arm clamped around his neck like a vise and squeezed.

Growling, Aethan elbowed the male in the sternum. He swung around, lashed out with his fist, and heard a satisfying crunch as the appendage broke again.

"My nose!" the male howled.

"Thank your deity that's all I broke, human." Aethan evaded another flying fist. A brutal kick sent the male slamming into a wall, where he fell and crumpled into a heap. Pivoting, Aethan found the remaining three on Blaéz.

Those stupid dumbasses had no idea the Celt could kill them with a single thought. Like ants, they crawled all over him, because the bastard was letting them get their licks in with his need to feel.

For fuck's sake!

Blaéz's proclivity for being used as a punching bag rubbed him raw right then. Aethan grabbed the shorter human with spiky black hair. His heart missed a beat. The hair, it was so like Echo's—

Stars exploded in his head as the ugly-ass bastard punched him in the face. That hauled his ass back into the game. Aethan shook his head clear and growled, clamping down on the urge to rip the human's head off. A fist to his temple, and he was out cold.

Inhaling roughly, Aethan wheeled around. "Blaéz, dammit! This isn't time for play. Send the fuckers to sleep, and let's get rid of this infestation."

Blaéz grunted. "Hand-to-hand combat should be fun, right?"

"That's not fun-fucking anything. You should be kicking their dumb asses—" Aethan dragged another human off Blaéz and pounded him into oblivion. "Instead, you stand around and let them kick yours."

Blaéz made short work of knocking out the last male on him. A knee in the groin, an upper-right cut,

Georgia Lyn Hunter

and he joined his cohorts in Slumberland.

"You want to know the sensation riding me right now?" Blaéz asked him as he straightened his coat sleeves. "Nothing. Same shit as usual." He glanced at his torn tee. "Another shirt ruined, and we still have to clean house."

They headed for the closed door farther down the hallway. The stench of death grew stronger.

"They must know we're here," Aethan muttered. "What the hell are they waiting for?"

Blaéz fingered the rip in his shirt. "A personal invite?"

Aethan pushed the door open with his booted foot. The tattoo on his arm hummed relentlessly.

The small square office reeked of death. It contained a desk and a filing cabinet. And in the chair pushed against the wall was the body of a female, her terror-filled eyes wide in death. Her throat was torn, as if savaged by animals. Blood soaked her pink sweater and matted her long blond hair. The demoniis had to be concealed somewhere, watching them.

Let's deal with this and the four outside before we track the bastards, he mind-linked with Blaéz.

"We have another."

Aethan turned to find Blaéz peering under the desk. He strode around to him, and there, under the desk, a young female, about ten, lay curled. She whimpered when she saw them, her hand clutching her ravaged throat. Tears rolled down her face.

She cringed farther away when Blaéz reached for her, her whimper more of a gasping gurgle. "Listen, female, if you want to live, then come out from under there."

The male had all the sensitivity of a rock.

Aethan pushed him aside and stopped. He had no idea what the hell he should do, so he willed her to look at him and held out his hand. Soon enough, she placed her small bloodied one in his. Gently, he drew her out, sent her to sleep, and laid her on the floor. Holding his hand over the wounds on her neck, he let the healing light flow out of him and into her. The light tingle of her psychic power brushed against his mind. His anger fired up again at the atrocity done to a defenseless little girl. The horror she must have lived through.

His tattoo stirred sharply on his skin. Grunts filled the air.

Glancing up, he found Blaéz tackling two demoniis through the open door. Good to know the Celt didn't play when it came to those shitheads.

Aethan concentrated on healing the girl. *Almost done.* He watched as the skin slowly sealed from the inside, knitting together.

He jerked forward, agony piercing his shoulder and crashing through his body in waves.

Shit! The same freaking shoulder, every fucking time! He rose and stumbled, weakness taking him over from the dark power of the accursed demonii-bolt.

"Somethin' wrong, Guardian?"

He wheeled around and glared at the fucker who'd nailed him.

The demonii smirked, revealing stained fangs. "We know you have the psychic mortal. She can't get away with killing us—I'm so going to enjoy taking her soul. Then we'll come after you." Another red bolt sparked in his hand.

That's what you think. With preternatural speed, he moved and grabbed the demonii by the shirt, giving the asshole no chance to release the bolt. Aethan's power flared. Unable to release it without Blaéz and the girl getting caught in its deadly light, he punched through the demonii's chest, pulverizing bone and flesh.

He seized the heart and let loose his ability. "Don't threaten what you can't kill."

Red eyes widened in horror as the flame of whitefire consumed him. The demonii disintegrated into ash seconds later.

The other demoniis' dusty remains lay scattered around Blaéz's feet.

Aethan brushed his grubby hand on his tee and pulled out his cell. "Damn, phone's fried again. Call 911. I'll deal with the dead female."

Aethan walked over to obliterate her. He couldn't leave this killing for human authorities to find.

"It's strange," Blaéz said, "that they didn't abduct these females, considering they were both psychic."

"This has nothing to do with the prophecy. These gluttonous fuckheads only wanted the rush consuming a psychic's soul would give them."

And Echo was damn well staying put, even if he had to ask Blaéz to take over her protection.

Chapter 14

Aethan arrived back at the castle in the early hours of the morning. After the incident at the Taekwondo studio, weakness overtook him. With his pain-in-the-ass injury fast deteriorating, he wasn't fit to fight a damn roach.

He stood on the portico and let the silence and the briny air seep into him. Exhaling roughly, he scanned the perimeters of the boundary. Satisfied all was quiet, he pushed open the front door and staggered into the foyer.

It took every scrap of his waning willpower not to look upstairs or let his mind wander to Echo. He shrugged off his leather coat and cursed. Pain raced through his shoulder and spread to his neck. Ripping off his skin layer by excruciating layer would have been far better. Dizziness plagued him. He inhaled a ragged breath and the acrid stench of burnt hair drifted to him.

He pulled the singed strands to the front. Wonderful! Not only had the fuckers destroyed another coat of his, but they'd ruined his hair too! Cursing, he lurched through the kitchen toward the butler's quarters.

Aethan left Hedori's room ten minutes later, his hair shorter, and a little steadier on his feet.

Echo was right, Lila's potion tasted like shit but it counteracted the weakness from the demonii-bolts. He rolled his taut shoulder. Damn thing hurt like a bitch, but he had something else to do before he treated his wound with the salves Lila left for them.

As he made his way back to the kitchen, he found Blaéz and Týr there, chowing down on humongous roast-beef sandwiches. Týr reached out for the mustard, slathered it on his bread, and added several more slices of meat before slapping the thing back together and took a bite.

Blaéz looked up from his meal. "Joining us?"

"In a moment." Aethan took a bottle of water from the fridge and leaned against the counter. He couldn't put this off any longer.

"There's something I need to discuss with you. The female here…" He had to force himself to continue and speak of Echo like she didn't matter to him. "Her name is Echo Carter, and there's a demon after her. He tried taking her through a portal a few nights ago. He didn't succeed. But he scored her arm, so he can track her."

"Like a demonii-bolt," Blaéz said, pushing his empty plate away. He picked up his squat glass and took a swallow of his whiskey. The bruises on his face from the fight with the humans had faded to yellow.

"Why does the demon want her? Is she psychic?" Týr asked, his expression cool.

The warrior wasn't ready to forgive him, but he

understood their work always came first.

"Yes. And no. She's not the one we search for. She has no abilities of *pyre and rime*." Aethan unscrewed the bottle cap, his gaze on Týr. "That night I tracked the demonii I wounded?"

Týr nodded, eyes flat. "He's dead, right?"

"Yeah, the bastard's dead, but *I* didn't kill him. She did."

Týr stilled.

Blaéz stared.

A trace of his old humor flickered in Týr's gaze. "You've gotta be shitting me."

"It's how our paths crossed and now there's this." Aethan told them what the demonii in the Taekwondo studio had said.

"So they want the female you protect?"

"And our collected arses, it seems," Blaéz murmured.

"Well then, good thing she's here, if they're coming after her." Týr polished off the rest of his sandwich.

Hell, it wasn't the only reason he'd brought her here. And talking about her pheromone problem to the males was not something he wanted to do. He had to remind himself that her safety came first.

Now if he could just unclamp his damn jaw, he could get this over and done with. Then he'd ask Blaéz if he'd see to her protection. He took a drink of water then left the bottle on the counter. "There's something else you should know. Why she'll always be their target... Her pheromones. That crap draws them to her."

Stunned silence filled the place.

"Well now. That's what it was." The grin on Týr's

Georgia Lyn Hunter

face had Aethan jamming his fists into his pants pockets so he wouldn't be tempted to knock Týr's teeth down his throat.

He told them the rest. "She uses her pheromones to lure the bastards out, then she kills them."

"Damn, I was right. She's a feisty one, all right." Týr rose and took his dishes to the dishwasher. He packed the thing in, before heading for the door. Turning, he met Aethan's gaze. "Just so you know, she didn't touch me—she punched me."

"Why?" There was only one reason for Echo to do so.

"Asked her for a kiss. She didn't oblige—"

Aethan leaped for Týr, blood rushing to his head, only to find himself tethered in place by Blaéz.

"Get the hell off me!"

But the Celt remained like a freakin' oak tree. One Aethan was quite prepared to uproot and hack up for firewood.

"He never did share well," Týr muttered and left.

He'd wipe the floor with the bastard. Muscles straining, Aethan tried to break free of Blaéz's hold, but the warrior's arms were like steel clamps around him.

"You are your own worst enemy," he told Aethan. "You want the female? Claim her or let her go. I warned you to be prepared for the consequences of the path you've chosen."

Aethan finally shoved Blaéz off him, and dematerialized upstairs, his mind furious with resolve.

Had he really thought he could walk away from his mate and not want to kill every male who looked in her direction?

***

Echo paced the bedroom. Her eyes narrowed.

Yup, definitely closing in on her. Each time she turned around the walls took another step closer. She glanced at her cell. *4:07 a.m.* Darn. Only a minute had passed since she last looked, like, an hour ago? She rubbed her palms over her sweats, stopped at the window, and stared into the darkness.

Why did Hedori insist on waiting until daybreak to take her back to the city? A cab would do just fine. She wanted to be gone before Aethan got back. How could she look at him and know everything, every look, every touch, had only been in her mind?

"Stupid, stupid Echo," she muttered for the hundredth time. *As if he'd want me.*

He'd been clear right from the get-go about only keeping her backside safe. Seems she'd forgotten that.

A frisson of awareness darted through her. Her heart kicking up speed, she spun around.

Aethan watched her from across the room.

Crap. He was back earlier than she'd expected.

His unrestrained hair skimmed his shoulders now and framed his striking face. Anger and something else—probably irritation—blazed in his gray eyes. He strode to her.

Echo backed away. Not in the mood for a fight, she picked up her backpack from the armchair. "I'll wait downstairs."

He blocked her path. The next second her backpack disappeared and landed on the chair again. "You're not leaving."

So the orange-eyed snitch of a butler had ratted her out. It didn't matter. She'd walk if she had to. "You can't stop me."

All she wanted was to get out of here without making a bigger fool of herself.

His jaw tightened as if to keep himself under control. "Gods, Echo. Don't make this any harder."

Of course it was her fault. It pained her to admit the truth. "I'm sorry for what happened in here. I-I wasn't thinking. It's just the pheromones at work. Once I leave, everything will go back to normal." She looked away, unable to meet his gaze. "And you won't feel this compulsion to be with me, or the guilt afterwards because it wasn't what you wanted—"

"I don't want your apology." His growl reverberated through the room, startling her. He dragged her to him and clamped his arm around her waist when she tried to break free. "I want you so damn much."

His words pierced the walls around her heart and stopped her struggling. Her voice came out in a croak. "What?"

He didn't answer but bent his head and kissed her on her nape—right on the spot where he'd bitten her the first time she dared him. Her body came alive, needs surging at the touch of his warm lips on her skin. Her breath hitched. "Why? You accused me of going after your friend just a few hours ago."

"No." He pulled back to look at her, a tick beating rapidly in his jaw. "I asked if you touched him. I'm sorry for that. I find I don't deal well with jealousy. Why didn't you tell me you punched Týr?"

Her eyes widened in shock. "You were jealous?"

His mouth tightened. "Do us both a favor, Echo, and never test that theory."

"Then why did you walk away from me earlier?"

***

Aethan let her go and raked a hand through his hair, frowning at the shorter length. That question needed to be answered.

"I'm not good for you. But no matter how much I convince myself of it, I find I can't give you up." He took a deep breath, hoping it would help settle him.

No such luck.

"This is your last chance to escape me. Free will, I'm told, is important to mortals. It's your choice. If you choose us, Echo, I have to warn you, it's not going to be easy." She would have to know the truth about him eventually, but no way would he risk telling her now. "Or you can take another room, and I'll keep you safe until this threat is over and you can leave."

It's a wonder he didn't shrivel up from his lies.

She chewed on her bottom lip as she studied his face, and he damn near growled again.

"So, I can choose another room?"

Something deep inside him shifted, protested. No matter her decision, he'd let her keep the illusion of choice, but he would never, ever let her go. *Mine.* The word seeped into his blood and embedded in his soul. "Yes," he bit out.

Her brow arched. "You just said you couldn't give me up, now you say you'll let me go?"

He shrugged. "I did. But if you choose to leave, I planned on changing your mind."

A smile tugged her mouth, then her brow wrinkled in confusion. "What do you mean, 'mortals'?"

Gods, so many questions.

For a male who'd waited several millennia for his

Georgia Lyn Hunter

mate, Aethan found he wanted her y*es* with a desperation that clawed at him. He did the only thing he could. Closing the gap between them, he slid a hand around her neck and took her mouth in a hungry kiss.

The taste of her made his head spin. Warm and silky, he could spend hours kissing her. Her hands fell to his shoulders, and he cursed as pain surged.

She jerked back, her gaze widening in alarm at the blood smearing her fingers. "You're bleeding."

Right. He'd forgotten about that. "I need to take care of this, and Echo"—his eyes held hers—"I need your answer." Stripping off his tee, he headed for the bathroom.

***

Echo took a moment to get her racing heart under control and tried to focus. Moments ago, she'd been ready to leave, and now everything had changed. At least all these feelings hadn't been all one-sided. But she didn't understand why he thought he wasn't good for her.

Needing answers, she followed him to the bathroom.

Seeing her, Aethan straightened from the counter. Echo opened her mouth to question him and then simply closed it when no words came out. Every single thought she had dissipated like mist. The man had a body that would make most men slink away in despair.

Rope after rope of sleek, tawny muscles flowed into each other. His leather pants rode low on his hips. Banded blue hair no longer flowed down his back but swept over his shoulders. He shoved the strands back from his face, drawing her eyes to ripped abs. The few nicks and old scars just added to his appeal.

"What is it?" he asked her when she just stood there.

I want to lick every inch of you.

"Nothing." She swallowed, since she could do little else to temper down her desire. "How did you get hurt?"

His gaze lowered to her arm. He didn't seem interested in his injuries, only hers. "Where's the dressing?"

She scrunched her nose. "The thing itches, drives me crazy—I'll put another on before I go to bed."

He examined the angry welts of newly knitted skin and stroked the redness surrounding the injury with his thumb. His gentle touch sent another jolt of need through her body. "Make sure you do."

He turned back to the counter and picked up a brown bottle. Echo spotted the tattoo of a sword on his biceps. She wasn't surprised he had one. The man had blue hair and earrings. Why not a tattoo?

The inky lines etched into his skin were intricately detailed, almost ethereal. She reached out and stroked a finger down the tattoo's compelling design. Myriad patterns made up the sword. It was unlike anything she'd ever seen.

Moving in for a closer look, her gaze fell on his wound instead. She gasped. "Aethan, your shoulder's really bad."

Whatever had hurt him had seared right through the thick muscles, leaving a gaping wound. Her stomach churned at the pain he must feel. "What happened? Did the demoniis do that?"

He shifted away so she could no longer see the damage. "It's nothing."

Georgia Lyn Hunter

"How can you say that? It looks awful. You need a doctor."

"It's not that bad. It will heal." He picked up a cotton gauze, saturated it with the solution from the bottle, then angled his body, so he could see his injury in the mirror and started to clean it.

Not that bad?

Irritated, she pushed him down onto the closed lid of the toilet seat. The wound looked like someone had stuck a blade through him, sideways. He didn't seem to care that he could bleed to death.

"What is it with you men?" she snapped, picking up another piece of gauze. She wet it with the solution and gently cleaned the blood from his injury. "Are you born thick-headed, thinking macho pride will make this better?"

"Macho pride?" he repeated, raising a dark eyebrow. "Hardly. Echo, nothing can happen to me. I've had worse. Getting hurt is a side effect of what I do."

"What? You have nine lives now?" She tossed the bloody cotton gauze on the counter. Why couldn't he ever answer her questions in straight English?

His silver-flecked eyes skimmed over her face. Warm and inviting, they made her want to drown in them. She huffed out an annoyed breath. Lethal is what he was. He made her forget why she was mad.

"Nothing's that drastic when you can't die."

She glared at him. "Did taking too many demonii-bolts make you delusional, too?" Pouring more solution on another piece of gauze, she slapped it on his wound, making him wince. Then she threw him a venomous look before stalking out.

He thought he was so damn funny. Giving her

crap about *her* safety. Demanding *she* not spend her nights hunting demoniis. While *he* could do whatever he liked.

And now he can't die? *Ah!*

***

Damn, his female was fast. Aethan caught her before she'd made it halfway across the bedroom and swept her up into his arms. She yelped, her flailing arms fastening around his neck. "Put me down."

"No." He carried her back to the bathroom and let her slide down his body until her feet touched the floor.

"Are you crazy? Your shoulder's bleeding again!"

Aethan sat down and tried to ignore his erection straining against his leathers.

She reached over for more gauze and staunched the slow trickle of blood he could feel trailing down his shoulder. Whatever she did to his wound stung big time, but it paled in comparison to the emotions churning inside him.

He took in her flushed face, her eyes sparking with irritation. Oh, yeah, she was pissed as hell, and it only made him want her more. Had he really thought he could walk away from her? Let her go?

Tenderly, he brushed the hair away from her eyes. And a heart he'd thought long dead started to beat once more. Emotions crowded him. He wrapped his arms around her waist, pressed his face to her chest, and simply held her.

After a moment, her tense body relaxed into him, and she sighed. "I'm sorry if I hurt you."

"I hardly felt it."

"Liar."

Georgia Lyn Hunter

But he heard the smile in her voice. Gods, no one made him feel this way. Ever. Her scent, her warmth crowded him. He slipped his hand under her tee, needing the skin contact. "You wear too many things."

She laughed. "It's a t-shirt. You can hardly get any less than that."

"Like I said, too many." He grasped her around her nape, his thumb stroking her quickening pulse, and brought her mouth down to his. He nipped at her bottom lip. The catch of her breath had his sex growing harder. Clamping down on his needs, he licked away the pain and trailed his lips along her jaw.

Her fingers combed through his hair, gently tugging at the ends. Distracted as he was, he almost didn't hear her soft murmur, "Why did you cut it?"

Grateful at least some part of his brain was functioning, he answered, "A demonii-bolt scorched it. Hedori sorted out the mess."

He ran his tongue over the rapid-fire pulse at her throat. She shivered. "The fiends," she muttered, leaning against him as if her legs could no longer support her. "Next time, let me cut it for you."

"I'll end up with hair like yours."

Her laugh was a husky caress on his already sensitized skin. He took the hand destroying his peace of mind and pressed a kiss to her palm. "Your answer, Echo?"

"All right. I will live here with you."

"Why?" He held her gaze, wanting more than just those words.

"Because I want you, too," she said softly. "God knows why. You're bossy, arrogant, and you like getting your own way far too much." She stopped when she saw him smile. "What?"

Aethan shook his head. "You make me happy."

The twitch at the corner of her mouth slipped into a reluctant smile. "See. There's something wrong with you. No one likes me—at least, not the real me." Her mouth snapped shut. Uneasiness crossed her face. The pain behind her words was like a physical blow to his gut. Memories of what Lila had showed him came rushing back.

"I don't care what others think. You are what matters to me and all I want." He skimmed the dent in her chin with his thumb, pleased when the sparkle reappeared in her eyes. "Will you do something for me?"

"What?"

"Take out your contact lenses. You don't really need them, right?"

She stiffened. Color drained from her face. "I need them." Her gaze skated away from his and she tried to step back.

Aethan didn't let go. He searched her face, her mind, and didn't like not being able to read her thoughts. This had to be about her foster family. "Who hurt you?" he asked, unable to control the roughness in his voice.

She shook her head. "It's not important—all in the past. You were telling me about yourself."

The pain, the desperation she tried to hide, hammered at him. Aethan clamped down on his frustration when she refused to say more. He'd let it go. For now. "Whatever I say, no screaming or running out of the house, okay?"

"Yes, I'm the type to run from danger."

He narrowed his eyes. "You really don't want to remind me of that."

She sighed. "I've known demoniis existed from a young age. What can be scarier than them?"

Me.

He looked at her for a long, silent moment. He could lay down all the rules he wanted, lock her up for the rest of her life so nothing could ever harm her, but could he save her from himself?

"I am one of the Guardians of this realm. We protect this world against any supernatural evil—keep the innocent safe."

"What do you mean 'this realm'?"

"There are many, Echo. Earth is just one of them. I come from a different world called Empyrea."

She pushed away from him. "Aethan, I was attacked by a demon. I might've hit my head but I didn't lose my mind. Do you honestly expect me to believe that old fairy tale?"

He frowned. "What fairy tale?"

She rolled her eyes and gathered up the soiled gauze from the marble counter. "Okay, maybe not a fairy tale exactly. But, you know, the story about a race of immortal beings with unbelievable powers who live in a magical place called Empyrea."

Echo couldn't have shocked him more if she picked up a tanker and dropped the thing on him. She knew about his world? "Who told you this?"

Her brow puckered into a tiny V. She rubbed the scar on her forehead, as if trying to remember. "I...I don't know. Look, they're just tales told to a little girl who needed to believe something else existed out there. Something wonderful, instead of demons and cruel people. Tell me the truth, Aethan, or drop it. But don't lie to me."

"It is the truth," he growled. "I'm immortal. That's

why this"—he gestured to the bloody hole in his shoulder—"isn't a big deal."

But Empyrea, *magical*?

Gods, he'd hate to disillusion her on that score.

When she learned the truth about him, the whole thing would blow up in his face and shatter her dreams. A helluva gift for an unsuspecting human mated to a nuclear weapon.

***

Immortal? Why would he say that? Sure, his aura was different. But that had to be because of his strong psychic abilities.

"Aethan, look, I don't—" Echo broke off as an eerie sensation snaked through her. The hair on her arms rose. "Something's wrong." Her gaze darted around the bathroom, then veered back to him. The annoyance in his gaze was replaced by something so lethal, it scared her. "Aethan?"

He didn't answer, just moved her aside and rose to his feet. Grabbing his discarded, bloodied shirt, he yanked it on.

The tattoo on his biceps shifted, startling her. She leaped back. *Holy crap!* The thing was real? Riveted, Echo watched as it shimmered and materialized in his hand as a six-foot sword. The intricate markings of the tattoo slid down his arm, and settled onto the sword's guard and blade.

"Stay here. Don't leave under any circumstance, understand?"

"Wait-wait-wait! Aethan, what's happening?"

When he didn't answer, her gaze raced to the trio of elongated windows above the bathtub. All was still dark outside, and she suddenly realized the truth.

"*Demoniis.*" She sucked in a harsh breath. "They found me. I told you they would. I shouldn't have come here."

"Lose that thought, Echo. Here is where you belong."

"No, I don't. I just bring trouble wherever I go. You're hurt and now, because of me, you have to go out there—"

"Echo," he cut her off. "I've been doing this for three thousand years. I'll be fine." He leaned down and kissed her hard. The next minute, his body wavered and dissolved into a shimmer of blue sparks as he vanished.

Rooted to the floor, her lips still tingling from his kiss, Echo stared at the spot where Aethan had been only moments ago, feeling as if she'd just been shoved off a mountain.

Chapter 15

Immortal?

Three thousand years?

Echo exhaled sharply, the reality of her situation overwhelming her. There was no way she could deny what she'd just seen. Her heart raced at the implications. Was everything Aethan had told her true?

He'd become irritated when she called Empyrea a fairy tale. But how did she know about Empyrea to begin with? Even she couldn't dream up something like that. Someone had to have told her...

That old childhood dream.

The tall man in the navy robes, carrying her after Clyde had hurt her. She struggled to put the pieces together and thought back to her dream from yesterday morning: men fighting, there were flashes of light, and he told her something... Something she was capable of doing...

Argh! Unable to recall past the fog in her mind, she pushed those thoughts aside for later. Aethan was out fighting demoniis with a gaping wound in his shoulder.

That got her moving. Hurrying into the bedroom, she saw the obsidian dagger on the bedside table, grabbed the thing, and sprinted from the room.

She leaped down the stairs, grateful she didn't trip and break her neck. Sliding down the corridor, she skidded into the study and hurried to the huge windows, but all was quiet and dark outside. She tried the rec room next. Still nothing. Panicking now, she stopped in the enormous library, and through the windows, she saw demoniis wrecking the gorgeous, landscaped garden.

Frantically, she searched for Aethan. The knot in her stomach grew when she couldn't find him in the swarming horde. Then she saw him—them. Her mouth dropped open. She'd never seen anything like it. Aethan, Týr, and another man fought like a symphony in motion. Swirling through the masses, they attacked, charging into the demoniis at a speed she hadn't believed possible.

Aethan, she easily made out, his sword blazed with the white light she'd seen once before. Týr's one glowed a deep amber. The dark-haired man, she hadn't met yet, fought the fiends with…fists? Surely, he must have a sword or some weapon, too? Blood oozed down his face, but he didn't seem to care as he dove into the mass of demoniis.

Her gaze darted back to Aethan and stayed, glued to his every move. Her heart seized when a demonii slammed into him, and he staggered back.

Nooo! She flung open the French doors, leading from the library to the sweeping terrace, and sprinted toward the horde.

Oh, please, please, let him be all right. How could

he hope to defeat them with that horrid wound on his shoulder?

A demonii darted for her, his gaze filling with lust the moment he got a whiff of her scent, and for the first time, Echo thanked God for her pheromones problem.

Her moves instinctual, she spun around, sweeping the demonii's legs out from under him with her own. She grabbed his hair and slit his throat in one swift motion. Sticky black blood spurting from his neck, she plunged the blade into his heart. As the demonii fell, another grabbed her from behind. She elbowed him in the belly, swung around, and kneed him in the crotch before driving her blade into his chest.

She went for a third, but a dagger came winging through the air and embedded itself in the demonii's chest.

Aethan flashed to her side, his eyes blazing in fury. He grabbed her and slung her over his shoulder. The breath exploded out of her flattened lungs.

"Dammit, Aethan," she wheezed. "Let me go—I can help you!" She pounded his back with her fists. Then the air around her shifted. Gasping, she grabbed on to his shirt as she was sucked into a whirlpool of nothing. Her body felt strange, weightless. The next moment they were back in the library. Aethan set her down.

She moaned, clutching the back of the couch, and tried not to hurl as the room continued to spin.

"Keep her here," he said, his voice so cold, a shiver darted along her spine. He vanished again before she could speak. And realized he'd spoken to Hedori who came up beside her.

Swallowing her annoyance along with her nausea, she stumbled to the window. Týr and the dark-haired man left dead demoniis in their wake as they worked their way out of the hordes. But there was no sign of Aethan. Once clear of the swarming mass, the two vanished.

Had they left him alone with all those demoniis? Her heart thudded in fear, her anger at Aethan dissipating. What the hell was wrong with them?

No matter. She'd help him. She shoved open the door, but hands grabbed her and held her back before she could take a step out of the house. Echo wheeled around.

Hedori. Dammit. She'd forgotten he was there.

"Let me go—he's out there fighting alone! They left him." She struggled against his grip. "I must help him."

"No, m'lady," Hedori said, his voice as calm as his expression, as if he'd seen this many times before. "He has to do this unaided."

"Unaided?" she yelled at him. "Can't you see—" Before she could finish her sentence, a familiar glimmer of light caught her attention. Her gaze snapped back to the chaos on the lawn. A white glow expanded from the center of the horde. The demoniis stopped abruptly, then began scrambling away.

That's when she saw him. Her eyes widened in shock. His body glowed, filling with light. His hair drifted around him as if he was underwater, his body silhouetted against the pulsing energy.

Then Aethan disappeared as an explosion of white light left him. In a silent wave, it spread through the gloom of early morning, incinerating all in its way. But it never touched the house, staying within the parameters of the grounds. Like a veil, it covered and destroyed every demonii.

There was no black goo left behind when it was over, just ash that scattered about. The light wavered, and Aethan became visible again, the fading white glow absorbed back into him.

"Oh, God," she whispered. "What was that?"

"It's who he is. This way, there is no escape and the demoniis can't regenerate," Hedori explained, releasing his grip on her arm.

Aethan stood in the center of the lawn, his head lowered. Echo could feel the weariness bleeding out of him as if it were her own. She took a step forward, wanting to rush out there and comfort him. But when he turned and looked straight at her, as if to say, *This is what I am,* she pulled in a shaky breath. She finally understood the caliber of the man she wanted so badly.

He was utterly lethal. And it scared her.

How did one—how did she handle a man like him?

"Don't, m'lady." Hedori's quiet voice stopped her.

Echo blinked, surprised to find she'd taken several steps away from the window and Aethan.

"I've known him since he was a young lad. Because of this power, he suffers much."

"What're you talking about? Didn't you see what just happened? He-he took out a freaking army of demoniis in a matter of seconds."

"Because he was afraid for you," Hedori pointed out. "Those wounds on your arm led them here. However, they didn't know you were inside. The castle is warded against supernatural invasion of any sort, but you left its protection."

Annoyance replaced her shock and wariness. "Why didn't he just say so? Why must he order me about?"

"It's what he is."

"What? Arrogant and bossy?"

"No." Amusement flared briefly in Hedori's orange-green eyes. "He's protective of the one he...ah, cares about."

She snorted. "Like I said, bossy and arrogant."

The fight drained out of her, Echo sat on the couch and rubbed her temples. But all she saw in her mind was the white light taking over Aethan's body. It had been the most frightening, the most beautiful thing she'd ever seen. Why did he bother with a sword when he had such a formidable power?

"Hedori, that sword on his biceps, what is it?"

"It's a gift he received when he became a Guardian. Like the sires, Týr and Blaéz."

Her gaze strayed to the tall window again. Týr, along with the dark-haired man, headed for Aethan. "But who would give such a gift? It looks painful."

"Gaia."

Frowning, she turned to Hedori.

"And no, it's not painful." He smiled. "Not when evil is present. Only then does it become sentient. It's important that, as Guardians, they are always armed."

"Gaia?" she repeated.

"Yes. I believe humans refer to her as 'Mother Nature'. She er...drafted him as one of her Guardians. His abilities serve him well in what he does."

Echo stared at him. "Mother Nature? She's real? She actually exists?"

Hedori nodded.

She wanted to pinch herself to make sure this conversation was real and not a dream. But after all that happened this morning and what she just saw, how could she doubt any longer?

Echo glanced at the men again. They stood there, looking around the grounds and talking. As if nothing earth-shattering had occurred just minutes ago. For them, this must be a normal occurrence, she realized.

"You said you've known Aethan since he was a little boy. Are you like him, too?"

"I would never claim to be one such as he." There was a reverential tone in Hedori's voice. "But yes, I am from Empyrea. When Aethan left, I followed."

"Why did he leave?"

There was a moment of heavy silence before Hedori spoke. "He didn't actually leave. He was banished."

"Why—who would do something so cruel?" she asked, horrified.

"The high ruler of Empyrea." Hedori stepped away from the window. "My lady," he said softly, and with a nod, he slipped out of the door.

Echo pushed to her feet and turned.

Aethan entered the library from the terrace entrance, his gaze pinning her to the spot. His impassive expression had her trepidation coming back in full force, reminding her of what he truly was.

Deadly. Immortal.

He wasn't like her. Instinct, made her take a step back.

"You...you took out an entire army of demoniis," she whispered.

"Yes." There was no apology in his tone. For a tense moment, his gaze held hers. "Go to bed, Echo. I can taste your fear. Your heart pounds so fast, I'm afraid it will give out on you."

The next minute, he disappeared. There was no coercion, no emotion beneath his words. Either he was very, very angry with her, or she'd hurt him with her fear.

Left alone in the silent library, and surrounded by towering bookshelves, Echo bit her lip. No, she realized, she wasn't afraid of him. Wary, perhaps. Awed, definitely. But afraid? No. Her heart pounded not in fear, but at the thought of how much she did want him.

Unwilling to start their relationship on doubt, she headed for the stairs and jogged up to the third floor, down the corridor and into the bedroom. Breathless, she skidded to a halt as he came out of the dressing room wearing sweats and Nikes. He had a t-shirt in his hand.

"Aethan, wait," she panted. "I know I shouldn't have gone outside—"

The gaze he turned on her flashed with silver ice.

Oh, yes. He was furious.

"You should have never left the safety of the house, Echo. And now, you should have stayed away until I calmed down. I'm seconds away from making good on my promise."

Her back stiffened at his threat to take her away to some unknown place. "I'm not a possession to be packed away because you fear it'll break. You want a relationship with me, you need to accept me for who I am."

"At the expense of putting your life in danger? Don't push me on this. You won't like the trade-off."

She bit back on the deluge that nearly spewed out at his threat. And said, "I don't like you very much, right now."

At her words, something shifted in his stance, his gaze. The chill in his eyes went into a slow burn, reminding her of a dangerous predator. He flung his t-shirt aside and prowled closer.

Hastily, she backed away. She wasn't a fool. Whatever he planned wouldn't be good for her. Then she met his eyes, and fear gave way to anticipation. Breathing became harder, aware she'd unleashed this dangerous side of him.

"You don't like me, do you?" He stalked her until her back hit the wall. Hands slapped down on either side of her head, locking her in. "Let's see about that, shall we?"

His eyes glowed fiercely, filled with possession. He lowered his head. His nose trailed lightly along her jaw and down her neck.

Echo stilled, unprepared for the sensual feeling of his lips lightly grazing her skin. The heady scent of rainstorms, his masculine heat, and raw sex surrounded her. She could almost taste him on her tongue.

"Aethan," she whimpered, desire surging through her veins. If he could do that without even touching her, she truly was in trouble. But she didn't care. She only knew that if he didn't kiss her, she would burn up from her own heat and die, and then he'd be sorry. She tilted her face toward his, seeking his lips.

Soft laughter reached her ears as though he could hear her thoughts. "Still don't like me, do you?"

"Aethan, please," she moaned, her palms sliding up his muscled chest. But his body was too big, too hard to tug closer. So she grabbed his hair, her fingers wrapped in the silky strands, and pulled him to her.

He picked her up and braced her against the wall, her legs anchored around his waist. The warmth of his naked stomach against her center, the temptation of all those powerful muscles holding her up, made her heart

Georgia Lyn Hunter

beat faster. Unable to resist, her hand trailed down his chest and circled his flat nipple. A shudder rippled through his hard body.

His gaze, hot and possessive, skimmed over her hair, her face, to latch onto her mouth, then slid lower. Bending his head, he licked her nipple through her tee and blew on the damp patch. Her breath caught in her throat. He bit down gently before sucking on the nub, driving her out of her head with mind-numbing pleasure.

He let go of the tight bud and covered her mouth in a kiss so hot, it branded her to the very depths of her soul. Heat gathered and rolled between her legs. A flood of moisture dampened her panties.

Her hand slid restlessly down, pushing between them to stroke his heavy erection. He grabbed her hand.

"I want to touch you," she protested.

"No. You don't get to do that—your punishment for disobeying me."

Her legs tightened around him as he carried her to the bed. The moment her bottom hit the mattress, he reached out and ripped her t-shirt down the center.

Shocked, she gasped, "You tore my shirt."

Pulling off her tee, he flung the tattered remains away. "I'll buy you more."

Desire stole her breath at the thought of being the sole focus of a man this powerful. His scorching gaze trailing over her bare skin made her tremble. Going down on his haunches, he hooked his fingers into the waist of her sweats. "Lift, if you want them intact."

Her elbows braced on the bed, she lifted her bottom. He tugged her sweats down and tossed them aside, revealing the tiny white panties she wore. His hands stroked her skin from her thigh to her ankle.

"Move up," he ordered.

Echo dragged herself farther up the bed. A hand on her chest, he gently pushed her back. She broke her fall, bracing herself on her elbows again, and watched him. Holding her gaze, he ran his lips along the inside of her thigh, stopping midway. "Spread your legs for me."

At his words, Echo blushed, her face growing hotter. Unwilling to miss out on the experience of all he would show her, she parted her legs a little.

He spread them wider. And lowered his head. His hair like silken fingers, caressed her thighs as he licked the tender skin, trailing little kisses and sharp nips, making her squirm as a voracious hunger swept through her.

"I'm dying to taste you," he said, his tone raw. Edgy. "You smell incredible."

Any other time, she would have cringed knowing he could smell her arousal. But now, her lust spiked dangerously high, as anticipation of what would follow took hold.

He reached the juncture of her thighs and sucked the tender skin there, close to where she wanted him but far enough away to torment her. He ran a finger down the center of her cotton panties and cupped her heated core. Her breath caught. His gaze on hers, he pressed down with the heel of his palm and massaged her with strong strokes. Desire spiraled. She squeezed her eyes tight.

Lights exploded behind her closed lids at the pleasure flooding her. Echo wondered if she'd survive the storm he'd unleashed in her. A ripping sound filled the air, and her eyes snapped open. He tossed her

Georgia Lyn Hunter

panties aside. She no longer cared that she was exposed to his gaze. She wanted him, wanted more.

He leaned down and licked her, a slow, decadent stroke of his warm tongue down her cleft. A scream tore from her throat. She gripped his hair tightly, fighting for control against the overwhelming pleasure consuming her.

He tormented her with his intimate kiss and became single-minded in his focus as he lapped and suckled her. Pinpricks of desire sent tingles racing up her arms and down her body to pool in her core. Her pleasure heightened, driving her insane with need.

Her body a teeming mass of sensations, Echo let go of her grip on reality. She moaned and moved her hips, her legs sliding over his shoulders, giving him better access to her most feminine part.

***

Male that he was, Aethan took full advantage of her vulnerable state. He flicked his tongue over her sensitized nub, held her down when she would have squirmed away, and taught her what it was like to be possessed by an immortal like him. Her pleasure his ultimate aim, he licked and sucked, leaving no parts of her unexplored.

Slipping his hands under her bottom, he tilted her pelvis up to take more of her into his mouth. Her thighs fell open. Her surrender tasted as sweet as her honeyed skin. After today, she would never doubt to whom she belonged.

Beneath his sensual haze, he felt his powers gathering force. He clamped down on his shields as the pleasure in his mate drove him on. Her strangled scream deepened his own needs as he pushed her closer to the edge. He wanted her so badly, it became a testament of how much she mattered, and of his willpower, that he wasn't already sliding into her welcoming heat.

He glanced up; her eyes were shut tight. He didn't care for that. "Echo," he growled. "Look at me."

Her eyelids flickered open. Hazy with desire, they locked on his.

He eased a finger into her tight, silken heat. "Know always, how much I want you."

She cried out, her body arching off the bed. His hand splayed over her stomach, he held her down, felt the ripples at the start of her orgasm. He pushed another finger into her and her feminine muscles squeezed them. Sliding his mouth over her clit, he worked her with his tongue, his fingers thrusting in and out of her as he took her over the edge.

Her cry of passion resonated in his being as she fell into a mind-shattering orgasm.

Slowly, he eased off and gently brought her back down. His heart raced along with his rioting powers that battered at his shields. His vision blurred, became cloudy. A streak of pain shot through his head. And he knew; his eyes were changing, becoming inhuman.

She raised a hand and touched his face. "Come inside me, Aethan. I need you."

Her husky words, a whisper of seduction, tortured him. He squeezed his eyes tight. Anger filled him at the unfairness of having the only female he'd ever wanted with his heart and soul in his arms, yet being unable to love her with his body. Gods, he'd so foolishly thought he'd be all right. Thought he could finally claim her after expending some of that accursed power wiping out the demonii horde. His erection unbearably hard, with release nowhere in sight, the pain in him intensified. He had to get out.

***

Aethan rolled away from her and off the bed in a speed that baffled her. It took Echo a moment to realize he was leaving.

"Aethan, wait—" She scrambled off the bed, dragged the sheets with her, and nearly fell onto her knees, still shaky from her orgasm.

He turned, and she saw his eyes. White had trickled into the gray irises.

"What's wrong?"

It was a moment or two before he spoke. The tendons in his neck stood out, his big body tense, as if he was straining to hold himself together. "I have to go." His words were hard, flat, the sensual lover gone.

"What? Why? Don't you want me?"

A harsh laugh left him. He looked ready to tear something apart with his bare hands. The wall sconces sputtered, flickered on and off at an alarming rate. The air around him shifted, changed. He pivoted away from her. "I can't stay. I have to go."

In desperation, she hurried after him, nearly tripping on the trailing navy sheets. He was hauling on a t-shirt in the dressing room with none of the finesse she was used to.

"Aethan, talk to me. Please." She gripped his arm. "Tell me what's wrong."

This wasn't just about the abrupt ending to the most incredible experience of her life. Something was seriously off.

The tingles in her increased, and her legs trembled as his powers shimmered over her skin. Aethan turned, his irises more white than gray. But the horror filling his face when he saw her holding him, Echo knew she'd never forget as long as she lived.

"Don't touch me!" He reared back so fast it sent her stumbling to the floor. The recessed lights overhead shattered.

Her head spun, and her heart constricted in pain. *No.* This can't be happening. Tears welled in her eyes.

A blinding flash brightened the room, one so brilliant it hurt her eyes and left her reeling. When the white light had faded, she was alone in the dark.

Aethan had disappeared.

Chapter 16

Andras's veneer of patience evaporated. Agony spread from the pit in his chest and rocketed. He tugged at his hair as a shudder tore through him. Flames flickered from the torches on the wall, casting an ominous, orange glow throughout the black chamber.

He glowered at his brother. "You've been topside on the human realm, and you're telling me you haven't found her?"

Lazaar shrugged and shoved his hands into his trouser pockets.

At his careless action, Andras had to suppress the urge to tear off Lazaar's face.

"Bael," Andras snarled at the demon standing beside him. "Get me a soul."

He collapsed into his chair as the pain in his chest grew worse. Bael hurried out of the chamber, only to return moments later, dragging in a moaning human male. He tossed him on the floor at Andras's feet.

With a flick of his hand Andras callously cut off

the mortal's vocal cords.

Lazaar shook his head. "You cannot aspire to greater things if you can't see the big picture. You need a clear mind. Yours is clouded by the only thing you think about—when you can feed off the next human."

"Need I remind you to whom you speak, *little* brother?" Andras snarled.

"What is it you want?" Lazaar asked, his expression growing bored.

"Did you find the psychic girl?"

Lazaar rocked back on his heels and smiled. "Just one. However, free will makes it impossible to bring her through the portal. And she resisted my mind manipulation."

Andras glared at him. "What do you mean she resisted? We are powerful—we can make anyone do our bidding. Yet you stand there and tell me you cannot bring one from that feeble race to me?"

"She is under the warriors' protection. One came to her rescue."

"Guardians do not consort with humans."

Lazaar shrugged. "Then I suggest you go after her yourself."

"You think to mock me because I'm bound to this place? Be careful, brother. Be very careful you do not get on my bad side."

"Believe what you want, Andras. As always, you chase after rainbows in Hell. The girl can't break the curse of the binding. I'm done helping you." Lazaar strolled out of the chamber.

Andras scowled at his brother's retreating back, his hatred growing. Lazaar dared to mock him? He shifted his gaze to Bael and nodded. The demon followed Lazaar. A loud grunt echoed through the open

Georgia Lyn Hunter

doors, followed by a thud. A moment later, Bael reappeared, Lazaar's body slung over his shoulder.

Andras glanced dispassionately at his unconscious sibling. "Lock him up. I'll deal with him later."

Then he crooked a finger at the cowering human and captured his gaze. The human's eyes bulged in terror, his mouth open in a soundless scream. Andras smiled. Fear. It spiced up the mortals' wonderful energy, made them tastier. His eyes aflame, he allowed his true appearance to show. Black scales took over his skin, and his face stretched and reformed into a deranged parody of a dragon's. As his curled black claws embedded into the human's flesh, Andras slowly siphoned out the mortal's life force. He had to hold himself back from sinking his fangs into the man's throat.

Light filled Andras as the stolen soul settled into his psyche, easing the pain in his chest. He tossed the human husk away, basking in the intoxicating light, but already he could feel the dimming of the soul. No matter. Soon, he would have it all. "Bael? My new lair?"

"It's almost ready."

Andras smiled. "Good. Now, bring me the little oracle."

Chapter 17

Sunlight pushed through the cracks in the gray cloud cover, brightening the dull morning over Long Island. Echo floored the accelerator, the roar of the Reventón filling the quiet, tree-lined road as she left the island behind. Soon, she hit the mainland and connected to Route 25-A.

The instant Aethan had left, she had, too, unable to stay a moment longer at the castle, humiliation burning deep.

The exhilaration of driving this black beauty did little to ease the ache in her heart. Nickelback pelted out from the radio, and she cranked up the volume, attempting to drown out her thoughts. The smell of leather and wax inside the roadster choked her. She slid the window open, and the crisp fall air caressed her face. The tall, green trees soon gave way to splashes of warm, variegated colors that brightened up the roadside. Living in the city, she didn't always get to admire the beauty of this season. Nor could she do so today.

Her clammy hands tightened on the steering wheel to still the unsteadiness in them. Far better than pulling over to the roadside so she could lay her head on the steering wheel and let despair wash over her. Besides, she had company.

Hedori sat in the passenger seat, gripping the dashboard as if he were on a runaway freight train to Hell. Too bad he'd insisted on accompanying her. But she didn't want him picking up on her distress. She far preferred him worrying about her crashing the car.

Anger and hurt warring within her, Echo tried to understand what had gone wrong that morning. Aethan wanted her. He'd told her straight out that he did. He'd acted like he couldn't get enough of her. So why did he leave?

Was he afraid of hurting her with his power? Heck, she'd seen it firsthand. Yes, it did scare her, but he'd never hurt her, she knew that. She could still feel the tingles that had overwhelmed her body when the light vibration of his powers seeped through her. It hadn't hurt. So that couldn't be why he'd left.

Then what was it?

The thought hurtling into her mind made her heart drop to her stomach like a lead ball. Had he changed his mind about her?

The tension that had settled along her shoulders intensified. The dull throb in the base of her head grew.

"My lady, please—" Hedori cried out, "You cannot drive so recklessly!"

Crap. She'd forgotten all about him. Damn man was as bad as Aethan always telling her what to do. "Hedori, my name is Echo. You call me 'my lady' again, don't expect an answer."

She overtook three cars, and a screech of tires

pierced the air.

"My la–missy!" He grabbed the dash as she swerved to avoid an oncoming vehicle. Ignoring the irate honking, she slipped back into her lane.

Echo glanced at Hedori's pale face. "You're immortal. Why are you scared?"

"Aethan will have my head if you get a scratch on you. I've promised him I'd keep you safe. But you don't make my job easy."

She was a job now?

Her mouth tightened with hurt. Aethan had had time to contact Hedori, but she wasn't worth an explanation? He just dumped her on his butler instead?

Well, she didn't need him or his protection. She'd managed fine on her own for the past few years.

"My–Miss Echo," Hedori amended at her dark scowl. He lowered the volume of the music. "Normally, I would stay out of this. However, there is something I must say."

There was such an intense look on his face, her gut squeezed in anxiety. Jesus! What more could there be?

"Yeah?"

Hedori leaned back in his seat. "Aethan, he never speaks about this. And you being his—er…someone who cares about him, I feel it's best you know."

Echo had the distinct impression he had meant to say something else when he paused.

"You must understand, my lady, Empyrea is a peaceful place. It has to be. The powers most Empyreans have could easily destroy our world if there was no accord. So, violence is forbidden. It means death or exile if one is found guilty. To an Empyrean, banishment is worse than a death sentence, because some need the white boulders found only in that realm to Ground their powers."

She was quiet for a moment as her distressed mind tried to understand what Hedori was telling her.

"That's a harsh punishment. But why do you need to, er…ground?"

"It draws off the excess energy of those with immense powers. Makes it less painful and easier to bear."

"Painful?"

"The downside to those abilities. It's all about balance. Over the years, it becomes easier, as complete control is achieved."

"How do you manage?"

"I do not possess those kinds of powers. Mostly it's the ruling class Empyreans who do. Anyway, I digress…" He was quiet for a second, almost like he didn't want to talk about it. Then he said, "Aethan's sire arranged a mating-contract for him. It's like an arranged marriage—"

"Aethan's *married*?" Her heart crashed into her ribs as the car swerved violently. God, no wonder he didn't—

"No, my lady," Hedori hastened to reassure her. "He is not."

It took her a moment to collect herself. "What happened?"

"Aethan refused to consider the mating-contract, and an argument broke out with his father, Elyon Dandre.

Echo's eyes skipped from the road back to Hedori. "Elyon Dandre?"

He let go of the dash. "*Elyon* means 'most high'. He is what you would call a 'king' on this realm. Only, he rules all of Empyrea. Aethan is—was his heir."

Echo hit the brakes, and the car skidded. Her heart pounding, she pulled over to the curb of Northern Boulevard and pressed her fists to her eyes. God, she just wanted today to be over.

"Aethan no longer acknowledges the title of High Prince of Empyrea," Hedori continued, forcing her attention back to him.

"What are you trying to tell me, Hedori? Just spit it out. Please."

Hedori sighed. "Aethan was not yet twenty-one in his world years. Thousand years in your world are like a blink of an eye in Empyrea," he explained. "So when politics reared its ugly head. The ruling council wanted the old ways back. They didn't care for interspecies mating, from which offspring were born with unimaginable powers. Those offspring became utterly lethal when their gifts came into being.

"The council decided the young ones were too dangerous. They wanted the old ways back, to make Empyrea safe again. And who better to start the new regime than the prince? Aethan was ordered to mate with an Empyrean female from another ruling house. However, he didn't care for this. He wanted to wait until he found his destined-mate, like his father had.

"Elyon Dandre had little choice but to adhere to the new laws decreed by the council, since he, himself, had mated outside his race and begot children with treacherous powers. He understood the need for this law. He made the betrothal an order. Aethan refused. But Elyon Dandre would not be deterred." Hedori stopped, his expression lost in memories from long ago as he stared out through the windshield.

Echo's emotions warred within her. Her anger at Aethan made her want to yell at Hedori that she didn't care, but her longing to understand had her riveted to every word he spoke.

"Aethan has two younger brothers," Hedori continued, "but thousands of years later a sister was born to them. A gift from the Heavens, they called her. Ariana brought joy to the castle, the realm, and she adored her brothers, especially Aethan. She'd slip out and trail after him, and he indulged her.

"After the altercation with his sire, Aethan left the castle for the warriors' training ground." Another pause. Longer this time. Then, "My lady, it was the day Ariana died."

Shocked, the words tumbled out of Echo. "What? Why—how did she die?"

Hedori shook his head. "It's his story to tell."

"But how could she die? She's immortal."

"No, m'lady, Empyrean children are mortal in their early years. She was just five years old when she died and Aethan was held responsible."

***

Aethan materialized at the foot of the Catskill Mountains. Frigid air stung his face as he held his unsteady hands out to open the entrance that led deep into the earth's belly.

No! He jerked his hands back. He had to call Echo, see if she was okay, explain that he needed time to Ground. He patted the pockets of his sweats. Empty. Where the hell did he leave his cell?

Mind-linking with Blaéz, he shot his message to the other Guardian then he stared at his hands. The shit inside him made him glow like he was plugged into every freaking socket in the entire country. Gods, he hated this. More, he hated himself and what he was.

Terror roiled within him at the memory of Echo stumbling to the floor when she touched him and his power hit her.

Please be safe, Echo. Just be safe until I get back.

He willed the heavy vegetation to part, and a fissure in the rock face opened into a gaping crack. His molecules shifted. Once he became one with the air, he glided into the mountain. Going deep beneath it, he took form in a cavern no bigger than a closet and stumbled to his knees.

Pain rocked through him as his powers spiked, crashing against his shields. He fell onto his back. The musty smell of soil invading his nostrils, Aethan let go of his rigid control.

Powerful, lethal flashes brightened the cavern, scorching the rocks. His labored breaths easing, he lay still as consciousness left him and the white quartzite in the mountain siphoned off his excess powers.

***

Echo came to the conclusion that *all* Empyreans were protective and stubborn. Living with someone like Aethan, she figured Hedori would be as bad. She hated to be proven right.

He wouldn't leave until he walked her to the door.

She leaned against the doorjamb, crossed her arms over her chest, and arched a brow when he stood on the threshold and looked into her small apartment. "You're sure there's no one hiding in the bathroom or under my bed? Don't you want to get *inside* and do a thorough search? You might have missed something."

He smiled. "I would know if anyone was here.

Your apartment's safe."

"Are you sure you were just Aethan's butler back in the day?"

"No, m'lady. It's a position I took on this realm, since I am not a Guardian."

At his serious expression, she narrowed her eyes, took in his erect posture and unreadable eyes, and could only guess at the truth. "Wait, don't tell me. Since he's a prince, you were his protector?"

Amusement glittered in his orange-green eyes. "Back in the day, yes."

She rolled her eyes at having her own words tossed back at her and held out the car keys. "Here. Thanks for letting me drive the Rev."

He took the keys, nodding slightly. "That was...quite an experience, my lady." The smile lingered. "I'll return at four."

"No, Hedori." Her throat tightened again when she thought of the reason why she was back at her apartment. "I'll be staying in Greenwich Village for now."

Hedori sighed, staring at the keys in his hands. "Very well, I'll take you to the Oracle's."

"No. I have my own car, but thank you. Will you look after Bob for me? I'll—" She swallowed as tears threatened. "Look after him, please. I'll call when I'm ready to return."

"My lady—"

She shook her head. "I need some time away from the castle."

After Hedori left, Echo prowled around her apartment, her despair turning to annoyance and then to anger. Her call had gone unanswered again. Her cell clutched in her fist, she looked at the display once more, tossed the thing on the couch in disgust, and brooded.

If Aethan had waited this long for his destined-mate, then what was she? A passing fancy? Her chest tightened at the thought as she circled the coffee table.

For godsakes, she was human. Of course she'd be a passing fancy. Had she really been that stupid to believe it would be something more? Not only was he gorgeous and extremely powerful, he was an immortal prince! His mate would be like him, beautiful and special—

Christ, she couldn't stay here moping. She'd go crazy. Throwing a few things together, she locked up her apartment and headed for Kira's.

Echo pulled up in front of the brownstone a short while later. The front door opened as she parked her Volkswagen Beetle. A black-haired Kira rushed out, a pink streak weaving between the strands of her hair. A smile of relief brought out her dimples. She tugged open the car door and hauled Echo into a hug.

"I'm so happy to see you're in one piece and all better." Kira looked her over, as though to confirm she really was okay, with no new injuries. Another hug followed. "Don't you ever scare me like that again."

"I'm sorry—I didn't mean to." Echo hugged her back. She could never tell Kira the horror of almost being hauled into Hell. She reached into the passenger seat and pulled out her overnight bag.

Kira linked their arms as they walked toward the brownstone. "Now, tell me about the gorgeous hunk with the blue hair."

Echo's heart dipped at the mention of Aethan.

Kira nudged her playfully with her elbow. "Is it real? Man, he's really into you. Hey, how come you never told me about him?"

Echo didn't want to talk about him and had hoped some time with her friend would help ease her pain and confusion. But faced with Kira's questions, that wasn't going to happen. She'd have to tell her friend something. Only what that was, she had no idea.

***

"You're pacing again," Kira said from where she sat on the couch reading a magazine later that night.

"No, I'm just restless. Too much energy," Echo responded, turning away from the window. She had no idea what it was, but the urge to leave took hold like a compulsion. "I'm going out."

Kira tossed her magazine aside and grabbed her jacket. "All right, let's go then, before you wear a hole in the carpet." She patted Echo's shoulder. "Don't worry, you guys will work it out. It's just a little disagreement." When Echo didn't respond, she said, "Come on, Echo, even I agree with Aethan. You can't go hunting for demoniis, not with them looking for you."

Unable to meet Kira's eyes, guilt swamped Echo for lying to her best friend. She'd made up a story that she and Aethan were dating, but that they'd had an argument because he didn't want her on the streets at night. The humiliation of telling her friend the truth about why she'd left—ugh, she'd rather have a root canal done, without anesthetic.

Echo drove around in her Beetle, listening with half an ear to Kira, until she found herself in Times Square. It hadn't been her destination, but when she spied Starbucks, she pulled into a no-parking zone.

"You want coffee?" she asked Kira.

"God, yes. Need something to keep me warm. Your heater's busted," Kira grumbled, buttoning her jacket.

"I know. Damon said he'll see to it when he gets back."

Kira snorted. "His idea of fixing is to stare at the thing then call a mechanic."

Echo smiled. "Back in a sec."

She hurried across the chaotic street crowded with gawking tourists to Starbucks. A few minutes later, with a tall latte in each hand, she left the coffee house and headed for her car. The edgy feeling that had taken hold of her at the brownstone spiked again.

Stopping, she took a deep breath and searched the busy street. Cars swished by, people chatted. Dissonant sounds filled her ears, but still the sensation persisted. Echo glanced back to where she'd parked her car. Her gaze drifted to the dingy side street nearby.

As if under a compulsion, the dark gaping maw drew her. She walked down the seedy alley with its gloomy buildings and stopped near a boarded-up office front. Frowning, she swiveled around and searched the place. Something didn't feel right here.

She took a few more steps past the reeking dumpsters and gasped. Unexpected pain swept through her. She cried out and doubled over, the coffees falling and splattering on the asphalt.

Dizziness took her hard. She lurched into a crate and grabbed on to a dumpster then stumbled back to the mouth of the alley. Footsteps sounded, growing louder.

"Echo, what happened? What's wrong?"

"Help me—"

Georgia Lyn Hunter

Kira grabbed her around the waist. "Dammit, Echo, you're scaring me. For godsakes, tell me what's wrong?"

Echo heard her friend's frantic words, but couldn't answer as everything inside her seemed to shut down, and darkness claimed her.

Chapter 18

Aethan materialized at the front of the castle. For once, he didn't bother to scan the estate to check if the wards were still secure. He walked straight into the foyer and hesitated, glancing up the stairs.

Echo was probably out of her mind with worry or ready to tear into him for leaving so abruptly. But what choice did he have? If he'd stayed—

He scrubbed a hand down his face, unable to think about how badly things could have ended. He'd rather face her fury.

Footsteps echoed in the corridor. Moments later, Michael appeared, followed by Blaéz and Týr.

Did he miss a meeting?

Judging by their grim faces, oh, yeah, he had. Probably an important one, too, since they should've been out on patrol at this time of the night. Whatever. He'd catch up later. As soon as he reassured himself Echo was safe. Exhaustion beating at him, he headed for the stairs.

"She is not here," Michael said.

No, she wouldn't. Unwilling to believe she'd leave him, Aethan reached out with his psychic senses and scanned the castle for her. The emptiness, the lack of her presence floored him. Pivoting on his heels, he headed for the front door.

"Aethan."

"Not now, Michael. I have to go find her."

"She is safe."

Michael's clipped words penetrated the fog in his mind. Aethan eased his brutal grip on the doorknob and turned.

"This will not happen again." The Archangel advanced on him. "She needs a protector who's constant. Your emotions make you a risk factor. You cannot be relied on to safeguard her—you've been gone two days."

Risk factor? Like he needed that shitty reminder. With his accursed powers and his despair at being unable to claim his mate, it took everything Aethan had to keep from lashing out at Michael and proving him right. His hands fisted. "Who's going to take her from me?"

The air around Michael stilled. Ice formed in his eyes and seeped into every syllable. "You dare to override me on this?" The Archangel was at his coldest.

"She is all that stands between me and this city." The unemotional words were a deadly decree, his threat a serious violation of his Guardian oath, but Aethan didn't care. "I'm quite capable. After all, I had the best teacher in honing what I am."

Tension crackled in the foyer.

It had been on Michael's orders that he'd razed many towns and villages, killing the innocents along with demoniis, and staining his soul forever. But the bastard cared little for innocent lives lost as long as his war against evil was won.

The Arc nailed him with a cool stare. "This is about protecting Zarias's descendant. Had you been present for the meeting, you'd know this. If this female is—"

"Not *this* female," Aethan snapped. "Echo is *mine*."

"—who we search for, then she's the Healer," Michael continued, as if he hadn't heard a word. "The one who will traverse all the realms. It could be the reason the demoniis want her. I will meet with her."

Why the hell would Michael do this now? He had to go find Echo and bring her back so he could breathe again, when his rioting mind finally registered what Michael had said.

"*Healer*? No fucking way! She is not. She was here for three days—three fucking days and none of us felt a thing!"

Michael stepped closer, his expression rife with concern. "There was a spike last night—a big one. Whoever she is, her power has awakened. We have major problems. Those bastards will come out in droves, and your female is out there. Alone."

Like he didn't know that. But Michael insisted on keeping him here with his damn orations. All Aethan wanted was to find his mate and hold her, just hold her until his world was right again.

He headed for the door.

"Aethan?" Blaéz called out.

He growled and spun around. "What?"

"She's at the Oracle's. But I'd suggest a shower first. I don't imagine she'd welcome you with open arms seeing you as you are."

Aethan glanced down at his sweat-dampened t-shirt marred with dirt and grime, and ran a hand through his tangled hair. The grit there stuck to his fingers. He hated the time it would waste, but Blaéz was right. He probably looked like shit. His jaw set, Aethan headed to his room.

***

"For someone who just wants a roll with a human, he's got it bad," Týr muttered, staring up the stairs.

"A roll?" Blaéz repeated. "You ever stop to consider why he goes batshit crazy when it comes to that female?"

"He's too damn selfish to share is what I think."

Blaéz shook his head. "Not when it comes to his mate."

Týr's gaze sharpened in disbelief. "*Mate*? As in, destined-mate and all that crap?"

Blaéz merely stared at him.

"You gotta be shitting me. But she's mortal."

"Indeed, she is. Stranger things have happened."

Týr snorted. "How do we know if she's really his mate?"

"Every time he wanted to kill you for breathing the same air she did," Michael said, his tone dry as kindling.

Týr rubbed his nose and smirked at him. "My bad. But you rode his ass harder, Arc."

"I don't care for the imagery, but it's the fun part of my job," Michael retorted, heading for the kitchen.

***

A strangled scream tore from Echo's throat. She fought the tangled covers, struggling to sit up, her hand clutched to her chest. Her heart thudded too fast, seconds away from leaping out of her ribs. *Oh, God! Oh, God!*

The bedside lamp flickered on.

"Echo?"

She stared blankly at Kira, who sat on the bed and brushed her sweat-dampened hair out of her eyes. "Tamsyn," Echo whispered, wrapping her arms around her raised knees. "Her throat—the blood..."

Kira hurried from the room and came back moments later. "Here, drink this."

She handed her a glass of water. Echo gulped some. The cool liquid slid down her throat and eased her heart rate a little.

"Maybe this bug you picked up yesterday is more serious than we thought." Kira stroked her arm, her hazel eyes clouded with worry. "And you still haven't fully recovered from your injuries. That's probably why you dreamed about her."

Echo set the glass aside and raised her eyes to Kira's. *Bug?* Then she remembered the reason she'd given Kira for why she must have collapsed in the alley. She'd been dizzy and weak, and in pain...before she lost conscious. It had to be something she ate, she decided. And being so stressed out, something was bound to snap.

Now she was wound up again after her nightmare. Her dreams of Tamsyn had gotten more frequent lately. It had to mean something. She rubbed the scar on her upper arm where the demon had wounded her, and shuddered, a chill sweeping over her. Too edgy to go

Georgia Lyn Hunter

back to sleep, she shoved the covers aside and found her clothes. She had to get out of this confined space, to be able to breathe, and find her mind again or she'd go mad.

Changing into jeans and a sweater, she pulled on her boots and grabbed her jacket.

"Echo, what are you doing?" Kira rushed after her as she left the room.

"I have to go. I'm sorry, Kira."

Echo knew she had to go back to the place she'd avoided for five long years, the place where she'd found Tamsyn. Maybe then she'd get closure and the nightmares would end.

***

Aethan checked his cell again as he jogged down the stairs. He was heading for the front door, when Hedori stopped him. "Sire, we have a problem."

Aethan bit back his annoyance at the interruption. "What is it?"

"We have a visitor."

"Handle him, or have one of the others do it. I don't have the time." Aethan continued on his way, pushing his phone back into his pocket. The only urgent thing right now was bringing Echo back. Except for the three missed calls on the day he'd disappeared, she hadn't called him again.

"Aethan, it's a *her*."

He halted, his gaze narrowing. The only *her* he wanted was Echo, but at the look in Hedori's eyes, a low growl rumbled out of him. Who the hell was here? He hoped it wasn't one of the goddesses from the pantheons. He hadn't seen any of them in a long time.

And he really didn't have time to deal with that crap.

Hearing light footsteps, Aethan turned as Hedori left the foyer.

The vision coming toward him was like a punch to the gut, stealing his breath. Emotions cascaded, ripping him apart.

Resentment. Anger. Bitterness.

Memories locked away crashed through the walls of his mind and flooded him. His father's determination that he accept the betrothal contract with a female he thought of as a sister. The awful argument that followed, then storming out of the palace and heading straight for the training arena. And Ariana following...

There, he'd broken the first rule of Empyrea. *Never use your powers in anger.*

Now, his past stood before him, bringing back the tragedy that would haunt him for the rest of his life.

Elytani. The female the council had chosen for him to kick-start their new laws. And he, their sacrificial lamb. He swallowed hard and stared at the female in an elegant, dark green gown.

Long, moonlight-colored hair flowed to her hips, her face paler than the creamy gold he remembered. Dark eyes watched him warily.

"My lord, A'than," Elytani whispered. She stopped a few feet from him, looking as though she'd seen a ghost. "I thought you were dead."

"Why are you here?"

She flinched at the coldness in his voice, then she stiffened her spine. "A'than, I'm your betrothed. Are you not happy to see me?"

A nerve ticked in his jaw. He didn't have time to deal with this—with an engagement that never took place, one he never wanted. Why the hell couldn't his past just stay buried? Still, she was an innocent in Empyrea's machinations. She didn't deserve his anger.

"Elytani, the betrothal never happened. Just how did you get here?"

"I went to see the mage, Allatus, about my future, and he told me to seek what I desire." A blush pinkened her face. "I, er, was thinking of you, hoping you weren't dead, and ended up here."

Aethan shut his eyes and pinched the bridge of his nose. Great. He couldn't imagine his old mage letting Elytani come here. It had to have been an accident. After all, the old bastard had been the one to kick him through a portal into this realm after his banishment was declared.

"I'm sorry, but you cannot stay. You have to go back."

Shock widened her eyes. "You're sending me away?"

"You don't belong on this realm."

"But I'm an Empyrean. I can control myself. My powers aren't like yours—" The flush on her skin brightened as if she'd just realized to whom she was speaking. "My pardon, A'than..." Her apology died as footsteps sounded behind him.

He turned. Týr approached them from down the corridor. When Elytani's gaze rested on the warrior, she simply stared.

Týr stopped beside him. "Who is she?"

Aethan introduced her. "Týr, Elytani. Ely, Týr."

A look of awed curiosity crossed her face, then she curtsied. Týr responded with a half bow. Of course she'd be stunned by the Norse's looks. Most females were. Which was why Aethan had lost his head when he thought Echo had succumbed, too.

With little choice since he needed Týr's help, Aethan gave him a quick rundown of what had occurred, leaving out the more painful parts. Then he asked, "Would you see to her? Ask Michael to send her back? I have to go."

Týr nodded. Aethan turned for the door.

"My lord, A'than, the betrothal?" she said, stopping him.

He shook his head. "It never happened. Your family should have told you that."

"They did, but I thought—"

"I'm sorry you came all this way for something that doesn't exist." His cell vibrated in his pocket. He pulled out the phone. Frowning at the unfamiliar number, he answered. His vision hazed as he listened, his heart seizing in fear.

The phone still pressed to his ear, he dematerialized.

***

"I didn't know what else to do," Kira told Aethan, rubbing her hands down the hips of her jeans.

"I'll find her. Call me if she comes back."

Aethan left the brownstone. He tried to connect with Echo telepathically. A waste of time, he knew, but he couldn't stop himself from trying. It was a gift given by Gaia only to her warriors.

His gut tightened, desperation tearing through him. All he could see was her lying on the subway ground, hurt, demoniis tramping her. *Echo!* Her name was a roar in his mind. The air around him crackled and sparked.

"Aethan, man, what's going on? You flashed out of the castle, leaving an energy trail dangerous enough to turn a mortal to ash," someone said from beside him.

Aethan turned, trying to focus. He found Týr and Blaéz flanking his sides.

"What happened?" Blaéz asked.

It took a moment to get himself under control. "It's Echo. She had a nightmare, and she left the brownstone. She's not answering her cell. Her friend called me. I have to find her."

"A nightmare?" Blaéz asked him.

"Yeah. A demonii killed her friend several years ago. She's been hunting him ever since. It's why she goes after them with single-minded purpose."

Cold fury stoked his temper, warring with his fear as the stark truth hit him. Everything he knew about Echo's past, Lila had told him. Echo was like Ziploc. Now she was hunting this demonii fucker who'd killed her friend. He pinched the bridge of his nose in frustration.

Dammit. Lila should have warned him about this. His mate was out there, alone, while danger lurked in the shadows.

"Have to admire the female. She's got some moves in her. The way she took down those demoniis at the castle, never seen anything like it."

The admiration in Týr's voice scraped at his gut gone raw with anxiety. Aethan nailed him with a deadly stare.

The male shrugged. "She's damn good with a blade. But as much as I hate to agree with you, she shouldn't be hunting demoniis." He glanced at Blaéz. "Anything?"

"Indeed. I simply turn on my precognition at will

and have all the answers."

Týr eyed him in mock despair. "Useless talent. Let's go. If she's hunting for this fucker, then I'm thinking alleys, all their usual haunts—"

Aethan's fingers tightened around his dagger hilt, his stomach churning. "The obsidian."

"What about it?" Blaéz eyed the pewter dagger Aethan currently used. "Where's yours?"

"It's Echo's now. It should summon me. But dammit—" He scrubbed a hand over his face at the only reason why it would do so. "When the demoniis in the subway tried to take her through the portal, it yanked me to her, and just in time, too. I have to go."

Moments later, Aethan took form near her apartment building on the Lower East Side. With preternatural speed, he headed to the fourth level. Most of the mortals here were asleep. He scanned and picked up sounds of a baby crying, someone snoring, and coughing. But nothing of Echo.

It didn't matter. He had to see for himself. Touching the door of her apartment, he willed the locks to disengage. Shock pinned him to the spot as the door swung open. Across the doorway, a ward with a strong protection spell woven into it shimmered—one only a powerful immortal could cast. Similar to the ones they had at the castle.

He undid the ward, entered and glanced around the place. It reminded him of her, neat and efficient, no frills or fancy things that females often liked. Breathing in her scent caused pain to bloom in his chest. He ached to see her, to hold her.

Aethan stepped out of the apartment, redid the wards, then willed the locks to re-engage. Damn, he was running out of logical places to search, and desperation ate at him… He stopped dead. If she had a nightmare and she was determined to kill the demonii, then she'd go back to the place where it occurred.

He pulled out his cell and called Kira. The female answered on the first ring. "Where did her friend die?"

***

Echo drove down Canal Street and stopped near the filthy little alley leading off of it. Her stomach heaved, her skin still clammy from her nightmare. Closing her eyes, she waited, needing more from her dream—a clue, an inkling to help her find the demonii.

Nothing.

She rubbed her arms against the penetrating cold that seemed to have found a way into her car. And wished Aethan were there to hold her—God knew where he was. Or if he even cared.

Two days. Two horrible days had passed, and he hadn't bothered to return her calls.

Grimly, she pushed those thoughts away, switched off the Beetle and climbed out. She headed down the dark backstreet, which was concealed by a thick fog. The vapor clung to her hair and dampened her face. She shivered and tucked her frozen hands into her jacket pockets. She'd forgotten her gloves again. No matter, she couldn't fight with them on anyway.

She stared into the hazy, disturbingly familiar alley. Everything was just as she'd remembered from five years ago.

The stench overwhelming in the moist heat of summer, she could still smell the rotting garbage, merged with the aroma of soy-cooked food from nearby restaurants. While people had enjoyed their dinners, she'd found Tamsyn's body near a dumpster, lying among the filth, as though carelessly thrown out with the day's trash. Her bright hair still gleamed with life, but her eyes had been open and dulled with death.

Echo dragged in several breaths of icy air to ease the old ache in her chest and rubbed at her misty eyes, willing her anger at the loss of her friend to stamp out her grief.

She looked around her. It was a waste of time trolling for demoniis tonight. Visibility was close to impossible, except for a few feet in front of her. Not a single pulsing red glow to be seen anywhere. It was probably too cold for the fiends.

She turned to head back to her car and there in her peripheral vision, a red spark caught her attention. So, one was brave enough to leave the fires of Hell.

The glow, more crimson than red, came closer, pulsating like a beacon. Adrenalin shot savagely through her veins, sharpening her focus.

Then she saw him. Brown dreads hung loose around his shoulders. It was the demon from the subway station.

Lazaar.

Panic urged her to run, but the memory of Tamsyn's cold, sightless gaze and ravaged neck had her planting her feet to the asphalt. She slipped her obsidian dagger free from her jeans, the weight of it reassuring as the warmth of the hilt tingled through her hand.

He sauntered toward her. In blatant disregard for the weather, he wore only a dress shirt and pants this time. The fiend probably had Hellfire burning in him.

"Yesss," he said, sniffing the air. Joy lightened his pale, frighteningly handsome face—all the more

Georgia Lyn Hunter

macabre when he smiled, revealing a set of fangs.

But that wasn't right, he didn't have—

"I've been searching for you."

"I'm flattered by your devotion. Why don't you come and get me?"

He laughed in delight. "We're going to have so much fun."

His movements a blur, he attacked.

Familiar with their quick maneuvers, Echo danced back, barely avoiding his grasp, but a wet trail ran along her jaw.

Echo wiped the saliva off her face, her eyes trained on him. She didn't bother to curse this time as she waited for his next move.

"You taste absolutely luscious." He leered, circling her.

She countered, moving with him, the dagger hidden in her palm. "Yeah, yeah, that's me, luscious human. You're boring me. Let's cut the chitchat and get on with it."

He growled. His brown eyes filled with a darkness so malevolent, the hair on her nape froze.

Somewhere farther down the alley, a back door opened. The aroma of baking bread and voices yelling something in Mandarin filled the cold, smelly alleyway. Another door opened, and more voices joined the clamor as the backstreet came alive with merchants making an early start on the day.

"You're coming with me." Lazaar didn't seem to care people were within yelling distance, he must have thought he was safe in the cover of smog. Or that she was easy to get at.

She had to end this.

He launched himself at her. Evading him, Echo

swung around and lashed out, her dagger slicing the fiend across the chest. Her momentum sent her skidding on the wet sludge covering the ground.

"You'll pay for that," he snarled.

She bounced on her feet, her dagger braced for another attack. "Put it on my tab."

But he stepped back as another sinister growl left him. "Listen to me carefully, human. The next time I come, you *will* leave with me, or you won't like what will happen."

He didn't flash after his threat, merely retreated into the early-morning fog which swirled around him, thickening until it engulfed him. Echo struggled not to hurl at the stench of sulfur coating her tongue and skin—

She stilled. The fiend didn't smell right. No honeysuckle like the one in the subway. Instead, he smelled of...vanilla?

Her gaze darted around. She inhaled deeply, searching for his scent. Nothing. Just the aroma of baking bread crowded her nose. *Crap!* His smell was the one she'd hunted for five long years. But why did Lazaar reek of vanilla now—exactly like the one who'd killed Tamsyn? She *had* to be imagining things. Besides, the one who killed Tamsyn was blond. He didn't have brown dreads.

The tiny hairs on her neck prickled. A dark figure materialized in front of her. Her blade palmed, she attacked. A sharp hiss erupted from her assailant, swearing in a language she'd never heard before. But before she could locate the fiend through the fog, he grabbed her from behind, locking her arms and keeping her trapped against his chest.

She snarled and head-butted him, connecting with

Georgia Lyn Hunter

his jaw instead of his nose. A satisfying grunt of pain reached her ears.

"Stop that, you little hellion!" The air filled with more curse words. The next minute, her dagger was gone.

She inhaled sharply and the familiar scent of rainstorms and leather enveloped her. She glanced over her shoulder, her breath caught at the tight, hard features. "Aethan?"

"Yes, it's me." He whirled her around to face him. "Who the hell did you think it was?"

Before she could speak, he yanked her close and dematerialized them back to the castle.

Chapter 19

The thick walls of the small living room subdued the sound of the winds howling outside as a storm broke. Fat raindrops splattered against the windowpane, drowning out the crackle from the fireplace.

Echo felt as if her head was still detached from her body as Aethan helped her out of her jacket. She swayed. God, she hated this dematerializing. It made her feel like she'd left her head behind. He grabbed her arms, steadying her, then hauled an armchair close to the fireplace.

"Sit down before you fall."

Gratefully, she sank into it. Why was he so angry? He was the one who'd walked out.

She shivered as the warmth from the fire seeped into her frozen limbs and stared at her icy fingers. She hated that she was so aware of him as he crossed to the sideboard. Glass tinkled. He reappeared moments later, and wrapped her stiff fingers around the snifter of brandy, then he pushed up her sleeve to examine the wounds on her upper arm.

She pulled back. "It's healed."

Mouth tight, he cut her a dark look and turned away as if to gain control of himself. Her breath seized. The dagger-slash on the sleeve of his charcoal shirt gleamed wet with blood. Her heart tripped when she found him watching her with stormy gray eyes. "You're ble—"

"What the hell were you thinking, Echo? The demonii could have killed you. I leave you for one minute and you go get yourself into another dangerous situation."

"*One minute*?" She jumped up, the brandy spilling over her shaking hand. "How dare you? You left for two—*two* days, without a word or an explanation!" Her humiliation grew at how desperate she'd been to reach him, and she hated herself for being so weak. "I never expected this, you, me, to be a forever kind of deal—" The lie stuck in her throat.

"Wait one damn minute—"

"No! You changed your mind about us, fine, but have the decency to tell me instead of leaving." She set the snifter aside and wiped her damp hand on her jeans. Pain tightened her chest at the knowledge she didn't matter in the greater scheme of things in his life.

It was okay. She did better on her own, without a man in her life, anyway.

"If I could get a ride to the city, I'd appreciate it."

***

Aethan jammed his hands into his pockets so he wouldn't put a fist through the wall, and struggled to contain his fury. He despised the helplessness that still lingered from when he couldn't find her. Now she stood there making this his fault. It was, he knew for walking out without an explanation. But if she thought for a single second that he would stand back and let her leave him… Yeah, that wasn't happening.

She had to understand what it meant to be his mate.

"I didn't leave because I didn't want you—gods, it's the farthest thing from the truth." He closed the distance between them. "I had no choice."

"We all have choices."

"No, Echo. Not all are that fortunate." He cupped her chin and saw the pain she struggled to hide, and hated himself for putting it there. "I couldn't stay to explain two days ago. I didn't dare. I had to Ground, or it could have ended in disaster. You know what I am. You saw my power. There's a dark side to it, too." He brushed the silky smooth skin of her jaw with the pad of his thumb.

"You experience terrible pain if you don't Ground when your power spike."

Hedori had been busy.

Aethan didn't care. He pulled her into his arms, needing to hold her—needing to know she was safe.

"Yes, that's one part of it. When I Ground, I have to go to the mountains. The white quartzite there helps me stabilize. For that to happen, I must shut down completely, body and mind. I lose track of time. It's something beyond my control." He bit her earlobe in punishment for doubting him. For even thinking he didn't want her. The little gasp that left her made him feel better. "Echo, had I stayed, I would have hurt you. And that, I would never allow."

She leaned back and looked up at him. "I don't understand."

"Where I come from, Empyreans have various strengths and types of powers. Mine is of whitefire, the most lethal. It would be deadly to anyone if my shields so much as cracked open. Mortals and immortals alike would die. My job as a Guardian makes it necessary to use this ability to take out evil. You've seen this. Now do you understand just how perilous I am?"

"Only to demoniis," she insisted. "You won't hurt me."

Her trust sent a warm feeling flowing through him, but it didn't override his irritation with her refusing to recognize that every time his power surged, she could be trapped in a minefield.

He groaned. "Echo—"

"Your eyes, they turn white. It's because of what you can do, right?"

"No, that's because of what I am."

"What do you mean?"

He brushed a hand over her hair. "I don't want to frighten you."

"You know I'm not easily intimidated or scared. If I'm to understand this, you have to tell me."

Tension flowed right back into him. He let her go and walked over to the window to stare out into the wet night. Lightning flared, brightening the shadowy trees and drenched gardens. Rain raced down the windowpanes in tiny rivulets. The gentle touch of her hand on his back offered him comfort, one only she could give.

"It happened during my mother's transition," he began. His jaw tightened, remembering the first time he lit up like a damn specter. He'd been only sixteen at the time and completely terrified when, in a spurt of anger, a wave of light exploded out of him. Over half the countryside had been destroyed in the blast. He'd taken out dwellings, shrubs, and plants, singed skin, clothes, and hair off the people caught in the wave of light. His mother's look of horror when she'd realized the truth was burned into his memory.

"Her transition from what?"

Echo's voice pulled him back. He braced his fist against the windowpane. "My mother's a seraph. When she *fell*, she went through a brutal and fiery trial, unaware she was pregnant with me. I absorbed the whitefire that took her wings. A damn vicious punishment for falling in love with an Empyrean and leaving the order of the Seraphim."

***

A seraph?

"Aethan?" Echo drew his hand from the window and stroked her thumb over the calluses on his palm. "Your mother, what is she?"

"An angel. Only she was a divine one—unlike the Empyreans. We're angels of a different caliber, without wings, and a menace with the kind of powers some of us are burdened with."

Echo dropped his hand. She stared at him as his bitter words flayed her.

He's an angel! Aethan's an—

Her mind stuck on that line like a scratched disc.

"Whitefire is an energy belonging to Heaven. A horrifying power, one nobody should be subjected to, yet it's used as a punishment for fallen angels. No one should possess abilities like mine." He turned and took her cold hands in his, his warmth flowing into her. "Echo, I'm the result of an Empyrean and a high-level angel. Add whitefire to the mix—hell, I shouldn't even exist."

"Don't say that." Her grip tightened. "Then I wouldn't have met you. If I had to live my horrid life all over again just to be with you, I would."

He pulled her into a crushing hug, and the air left her lungs in a gush.

Argh, she didn't really need to breathe, did she? He could always revive her if she asphyxiated.

"Echo?" His breath ruffled her hair. "There's something I need to tell you."

He sounded far too serious. Her stomach dipped when he let her go.

His gaze held hers. "My powers don't only make my fighting abilities lethal. During times of intimacy, some of that power escapes. When I first came to this realm, before I became a Guardian, there was another, a human female. I never thought about how my powers might affect her when we became intimate. Not until it was too late.

"She—" He blew out a breath. "My powers filled her, and her heart gave out. I couldn't save her. I've never been with a mortal again. That's why I must be careful with you. Every time I touch you, it gets riskier. I fear my need for you will push me over the edge. Make me lose control. It terrifies me, what could happen to you."

Each heartbeat became more agonizing than the last. "What does this mean? You're afraid you'll hurt me, so you won't touch me? Won't make love to me?"

He captured her face in his hands before she could draw another pained breath, tenderness banishing the austerity of his gaze. "Hell no." He pressed his lips to hers. "I can't *not* touch you. I might as well stop breathing. I will find a way out of this, I promise. But we have to be careful."

Echo rested her forehead against his chest and squeezed her eyes tight. She wanted to cry, wanted to yell at the unfairness of her life. First her pheromones played havoc and ruined relationships for her, and now this.

Aethan could kill her. Not something she wanted to hear, especially from the man who'd chipped away the walls from her heart, a man she was falling for.

But he wasn't really a man, was he?

She pushed away from him and looked him over. Tall, muscular, and heartbreakingly handsome, even with the grim expression he currently sported. His thick hair tied in a ponytail, revealed the gleam of silver earrings. He was perfect.

She tried to understand what he saw in her, and failed. "Why me, Aethan?"

"You haunt me," he said simply. "From the first moment I saw you, there was no looking back for me. You are mine, Echo. My heart. My soul. My destiny. I will never give you up."

***

Echo walked into the bedroom wearing blue flannel bottoms and a darker blue tee. With a shaky hand, she smoothed her top. She'd hoped a shower would calm her nerves, help her come to terms with what she'd learned about Aethan.

His being an angel with scary-ass powers didn't matter to her. She was drawn to the man she thought him to be, had been from the moment she saw him in front of the stone angel statue. The irony of it brought a wry smile to her lips.

The fact he couldn't touch her, had her taking a deep breath. *One day at a time,* she told herself. And clung to the hope his possessive words gave her.

Running a hand through her damp hair, she stopped when she saw him come out of the dressing room. He'd changed, too, and wore jeans and a t-shirt now. Hardly anything remained of the deep wound she'd inflicted on his biceps, just a thin red line across the tattoo.

"Can you use your sword if you're wounded on the tattoo?" she asked, worried that she'd left him weaponless.

His gaze softened. With a hand on her nape, he drew her close and laid his lips on hers in a tender kiss. "No. But I'm always prepared, so don't worry about it. Here." He held out the obsidian dagger.

"It's yours—"

"No, it's not. It never was. I inherited that along with my tattoo. It's my mate's dagger—yours."

"You're with me because of a *dagger*?"

"No." Amusement brightened his eyes at her snippy tone. "I'm with you because you are mine. I don't need a mystical dagger to tell me how I feel. Besides, that's no ordinary blade but a Gaian one. It can't be stolen, ever."

"But I did, from you." She smirked, because she loved besting him. Taking the blade from him, she trailed her finger over the design on the guard and said softly, "It glowed the first time I touched it."

"I guess it would, since it recognized you. That blade will summon me if you're in grave danger."

"Like tonight?"

"Tonight I was faster," he retorted. He took the

dagger from her and tossed it on the table. "If it's ever stolen, just will it back. It will always return to you. Why didn't you tell me about your friend being killed by a demonii?"

The abrupt change in conversation froze her. He didn't look happy. Darn, Kira must have told him the truth.

A knock sounded on the door, and a gush of relief filled her at her momentary reprieve. Aethan strode across the room and opened it. Hedori walked in, carrying a tray which he set on the coffee table. "M'lady, I'm glad to see you unharmed."

She offered him a smile while embarrassment made her want to squirm.

Did they all know that Aethan had found her in an alley and she'd attacked him? Of course they did. Týr and Blaéz had helped him search for her, and Hedori had been oozing anxiety by the time they got back to the castle.

After Hedori left, Echo sank into the armchair, her stomach pitching. She didn't dare tell Aethan Lazaar had accosted her again. Avenging Tamsyn was too important to give it up. She frowned, the demon's confusing scent troubling her.

Still, she had to tell Aethan about those years on the street and hoped he'd understand. He had a right to know why she couldn't leave this alone.

Aethan stopped a few feet in front of her and waited.

She poured herself coffee, hoping it would settle her nerves, and took a sip.

"My parents died in a mugging when I was four," she said softly, staring at the steaming black liquid. "I had no other family, so I ended up in foster care. I hated it there, really hated it. But I was too young to do anything about it. Not for lack of trying. Complaining to social workers just made things worse." The memories of long nights locked in the cold, dark basement sent a shiver through her. She turned the mug in her hands, seeking fresh warmth. "A few years later, I ran."

She glanced up at him. Not a flicker of emotion showed on his striking face, but those eyes swirled with sympathy, with knowledge.

"You already know, don't you?" she whispered, her stomach cramping at the realization. Had he known from the beginning?

He nodded. There was no apology in his expression. "The moment I found out you were my mate, I wanted to learn everything about you. I think Lila must have understood that. It's probably the only reason she showed me."

"Showed you?" The spasm worsened. She pressed down on her tummy. "Everything?"

"No. Just your time in foster care." His expression hardened. "It makes me angry to know they got away with what they did to you. Gods help those humans if I ever find them."

"Don't, Aethan." She set her mug down, understanding that his anger was for her, for the way she'd been abused by her foster family. "It happened a long time ago."

"How old were you when you left?"

"Nine." She rubbed her arms again, unable to stop the shivers, despite the heat from the fire. She remembered every terrifying minute of the night she'd snuck out of her foster family's house in the dark hours with her meager possessions, never to return.

"It wasn't easy living on the streets, but I got by. Then I turned thirteen, entered puberty, and my pheromones created worse problems. Pimps, hustlers, anything with a Y-chromosome, came after me. I didn't know why back then, and I lived in terror whenever I saw a man. That's when I met Tamsyn."

She smiled, remembering the first time she'd met her friend, how fast she'd whipped out her stiletto and nicked the pimp in the throat, forcing him to let Echo go. "Tamsyn had already acquired a badass reputation on the streets. She was older, street savvy. She taught me how to defend myself. Of course, being so young, fighting wasn't always a good idea. Running and hiding was better, but she never left me alone." Absently, she rubbed the scar on her forehead, trying to ease the headache building behind it.

"One night, Tamsyn went out. She had to. We hadn't eaten in two days. I was ill so I remained behind. Then I saw him, the demonii, standing in the basement where we slept. He stood there sniffing the air. The other kids scattered, hid, but he wasn't interested in them. He came for me. He-he tore my clothes." She shut her eyes tight at the horrific memory, her voice a whisper. "I'm just grateful Damon found me when he did."

When warm hands covered hers, her eyes flickered open. Aethan sat on the coffee table opposite her. "What happened?"

She swallowed her tears and forged on. "After Damon adopted me, Tamsyn and I remained friends through the years. Five years ago, I met her in Chinatown for dinner, and afterward, we were heading for my car, when Tamsyn grabbed my arm and pulled me into an alley. She said we were being followed by demoniis, and that she'd handle them, but I had to get the hell out of there. She shoved me toward the back entrance of a bakery and ordered me to run because she couldn't be bothered to worry about my ass in a fight. But I knew why. At eighteen, I still had no idea how to use a dagger or fight well."

Unable to sit still, Echo pushed to her feet and looped around the couch to the fireplace. Arms wrapped around her waist, she stared at the flames. "I was half-way into the bakery, but I knew I couldn't leave. I had to make sure she was all right. I hurried back outside. She'd already killed one of them. But the other, he was stronger. He'd disarmed her and his mouth was on hers as he siphoned her soul, th-then he tore at her neck…"

"You can't blame yourself," Aethan said quietly, pulling her back.

She glanced at him, tears blurring her eyes. "You don't understand. Tamsyn was wearing my sweater." She choked on her words. "He didn't want her. He wanted *me*. He was drawn by the scent of *my* pheromones on *my* sweater. He said she smelled delicious."

Chapter 20

Aethan stared out the kitchen window as he waited for the others to come in from patrol. He hoped Echo would rest and get a few hours of uninterrupted sleep. The depth of her despair had him prowling the length of the kitchen. He understood her anger, her need for revenge, but he couldn't let her put herself in danger again.

Gods. He pulled out a chair and dropped into it. Shutting his eyes, he pinched the bridge of his nose. What a mess.

Footfalls sounded in the corridor, then the door opened. Blaéz and Týr walked in.

"Damn demoniis must be taking a break," Týr complained, crashing into the chair opposite him. He looked at Aethan, his eyes sparking with his old amusement. "The highlight of this evening was watching Echo make you run around in circles. It damn sure made my night."

Aethan let Týr's nearly friendly dig slide, grateful the warrior was speaking to him again. Not that he deserved it. Besides, they'd dropped everything and come to his aid when Echo went missing and that meant a great deal more than the jabs from Týr.

"She's okay, then?" Blaéz asked, as he shrugged off his trench coat. He tossed the garment on a chair and ran a hand through his clipped hair.

"If you mean unharmed, yes."

"Why did she leave the protection of the castle in the first place?" Týr asked. He pulled out his pack of M&M's, ignoring the snacks on the table, and tipped several into his palm.

Aethan ignored the question. Like he was going to tell them the reason, tell them that he couldn't claim his mate. Unloading his crap wasn't going to happen.

"Echo lived on the streets as a child," he said. Yes, that sure got their attention off why she'd left.

Týr paused in his selection of all things green. "You mean she was homeless?"

"What other way is there?" Blaéz asked.

"She was too young, and an older girl, Tamsyn, befriended her, and watched out for her, especially when puberty hit. Kept her safe from the Y's—"

"The what?" Týr asked, confused.

"It's what she calls the males."

"Damn, I like her," Týr said, grinning. His shoulders lifted in a shrug at Aethan's cold stare. "Don't go getting all fired up again. I know she's your female." He dropped the rest of the candy into the package.

The Norse's annoying habit of eating his sweets according to the Pantone Color Chart made Aethan growl, "Why can't you eat the damn things straight?"

"They're all the same beneath the fancy colors," Blaéz pointed out.

Týr glanced at them, his expression serious. "It's art. Each spectrum has to be enjoyed, savored, especially green." And the shit-eating smirk was back. It made Aethan realize he'd missed the bastard.

"After Echo was adopted," he continued, resting his arms on the table, "she kept up her friendship with Tamsyn, until five years ago when the demonii attacked them. And killed Tamsyn. Here's the thing: the demonii said she smelled delicious. Tamsyn was wearing Echo's sweater."

"Ah, hell," Týr murmured.

"Hard to live with that kind of guilt," Blaéz agreed.

The door opened. Michael entered. And behind him, Dagan followed.

The Sumerian warrior had finally shown up in all his menacing glory. His black hair, longer than the last time Aethan had seen him, had several warrior braids woven into it. Slitted yellow eyes flicked over them before settling into a look of indifference. Týr, he didn't even glance at.

The smirk that slipped off Týr's face when they entered was replaced with an expression one rarely saw, except when looking at the Celt. His gaze was like a void.

Michael tossed his shades onto the table. There wasn't anything angelic about his tough face and forbidding appearance tonight.

"Your female, she is well?" he asked Aethan.

A flash of surprise brightened Dagan's eyes, before they resumed their remoteness.

"Yeah." Aethan filled Michael in on the latest developments and the demon Echo was after.

"It's not unusual for a demon to fixate on a

human, especially one with pheromones at play," Michael agreed. "And it's normal to want to avenge a loved one."

Aethan cut him an annoyed look. What the hell did he know? Archangels were created for war. Love wasn't part of their makeup.

"Whatever. They won't get another chance at her," Aethan promised, tone deadly. "Can someone explain to me why her apartment would have protection wards? Like the ones we use? It's not the Oracle or her guardian, both are mortals." He glanced at them, hoping someone would have an explanation.

"What about A'Damiel?" Blaéz asked, reaching for a chocolate chip cookie. "He appears when you least expect it."

"No." Aethan shook his head. "He may be immortal, but he's too self-involved. Can't see one like him wasting his time to protect a mortal."

"I'll have a look at the wards," Michael said, heading for the fridge. He snagged a can of Coke. "Your mate will be protected here. But as for her safety, make her understand the seriousness of this. She needs to know about the demons hunting for a psychic mortal who ties into a prophecy. Since she's psychic too, she'll be high on their list."

Like he didn't know that. It wasn't frightening Echo that worried him, but what she'd do when more restrictions were placed on her. Restless, Aethan pushed to his feet and headed for the fridge. Raiding it, he found a can of juice. He popped the tab and was sucking back the orange nectar when he remembered something.

Shit! With everything that had happened, he'd forgotten about the information he'd received from

Riley.

"Michael?" Aethan flipped his chair around and sat astride it. "I met with my contact a few days ago, but never had a chance to bring this up before. He mentioned that the scroll the demon has is a prophecy relating to the angels. Care to share?"

Every sound in the kitchen drained out when Michael said nothing.

"Yes, Michael, care to share?" Týr reiterated, his tone glacial. "Wait, I get it. Latrine cleaners aren't good enough to know the truth, right? Meeting's over." He pushed to his feet, but Blaéz grabbed his arm and yanked the hothead down.

Michael never flinched from their accusing looks. "The Celestial Realm doesn't care to have its messes revealed, but no longer. It's time you know the truth." His words were as hard as his expression. He leaned against the island counter, Coke forgotten in his hand. "Zarias was the leader of the highest-level angels and the last to fall. His dying words became this prophecy. He cast an ancient spell protecting his bloodline, prophesying a *female* would rise again. And the very ones who annihilated them would be responsible for her safety. She cannot come to harm. If that happens, then every evil ever known will have free access to this world and others. In short, Zarias made sure his spell would cause us endless trouble."

A mortal Healer would guarantee them the *endless* trouble, Aethan knew. Demons would be on her like damn flies.

"Who was Zarias for this kind of shit to happen?" Blaéz asked.

"The leader of the Watchers."

Aethan stilled. "You're talking about those

powerful angels who were chosen to watch over fledgling mankind? Instead they fell for human females—the reason why the unspoken laws became Absolute?"

"The same."

"Who killed him?" Dagan finally broke his silence. He pulled a narrow black case out of the pocket of his biker jacket, selected a thin cigar, and popped the thing between his lips, but didn't light it.

"I did."

At Michael's disclosure, a hush descended over the room.

"Why?" Dagan finally asked around the unlit cigar.

A flicker of a shadow passed through Michael's gaze. Regret? Perhaps staying on the mortal realm had rubbed off on him.

"They broke the Absolute Laws, took mortal females as consorts, and bore offspring with powers no human should possess. Demons came out in droves, killing the offspring for that power, which enraged Gaia. Mortals are under her protection, and one does not anger a Being like her."

Aethan's mouth tightened. The similarities between himself and the Watchers didn't escape him. He'd nuke any fucker who dared to even think of touching Echo. He looked at the other warriors around him and hoped to the Heavens they didn't suffer Zarias's fate.

"Now, about the female," Michael said. "Once she's found, she will go to the Celestial Realm."

"You're talking about a mortal," Blaéz interrupted, pushing away from his seat. He rattled through cupboards, found the bottle of Blue Label, picked up a squat glass, and sat down again. "You imagine she'll happily go someplace and leave her kin behind?"

"She will. As long as whoever protects her makes her understand this: Demons will always be on the prowl for her. She will not survive long on this realm."

***

Later that morning, Aethan walked into his room to find Echo in the dressing room, with only a towel wrapped around her. Her damp hair was brushed back from her face. She hadn't seen him as yet as she took out a change of clothes. Then she dropped the towel. Desire hit him hard. All Aethan could do was stare at the sight of her toned, honey-colored body as she pulled on tiny panties. He desperately wanted to touch—to taste every inch of her—

Godsdammit! This wasn't helping his control. His powers surged along with the urge to claim her. Pivoting, he headed for the bathroom. He'd talk to her once he got this damn dangerous desire under control.

A little while later, he stepped out of the shower, and hesitated. The cold water did little to calm him down. His body still twitched with need. And Echo would be in the bedroom, waiting for him—

Jaw tense, he swiped a towel off the rail, hitched it around his hips, and strode into the bedroom, sweeping back his damp hair. He stopped when he saw her in the sitting room. Ready for work. Dressing could wait. He had to talk to her now.

This wasn't going to be easy. But after Michael's disclosure, he'd be damned before he let anything else happen to her. So far, he was doing a helluva job of keeping her safe.

She looked up from the book she was reading, and smiled. No visible sign of her torment from last night. Picking up the steaming cup of coffee from the table, she handed it to him. "You look far too serious this early in the morning."

He didn't answer but took the mug and sat on the couch beside her.

"What time did you come in?" she asked.

"I didn't go out." He set the coffee back on the table, turned to her, and realized there was no easy way to do this. "Echo, I want you to take a leave of absence from the gym."

She stared at him, like he was speaking a foreign language. "Why?"

"You know why."

She dropped the paperback, uncurled her legs and got off the couch. "I understand why you're asking me this. But I'm not running from some demon. I've fought too hard to live a normal life. My guardian wouldn't let me move out of the loft until I was twenty-one"—her expression tightened—"and now you would have me barred again."

"Is that what you think I'm doing?" Edginess crawling through him, Aethan rose. "You experience dreams that haunt you, leave you screaming in the night." At her betrayed expression, he snapped, "Yes, Kira told me. Did you think I wouldn't find out?"

"It's just a dream." She glared at him. "And now you're gift-wrapping a cage. I won't be a prisoner." She stomped into the bathroom and shut the door. The lock engaged, spiking his temper.

***

Her chest heaving, Echo leaned on the counter and stuck her clenched fists under the running water. She couldn't—wouldn't be trapped, held helpless again.

The bathroom door flew open.

She spun around. "I'm done talking."

"Then you can listen." He grabbed her by the waist, dumped her on the cold countertop, and shut off the faucet.

Furious, the towel riding low on his lean hips, he leaned over her like some wrathful angel and planted his palms on either side of her hips, muscles rippling beneath his tawny skin. But caged by his warm body, and with his minty breath caressing her face, desire stirred.

She bit her lip, struggling to shut off her yearning for him to touch her again, but nothing helped. How could it when she was almost sprawled over the counter and was forced to grab his biceps for support? She settled for glaring at him. "Let me up, Aethan. I'm in no mood for a repeat of the same conversation."

"That's too bad. I'm worried about your safety, and you think this is a prison?"

Her resentment rose. "Call it whatever you want. Keeping me here with restrictions makes it a prison, no matter how you dress it."

"There's a demon after you. There's a damn army of demoniis after you. But you don't care how I feel about this, do you?"

"That's not fair—"

"Nothing in life is fair. Your foster father locked you in the basement because he's an ignorant son of a bitch. But this is not a damn cellar. You'll have run of the entire damn castle, barring the other warrior's apartments. I won't lose you to some evil fucker," he bit out, his eyes a stormy gray. "Tell me, what do you think would have happened had I not found you in that subway station?"

She scowled, hating that he was right.

The ringing of a cell phone cut through the air thickened by fraying tempers. He didn't move, continued to stare at her when she didn't answer. What could she say? Because deep down, she knew she would have died in that tunnel.

His point made, Aethan let her go and strode from the bathroom, a nerve ticking furiously in his jaw.

Echo stared at the empty doorway. She didn't want to fight with him. There had to be a way out of this, a compromise. Dragging in a deep breath, she hopped off the counter and followed him to the dressing room. And stopped dead.

The sight of him yanking on jeans had her riveted. He didn't wear boxers, briefs, or anything. She only caught a fleeting glimpse of his perfect backside, and he made every part of her feel far too warm. He took a t-shirt from the shelf of a wall-to-wall closet and pulled it on. Then he snagged a thin leather strip from a drawer. Raking back his hair, he tied it into a short ponytail.

"If you have to go to work," he said, glancing at her, "then I'm not taking any chances on your safety. The night shift is completely out of the question. It's all I'm prepared to concede on. Or else Hedori stays with you as your bodyguard." He sat on the wooden chest and pulled on socks then his boots.

The fact that he'd relented meant more to her than anything else. Still—ugh! She certainly didn't want Hedori trailing after her every minute of the day. She went over and sat on the chest next to him.

"Aethan, how you feel matters to me. I never meant to brush off your concerns. It's just the thought—" She sucked in a deep breath. "Being locked up is too painful."

"I know, *me'morae*." He reached out and brushed the hair out of her eyes. "That's not my intention. I only want you safe."

"I know... What was that you called me?"

His gaze held hers. Quiet. Intense. "My love."

Happiness flowing through her, she rubbed her cheek against his arm. "I can arrange for someone else to cover my evening clients."

"I'd appreciate that. I'm on the edge where you're concerned," he admitted, brushing his lips against her hair.

She drew back, frowning at his quiet tone. "What's wrong? What aren't you telling me?"

He let her go and braced his elbows on his knees. "As Guardians, we not only keep the realm safe from evil but also from unfolding prophecies."

"Prophecies? I don't understand." It all sounded too much like a fairy tale to her. Ugh, what the heck was she thinking? Aethan was an Empyrean angel, of course there would be things like prophecies.

"You're psychic. And it doesn't matter how light your abilities are, demoniis will snatch anyone with a drop of power, hoping to find the one human female tied to an ancient prophecy, the one who'll have the ability to heal the rifts."

"What rifts?"

"All realms are protected by a mystical veil that keeps out supernatural intruders. But demoniis and other evil entities try to break through those veils. It's

Georgia Lyn Hunter

not easy to do, but some manage and they create invisible doorways."

"You're saying there's a rift here? Is that the reason for the surge in demonii activity?"

He nodded, his expression grim. "The fractures on this plane have begun. By guarding it, we give it a chance to heal, but it takes too long. We must find this female before it's too late. I can't go out and do my job if I'm worried about you. Demoniis will use anything to achieve their goal. And if one got you, I would come after you, no matter the cost."

She knew what he meant. He would die for her.

"You scare me more than my dreams do." She sighed. "Aethan, you know I can look after myself, right?"

"That is not the issue, Echo. You're mortal. A slip of a sword, a dagger, a damn bolt from a demon, and you can die. That, I will not risk. I won't lose you."

"You're not going to lose me."

His brow arched. "Yeah? All I know is the moment you're out of my sight, I wonder what condition I'm going to find you in."

"Ha, ha. You're a riot. What about you? You go out there risking your life, and I know you can get hurt. You think it doesn't worry me?"

"I'm immortal. I've survived worse."

"Just because you're immortal doesn't mean you're invincible. There's a difference." Then her scowl turned to a frown. "How exactly do you die?"

"Really? You're worried about how *I* die?"

"Of course. You matter to me, so yes."

He shook his head and indicated the closet opposite his with nod. "There's some stuff in there for you."

All she saw were colors and a crap-load of shopping bags, but she refused to let him sidetrack her with clothes. Slowly, she pushed to her feet and looked down at him. "Wait…is it by beheading?" Crap, of course it would be. The images that sprang to mind made her stomach churn. "Forget it, don't answer, I know."

He rose. Taking his cell from the dresser, he pushed it into his pocket before he faced her. "All right, but I'll tell you this. As destined-mates, when one dies, the other follows. Once our souls join, they cannot be separated."

She stared at him for a long, silent moment, hearing a far more painful revelation. "But ours aren't."

"No."

An ache started in her chest at his quiet word. For their souls to join, he would have to make love to her.

Chapter 21

Týr pushed open the door to the rec room and found Blaéz lying on the couch, booted feet slung over the arm. A recorded hockey game played on the flat screen TV.

"You didn't find her," Blaéz said, his gaze not leaving the television.

"No. I tracked Elytani to Park Avenue, then nothing. I looked all over the damned city. Where the hell can one lone female be? She doesn't know this realm."

"Guess she wasn't pleased Aethan refused her?"

Týr had no idea if the female was or wasn't. "Didn't look like it. She seemed more in awe of him than anything else." He dropped on the recliner, staring moodily at the screen.

Blaéz sat up and propped his feet on the low table. "I can't understand why you didn't send her off with Michael like Aethan wanted. It's dangerous for her to stay, you know that."

"Yeah." An annoyed rumble left Týr. "But it's

been so long since I've been in the company of a female like her. She reminded me of another life."

And reinforced the fact that you couldn't trust a damn female. Their beautiful façade was just a cover for a shitload of lies. She wanted to stay a few days and he'd agreed, as long as she remained at the castle. A fat lot of good that did him now.

Blaéz glanced at him. "What about the ones from the pantheon that queue at your door?"

Týr shrugged. "When they just fall onto your plate, it loses its flavor."

"So instead you dance on a blade's edge with mortals?"

"Make's life interesting," he said, glancing back at the game on the flat screen. "I hope to the Heavens Elytani doesn't cause any incidents out there. Gaia would kick our asses into oblivion then—*what the hell is he doing*?" he yelled at the screen. "Keeping the puck for himself—no! The bastard can't play for shit."

"You don't even follow hockey," Blaéz drawled, rubbing the tattoo on his biceps.

Týr smirked. "Yeah, but it's a good way to vent." He got to his feet and headed for the foosball table. "I need a break from chasing after the female."

Blaéz followed. He picked up the small soccer ball from the table and said, "I can't imagine *that*...changing."

Týr stared at him, then his eyes narrowed. "Oh, no you don't, you Celtic bastard. Go torment the Empyrean with that precognition shit, and stay the hell away from me. And that's a warning."

Blaéz arched a brow. "It's all about rainbows. They scare you?"

Týr shook his head in wry amusement. "You poor,

insane bastard. Let's put that mind to good use and play foosball. I win, your katana is mine."

"I win, then when you find your rainbow, you thank me. And you *will* do me a favor."

"Yeah. Right. Whatever."

"And I also want an elaborate gesture of appreciation."

Týr snorted and spun the rod of the yellow figures, starting the game.

***

As they left the kitchen after breakfast, Aethan stopped in the corridor and turned to her, his expression grim. Echo knew why—because breakfast had been tense. She'd pushed her food around her plate, and he'd barely touched his. After that realization in the bedroom, she knew he'd have to make love to her for their souls to join. But she didn't see that happening any time soon. He'd warned her it wouldn't be easy. God, she just hadn't realized how hard this would be, being so close to him, the waiting.

"Echo," he began. "We'll try, but—"

"It's okay. I understand."

In a strange way, she did. It had to be difficult for him, too. She didn't want him hurting emotionally, as well, not when his powers did a good job of keeping them apart. She changed the subject. "Could we leave a little early? I left my car in Chinatown, I need get it."

He didn't say anything for a second—just stared at her. Then sighed. "I'll see to your car."

"Thank you. Leave it at Gran's. Tell Kira it's hers."

He reached out and skimmed the shallow dimple

in her chin with his thumb, his gray eyes tender. "All right. I have some business to take care of first, so I'll see you in a little while."

"Business?" she repeated.

A smile tugged at his mouth in amusement. "Did you think that's all we did? Killed demoniis and kept mortals safe?"

She wrinkled her nose. "Actually, yes. So what is it you do?"

"Being a Guardian is first priority, but we need hobbies. So we act human, have other interests, too. It keeps ennui at bay."

"Like what?" she asked, her curiosity aroused.

"Nothing exciting. I acquire properties, vineyards, rare books, and play the stock market." He pulled his cell phone from his pocket and cursed.

"What is it?"

"Damn thing died on me."

"You want to use mine?"

A smile. He shook his head. "I have others."

He pulled her to him and took her mouth in a quick kiss, before heading off to the study.

Echo stared at the empty hallway and struggled to get her breathing back under control, her fingers on her still-tingling lips. *Patience, Echo. Patience.*

Sighing, she called Kira and winced at the barrage of words that assaulted her ears. After reassuring her friend she was fine and promising to be careful, she ended the call.

Sounds drifted to her from down the corridor. She followed them to the rec room.

The scent of leather, male, and cherry tobacco permeated the air. French doors opened onto a terrace, which led to a sprawling garden. At one end of the room, leather recliners faced an enormous flat screen TV that showed a hockey game. On the other side stood a pool table, a few arcade games, and a bar.

The slamming of metal rods and the crack of something hitting a wooden surface, along with grunts and curses drew her attention. Týr and the dark-haired man she saw fighting the demonii horde were attacking a foosball table.

Týr looked her way and his dimples winked to life. "Mornin', gorgeous. Where's your shadow?"

"He'll be here soon," she said, thinking that if anyone should be called gorgeous it was him. She shut the door behind her and wandered over.

Her gaze settled on the other man. Blaéz. That's what Hedori had called him. It must be an immortal thing, she decided, to look that handsome. Hell, even those nasty soul-suckers looked good.

Dressed in black jeans and a short-sleeve t-shirt, Blaéz sported a similar tattoo to Aethan's and Týr's, except the design was different. His black hair, cut an inch from his skull, showcased a face that appeared as beautiful as marble. But it was his eyes that drew her attention. A cold, pale blue, they made her feel as if she'd stumbled into a void.

There was nothing in those eyes, as if every bit of light had been sucked out of him. And his aura, it was a mere flicker. The blue was so faded she wondered if he was ill.

"Ah, right." Týr's dry tone cut across her thoughts. "Guess that look means you haven't met Blaéz yet."

Her face heated at Týr's amusement.

"That's Blaéz. Just make sure your other half doesn't see you eyeing him. I happen to like his face the way it is."

Something slammed into Týr's head, and Echo realized it was Blaéz's fist. Jesus, they all moved like the wind.

Týr rubbed his head, laughing.

"Echo," Blaéz said by way of greeting and went back to the game. A few swift moves of his hand, in that eerily fast way she was now familiar with, and he won. He looked at Týr. "Don't forget our deal."

Týr snorted, rescuing the small ball from a side slot in the table. "Never gonna happen, man."

"Can I try?"

Both the men looked at her.

"You know how to play foosball?" Týr asked her.

"They're plastic men on sticks. How difficult can it be?"

Týr grinned. "Actually, they're wooden men on a metal rod."

"Same difference."

"Take my place," Blaéz said, stepping back.

"What do I have to do?"

Týr answered. "Your main objective is to pass the ball through your opponent's—"

"Just kick him out of the game," Blaéz said. "Get the ball onto his side, past his goalie, and into the slot here." He pointed to the opening in the wooden structure.

She looked over the rows of black and yellow men. "Gotcha."

"Do a practice run," Blaéz suggested.

Echo took over the black team. She soon realized it simply needed hand-eye coordination, just like fighting with a weapon.

"Ready?" Týr asked after the tryout, ball in hand.

"Bring it on."

He dropped the ball. And they started. Exhilaration filled her as she played... When he dared to cut her off, she growled, then twisted the rod and smashed the ball into her opponent's side. It slid smoothly into the gap.

Her fist punched the air. "Yes!"

Blaéz nodded as if she'd done him proud. But she couldn't be sure, when he looked about as excited as the wooden men on the metal rods.

"You're ready?" At the sound of Aethan's voice, she turned to the door, and grinned. "Yeah. I knocked Týr right out of the game—" she looked back at Týr, "and if you went easy on me, too bad. As long as I won."

Chuckling, Týr tossed the ball back on the table. "Best loss I've ever taken."

Aethan crossed to her side, his eyes narrowing in suspicion. "What did you bet her?"

"Nothing," Echo reassured him, straightening her hoodie. And realized playing foosball gave her a moment of respite from her problems.

"Relax, Empyrean." Týr smirked. "It was a friendly game."

But the twinkle in his toffee-brown eyes warned Echo, now he knew she was a worthy opponent, he'd definitely be reconsidering his options in the next game. She shot back, "My limit's a buck."

Týr burst out laughing. "Now, I can't wait."

Aethan snorted and dropped his arm around her shoulders. "C'mon, let's get you to work before you become as bad as he is playing this game."

***

Blaéz picked her up in the Range Rover later that afternoon, since Aethan was on rift duty. One thing she knew, they didn't budge from their schedule of guarding that place unless a dire emergency demanded their attention.

"Blaéz, do you mind taking me to Greenwich Village?" she asked. "I'd like to see Kira."

He nodded. As he headed toward her friend's home, she realized Kira wasn't the only one she needed to apologize to. "Blaéz, I'm sorry I worried you all last night."

Winter-blue eyes glanced at her. "Don't trouble yourself over that. Added some interest to the job. You're important to Aethan," he said, his gaze returning to the road. "It's rare that ones like us are blessed with finding our mates. We will do all it takes to ensure your safety, even after the demon that wants you is destroyed."

Right. She'd already figured that out. Hard as it was for someone as independent as her, she accepted it because Aethan mattered a great deal to her. She glanced back at Blaéz and realized she knew nothing about him, or Týr for that matter. If Aethan was an Empyrean...was he the same?

"Blaéz, where are you from?"

His gaze shifted briefly to hers again and when she saw the ice swirling in them, she hastily recanted. The man didn't care for her probing.

"It's okay, I just wondered."

But he surprised her by answering. "I'm from the Celtic pantheon."

She stared at the stark lines of his handsome face. *Wait.* He'd said pantheon, which meant like a realm where the gods lived.

"You're a god?" she said, shocked. She never thought about where the other warriors came from. She'd been too wrapped up in her life.

A long stretch of silence filled the vehicle. Stopping at a traffic light, Blaéz finally spoke. "I am a warrior. My allegiance is to Gaia."

No emotion, just facts. Which made her more curious, but she let it go. Aethan had sworn his allegiance to Gaia after he'd been banished. Had something equally devastating happened to these warriors?

Moments later, Blaéz parked the Range Rover in front of the brownstone where Aethan waited at the entrance.

"I informed him of the change in plans," Blaéz said.

***

The day had been a long one, and relief settled in Aethan when he saw Echo. He'd spent most of it in the gym, working through rigorous circuit training, surprised he could still walk after pounding the treadmill for several hours. Going on duty at the rift and just keeping watch hadn't helped settle the restless energy growing within him.

After Blaéz had sent him a telepathic message that he was heading to the Oracle's at Echo's request, the warrior agreed to take his shift an hour early, leaving Aethan free to be with Echo.

He opened the Range Rover door and scanned the street as night crept in. The winds had picked up, sending debris and dust flying around him.

"I thought you were on duty."

He turned to her. "I was, until a few minutes ago. Blaéz is taking over."

"I'm not going to be long. I just want to reassure Kira and Gran that I'm fine."

"Let's get you inside, then." He helped her down, trying not to rush her. He didn't care for her to be out in the open when the demoniis could just flash in. Using his body as a shield, he followed her up the stairs.

"You know what's totally weird," she said, glancing at him over her shoulder as she mounted the stairs, "is that you've known Gran for so long, and I never once met you."

"We don't usually go to mortal homes for safety reasons. Lila comes to the castle when we need her."

"So she knows what you are?"

"Yes."

She pushed aside the overhanging creepers and knocked on the door. As she turned back to him, a stray vine swung into her face. "Darn!" She brushed the creeper aside and rubbed her stinging eye.

"Let me see." Before Aethan could examine the damage from the attacking vine, the door opened. Kira grabbed Echo's arm and pulled her inside. "I was so afraid."

"I'm fine, Ki—really."

Aethan followed them into the house, the smell of crushed herbs and incense adding a soothing ambience to the place. He shut the door behind him.

Lila entered the living room from the kitchen. A smile of relief lightened her face when she saw Echo. These two females were her family. Aethan understood that, but witnessing their deep affection for her touched him. It comforted him to know she'd had people who cared about her before he'd come into her life.

She would never be alone again now that he was here.

"It's good to see you, warrior," Lila said, then she turned to Echo, concern filling her dark eyes.

"Gran." Echo hurried to her. She kissed Lila's cheek and hugged her. "I'm so sorry I worried you."

"What happened, child?"

"A bad dream. That's all." Echo stepped back, shrugged off her coat, and hooked it on the coatrack in the corner of the room.

"Kira told me what occurred. You shouldn't have left."

"I know, Gran, but I had to. I just wanted to find a way to deal with it. I thought if I went there, to the place where it happened, maybe I'd understand why I keep having these dreams."

"In the night?" Kira snapped.

"Yes. It had to be."

"And did you?"

Echo shook her head. "No."

Kira growled.

Lila sighed. "Kira dear, let me talk with Echo. Go prepare a tea tray for us."

Harrumphing, Kira flounced off.

Echo turned to Lila. Aethan sensed her relief her friend wasn't there to pick apart everything she said. "Why, Gran? Why am I having these nightmares? Reliving Tamsyn's death nearly every night is just too hard. And there's this man with braided hair in a navy robe who—"

"What man?" Aethan asked her.

Frowning, she turned to him. "When I was six, my foster brother hurt me and left me lying in a ditch."

Aethan's mouth tightened. He remembered what Lila had shown him of her foster family. He had to force himself to listen and not go out there, find those abusive humans, and make them pay as his heart demanded. This was about her, he reminded himself.

"I don't remember much," she said, rubbing her eye. "Just the pain before I blacked out. But when I awoke, I had no injuries. I always thought it was a dream. Except recently, I've been having flashes of this man, healing me and telling me he'll take away the pain..."

Aethan felt as if something cold had slithered over him. The only man he knew who matched Echo's description was worlds away. The one who'd kicked him out of Empyrea.

Allatus, the high mage.

No. Way. That old bastard never left Empyrea.

"Being psychic, you're always going to touch on the supernatural side of things, even in your dreams," Lila said, stroking Echo's arm, her expression tender. "But Tamsyn, you need to let her go. It's why she haunts you. Let her soul find rest, and you will finally have peace, too."

After a long moment, Echo sighed and nodded. "It's hard, but I'll try." She blinked and rubbed her eye again. "Gran, do you have eye-drops? One of your vines attacked me on the porch."

A smile tugged at Lila's mouth, easing the strain on her face. "Let me have a look." Angling Echo's face to the light, she examined her eye. "There's a rip in your contact lens," she murmured. Then she cupped his mate's face. "It's time, child."

Echo stiffened. Aethan felt her distress like a huge wave crashing over him. He failed to understand why she was upset over torn contact lenses. Hell, he hated the damn things.

After a long moment, she nodded. She reached for her coat and withdrew a small case, then headed for the mirror in the hallway. A few minutes later, she made her way back into the lounge. But sensing her unease, he crossed over to her and brushed a hand over her lowered head. "I'm glad you've taken them off—"

She looked up.

And the world around him stopped. Aethan felt as if someone had taken a vise to his chest. He couldn't breathe.

She stilled. Pain seeping into her eyes, she turned and walked away.

Aethan stared after her in utter shock.

No!

Dammit! No. Not her. Not his mate.

Chapter 22

Andras paced around his concealed chambers. No one, not even a smidgen of light, was allowed in this walled-off room, except for the torches he burned while it was in use. He had planned and plotted too long for this and would allow nothing to stand in his way. As for his brother—locked up safe in the outer caverns of the Lower Strata of Hell—too bad, really. Couldn't have him running to their sire with what little knowledge he possessed.

Andras spread out the tattered piece of parchment on the table. Finally, after five years, he knew what the scrolls had hidden.

A true soul's joining will set her free.

A whimper at his feet drew his attention. "Is this true, what it says here?" He flicked a finger at the ancient scroll. "I must mate with the *prophesied one* to bind her to me? Lie and you will never see daylight again." He smiled at the female and let his lips peel back from his teeth, baring his fangs. Fear was a motivating factor, and one he relished.

The girl, cowering on the ground, nodded, her long, dark hair obscuring her pale face. Her fear filled the chamber.

He didn't want to have a mortal tied to him. But no matter. He would go after the female himself and do what needed to be done. That way, he could complete the joining as soon as he captured her.

During the short test run he'd made to the mortal realm, he'd gone to the alley in Chinatown, where he'd been five years ago when he'd made a crucial error and took the soul of the blond female. Now, he was thankful for the first time that he hadn't killed the prophesied one. For five years, she'd stayed in his thoughts. Finally, he knew why. It was meant to be. Great things were destined for him. And she did taste delicious. The excruciating pain of leaving the Dark Realm had been worth it.

Andras grabbed the terrified female off the floor and looked into her pathetic little face. "Taking on my brother's image worked the first time. But I don't care for the short time span it gives me. I want longer."

The glamor had worn off far too soon, and his binding hauled him back to the Dark Realm. Just in time, too, because that blue-haired bastard Guardian had arrived.

"Y-you must drink your brother's blood." Her pale green eyes blinked in fear. "An ounce of it to take on his essence. It will fool the magic that keeps you locked on to this realm. Th-three drops of the mixture I-I made will keep your eyes clear, too. But it will fade after a few hours."

"I'll just replenish that. Will the sun affect me?"

She nodded. "I-I can't change what is. It's only a glamor."

That meant sunlight would burn his corneas and kill him. It didn't matter. He would fix all that soon. "If it doesn't work, I'll take your weak little soul. And I won't spare you the pain."

His second-in-command had done well, finding him this little oracle. He dropped her back to the floor, strolled around her, and nudged her bare foot with his shoe. "Why don't you beg me for your life, little human? Everyone else does."

He grabbed her hair and dragged her across the floor, taking pleasure in her cries of pain. Black claws split from his fingers. He raked one down her face and watched as blood dripped from the gash. He leaned in and licked the trail, enjoying her terror.

"My lord," Bael said from the chamber entrance. "We found the female."

Andras shoved the oracle aside. "Well, little human, it's your lucky day."

Time to get to work.

Chapter 23

Echo stood by the open door, listening to Kira hum as she gathered teacups from a cupboard.

Gran's kitchen usually made her feel better. The myriad scents of roots, herbs, and flowering plants infused the air. Copper pans hung from the low ceiling. But the familiar smells did nothing to loosen the constriction in her chest or ease her throat gone tight with tears.

The shock on Aethan's face hurt. She'd known it would, which was why she never wanted to reveal her eyes to him. To anyone.

Kira turned and smiled when she saw her. "I'm sorry I yelled at you before—hey, what's wrong?" She left the cups on the counter and hurried over. "Ah. You took out the lenses." She reached behind her and shut the door. "If he's weirded out because of your eyes, better you know now, right?" She rubbed Echo's arm in a soothing gesture.

Her heart twisted in denial. Kira's words, meant for comfort, hurt far worse than if she'd said nothing.

Echo closed her eyes, trying to will the pain away like she'd done so many times before. Only this time, nothing worked. It went too deep. Old hurts pierced her protective shields.

Devil's eyes.

She's Satan's spawn. That's why she ain't got no parents.

Freak. Weirdo.

The kitchen door opened. The air changed, became charged with his presence, and she knew Aethan had come after her. She didn't want him to see her so devastated, but there was nowhere to go.

"Give us a moment," he said to Kira.

Echo gripped Kira's hands tightly as if that would prevent what had to be faced. But confronted with her friend's anxious expression, she managed a little smile. "I'll be fine."

"All right. I'm just a yell away, if you need me."

After the door closed behind Kira, Echo felt his warmth surrounded her. "Are you going to look at me?"

His breath stirred the wispy strands of hair on her neck and a frisson of desire flared low in her belly. God, no. Not now. She couldn't handle wanting him, too, when all this was happening.

His hands settled on her shoulders. "Echo—"

"Don't." She broke away from him and spun around. "Let's not pretend, all right?" She kept her gaze on his chest, unable to stop the bitterness of her past from spilling free. "I can't blame you for being weirded out. I know, they're real freaky. People always react the way you did." Her voice hitched, but she plowed on, determined to get it all out. "Did you know they glow? Just like an animal's do at night, when I'm upset, excited, take your pick. Don't worry, you won't see them again. I have a spare pair of lenses."

Then she waited for him to walk away. Like they all did.

***

Aethan knew he had to put right the unintentional hurt he'd caused her with his moronic moment of shocked gaping because of what he suspected. "You think I care what a person looks like?"

She rubbed the scar on her forehead. "It doesn't matter."

"It damn well does, when you won't look at me."

Her gaze snapped to his. "You want to take a closer look?" She glared at him. "Go ahead."

She was looking for a fight, but he refused to give her one. Gods, but her eyes were a punch in his gut. Some humans were born with bicolored eyes, but hers were different. One was a pale, pearly gray, and the other burned brightly, like golden flames. Then he saw the amber-colored ring around the pale iris. *Urias,* but they were stunning.

Pyre and rime.

Fire and ice.

It had never been about her powers. It was about her eyes. She'd be able to see into the supernatural, see right through any kind of glamor, into other worlds.

She'd see through the veils where the rifts formed.

She dropped her gaze.

"Do not hide them from me, Echo. They're exquisite."

Bitter laughter spilled free. "You say that because you know I'm upset. At least you didn't stone me—"

Her mouth clamped shut.

Aethan grasped her upper arms. "*What?*"

"Nothing."

He tilted her face up with a finger and brushed her bangs aside. Finally, he understood why she kept her hair so long that it fell into her eyes. He traced the star-shaped scar just above her left brow. "Echo, who hurt you? Who did this?"

She stepped away from him, her voice so soft, he was grateful for his heightened hearing. "Some kids in the neighborhood didn't like the way I looked. Stoning me was their way of making it known. My foster brother would egg them on by calling me names." Her words spilled out, her expression rigid, as if caught in the past. "It was the same day he snapped and came after me because his father caught him touching me the day before and punished him. He-he punched and kicked me. It hurt really bad. I lost consciousness…"

Aethan pulled her stiff body into his arms, finding it difficult to hold on to his fraying temper. There was little he could do to make it all better for her. Despite his formidable abilities, he couldn't turn back time. Instead, he hugged her.

After a long moment, she let herself relax against him, sliding her arms around his waist, and told him the rest. "After Damon adopted me, he seemed to understand how I felt…well, mostly because I refused to go to school or leave the loft. So he got the lenses for me, and life became bearable again."

Aethan raised her face to his and brushed the shadows under her eyes with his thumbs. Now that she no longer shielded her eyes, an ethereal quality seemed to settle over her. He pressed his lips to the scar on her forehead. "You're amazing." He kissed the tip of her nose. "Beautiful." He kissed her lips. "Smart and brave. A little less brave and I'd probably be able to sleep at night, but I wouldn't change a thing about you."

A reluctant smile curved her mouth.

And his heart eased to see her smiling again. "Come, let's get out of here." He ushered her out of the kitchen. "There's something I want to check out."

***

A while later, Aethan drove through Times Square and parked the Range Rover across from Starbucks, a block from Demon Alley. Nightfall settled in like a shroud, and people rushed about, wanting to get home before the evening got too chilly. Aethan came around the vehicle and opened the door for her.

It surprised him when she refused to get out. "Why are we here?"

"This won't take long."

She arched a delicate brow at him. "Aren't you afraid demoniis will come after me?"

"I won't let them. Come on."

She sighed and got out of the Range Rover. After locking the vehicle, Aethan draped his arm around her shoulders and headed into the alley, which looked like it suffered from a bad case of diarrhea. The damn place stank to high heaven. He carefully maneuvered them away from the sludge coating the asphalt.

His tattoo remained still. Except for the rift, he could sense nothing supernatural in the area. But something felt different. It tugged at his psyche. Not evil, more like it waited in anticipation. Whatever the hell it was, he wasn't keeping Echo here another minute.

"Aethan?" she murmured. "I was here the other night—"

At her words, blood pounded in his veins and snagged at his temper. "Dammit, Echo. You came here alone?"

She pulled away from him. "Don't yell at me. It wasn't by choice. Something drew me here, and no, I didn't get hurt."

"Gods, I'll be the first immortal to suffer a heart attack," he growled.

He scanned the area and picked up on Blaéz's presence farther down the alley. The Celt sat on the rooftops, keeping guard. It probably was better than wading through this sea of crap.

"What was it you felt?" He turned when she didn't answer and found her with a hand pressed to her stomach. "Echo?"

She shook her head and glanced around the shit-pit.

"What is it?" He shielded her with his body, his senses scanning furiously, but he picked up nothing.

"I don't know. It feels the same. Like the last time." She rubbed her middle again, as if in pain.

"Come on, let's go back."

"No. Wait." She laid a hand on his chest, stopping him, and inhaled deeply. "It's–it's okay… I need to stay."

His senses on alert, he waited, ready to grab her and dematerialize if need be. It was the worst damn idea, bringing her to this place with the tear in the veils. She wasn't ready for this encounter. But Echo seemed to want to stay. Did she feel it, too—did she sense the rift?

Georgia Lyn Hunter

As he kept watch, her body went still. Her eyelids drifted shut.

"Echo?"

She didn't respond. He waited; his gaze pinned on her, his edginess increasing with each passing second.

Then, like a fading bulb, her knees buckled.

"Echo!" He grabbed her and she fell limply into his arms.

***

Aethan muted the flat screen. He pulled out his cell and called Blaéz. They rarely used their mind-link, except in dire emergencies. Besides, it gave him something to do other than wear out a hole in the carpet while Echo remained in a deep sleep.

"I left the Range Rover near Demon Alley," he said when the warrior answered.

"No problem. I'll get it."

"Thanks, man. Owe you one."

"What happened?"

He scrubbed a hand over his face. "I took Echo there. Don't know what the hell I was thinking."

"That makes two of us. She's okay?"

"Yeah. She's asleep. I'm at the castle with her." Cell pressed to his ear, Aethan walked to the window and stared out into the night.

"All right then." A pause. "You think she could be The Healer?"

"I'm not sure. Gods, I hope not."

Another pause. "Right, later then."

"Yeah, okay. You need me, call."

***

Aethan smelled her before he saw her. She pressed a soft kiss to the corner of his mouth. He breathed in her scent, let it settle into his lungs, then opened his eyes to take in her smiling face. She kneeled between his spread thighs, her arms resting on them. She still wore the navy t-shirt he'd put her to bed in. The possessive male in him liked seeing her covered in his things. He reached out and caressed her cheek.

"Why didn't you come to bed?"

"I am on call. Easier to sit here and keep an eye on you."

Her brow creased. "You didn't have to stay, Aethan. I'm fine."

"And deny myself the pleasure of watching you sleep?"

She still had no idea of what she meant to him. Seeing her lying there, almost comatose in sleep from whatever happened in the alley, he wasn't leaving her. The only reason he didn't panic was because he'd scanned her and knew she hadn't been hurt in any way.

"You need a new hobby," she said with a wry shake of her head, her fingers stroking his thigh.

At her touch, his sex strained painfully behind his leathers. He wanted to touch her, wanted her to touch him without the barriers of clothes, wanted just the slide of her skin against his—

He shifted in his seat.

She pulled back and glanced around the room. "No snacks? And I'm starving."

"Hedori's been hovering, waiting for you to awaken. I'm sure he'll have something ready." He called Hedori and told him to bring up food.

She turned those striking eyes on him, her brow

creasing. "What happened to me?"

"First, I need this." Unable to hold out any longer, he pulled her to him and took her mouth in a starving kiss. A deep sigh left her and she slid her arms around his neck, pressing against his erection. The seductive taste of her crowded his senses. Beneath his skin, his powers surged, battering against his psychic shields—

Gods, just one damn minute—one godsdamn minute!

He wanted to be able to hold his mate and kiss her the way he wanted. But he couldn't even have that. Clamping down on his frustration, he gentled the kiss and eased back.

She stared at him with slumberous eyes, then ran a shaky hand through her messy hair. "What happened last night?" she asked him, drawing back. Already, he hated that small distance she put between them.

"Echo, you've been asleep for eighteen hours."

"But I don't sleep that long…" She frowned. "I remember we were in the alley before everything went dark. What happened?"

Aethan skimmed her face with the back of his hand, the need to touch her almost as vital as breathing. Seeing her fall limp into his arms had terrified him. "I never should have taken you into Demon Alley. Do you remember anything?"

Her brow creased again and, as was her habit, she rubbed the scar on her forehead. "I don't know. I felt pain… I could see the wound."

"Whose wound?"

Her gaze shifted back to him, but Aethan knew she wasn't seeing him. She waved her hand to encompass everything around them. "I saw it in my mind, torn in the middle, like a long rip in a thin piece of fabric. I felt drawn to it...then I heard it sigh, as if the ache eased when I touched it with my mind, but I started to feel ill... I don't remember anything after that, except waking up here."

She focused on him again. "It felt like the other time I was there, only, I guess I was a little more prepared this time when I felt that tugging sensation again."

Fear plagued him. She'd not only *felt* it but described the rift in Demon Alley just as he'd seen it. He knew exactly why the demon bastard wanted her.

"Echo, after you've eaten, there's someone you should meet."

"Who?"

"His name's Michael."

***

A little while later, Aethan headed for the study with Echo, the cat trotting along with them. He was finding it damn hard to keep his hands off her. It had to be that damn loose sweater she'd pulled on. One that didn't hide but instead hinted at the curves he'd seen, touched, and tasted—

Shit. He pushed those thoughts aside, aware of the looks she cast his way.

Then she turned and walked backwards so she could look at him, her hands tucked in the back pockets of her jeans. "What's wrong?"

I'm afraid meeting Michael will change everything. "Nothing."

"So the sound of gnashing teeth filling this silent corridor is not you? Guess it's me then."

"Smart-ass." He hauled her to him and kissed her,

feeling her smile against his mouth.

He didn't say anything. Why ruin whatever was left of life as she knew it?

All he wanted was to find a way to claim his mate and finally have some peace. When Echo had lived her mortal years, then he would end his life with hers. *Gods*, he was thankful for the destined-mate loophole, because he wouldn't be able to go on without her.

You have to make love to her for that to happen.

Damn the Fates! Being unable to claim her was like acid corroding his gut as his hunger, his need for her, grew. His greatest desire was his biggest fear.

"Is this Michael like you?" she asked, sweeping aside the wispy hair falling into her eyes.

Aethan snorted and pushed opened the study door, the cat streaking in ahead of them.

***

A tall male stood before a desk, talking to Týr. As the door shut behind Aethan, they both turned.

Týr greeted her with a wink. "Hey, gorgeous." Shock flared across his face as he looked at her, then it gave way to a flirty smile once more. "Like them way better. Sexy." He smirked at Aethan and sauntered out of the study.

Echo didn't respond, her gaze riveted on the man near the desk. An inch or so taller than Aethan, the sheer size of him dumbfounded her. Good-looking, sure, but Jesus, if he wasn't the most intimidating man ever. Black hair fell in thick, careless layers to his shoulders. His face, tanned to a golden hue, was sculptured in granite.

But something about him pulled at her, demanding

that she respond. Her toes curled in her leather boots, digging for purchase on the carpeted floor. Why was he affecting her like this? Aethan was the only man she wanted in that way. She concentrated on that thought as awareness flickered to life, and then she realized what it was.

The man's sexual aura was a hypnotic lure. For the first time, she wondered if all men felt this way when she wasn't on her pheromones suppressant.

However, it was his eyes that caught and held her. Vividly blue, they were unnerving to look at, like a mirror that had been shattered and haphazardly put together again, the pieces never quite fitting, allowing an eerie silver light to escape.

"Echo, this is Michael."

Her greeting died in her throat as Michael strode over. She eyed him warily. With a finger, he tipped her face to his. She felt helpless. The sheer power of him overwhelmed her as he stared at her.

"Zarias. The bastard made sure I would know," Michael said softly.

Echo frowned. *Zarias?* Before she could ask who he was and what he had to do with her, Michael stepped back and said, "You are Eshana Eklyn Sostratos."

She blinked in surprise. She hadn't heard that name in a long, long time. "Actually, it's Echo Carter now. My friend Tamsyn called me that when I lived with her. Damon changed it when he adopted me."

Aethan slid his arm around her waist and drew her to him. His tension wrapped around her like a spring. She glanced at him. Something was going on, it made her uneasy. More, she didn't like the angry tick in his jaw or the hard stare he pinned Michael.

"Aethan," she said softly.

After a moment, he looked at her. His gaze softened. "Yes, *me'morae*?"

"You okay?"

"Yeah, I'm fine."

Still, her anxiety didn't ease. She turned and found Michael studying her. "Are you from Empyrea, too?"

"No," Aethan muttered. "He's the Archangel."

That would explain the difference in their auras. While Aethan's was a stunning silvery blue, Michael's was a spectacular silvery white—

Oh, dear God! She went motionless. She was in the presence of not just any angel but *the* Archangel!

Her mind tried to accept what her psychic sight revealed when she looked at Michael's aura. Like his eyes, it had the same hairline fractures, as though his soul had shattered. Something really bad must have happened to him. Then she realized what else was missing.

He had no wings.

Did he hide them? Had he given them up to live on this realm? Aethan had said his mother's wings were taken when she fell from Heaven. But whatever Michael's reasons were, he was one being she would never forget.

Her cell phone rang. She ignored it.

Michael leaned against the desk, his arms crossed over his chest. The tattoo of a sword, a lot like Aethan's, peeked out from beneath the short sleeve of his t-shirt.

"Go. Take your call," Aethan told her. "I have a few things to take care of. I'll see you later."

"All right." She pulled her cell from her pocket. "Hold on a sec," she told whoever it was. She had no idea why he worried about her meeting Michael. "See?" she told him. "You fretted over nothing."

His brow shot up at her teasing, and his tight expression eased a notch. He caressed her cheek with a finger. "I don't *fret, me'morae.* Concerned? Maybe. Troubled, yes. But I never fret."

"Right." Smiling, she headed for the door. "Come on, Bob," she called out.

Her pet uncurled himself from the rug near the fireplace and trotted out beside her.

***

Aethan forced his gaze away from the door after Echo departed and wandered over to the French doors to stare out into the gardens. Noon sunlight streamed through thick layers of clouds. A breeze ruffled the trees, sending the fallen leaves scattering about.

She worried over him, when it was all about her. He didn't even ask Michael if she was the one, because he knew.

"Her eyes, it's like looking at Zarias," Michael said, as he joined him by the door. "Her power increases. I feel it."

"I know." The psychic vibrations he'd scanned her for while she'd been asleep were stronger, brighter now.

"It is not a dangerous type of power that can put mortal lives at risk, but that of a *Curantii.* A healer." Power swirled in the Archangel's ruined irises as he spoke. "It is what she's been born to do. She will need all her strength when she has to travel to other realms, going to places some of us have never been to."

Everything in Aethan tensed. "You do realize I

won't let her go alone?" he said, prepared for a fight.

"I did not expect any less. I recant what I said the other day. Besides being her mate, *you* will be perfect as the Healer's guardian on these missions. It's just as well. Cannot have you killing my warriors, if it were another," Michael added drolly, before his expression settled back into a serious one. "She needs to know. If this demon captures her, he will attempt to bind her soul to his and it would be disastrous. We cannot have her going after demoniis, knowing how important she is. I think she'd take it better from you. I will speak with the others."

Michael headed for the door, only to turn back. "Oh, and that's not pheromones she suffers from." He regarded Aethan with a steady look. "She's like us. She has the same angelic allure." For the first time ever, Aethan saw the Archangel smile. "You need to teach her how to shield."

For fuck's sake! He glared at Michael's retreating back. *Angelic allure?* That shit was worse than pheromones, and it would only get stronger. He swore again when he thought of the males going after his mate. Gritting his teeth, he headed for the gym. He found Blaéz already there, in the process of pulling on his sweats.

"Everything go all right last night?" Aethan asked him as he changed.

"We had our moments. Same old crap. Broadswords or katanas?"

"Katana."

"There's something else," Blaéz continued, removing the swords from the reserves. "When I went to pick up the Range Rover, I did a recon in Demon Alley and found the oddest thing. The rift there, it's decreased. Seems to be mending at a faster pace, too."

Aethan pulled back his hair and tied it with a leather strip. "It's Echo. She's Zarias's descendant. Michael just confirmed it."

***

Echo ambled along beside Aethan through one of the castle's lush gardens she had yet to explore, drinking it all in. She'd only seen the manicured grounds from the bedroom window. The cold breeze stung her cheeks. She pulled her beanie down over her ears and stuffed her hands into her coat pockets.

They passed a freshwater pond. Streams of silver flashing near the surface caught her eye. Then the tiny fish darted away.

"Are you going to tell me what this is all about?" she asked, glancing at him.

A smile tugged at his mouth, but his gray eyes were grave. "So impatient."

She wrinkled her nose and turned away to take in the glorious view. "This entire place is so amazing, but that," she said, pointing to a wood and glass enclosed gazebo situated on a small, man-made island in the middle of the lake, "has to be the prettiest thing I've ever seen."

Wisteria, weeping willow, and other trees she didn't recognize grew in abundance around the lake, their branches dipping into the shimmering water. Aethan led her across the wooden bridge to the island. The place was barren of flowers, the grounds prepared for winter.

"So, what normally grows here?" she asked, looking around. "It must truly be beautiful in the spring."

"Wildflowers."

Echo glanced back at him but couldn't read his face. Shadows clouded his eyes. She looked back at the gazebo and, on the wall, spotted a small, engraved gold plaque. She stepped closer and traced a finger over the old script, unable to decipher the language. But one word stood out.

Ariana.

His sister. He'd dedicated this place to her memory.

Tears clogged her throat. "It's beautiful, Aethan."

"It's just a building. Come," he said, his tone abrupt.

Hedori hadn't told her how Ariana had died. But it must have been bad, if Aethan was banished. Echo hoped he'd talk about what happened, about the past that put such bleakness in his soul. All she wanted was to ease his pain.

He pushed open the door to the gazebo and waited for her to enter. The warmth of the interior startled her, the décor even more so. A semi-circular, wicker lounge set lined the wooden walls, the cushions a harmonious blend of blues and greens. It was peaceful, a place to escape to.

Aethan shrugged off his coat and tossed it on the armchair, and helped her out of hers.

She pulled off her beanie and combed her fingers through her hair. "This place is so..." She searched for a word.

"Isolated?"

She laughed. "No. Beautiful." Dropping her hat on her coat, she crossed to a window to stare outside. Tall, dark trees surrounded the place. Maples added a splash of color with their variegated leaves, most of which littered the ground. Squirrels darted about, stirring the colorful carpet. "And peaceful. Usually when I need to unwind, I go to the roof of my building. Just me and the stars—" She stopped, realizing she sounded melancholy.

He joined her near the window. "It's yours."

"Aethan—"

"Echo, everything I have is yours," he said, tone implacable. "Protesting serves no purpose. Come and sit down."

Sighing, she glanced around. On the square, glass-top wicker table stood a black thermos coffee pot and silver-covered dishes.

"A *tête-à-tête*?" she teased.

The predatory look she knew so well was back in his eyes. "I guess talking can wait a bit."

Her teasing died a quick death. Remembering the wicked things his mouth could do had her sitting down and clamping her thighs together. It made her hot and left her wanting.

His expression tightened when she didn't respond.

What was she supposed to do? He'd give her the orgasm of her life, she knew, but he'd still be unfulfilled, in pain. She pushed those thoughts aside.

He raked his fingers through his unbound hair, giving it some semblance of order, exposing the silver hoops in his ears. His crewneck sweater revealed every ripple of muscle with his movements. He made one heck of a sight for a woman who hungered for him.

She fought down her desires. It was damn difficult to do with him just a foot away. So she concentrated on why he'd brought her here. "Feels like I'm back in school, and in trouble. Okay, what did I do?"

Gray eyes held hers. He didn't answer, just pushed his hands in his jeans pockets, which was so unlike him.

"Aethan? You're scaring me."

"You recall what I told you about the demons looking for a psychic female relating to a prophecy?"

She nodded, slipping her hands under her bottom to keep them warm. "I remember. She'll be able to heal rifts."

"Yes. She is *the* Healer, a descendant of an angel annihilated eons ago. A certain demon believes binding this female to him will allow him the freedom to enter all the realms. Since no one can reap psychic powers, he will use her abilities to fulfill his goals."

"What are you going to do?" she asked. Darn, but her hands were still so cold. Getting off the couch, she headed for the heater.

"What we have to do is keep her safe and away from demon clutches, but she makes that difficult to do."

"You found her?" Her gaze rushed to his. She smiled. "But that's wonderful—wait, you said bind her, how?"

"There's only one way to do that in the supernatural world. Through the most intimate act possible."

She frowned, then heat flooded her face when she realized he was talking about sex. "Oh. Right. Then where is she?"

Aethan didn't say a word, and when he just stared at her, uneasiness prickled her skin.

Why was he looking at her like that? As if he didn't want to say this—as if—

Her eyes widened as understanding dawned. *No*—

no!

"Yes, Echo, you are the Healer."

"No—no way!" Shaking her head, she shot to her feet, flung open the door, and sprinted outside, feeling as if she couldn't breathe.

The urge to run, to escape from a destiny she didn't want, took hold. Instead, she stopped near the bridge and wrapped her arms around her body, shivering as icy air pierced her skin. She stared blankly at the trees in the distance, the words reverberating inside her head like a death toll. *You are the Healer.*

Warmth surrounded her as her coat was draped around her shoulders. Aethan's hands tightened on her shoulders.

"I don't want this," she whispered. "You guys made a mistake, that's all."

"There is no mistake, Echo."

Of course there wouldn't be. These powerful immortals would not make such a foolish error. She wanted to rant at him, at the unfairness of it all. The only thing she longed for was a normal life.

Normal? For *her*? A dark laugh trembled on her lips. That was never on the cards. Not since the day she was born, it seemed.

She slid her hands into her jeans pockets, but even the stones didn't work their magic on her this time. After a long moment of silence and his reassuring presence giving her the comfort she needed, she took a deep breath and met his concerned gray eyes. "How long have you known?"

"About the prophecy? A while. About you being the one? The moment I saw your eyes."

Georgia Lyn Hunter

Chapter 24

Aethan steered her back into the warmth of the gazebo and waited for the explosion. He understood his mate all too well. She paced to the window, her movements stiff, her hands bunched in her jeans pockets.

"I want you to say this is all a mistake, but…"

He saw the fragile line of her throat move as she swallowed. And wished to hell that was true.

"All right." She turned to him, her face still far too pale for his liking. "Hit me."

"What?"

A tremulous smile touched her lips. "I mean tell me everything. I have to know what this is all about, right?"

Right. His heart settled. "Remember the name Michael said when he saw you?"

A crease marred her smooth brow. "Zarias?"

"Yes. He was the leader of the highest level of angels. You are his descendant," Aethan said, deciding to leave the history lesson of the Watchers for a later time. "The prophecy states one will be born of fire and ice and will see into the supernatural."

Her eyes widened, her mouth dropped open in shock. "No."

"Yes, Echo. You have Zarias's eyes. It's how Michael recognized you. Being who he is, he would know, since he knew Zarias at one time."

"Oh, God!" She pressed a hand to her stomach. "Aethan, I don't want this. I don't want to be a descendant of any angel, I don't want this responsibility."

He cupped her face and held her gaze. "It will be all right. You've already started, it seems, and all on your own, too."

She pulled away from his hold and narrowed her eyes. "When did I do this impossible feat?"

"Last night. The alley I took you to? A rift had been there until recently."

"What do you mean 'until recently'?"

"The fissure shrank. Demoniis can't use it as a gateway anymore."

"Why— How?"

"Because of you. You didn't get sick, Echo. Your energies were depleted when the magic in the psychic veils recognized you. It drew from you, from the healing abilities that lie in your blood, those of Zarias. When your powers get stronger, you will be able to leave this realm, go to others that need your help and heal them."

Her eyes clouded with unease. "I can't be responsible for things of such magnitude. I can't. I'm just someone who had a rotten childhood and managed to create some semblance of a life in my adulthood. I'm only twenty-three. Why me?"

"Because fate's a bitch," he said, reaching for her.

She wrapped her arms around his waist as if seeking his strength.

"I understand," he said after a while, when it appeared she wouldn't leave the shelter of his arms. "This will be hard on you. I mean, it's one thing to kill demoniis, but something that needs the magic of your bloodline to heal is scary."

Her pliant body stiffened. She pushed away from him. "Is that what you think I am? Scared?"

He shrugged.

Her eyes fired up in irritation. "I'm not scared. Not of that—well, not anymore. I just don't want to be liable…" Her eyes narrowed. "For so many…"

He waited.

Then she scowled and smacked him in his stomach with her palm. "Owww!" She pulled her hand back and glared at him. "I'm not talking to you for that cheap trick. And for the pain in my hand." She turned away, shaking her fingers.

He'd made the right call, bringing her will and strength into question, for her to accept what she was. Heavens, if he had his way, he'd take her away from this insanity, away from the danger that would now surround her.

He took her sore hand and tenderly massaged it. "Look on the bright side. It'll be a vacation for us when we go on this *Curantii* business."

She looked up at him, eyes hopeful. "*Us*?"

As if he'd ever let her face danger alone. "Of course. I'll always be with you, Echo."

A relieved sigh escaped her. "Only you would take something this mind-shattering and make me feel stupid for overreacting."

"You aren't stupid, *me'morae*. It's normal to fear the unknown. But you were never destined for the ordinary." He brushed his lips against her knuckles. "Tell me, now that you've done some healing of the rifts, how does that make you feel?"

She thought for a moment, a wry smile lifting the corners of her mouth. "It does feel good to help something so fragile yet so strong as to keep an entire realm of people safe."

His mate humbled him with her courage.

***

Aethan got back from patrol in the early hours of the morning. He found Michael waiting for him in the foyer, sitting on the stairs and studying the stained-glass windows, a Coke in his hand.

"We do have chairs in this place," Aethan drawled.

But the expression on Michael's face didn't bode well at whatever was about to be dumped on him.

"We need to talk."

"You could have done that at the meeting, before I left on patrol."

"Not about this." Michael set the can between his feet. "It's about Eshana. She cannot come to any harm."

"Yeah, I got all that." Aethan headed for the stairs.

"That's not all." Michael rose to his feet, forcing Aethan to stop. "The mortal realm is too dangerous for her as she is. Demons will always try for her, hoping to tie her soul to theirs, you know this." His shattered blues were hard as granite.

And there it was, the unspoken message. *Mate*

with her to keep her safe, or she will *be taken to the Celestial Realm.*

Fury buzzed through his veins. If Michael thought for one fucking second he'd let Echo go, he was in for a rude awakening. "I will decimate any who attempt to take her from me."

Pivoting, Aethan headed for the gym instead, barely able to leash his anger.

When he finally hauled his tired body upstairs a while later, Echo was still asleep, curled up on the far end of the bed. He crouched at her side and brushed the hair off her face. But Michael's words gnawed a hole in his head.

No. No fucking way would he let anything—*anyone* separate them.

A tail flicked over her face, breaking his dark thoughts. Bob lay coiled around her head like a furry scarf.

"C'mon, let's get you to your own bed." He scooped up her pet and set the feline in a basket near the fireplace. With a low rumble, Bob shot Aethan an annoyed stare before going back to sleep.

After a quick shower, Aethan pulled on a pair of sweats. He usually didn't bother with clothes for sleeping but, gods, he had no choice, not when that part of him he had no control over made lying naked next to Echo impossible.

Sliding in beside her, he reached over and drew her to him.

"Aethan?" she murmured drowsily.

"Yeah, it's me."

A soft sigh escaped her as she settled into his arms.

His first night with her and she was sleeping. He

blew out a rough breath. Better this way, for now. If she were awake, he knew himself well enough to know he'd touch her...and yeah, then he'd have to leave if things got out of control.

He pressed his lips to her hair. And his damn cock hardened. Breathing in her evocative scent wasn't helping matters. His sweats felt like a boa tightening around his groin. Absently, he caressed the arm she'd slung over his waist and tried to let his body relax enough so sleep could pull him under...

***

The clashing of swords reverberated off the white cliffs surrounding the valley. Flashes of white light brightened the arena.

Anger tore through Aethan that his father would order him into a betrothal he didn't want. He wouldn't do it—he refused.

"Is that all you have?" Reynner grinned, brushing back his pale hair. "You fight like a female."

Snarling, Aethan attacked, perspiration dripping from his face. His damn friend had no idea of the horror he faced. Laughing, Reynner leaped back, blocking the strike with his sword. Aethan spun around, wanting to hack his friend to pieces. His power consumed him, needing an outlet, it fired through his arm and lit up his sword.

No—no! Too much power.

"A'than!" A childish voice swept through the arena. "Here, for you."

He wheeled round, his sword flying from his sweat-drenched hand. His blade, blazing with his deadly power, went winging through the air as Ariana

Georgia Lyn Hunter

came careening toward him, a bright smile on her cherubic face, the wilted stems of a few wildflowers she'd offered him earlier dangling from her fist.

His heart shuddered in terror. 'Ariana, no! No! Get back!' They were frantic words she couldn't understand. He tried desperately to shield her.

Too late.

The sword struck her in the chest, the power of it flinging her several feet away before she lay still on the ground...blood seeping from her chest.

So much blood—

A cry of anguish escaping from the depths of his soul, Aethan jack-knifed awake. His throat tight with unshed tears.

"It's okay. It's okay," a soft voice soothed. A warm hand rubbed his back, sliding over his bare shoulders in a comforting caress. Only one person gave him that.

Like a blind man, he reached for her and buried his face in the warmth of her neck. He breathed in her sweet scent. Gods, how had he survived the last few millennia without her?

After a long stretch of silence passed, his heartbeat gradually eased into its normal rhythm. He shifted and lay back on his pillow, pulling her into the crook of his shoulder.

"Aethan?" She rested her chin on his chest, her gaze on his. "Tell me about her. About Ariana."

She knew his blackest sin.

Instinct made him draw back, to shut her out. It wasn't something he ever spoke about. He pinched the bridge of his nose. "You would have me retell this horror?" He dropped his hand, his pained gaze on her. "I guess I deserve your disgust, too. Why not? After all, an entire realm couldn't stand to look at a killer."

"Stop it, Aethan. Just tell me what happened." There was no censure in her eyes. "If you don't want to, then that's all right, too."

His mouth tightened. It took him a while before he could speak again. "Ariana was my sister," he said, staring at the ceiling. "She died a long time ago." His voice turned stark with grief. "I…I killed her."

"Aethan, no—"

"Yes!" He shoved off the bed and stalked to the fireplace as memories, vivid and bloody, surged back. Ones he had no way of shutting out. Gods, he slammed his palm against the stone hearth, pain slicing through him.

***

Echo slid off the bed and hurried over to Aethan, shock still reverberating through her at his disclosure. But she refused to believe that. The man she was coming to understand, to love, would never deliberately do something so horrifying.

"Aethan, no matter what you *can* do, you would never intentionally hurt anyone."

A rough laugh left him. His gaze fixed on the crackling embers of a dying fire. "But I did. And Empyrea banished me. Apparently, execution's too good for the likes of me. I have to live in a fragile realm where I have to let go of all emotions to keep those around me safe. No Grounding stones or Rean trees in this place to stabilize my godsdamn powers." He ran a shaky hand through his unbound hair.

"What happened?" she asked softly.

"The council wanted the old ways back…" He told

her the same things Hedori had. Though her heart ached for him, she listened, waited for him to get it all out. "My father made the betrothal an order. I refused. We fought, and bitter words were said.

"Furious, I left, but Ariana waylaid me in the courtyard, clutching a few wildflowers in her fist. She wanted to play." A humorless laugh left him. "But I...I was curt, told her I didn't have the time, and handed her back to her nursemaid.

"I let my emotions control me and took on my friend in a sword fight. But Ariana had followed me into the fighting arena—" He scrubbed a hand over his eyes as if to wipe away the images. "She was still carrying those damn flowers she'd picked. She came to give them to me because I was upset."

His deep-seated pain made her chest constrict. Echo reached out, wanting to comfort, but he shook his head. Refusing to let him push her away, she grasped his arm. "Aethan, it was an accident. You've lived with this for three thousand years, and it's destroying you—"

"It was my sword," he cut her off. "My mistake. I should have stayed with her, then she wouldn't have followed me to the arena. She wanted a few minutes of my time, and I didn't give her that—too wrapped up in myself. She was my sister, and I killed her. *I* killed her." He sank to the carpet in his anguish. "They wouldn't let me near her..."

At the immensity of his grief, her own throat tightened. She dropped to her knees beside him and wrapped her arms around his shoulders, so he'd know he wasn't alone anymore.

"Aethan?" She held his face in her palms and waited until he raised those anguished eyes to hers.

"Ariana loved you. She would never hold this against you. *I* don't."

After a long moment, his arms came around her, and he held on tight. Echo pressed her lips to his hair, tears misting her eyes.

So much pain in her warrior. He'd suffered for so many millennia, bearing the deepest **wounds** and the scars of a never-ending war while fighting supernatural evil to keep this realm safe for humans. But peace was never his.

***

The soothing movement of her hand brought Aethan back from his deepest, darkest despair. He didn't deserve absolution. Hell, he didn't deserve her. But her love and empathy enclosed him like a soft blanket, cloaking him with warmth. Choking down his emotions, he tightened his hold and buried his face in her neck.

Gaia was right. Echo was his salvation. For the first time in three thousand years, the heaviness, the ache in his heart eased. Then something wet hit his cheek. He looked up and saw the tears sliding down her face. Tears that fell for him.

His chest constricted. "Don't, *me'morae*." He brushed his thumb across her damp cheek. "Don't cry for me."

She lowered her head and pressed her lips to his, offering comfort. He needed her desperately. She was his redemption, his Achilles' heel. His life.

Pressing his lips to her in a soft kiss, Aethan rose, swept her into his arms, and walked over to the couch in the sitting area and sat down. Needing to just hold her and ease away the pain from his past. After a long moment, she pulled back from him and stroked his jaw. Her beautiful eyes searched his face. "You okay?"

In response, he brushed away the hair dipping her eyes then slid his mouth over hers. She shifted and straddled him. Her center hit his crotch. His cock jerked in reaction, tenting the soft fabric of his sweats.

Her gaze filled with needs as stark as his own. She ran her palms down his chest, then lower. Aethan went motionless as she pushed her hands between them to stroke his sex over his sweats. Then he nearly lost his mind when she slid her hand inside to grasp his painfully rigid cock.

Biting back a groan, he growled and nipped her earlobe. "You don't want to do—"

"Why not? I like touching you." She tightened her hold, stroking his length.

Urias, she was going to kill him. Shifting, Aethan laid her flat on the couch, forcing her hand away from his sex.

Slowly, torturously slow, he removed her top, despite dying for a look at her. But he refused to rush. A light flush covered her face as he drew her flannel bottoms down her legs and tossed them aside, revealing tiny pink panties.

The soft sconces light highlighted her slender body, strong with feminine muscles. He glided his hands up her smooth, honey-hued skin in a languid caress. Squeezing her breasts, he lowered his head and bit the under curve—she gasped.

He soothed the tender flesh with a slow lick.

She tugged him to her nipple.

A smile pulled at his mouth, he knew exactly what she wanted and avoided the tempting taut bud begging for his attention. Ignoring her glower, he ran his tongue over the curves of her breast instead, then kissed his way up her neck to her jaw, evading the mouth she turned to him.

Those slumberous, cat-like eyes narrowed. She trailed her fingers down his back, sliding into his sweats. A light dance of her fingers over his ass and desire, hot and smoky, made his erection go from painfully hard to near exploding.

"Kiss me." The demand left him in a hoarse rasp.

She smiled now. Her fingers stroking his backside moved between their bodies to squeeze his cock. Growling, he grabbed her hands, pinned them over her head, and covered her mouth in a deep, carnal kiss.

The white heat of his powers raced in him, along with the iridescent light of the mating bond, urging him to claim her.

Her leg slid restlessly over his hips. He let go of her mouth and turned his attention to that tempting nipple, sucking and teasing the taut bud.

She whimpered, "Aethan, please..."

He quickly got rid of her underwear, then moved lower and parted her thighs. Focused only on her pleasure, he ran his tongue up her center with a languorous stroke. Once, twice, then he clamped his lips around her clit and sucked hard. She nearly came off the bed, her cries of pleasure filling him as her orgasm hauled her over.

***

Her body trembled. His power skimmed over her like tiny pinpricks, hiking her arousal. Her fist tangled in his hair, Echo pulled him up to her, and then she saw his eyes. Her heart kicked up in panic. The gray irises were mere specks of color as a burning white took over.

They changed so fast?

Fear surged through her. *No, no, no!*

She didn't care if she blistered or burned, she needed him. Reaching up, she clamped her mouth on his and deepened the kiss. She tasted herself as he sucked her tongue. More sparks tingled through her, amping up her arousal again. She pulled at his sweats.

He clasped her hand, stopping her, his eyes squeezed tight. "I can't, Echo."

His words were like a sword in her heart.

"No. Don't say that. I can't stand this, being unable to touch you, to love you."

He sat up and dropped his head in his hands. His hair fell forward like a dark blue veil, hiding him from her.

***

Sparks shot through him and battered against his shields. His cock strained painfully. *Urias*, he was desperate for her but he couldn't take a chance.

"Why won't you believe me when I say your powers don't hurt me?" He felt her crawled up behind him and laid her cheek on his back. At her touch, a burst of light flooded his vision.

He jerked away so fast he fell off the couch and landed on the floor. Shit, he was glowing like a light bulb!

"Aethan!" She dropped to the floor a few feet from him. "Please, let me near you. Your powers don't hurt me. It just tingles. See?" She crawled closer, the light enclosing her fingertips.

"No!" he roared, fear grabbing him by the throat. "Get out *now*!"

She froze. The pain in her eyes ripping him apart.

A tormented groan escaped him. "This is one light you can never walk into. It's fucking treacherous. It will eat you alive. You die, I will wreak havoc on the planet unlike anything seen before. Now go. *Please*."

A heart-wrenching sob escaped her before she snatched up her discarded clothes, wheeled around, and left the room.

Aethan squeezed his eyes tight, feeling as if he couldn't breathe as the door slammed shut behind her like a death toll.

Chapter 25

After work, Echo crossed over to East First Street and headed for the Peacock Lounge.

Her head pounded despite the pain meds she'd taken earlier. She wanted to be among people, get lost in the crowd, and forget her misery for a while—forget the disaster her life was shaping out to be. Thank God Kira had the afternoon shift. Being with her friend would give her some much-needed time to get her emotions under control.

She hefted her gym bag over her shoulder, zipped up her windbreaker, and shoved her hands into her pockets, encountering the soothing warmth of her stones.

It was just past noon, so she'd be safe from any demonii attack. Those fiends didn't come out during the day, since it was lethal for them—the sun incinerated their sensitive corneas and caused instant death.

Pushing open the door to the lounge, the smell of

fried food and alcohol welcomed her.

At this time of the day, the bar was relaxed. There were a few empty tables but that would all change and the frenzy would set in, in another hour.

Waving at Kira, Echo took a seat in her friend's section. Moments later, Kira danced over, her hazel eyes sparkling. She set a Pepsi down.

"On the house," she said. Then her eyes narrowed. "Actually, by the looks of you, definitely something stronger." She grabbed the Pepsi before Echo could open her mouth and bopped off again. On her way to the bar, Kira laughed and flirted with some regulars.

Why couldn't she be more like Kira? Carefree, taking life as it came? And maybe all this wouldn't hurt so much.

Exhaling roughly, she traced the grooves of the wooden table with a finger then stopped to look at her hands. They appeared to be normal, the tanned skin smooth, her fingernails cut short. No, she wasn't hurt. When she'd touched Aethan, a light current had streamed through her, more arousing than painful. It was only when *he* grew aroused that the tingles became sharper and sent her libido skyrocketing.

Her fingers balled at the sudden, sharp ache in her chest. What was the use of being the descendent of an angel when she couldn't even be with Aethan? It hurt far worst to know he would never belong to her, never be part of her in that most intimate way.

"Here you go." Kira set a quarter glass of clear liquid and ice before her. Echo glanced up from the scarred table, as Kira popped open a bottle of tonic and poured it into the glass, a slice of lime floating happily in the fizz. She pushed it toward Echo. "A good antidote for what troubles you. Drink up. Ten more

Georgia Lyn Hunter

minutes, then we can leave, and you're talking." Her warning delivered, Kira bounced back to work.

Talk? She didn't want to talk. Talking would only bring back the pain she was desperately trying to bury. And which disaster of her life would she tell her friend about? How Aethan wouldn't touch her, because he feared he'd hurt her? Or that she was "the Healer", the long-awaited descendant of an angel? Hell, she seriously doubted Kira would believe any of it.

Echo glanced up to find Neal watching her from across the bar, his brows lowered in a scowl. Argh, definitely not the person she cared to look at right now, let alone think about. She had too much going on to worry about his spiteful little digs. She turned away and picked up her drink, taking a tentative sip.

"Echo?" Jon slid into the chair opposite her.

She smiled, glad to see a friendly face. "You just got here?"

He nodded. "I have a few minutes before I clock in, so—" His gaze widened.

She'd forgotten she was no longer wearing her contacts. "That bad, huh?"

Color rushed to his face. "No–no, I like them. I'm guessing they're real, right?"

She nodded.

"I'm glad you got rid of the contacts," he said. "So, hey, it's Kira's birthday soon and I managed to get a table at Anarchy for Saturday. I told her about it, but she's worried you won't agree."

Echo groaned and dropped her head on the table. Kira had that right. Club Anarchy was the last place she wanted Kira to go. The only reason *she*'d ever gone there was to hunt demoniis.

She lifted her head and glared at him. "She's right.

I don't like that place. What about the one in Soho? I hear Blitz is good." And safe.

"For my gramps." Jon snorted, but his blue eyes caressed her face. "So, will you come?"

Echo lowered her gaze to her glass, wishing Jon wouldn't look at her in that way. "Who's going?"

"A few of us from here."

"Neal, too?"

"No." A short pause followed before he asked the question that was a long while in coming. "What happened between you two?"

She sighed and traced her fingertip over the rim of her glass. "One date. He doesn't like the word 'no.'"

"Asshole—" Jon grimaced, brushing at his blond hair. "Sorry."

"Don't be. I slapped him."

"*Ah*. That explains the venomous attitude toward you."

"He doesn't bother me." She shrugged and glanced around the bar. The place was starting to fill up fast with the happy hour rush. "About Kira's birthday, count me in." Someone had to keep an eye out for them. Might as well be her. Then she winced. There'd be hell to pay when Aethan found out.

"So, what time are we meeting?" she asked.

When he didn't answer, she turned to Jon and found him staring at her with a glazed look. "Jon? Hey, what's wrong?"

"He's under my control. They all are."

The hair on her arms rose. She became aware of the abrupt silence and the acrid odor of sulfur stinging her nostrils. Her head snapped to the right.

And there, among the still figures of the bar's customers and staff, stood Lazaar. The demon leaned

Georgia Lyn Hunter

against the bar, dressed in black slacks again and a button-down shirt. His dark dreads hung about his face.

She knew about demoniis' proclivity for bars and clubs, but they never came out during the day. And yet here he was. No demonii horde with him this time. She tried to look past his aura to see his demon self and failed. Realizing just how powerful he must be to have such complete control, Echo stiffened her spine, her heart thudding in her ears.

"Let's go." He beckoned her with his head.

Please let Aethan be right and about free will preventing him from taking her to Hell. But the motionless bodies around her didn't bode well for that theory. She held onto her composure. "I'm not going anywhere with you."

In response, Lazaar strolled to her then shoved a nearby man, who sat frozen with a glass to his mouth, off his seat. The man toppled to the floor, liquor spilling down his shirt. Lazaar dragged the chair close to her and sat. The stench of sulfur was so strong, she nearly gagged. But she remembered what had happened the last time she did and swallowed hard.

She didn't dare look for Kira and risk him noticing her friend.

"Here's the thing..." He crooked his finger, and a girl sitting at another table walked to him like a puppet on strings. Sharp black claws extended from Lazaar's fingertips. He smirked and traced a talon down the girl's arm.

"Refuse me again and I'll kill her."

Echo's throat constricted in fear, her mind trying desperately to find a way out of this nightmare.

Flames leaped from his eyes at her silence. His brow cocked.

"Very well." He pointed to the floor. The girl knelt. A blur of movement and blood seeped from the gash in her neck that stopped just short of her carotid. Several more slashes appeared on her chest, saturating her white sweater red. "Shall I release her from my command and let her feel the full effect of my fun?"

Echo glared at the bastard who was looking around the bar as if he was enjoying a relaxing afternoon and wanted nothing more than a frothy beer. He flipped the dreads back from his face with an impatient hand.

"Hmm, let's get another to join in, shall we?" Lazaar glanced around, his flaming gaze settling on Jon. "He'll do."

No! Terror rushed through her as he seized hold of Jon's hand across the table and stroked his pinkie. "Each time I call and you don't respond, I will do something to them."

The sound of a bone snapping filled the quiet place.

"Stop it!" She jumped to her feet. Jon sat there, not a flicker showing on his face to pain that must be excruciating.

"I'm glad you see this my way," Lazaar said, standing.

Breathing hard, she met those malevolent eyes. The bastard thought he'd won, did he? Echo reached slowly to the back waist of her jeans and palmed the obsidian dagger. She flew at him, rage fueling her. He evaded her attack, swung around, and grabbed her wrist, twisting it behind her back. She inhaled sharply, gritting her teeth against the pain and puke-inducing reek of sulfur and…coppery *vanilla*?

Her heart pounded with a fresh surge of adrenalin.

Georgia Lyn Hunter

This was the son of a bitch who'd killed Tamsyn. She didn't care how he changed his appearance; his stench didn't lie. Echo elbowed him in the ribs, then head-butted him and, hearing a satisfying grunt, she hoped she broke his fucking nose. His grip loosened a fraction. She wheeled around and drove her dagger into his chest.

And missed. *Crap!*

He snarled and flashed several feet away, sending furniture scattering about. She jumped over the fallen chair, anger blazing through her, and attacked. His eyes changed, the brown became the eerie red of demoniis. He released the patrons from his hold, and the bar came alive again, buzzing with noise and confusion.

Screams started. People got in her way as she hunted for him.

"Echo!" Like a squall, Aethan appeared at her side in a flash. He grabbed her arms. "Are you hurt?" The words were a hiss of power.

"I'm fine, I'm fine—Lazaar, he's here!" She pushed away, searching frantically for the fiend.

"No, Echo. He's gone—"

A sudden hysterical scream of pain broke from the girl kneeling on the floor.

"Don't move." Aethan left her and headed for the wounded girl as the ruckus in the bar grew. He crouched in front of her and laid his hand over the lacerations on her chest. Familiar healing light seeped out of his palm and the girl stared at him in a daze. The noise level dropped as the other Guardians suddenly appeared in the bar.

Týr took over from Aethan. The girl transferred her dazed attention to him. At least his beauty would keep her mind off her pain. Echo turned, searching the crowd for Jon. When she found him, the agony in his blue eyes had her hurrying to his side. He held his hand against his chest, his pinkie sticking out at an odd angle.

"Oh, Jon, I'm so sorry."

"I broke my finger?" he asked in confusion, his voice thick with pain. Guilt and anger raged like a whirlpool, making it hard to answer. Echo did the only thing she could. She put her arms around him, offering comfort, and looked around for someone to heal him.

"Echo?"

At the curt tone, she turned her head and met Aethan's stony gaze. "Heal him," she begged. "Please. He doesn't deserve this."

"Then you should let him go."

She stepped back from her friend and reached for the stones in her pocket, her fingers tightening around them. But nothing could calm her.

Blaéz came over and nodded to Aethan. "I'll see to him."

She was responsible for all this. By wanting to get away from her own pain, she'd hurt others.

Aethan drew her aside.

"It's my fault," she whispered. "I was waiting for Kira, so we could leave. I didn't expect any demoniis to be out here at this time of the day—" She broke off when she saw all the bar's patrons were back in a trance-like state. Jon's expression had glazed over again. "What? What is it now?"

"Dagan. He'll hold them while Blaéz and Týr do a mind sweep. We can't let them retain their memories of this."

Knowing Jon and the girl wouldn't have any memory of the horrible experience gave Echo a small measure of relief. Her eyes swept over the still figures of the customers.

"Kira! Where is she?" In panic, Echo broke away from Aethan and stumbled into Dagan. The dark warrior didn't even look at her. He merely stepped back. With a wave of his hand, he cleared the blood off the girl's sweater, but the tears remained.

Echo mumbled an apology and rushed past him into the passage leading to the staff bathrooms. Shoving open the door, she hurried inside and looked into each stall.

Nothing.

She dashed back into the corridor. Aethan grabbed her arm, stopping her. "Echo, slow down. She's all right."

Meeting his steady gray eyes, she closed hers in gratitude. He'd know. She didn't resist when he pulled her into his arms. The strength of his embrace steadied her. His earthy scent calmed her. But his hand caressing her back had desire flaring again.

Hating her treacherous body for reacting so easily to him, she stepped back. "Where is she?"

A muscle ticked in his jaw at her retreat. "In a room farther along this corridor."

Echo hurried to the locker room and found Kira humming an off-beat tune while she swapped her black work shoes for her fur-lined Uggs.

A smile lit her face. "Hey, I'm almost done here, and we can leave—" Kira glanced over Echo's shoulder. "Hi, Aethan." Then a wry smile curved her mouth as she looked back at Echo. "Guess this means you're not coming home with me, huh?"

Echo grabbed her in a fierce hug. "I'm sorry. But something's come up. I'll walk out with you."

A short while later, she watched the taillights of Kira's cab disappear down the street. "I did this," she whispered. Standing on the busy roadside, the sheer horror of what had happened crashed over her, adrenalin finally flatlining. "Go ahead tell me what a fool I am for insisting on having something that was never mine."

"You're not a fool for wanting normalcy or for caring, Echo. Just human."

"I want to kill him so bad, make him hurt for what he did in there."

"I know, *me'morae*, but he's an old one. They're much harder to kill. It will take time, but we will get him, make no mistake." Aethan dropped his hand to her lower back. "Come, let's get out of here."

"Aethan, wait." She stepped in front of him and frowned as she looked him over. His shirt and jeans had dirt smears. His hair, freed of its tie, hung limp over his shoulders. The scent of earth clung to him, as if he'd rolled in soil. "Where were you?"

A nerve kicked up in his jaw. "Detained."

Her chest tightened when she realized the truth. He went to Ground because of what happened between them that morning.

She pushed aside her troubled thoughts, took a deep breath, and continued. "This demon, he looks like the one from the subway, but he's not the same. This one killed Tamsyn."

"You sure?"

"It may have happened five years ago, but I could never forget his stench. He smells like blood and ice-cream. The one from the subway smelled like honeysuckle, and his eyes weren't those of a demonii."

"Echo, you can't go after him."

She already knew that, had it drilled into her in the worst possible way as she watched innocent people get hurt because of her. And she hated that *she* could never avenge her friend. She held Aethan's gaze. "But you will, right? For Tamsyn?"

"Yes." No hesitation.

She didn't have to be the one to kill Lazaar. As long as the bastard died.

***

Echo made her way down to the kitchen the following afternoon.

She was now without a job—or she soon would be. Tomorrow, she'd hand in her notice at the gym. She couldn't put anyone else at risk and give that fiend, Lazaar, another way to use the people she cared about against her.

She exhaled a rough breath, and when she thought about Aethan, a hollow pit opened in her stomach. He'd stayed out *all* night on patrol. He hadn't even come to bed this morning. Her heart dipped at the reason why.

Echo entered the kitchen, and heard the sound of clattering dishes. Hedori had started on the evening meal. Needing to keep her mind occupied, she wandered over to the island counter that separated the kitchen from the dining room and watched as Hedori set aside lobsters in the prep area.

"Can I help? I'm not good at cooking and stuff, but I can clean, peel, and stir," she said, eyeing the shellfish and hoping he wouldn't ask her to…well, she had no idea what to do with *that*.

Hedori smiled. "No. I enjoy this. It's not

something I would have thought to do had I been in Empyrea. But I find human culinary arts to be quite relaxing." He nodded his head to a small television where *The Food Network* was on.

Okay, that was far beyond her skills, she decided, watching the chef on the screen chop up stuff so fast, she was surprised he didn't dice his fingers along with the vegetables.

"M'lady? I've been known to be a good listener to whatever troubles a soul."

Echo glanced back and met his understanding look. "I'm all right, Hedori."

He nodded, then set out the ingredients for a salad, and began slicing up the carrots as fast as the chef had.

Týr sauntered in, winked at her, and dropped his jacket on a chair. He nabbed a carrot stick from Hedori's stash and popped it in his mouth. Opening the fridge, he took out a can of Red Bull and came over to lean on the opposite side of the island counter, his dark eyes grave. "You okay after yesterday?"

She nodded. "I'm fine. I guess I just forgot a key factor: that there are demoniis who move about during the day when the weather's gloomy."

"Yesterday wasn't dull or overcast, Echo. The bastard flashed into the bar. We found his point of entry. He's desperate to get you. But there's not much a demonii can do if he gets you now," he said, smiling. "You're mated. Your soul's bound to Aethan's, so—"

Her mouth tightened.

Hedori moved over to the prep area to work on the lobsters.

Týr stared at her. Shock, then understanding crossed his face. Echo dropped her gaze to the beautifully diced vegetables, unable to take his pity.

Georgia Lyn Hunter

"Damn, I'm sorry. I didn't mean to—"

"It's okay," she said, in no state to talk about the thing that pained her.

Týr cracked open the Red Bull, bringing her attention back to him. "Can I ask you a question?"

"Shoot," he said, swallowing the liquid caffeine from the can.

"Do you have to Ground, too?" she asked, reorganizing the apples in the bowl on the counter.

"No. We aren't as dangerous as your Empyrean. We're pussycats really, more docile than Bob."

That made her smile. "I'm sure you are… Is that the only way?"

"Well, there's fighting but bed-sport's far better, a damn good way to get off, I'd say—ah, hell." Consternation darkened his eyes. "Echo, look, you're all he wants. He nearly rearranged my face for hitting on you. That's my fault, though. I just wanted to settle a score. Things will work out. Aethan Grounds at the Catskills when the need arises. The mountain does the job just as well. Now, before I put my size fourteen back in my mouth, I'm gonna go."

He grabbed his biker jacket off the chair, his expression pained, as he strode out of the kitchen.

Echo stood frozen beside the counter.

Bed-sport…*sex*. The one thing Aethan wouldn't risk with her just yet. A crushing pain filled her.

This was so damn hard.

Chapter 26

Aethan changed into his work clothes, his mind still on the close call that had occurred yesterday. The demonii's desperation was growing. He'd risked coming out during the day when it could mean his death.

With unsteady hands, Aethan tied back his hair and exhaled a rough breath. Breaking free of his mountainous prison had left him raw. Pain ate at his psyche with his powers roiling close to the surface. But until he killed the bastard, he couldn't take another chance of Echo being unprotected while he Grounded.

Aethan picked up his cell and walked out of the dressing room, only to stop in the bedroom. He'd not shared the bed with her this morning. Right now, he was too dangerous. Instead, he'd spent time in the gym. He'd promised Echo they'd try. But how could he, when he was unable to Ground his cursed powers?

Leaving his quarters, he headed downstairs.

"Aethan, hang on a sec, man," Týr called out.

Aethan glanced at him as he jogged down the

stairs. "What is it?"

"You're not gonna like this. Elytani's gone. She's missing."

"What do you mean she's missing? Didn't Michael take her back?"

Týr rubbed his neck, looking a little uneasy. "She wanted to stay a day, I let her."

Aethan growled. "Dammit, Týr! You know what can happen. Let's go—wait, I'm supposed to take Echo to her apartment." He scrubbed a hand over his face. "Okay, give me a minute, then we'll do this."

Aethan found Echo sitting cross-legged on the kitchen floor, talking to her pet, who seemed more interested in inhaling his food than the hand stroking him. She lifted her head. When she saw him, her gaze slid from his as she rose to her feet. "I was feeding Bob and forgot the time. I won't be long."

"That's okay, no rush. I have something to take care of first."

"Oh...okay," she murmured. Before he could kiss her, she sat back on the floor.

"Is something wrong?"

She cast him a quick look and shook her head. "No. I'll see you later."

Frowning, Aethan left the kitchen, meeting Týr out on the portico.

What the hell was going on? He felt like he'd hit a brick wall when he tried to kiss her. If she thought to push him away just because they couldn't—

His teeth snapped together.

"What did you tell Echo?" Týr asked him.

"That I had to clean up your mess." He ignored the warrior's narrow-eyed stare. "Let's do this fast."

"Fast? *You* know where she is?"

Týr's suspicious tone was starting to irritate the shit out of him.

Finding Elytani wouldn't be difficult, he hoped. He recalled she liked spending her time in the open grasslands and forest back in Empyrea. "Let's try CP first."

He and Týr dematerialized to Central Park.

"She has a proclivity for these kinds of places," Aethan said as they took form again in a shadowy thicket of trees.

"And you remember that?"

Oh, he knew where Týr's thoughts were heading. Aethan nailed the Norse with a cold look. "There was never anything between us. Her brother, Reynner, was one of my best friends. She would constantly get lost, forcing her sire to send out the guards to find her. But we were the ones who always did, in parks or on the moors."

"Just checking," Týr retorted. "You have an amazing female. Don't hurt her."

Aethan said nothing as they searched the park. He was already hurting her by not consummating their relationship. He was just too afraid of losing her.

Scanning the park, he soon located Elytani. Late-afternoon sunlight lit her pale hair like a halo where she sat on the grass near the lake, feeding the ducks. Children ran around her, and she laughed, seeming quite in her element.

"She's been here all this time while I've been searching every freakin' hotel in the city," Týr muttered in annoyance.

She looked up, and a smile brightened her face when she saw Týr. But the moment her gaze fell on Aethan, the glow faded and wariness settled over her.

She pushed to her feet and brushed the grass from her gown.

"You cannot leave the castle unchaperoned. It's far too dangerous," Aethan told her, his tone terse.

She sighed. "It's so beautiful here. I like it, in all its entirety." She tossed more crumbs into the lake, her smile wistful as the ducks dove for the food.

"How did you get food for the ducks?" Týr asked.

"Oh, that man…" She looked toward a bench along the edge of the lake. It was empty. "There was a man there. He gave me some when I asked."

Elytani had the same angelic allure he did, so Aethan wasn't surprised that the man had given her what she wanted.

"I see," Týr murmured. "You've been gone a few days. Where did you stay?"

"At that castle." She pointed a finger across the lake where parts of a building showed. "And the other night, I saw a fight—people fight without powers here, did you know?"

Týr glanced at the ducks, hiding his grin.

Aethan sighed and shook his head. She still was as amusing as he remembered. "Come on, we have to leave," he said, leading the way to a secluded grove of trees so they could dematerialize. He was damn grateful no one had accosted her, because it would have been devastating for the human. She wouldn't intentionally hurt anyone, but accidents could happen, and on a very bad scale.

***

Aethan stood at Echo's bedroom window later that afternoon, his gaze on several youths playing basketball on the eroded court below her apartment building. The yells and curses reached him since he'd opened the window. While he followed the game, his senses were tuned to his mate.

During the drive to the city, she'd remained silent, staring out of the side window. He'd never seen her this quiet.

He turned. Leaning against the sill, he crossed his arms over his chest and watched as she tossed some clothes onto the bed. "You want to tell me what's going on?"

She picked up a sweater and looked at it, her brow furrowing. Either the sweater confused the hell out of her or his question did.

He knew damn well which one it was.

"Why would you ask that? Nothing's going on."

"Something has upset you. I want to know what." Then he narrowed his eyes. "Is it because of yesterday morning?"

"No." She stopped folding the sweater and finally met his gaze, but hers swam with despair.

Fear took hold of him. "Echo, what is it?"

"Týr told me what helps you to fully Ground," she whispered.

All his anger drained out of him, only to come rushing like a backdraft when he realized what she was referring to. He shoved to his feet. "You think I'll betray you because we haven't consummated our relationship?"

"No…"

Her hesitant answer made him curse. "Echo, before I met you, I hadn't been with a female for a while. Grounding in the mountains was far preferable to the emptiness inside me after one of those encounters. Being with you is all that holds me together. It's when you're not here, or keeping me at arm's length, like now, that messes me up."

"I'm sorry. I'm trying to make this easy on us. But I feel as if"—she swallowed—"as if I'm going to lose you."

"That will never happen." He drew her into his arms. "Gods, Echo, talk to me. Don't build walls. It just hurts us both then."

She held him tightly. His heart settled as the barriers between them faded. He sat on the windowsill, pulled her between his thighs, and took her mouth in a tender kiss.

"Echo, are you home?"

Aethan's head jerked up at the intrusive sound of a male in her apartment, and every possessive molecule fired up.

Her face flushed, her mouth swollen from his kisses, she blinked.

"I'll be there in a moment," she called out, her gaze on him. "It's Damon. He's been away on business. He must have just gotten back."

"And he came straight to you?"

She frowned, brushing at her wispy bangs. "Yes. Most times he does. Aethan, I haven't told him about us yet. He's a bit protective, so…please?"

She wanted him to what? Tone down his…aggression? Did she think he'd hurt her guardian?

Her hand stroked his chest. "Aethan?"

He nodded.

Yeah, he was grateful the male had kept her safe, but he hated his guts. Hated him for being all the things *he* should have been. Why the hell hadn't Fate let *him* find her all those years ago?

Truth was, he would have walked right past her. As long as he kept the streets safe, he never interfered or took an interest in the homeless—the street kids. And that, he realized, stung more.

"Echo, I need to talk to you," the male called out again.

"Hang on a sec. I'm coming."

"Wait." Aethan caught her hand when she turned to leave. "Tell him about us. No need for details, but he has to know."

Sighing, she nodded, and left the room.

He heard the murmur of voices and dragged in a rough breath. He'd let her have a minute before he interrupted the reunion. Then he heard the male laugh and say something about being glad she'd gotten rid of her contacts.

Dammit, the human was her guardian—like a father. Aethan hauled in his possessive shit. Unable to claim his mate was screwing with his perception. And jealousy was a damn bitch.

He walked out into the lounge. What happened next became a blur. He saw the human, who looked far too young to be anyone's guardian, touching his mate. Then he got a good look at the male, and his stomach lurched as he realized the enormity of what faced him. This fucker was responsible for Echo's safety? The one who'd stood by and watched a Guardian die?

A'Damiel.

Centuries of animosity broke free. Aethan's dagger was drawn and pressed against the male's throat.

***

"Aethan, no!" Echo cried out. Fear for Damon tearing through her, she shoved at Aethan. She had no idea what had happened. One minute she'd been talking to Damon, and the next Aethan was there, looking ready to skewer him.

Unable to move Aethan, she grabbed the blade and tried to pull it away from Damon's throat. A burning sensation slid across her palm. "Dammit Aethan, let him go!"

"Echo—" Damon put his arm around her waist, pulling her away. "Step back." He didn't seem to care about the blade at his throat.

Aethan lowered his dagger and smashed his fist into her guardian's face instead.

Damon staggered and hit the couch. Eyes narrowing, he wiped at the blood trickling from his mouth. Unease surging, Echo rushed over and slapped a hand on Damon's chest, keeping him back as he straightened.

"Stop it, both of you, and tell me what the hell's going on!"

They both looked at her. Then Damon crossed to the kitchen. Her gaze snapped to Aethan. He didn't respond. He sheathed his dagger and reached for her hand. But Damon was already there, wrapping a dishtowel around her palm. Only then did she realize she was bleeding and Damon's white shirt was stained with her blood.

His expression stony, Aethan headed for the door.

She broke free of Damon's hold and hurried after him. "Wait, wait. Where are you going?"

"I think it's best if I wait in the car. Call me when you're ready to leave."

The look he shot Damon before he left the

apartment made Echo feel as if he'd completed the job of slitting her guardian's throat.

She wheeled around to Damon. "What's going on? Do you know Aethan?"

Damon didn't answer, but his violet eyes narrowed. "What did he mean, 'call him when you're ready to leave'?"

The pain in her palm stung like acid had crawled into it. She curled her fingers around the cloth, trying to ease the ache. "Answer me first."

"Yes, I know him." He crossed his arms. "So explain, Echo, what did he mean?"

Damon knew Aethan? How?

Aethan was an Empyrean, and Damon was just...well, Damon. Questions pounded in her, but when she saw the concern on his face, she caved. No matter her anger, Damon was still her family.

"I would have told you about him, but you were gone and things happened... I'm sorry, I didn't." She inhaled a trembling breath. "I...I love him, Damon."

He stared at her in disbelief. "You barely know him."

"Don't tell me how I feel."

"It's just infatuation—"

"How can *you* say that?" she snapped, riled at his attempt to dismiss her feelings so lightly. "In all the time I've lived with you, I've yet to see you in a relationship."

"This is not about me," Damon shot back. "It's about you and him. And that's asking for trouble. How do you think it will turn out? Their foremost priority is to protect this realm. Where do you fit into all this? I'm surprised he's with a human, when they've always kept their distance before. What's changed?"

His tone, his expression had a stillness that finally pierced through her chaotic emotions. Echo searched his face, finding nothing there to tell her what was wrong. Her stomach dipped with uneasiness as she finally answered his first question, "I'm living with him."

"You *what*?"

She bit her lip at Damon's anger. Why did she think this would be any easy?

Then a heavy sigh left him. "Why, Echo? Why him?"

She opened her mouth to respond, but Damon shook his head and turned away. Hands on his hips, he paced around the room then stopped in front of her again.

"He'll hurt you. He won't stay. He can't."

She didn't think so, not when Aethan had made a point of telling her he'd never let her go. "I'm his destined-mate, Damon. But whatever happens in the future, I'll face it when the time comes."

He squeezed his eyes shut at her revelation and shook his head. A long sigh left him.

"Why did Aethan hit you? Why does he hate you?" she asked, unwrapping the dish towel from her burning palm. Maybe it needed a Band-Aid or something. She examined the cut, not realizing it was so deep. Blood still oozed out of the wound.

The next moment, Damon came over and gently grasped her injured hand. She looked up, meeting unreadable violet eyes. "Because of something that happened in the past."

Before she could continue her questions, he laid a finger on her open wound. A pale blue light streamed out. Warmth surrounded the injury, and before her very eyes, the skin knitted together.

No. Her chest constricted in denial. *He's like Aethan?*

She exhaled harshly, shaking her head. "No…"

"Yes, Echo," he said quietly, his grip tightening when she would have pulled away. "I am immortal. But I'm not as self-sacrificing as the Guardians are. I like my life the way it is. Centuries ago, this world was different back then. The humans call it the Dark Ages. It was dark, all right. Demoniis roamed all over Europe, destroying humans and spawning demonic offspring with the females. I could have helped them…" He frowned, staring at her healed palm. "Many lives were lost, including a Guardian who protected that region. They've never forgiven me."

"You let a warrior die?" She stared at him in shock. "How could you?"

He met her gaze, his expression flat. "I'm not a Guardian. It's not my fight."

She snatched her hand away. This wasn't the man she knew and loved. Aethan put his life on the line every night that he went out. How could Damon be so callous?

But hearing his cool, detached words, she wondered if she'd really known him, except for what he allowed people to see.

"Echo, in some things we don't have free will."

"Free will be damned," she snapped. "There's a thing called compassion."

A sigh left him.

Fisting her healed hand, she stared at him long and hard. "Why didn't you tell me the truth about you?"

He shrugged. "It didn't seem important at the time. You were a child. You had nightmares, and hated anything to do with the supernatural. It surprised me when I found that I didn't want you to hate me, too. So I chose not to."

How could she believe him when he'd kept so much from her? She opened her psychic sight and searched for his aura but, like all the times before, it remained hidden.

"Why can't I see your aura?"

He sighed again, as if he didn't want to do this. Too bad, because she wanted to know who she'd been living with all these years.

"It's there," he said. "Look closely."

She turned disillusioned eyes to him, forced her anger down, and opened her mind once more. It was almost transparent, like Blaéz's. Her breathing hitched. "What are you, Damon?"

"Someone who cared enough to adopt you."

Damn him for that cheap shot. "Was that even real? The adoption?"

"Yes."

"Why? You couldn't be bothered to save a Guardian but you saved me?" she asked him dully.

He shoved his hands into his pockets, a gesture she'd rarely seen him do, as if to contain his emotions.

"Nothing is what it seems, Echo. Some just ask for trouble, but with others, it finds them."

"If I was trouble, then why did you kill that demonii in the basement and take me?"

"You were never that." His steady gaze held hers. "I was in the area. I heard a scream, one I couldn't ignore."

She shook her head. "But I didn't yell. I couldn't. I was paralyzed with fear."

"I felt you on a psychic plane. That's why I

couldn't ignore you. I traced the scream to the basement. Just in time, too. When I saw what that bastard was going to do to you, I killed him." His gaze softened. "You were so traumatized. I looked into your eyes and felt something I'd never felt before."

"What? Pity?"

"No. Concern."

A part of her wanted to hold onto the only family she'd ever known, to forgive him. "I guess I should thank you then." Her words came out harsher than she'd intended.

"You already did." Violet eyes held hers. For a fleeting second she saw something move in them. Tenderness? She couldn't be sure because it disappeared. "You kept me a little human." He traced a finger down her cheek, the usual easy-going smile no longer evident. "You were all that was right in my life. Be happy."

He shimmered and dematerialized right in front of her, shocking her again.

How had she missed the signs? She looked at her healed hands and remembered. After she started living with Damon, if she got hurt, her injuries would mysteriously mend in a few hours. He'd said it was because she was a fast healer.

Another memory filtered through. When he'd first brought her to his home, he had no idea what to do with her. Her mind had been so fractured from her ordeal, she barely hung on to reality, but she remembered the warmth surrounding her, unbelievable warmth that pulled her back to life again. Damon had set her in front of the fireplace and wrapped her in a blanket when she couldn't stop shivering.

Then, he'd made her cocoa—no, he'd first phoned

someone to find out how to make cocoa because he didn't know how. He always made her that chocolaty drink when nightmares troubled her. If things got too bad for even cocoa to fix, then he took her to Gran and Kira—it was how she met them. She sniffed as tears fell, her anger fading.

He'd been patient, waiting for her to trust him enough to open up. Years later she'd told him about her past. And he was there when the nightmares about Tamsyn started.

No, nothing else mattered, she realized then. He'd been the only one to take her in when no one else wanted her. The secrets were no longer important. He was her family.

She pulled out her cell and dashed at her tears as she called his number. She had to tell him she was sorry. It went straight to voicemail. Her stomach dipped at the horrid feeling taking over and more tears sprang to her eyes.

Damon had just said goodbye.

***

Halfway to the castle, Aethan reached for her hand and saw the wound on her palm had healed. He wasn't surprised. He stroked his thumb over the new scar. The tears that ravaged her face gnawed at him. He didn't like to see her this way, and more, he wanted her to talk to him.

Night had fallen when he finally drove across the bridge and through the thick fog to the gates of the estate. Once he parked the car in the garage, he turned to her, unable to stand the silence. "What happened?"

"Please, Aethan, not now." She got out of the

vehicle and headed for the door that led to the basement.

His temper, already on a thin leash after that encounter with A'Damiel, fired up. He went after her. "Don't brush me aside, Echo."

Echo raised anguished eyes to him. "I know you can't understand my relationship with him. But he matters to me. I was angry with him for keeping me in the dark about who he was. But how can I hate the one person who cared enough to take me off the street and give me a chance at a different life? The only one who didn't ask me for anything in return? It took a long time, but he earned my affection, my trust." She swallowed her sob. "Now he's gone because of my harsh words, and I don't know if I will ever see him again."

Her pain hit him hard. He hated to see her so torn apart.

"Do you still want him in your life?" he asked, despising the words.

She stared at him, her mismatched eyes dark with unhappiness. "Will you accept him as someone I care about?"

No. "Yes."

She blinked at his answer.

Aethan couldn't blame her for her suspicion. Hell, he couldn't believe it himself, but for her, he'd do anything. She came over and pressed her damp face against his chest. Her tears, like the scent of rain, enveloped him. Yes, he would chain the bastard to their side if it made her happy.

***

Damon opened a portal to the Dark Realm and went straight to the lower levels. Once in the strata of Hell, he headed for Andras's chamber.

The upper levels where the Otium demons resided were far better than this shithole. The dank walls of the passageway gleamed wet as the coppery scent of blood hit him. Screams of the damned echoed through the tunnel lit only by veins of amber flickering behind the rocky walls.

He moved swiftly through the caverns until he reached a black granite wall. He flicked his hand, and the door to Andras's chamber opened. It wasn't the ruined furniture or the sheer evilness that resided in this place that had him clenching his jaw, but the fact that Andras dared to take on the role of the Sins. He punished the so-called damned souls in his abode. In that bloody Wall of Screams.

The chamber was silent, empty, except for the cries coming from the black wall. He stared at the thing in disgust.

"Admiring the decor?" The disembodied words drifted in the air. Belphegore waddled to his side still in his animal form.

The demon had made a good protector for Echo, by taking on her pet's shape, when Damon had had to leave the mortal realm on business.

"Just say the word, and you can *be* Bob," Damon said.

At the threat, as quick as a wink, Bel shook free of his fat, gray feline shape. The young demon straightened and raked back tousled, iron-colored hair from his grinning face.

Damon sent his senses out, scanning beyond the chamber for the fucker he'd come for.

"Doubtful he's here," Bel said. "Place looks deserted. So are you going to release these souls?"

"Why? They chose their paths. Not my business. But Andras is." After all, he'd bound the shithead to this place.

Damon's heightened hearing picked up a reedy moan. Narrowing his eyes, he stared at the wall on his left. A wave of his hand and the marble slid open to reveal an inner chamber, so dark he couldn't see a bloody thing. But in seconds his eyes adjusted to the blackness all around him. He found a table in the center with papers strewn about it, and there, in the far corner, a figure cowered.

Female. The ripped tunic she had on barely covered her thin body. Blood trailed down her cheek from a deep laceration, and more slashes crisscrossed her arms and chest. She scooted away as he came closer. She appeared to be around sixteen. The scent of fear thickened the dank air and skyrocketed when he crouched in front of her. Damon pushed aside her greasy hair, surprised to see her neck untouched. Just as well, because he wasn't in a mood to clean up Andras's mess. This female would have turned into one of his minions.

But looking at her took him back to when he first found Echo in that basement. She'd been so young, traumatized, and almost in a catatonic state. He pushed away images of a charge who no longer belonged to him. "Let's go," he told the girl and rose to his feet.

Wary eyes peered up at him from behind chunks of dirty brown hair. "I can't leave. He's put a spell over the doorway. It hurts when I try."

"You can either attempt it again or stay here." Damon walked out into the main chamber.

"Wait." The girl lurched to her feet, stumbled, and grabbed the table to steady herself. She scooped up the papers on it, clutching them to her chest, before shuffling to the door. Then she just stood there, dread in her pale eyes.

Damon reached out, grabbed her skinny arm, and hauled her out, ignoring her screech of panic. The instant she passed through the opening, her fear abated.

"Thank you," she whispered.

Damon didn't respond. He opened a portal and sent her off to the mortal realm. Once the gateway closed, he headed out of Andras's hole of depravity, Belphegore trailing behind him.

"Report on what happened while I was away," Damon ordered, heading toward Greed's dwelling.

"What can I say? I miss sleeping on Echo's bed, since she's moved to the castle."

Damon cut him a hard look.

"Just saying," Bel said, grinning.

"If Echo ever told me otherwise, I would have to kill you. Where's Bob?"

"I sent him back in all his pudgy glory since I can't enter the castle. Anyway, I did a little snooping when I got back after Echo got hurt in the subway." Bel stuck his hands in his pants pockets. "Where were you anyway?" he asked. "I tried to get a hold of y—"

"I had business to take care of." Damon cut him off. His hands fisted, easing the pain in his palms. No one could ignore a summons from one of the Ancients. Least of all, him.

Bel nodded. "Lazaar acted on his brother's behest. What is wrong with that stupid fuck? Andras is bound and a damn demonii. Why would Lazaar risk the wrath of the Ancients?"

Damon hadn't liked it at all when he was ordered by the Ancients not to kill Andras, but instead to bind him. The bastard was up to something. "What else did you find out?"

Bel shrugged. "Not much. Lazaar ran off when that warrior of Echo's flashed into the subway. She got hurt and the Oracle patched her up. But her mate refused to leave her behind with Lila. That's about it."

"About that mate thing. Why didn't you warn me?"

"You said to keep her safe when you weren't around, not tell you who she fell in love with."

Damon glared at the wiseass. His hand brushed the paper sticking out of his coat pocket. Retrieving it, he frowned, and realized the female must have slipped it in his pocket before she left. Her stealth surprised him. He opened the scroll and scanned the contents.

Shit!

So not what he wanted to do, but the blue-haired bastard had to know about this.

Chapter 27

Echo awoke to a dull morning. Her head ached a little, and her eyes still burned from the tears she'd shed last night.

Expecting to be alone in bed, she turned and found Aethan asleep beside her. He'd gone out on patrol after they'd arrived last night. She let her gaze drift over him, enjoying the moment because she rarely got a chance to see him unguarded and vulnerable.

The navy sheet pooled low around his waist, revealing miles of tawny-gold skin. His chest rose gently with each breath he took, his lashes resting like dark arcs against his skin, and his sensual mouth relaxed in sleep.

She played with his hair. The strands, a striking blend of different shades of blues and black, slid like a silken waterfall between her fingers.

His heavy arm reached out, looped around her waist, and brought her closer to him. The feel of his hard, warm body against hers, his erection pressing on her thigh, and just like that, desire awoke. Unable to help herself, she leaned in and brushed her lips across his.

Gray eyes flickered open, filled with warmth. Desire. His mouth took hers in a slow, heated kiss. His hand skated down her body to caress the curve of her hip. He pushed her on her back and deepened the kiss. Sliding his hand under her nightshirt, he cupped her naked breast, squeezing gently.

A moan escaped her as need spiraled.

He shifted and settled between her thighs. Pushing her nightshirt up, he trailed kisses down to her stomach. His lips glided around her navel, to the edge of her panties, over them, and down to the center of her damp core. He pressed down with his tongue.

Echo grabbed his hair and hung on as sensations consumed her like a tidal wave.

"Aethan. Wait—wait." She didn't want to do this if he wasn't prepared to go all the way. She didn't want a one-sided lovemaking, unable to touch him.

Too late. He yanked her panties down her legs and tossed them aside. His mouth came down on her. Echo gasped, forgetting what she wanted to say as he drew her passion right to the edge, keeping her there with his relentless torment. Driving her wild with his touch, he made her sob for release. Her hands fluttered over him, pushing at him, then tugging on his hair as desire built to a fever pitch and she fell, her orgasm pulling her over.

While shudders still racked her body, he came back up, kissed her gently and lay beside her. Tears tightened her throat. The emptiness filling her chest made her stomach pitch.

Is this how it would always be? He'd satiate the needs of her body but not her heart? Pleasure her and watch her fall while he stayed apart from her. Every sensation she'd come to associate with him, the sparks that heated her blood, the tingles that normally raced through her, were missing. Almost like someone else had made love to her.

She rolled away from him to face the window. Her skin burned in humiliation as icy numbness filled her chest.

The mattress dipped. His hand touched her hip. "Echo—"

"Don't." She slid off the bed and hurried to the bathroom, aware his brooding gaze tracked her. And prayed he wouldn't follow.

He didn't.

Standing under the cascading water in her nightshirt as steam fogged the shower, she blocked out everything but the gaping hole in her chest. When she found she could breathe again, she shut off the water, pulled off her soaking nightshirt, and wrapped a bath towel around her. She walked out of the shower and hesitated.

No use hiding.

Stiffening her spine, she opened the bathroom door, and stepped into an empty bedroom. Unbearable pain took hold of her. No. She wouldn't fall apart, she wouldn't—but tears flooded her eyes and slid down her face. She couldn't do this anymore, couldn't be in a relationship that had no future. No hope.

***

The day at work passed far too quickly. Jimar hadn't been happy about her sudden resignation. He'd insisted on a two weeks' notice. She just wanted to get it over with and, with misery eating at her, she'd agreed.

She dragged her feet when it was time to leave, knowing Aethan would be waiting for her. Unable to put it off any longer, she left the gym and headed up the steps, her heart thudding dully.

He'd parked the Range Rover on the opposite side of the street and was leaning against it, watching the gym entrance with a grim stare. Men passing on the sidewalk eyed him warily. The women gaped at him in sheer fascination, drawn to his sexual magnetism and that angelic allure.

Aethan had tried to teach her to shield her allure, but it was a miserable failure. It wasn't pheromones, after all. Well, she didn't care. She'd been taking the suppressant Gran made for her, so she'd just stick with it.

He straightened when he saw her.

Echo stood on the curb, watching the afternoon traffic, her heart not ready to face what was to come. She buttoned her coat against the chill that seemed determined to take over her body. Clients shuffled up the steps behind her, and she mumbled in response to their goodbyes.

Aethan crossed the road and took her gym bag, ushering her toward the SUV. She'd expected some kind of argument, about leaving that morning without informing him. But he remained silent for the entire journey, one hour of sheer torture.

Finally, he parked the car in the enormous garage. She didn't get out. Instead, she wrapped her arms around her waist and stared at the black Reventón parked in front of them. The one she'd driven a lifetime ago.

"We..." She swallowed past the lump in her

Georgia Lyn Hunter

throat. "We need to talk."

"Echo, I know you're upset."

Upset? It didn't even begin to describe how she felt. She couldn't be near him without begging him to make love to her. She was wound up so tight, any more and she would snap.

"It's beyond that now. I can't do this anymore, Aethan. I tried, and I just can't—" She fumbled with the door handle and scrambled from the vehicle, slamming the door behind her.

He caught up with her seconds later and grabbed her arm. His eyes flared with frustration. "Don't make this any more difficult than it already is."

"*I'm* making this difficult?" She glared at him. "Tell me how? 'Cause you sure as hell won't let me touch you!" She tried to hold back the bitterness and failed. "If I needed just sexual satisfaction, I could see to it myself or find a one-night stand. It's just as gratifying and empty. At least then, I don't have to suffer the humiliation afterward."

"Echo, no—"

She shook her head, cutting him off. "Do you know what it feels like, yearning for the one person who means more to you than anything else in this world, but he won't let you in? You're left with nothing but a longing for what could have been—" She stopped and took a deep breath. "I can't live like this anymore."

Breaking away from him, she pushed open the door to the basement and hurried past the gymnasium to the elevator. She stepped inside. He followed. The silence hung heavy and strained between them as the door swished closed.

"Echo—"

She shrank into the corner of the metal box they were caged in. She didn't want to breathe in his tormenting scent—didn't want his excuses. "Every time I reach out to you, are you going to disappear or tell me to get out? I've touched you, felt your powers sweep over me. *I. Didn't. Get. Hurt!*"

"Don't you get it? I will be inside you—*inside* you. There's no escaping then. And I will not take that chance."

"So your solution is to touch me with no emotions involved? Like you did this morning?"

"What the hell would you have me do?" His temper blazed. "Tell me! I saw what my powers do, how it shocks the human heart. I can't risk you. I won't!"

Pain made it hard to speak as she asked the question that had been gnawing a hole in her heart since their first night together. "Where do you go when *you* need relief, Aethan?"

His mouth tightened, he didn't answer.

She nodded, battened down her emotions, and met his turbulent gaze. "We both know you *will* go to someone else soon. You may not want to, but you'll have to. I can't live with that. I won't." She took a deep breath. "So for both our sakes, let it be. We are over."

"Echo, don't do this. I don't want anyone but you."

The pain in his voice, the devastation in his eyes was a punch to her stomach. She couldn't breathe. Better to rip the Band-Aid off now, she told herself. She looked at him through a haze of tears. "I'm sorry, Aethan…I love you too much to destroy us both."

Back in their quarters, Echo made her way to the dressing room and silently collected some of her clothes, struggling not to let her tears fall. With her arms full, she turned and found him standing in the doorway.

"I'm—" she swallowed hard, "I'm moving to another room."

Biting her lip to stop the trembling, she walked toward him. He reached out to touch her then dropped his hand. His expression changed, morphing into one of icy detachment. "Stay here, I'll sleep elsewhere."

She shook her head, unable to bear being in this bedroom with so many memories. "No, I can't. I'll move—"

Aethan pivoted and walked out. Moments later, the bedroom door slammed shut, the sound reverberating through the empty room. She squeezed her eyes tight as the tears fell.

***

Aethan materialized in a building under construction on the Lower East Side. He headed outside, no particular destination in mind. Anger, frustration, and misery pressed down on him. He didn't know what to do, had no idea where to turn. She'd left him because she thought he couldn't keep his damn fly zipped and would go after another.

No. She left you because you wouldn't take a chance and make her yours, dumbass!

Fuck off!

His control teetering on a blade's edge, he saw Blaéz and Týr waiting for him at the corner of Broome and Eldridge Streets. He should have headed in the opposite direction.

He slipped on his shades, knowing his eyes were

inhuman just then, since everything he saw was hazy.

"Your demon wants to speak to you. Said you weren't answering your cell," Blaéz said, his ice-pale eyes watching Aethan closely. "Said he'll be at the usual place."

Answering his cell was the last thing on his mind, when Echo was ripping his heart out. He shook his head. "I can't. Reschedule. Speak to him. Whatever. I don't care—"

The tattoo on his biceps shifted. A cold, insidious vibration snaked over his skin. Demoniis were on the prowl.

Fuck, yeah! He was so on board for this shit. A cold rage emanated from him, stirring the debris at his feet as he dematerialized.

Chapter 28

Later that morning, Echo made her way downstairs and tried not to think about Aethan, or the fact that she hadn't seen him since he'd walked out last night. At the thought of never seeing, never holding him again, anguish swept through her. She clung to the balustrade for support just as a haunting tune drifted to her.

A piano? She couldn't imagine any of the warriors having the temperament for such a pastime. Drawn by the poignant melody, she made her way in the direction of the sound, pushed open a door, and stepped into the music room.

A woman sat at the piano, immersed in her music, her elegant fingers dancing lightly across the ebony and ivory keys. Her silvery hair glimmered in the softly lit room and trailed down her back to pool on the bench. She stopped playing and looked up.

With creamy-gold skin and dark brows arched delicately over coppery-colored eyes, her ethereal features were a study in perfection. She rose to her feet. Her silky, pale-blue gown flowed sinuously over her tall, willowy body.

"Hello, Týr," the woman said softly, but her gaze remained locked on Echo.

Only then did Echo become aware that the warrior was behind her and unusually silent. "Hi," she said, turning back to the woman. "I'm Echo Carter."

The woman looked at the hand Echo held out before she grasped it in both of hers, her touch as gentle as her voice. "I am Elytani of Ademéras."

"Ademéras?"

"Yes. It's in Empyrea."

Echo froze to the spot in shock. Then she yanked her hand free, dread crashing through her as she took in that pretty hair and stunning face again. "You're from Empyrea?"

The woman nodded. "I er, I am spending some time here with Aethan."

"You are?" A whisper.

"Yes. I am his…betrothed."

Something inside Echo splintered and shattered into tiny little pieces, making her realize she'd still carried hope that somehow she and Aethan would work this out.

Strong hands grabbed her by her arms as she swayed. What do you know? She was still able to stand while crippling pain swept through her.

The fact that Elytani was here meant Aethan had to know. How could he not, when the woman was staying in his house?

And he hadn't even bothered to tell her.

"Echo, we should leave," Týr said quietly from behind her.

Composing herself, she pulled away from Týr and faced Elytani. "I hope you'll be happy here. Excuse me, I-I have to get to work."

Pride forced her to take normal steps to the door, but her fragmented heart insisted she hurry.

Týr followed. "Echo, hang on a sec."

She ignored him and headed for the front door, but he slipped his arm around her shoulders and steered her into the study.

"Sit down," he ordered.

She didn't, just wrapped her arms around her waist, wishing the agony would ease, and give her a moment to breathe, so she could function again.

"This is not what you think," Týr said, his expression drawn.

She turned away, didn't want to hear what he had to say. Or see his pity. She gazed through the window. Mist obscured most of the garden this early in the morning.

"She's the one, isn't she?" she asked dully. "The one Aethan's father wanted for him? She's an Empyrean. He...he wouldn't have any problems being intimate with her, right?"

"You think he'd cheat on you?"

Her laugh was harsh. "It's not a matter of cheating, and you know it. I'm the other woman, and she's..." Echo trailed off unable to say the word fiancée. "After all, you told me exactly what helps Ground him."

Týr winced. "Echo, she isn't who he wants."

"But she *is* what he needs." She pivoted and headed for the door. She didn't want Týr to see her weeping for a love lost.

***

After he'd seen Echo safely to work, Týr came back to the castle. Anger and guilt clawed at his gut. Aethan had asked him to do one thing, get Michael to send Elytani back. But he'd lost the female the very day after she'd arrived. It was time he kept his promise.

He found Elytani in the garden, near the lake. She turned, her bronze eyes pensive. "Why did she leave?"

How did he answer that? There were no words to explain this tragedy. "Come on, sweet girl, it's time you went home. Michael will be here in a few minutes."

"I don't want to go back. I like it here."

"You can't remain."

A weary sigh left her. "Humans get to do what they want on this realm. Have lives."

"It's called free will. Something we cannot have because of who we are."

"Yes, I know..." Then she brightened. "We spent time together. I've enjoyed your company. Perhaps,"— she blushed—"you could mate with me, then I could stay?"

A smile tugged at his mouth. "The offer is tempting, but I must decline. Elytani, remember *you* came to another realm, went on an exploration of a strange new world all on your own. I think—" Týr broke off as the air shimmered.

Michael took form before them, his disarrayed hair settling over his broad shoulders, aviator shades shielding his eyes. Elytani stepped back, eyeing the dark, massive male warily.

Stop frightening the female, Arc.

Michael ignored him. "Ready?" he asked Elytani.

She turned to Týr. "Won't you change your mind?"

The female was too damn sweet for her own good.

"Trust me, Elytani. You don't want one such as me. Besides, this world is not for you."

"But if Aethan—"

"No." Michael cut her off. "You cannot." Then he shifted, looking her up and down, as if measuring her. "However, if you wish to remain, there is a way."

Týr's amusement vanished. "No! No way. You can't be considering *that*."

"Why not?" Michael asked. "She'd be perfect. It's time we had one of the fairer sex."

"Dammit, Michael, just because Echo kills those fuckers, doesn't mean she'll—" He gestured to Elytani's timid and gentle appearance. "Doesn't mean she would be able to."

"I'm quite capable of doing any task you would have of me," Elytani said.

They both stared at her.

"No need to look so surprised, Týr. The males of Empyrea aren't the only ones who can fight. Besides, I'm a quick study." She smiled a little and turned to Michael. "What must I do to stay? I don't want to go back to Empyrea." Her delicate jaw tightened. "It's not the same since my brother left centuries ago."

Michael stared at her for a moment then nodded. "Very well. There's someone you have to meet first, before the green light's given. However, remember, once you agree, there is no going back."

"Ely, wait." Týr stopped her, determined to save her from herself. "The life Michael speaks of is brutal. There's no pretty dresses or walks in the park. You'd have to kill or be killed. You'll be bound to this realm, cut off from everyone you ever cared about." Týr didn't want her to have any regrets. The gods knew, he and the others didn't have much choice. "It will be lonely."

She smiled and smoothed a hand over her gleaming hair like he'd just promised her a trip to paradise or back to Central Park. "I understand perfectly."

"Let's go." Michael touched her shoulder, and they both shimmered then disappeared.

***

Echo had spent the last hour on a barstool in the Peacock Lounge, as if she'd grown roots in the seat. The noise and the laughter of inebriated men increased the throbbing in her head. The smells of food combined with alcohol made her feel slightly ill. She took another sip of her ginger ale.

Despite the danger of Lazaar finding her, she'd come anyway, a chance she'd taken to forget her despair for a while. She needed to get lost in the crowd for a bit before Hedori came for her.

"Echo? Haven't seen you in a while."

She glanced up and smiled at the blonde bartender. "Hey, Jess. Yeah, been busy. How's Paul?" she asked about the woman's three-year-old son.

"He's good—" Jessie stopped and stared. "Your eyes. Wow! They suit you far better." She grinned. "Makes you look sort of mysterious and sexy."

"Exactly what I always told her," Kira said, stopping to pick up her drink order.

"More like a freak," Neal added.

"Shove it, Neal," Kira snapped. "Who pissed in your beer?"

Jessie leaned closer to Echo. "The guy's weird.

Half the time I don't know if he wants to get horizontal with you or kill you."

Echo laughed, sputtering out the ginger ale she'd just sipped. "In his dreams. Besides, you're more his type," she added, looking for napkins to clean up the spills. "Heard he likes them blonde and curvy."

Jessie snorted. "I'd date Jon. Hell, even Brian, the old geezer," she said of the bar's manager, "if I wanted another relationship, which I don't. Paul is more than a handful right now and about all the man I can handle. One sec." She went off to serve another customer.

Ignoring Neal's malicious glare, Echo reached for the napkins in front of her, when he grabbed her hand, squeezing painfully.

"You laugh now, but I will have you," he hissed. "Jon's not here to hide behind today."

She stared into his angry eyes. "When hell freezes over," she said coolly. Didn't bother tugging free. She wouldn't give him the satisfaction of doing so. He flung her hand away and stalked to the other end of the bar.

"What was that about?" Jess whispered when she came back.

"A difference of opinion." Echo wiped up her spill.

"Right. He wants you, and you want to kick his ass. Echo, you need to be careful. I'd hate to think of what could happen, if he got you alone or—" Jessie's mouth dropped open as she looked over Echo's shoulder, her eyes widening. "Oh, there is a God. Get a load of him."

Hearing the awe in her voice, Echo smiled in relief, grateful for the change in topic. In this place, there were always good-looking guys about.

Musicians, sometimes models. Heck, even the occasional movie star liked to come in, kick back, and chill—the deciding factor in Kira's decision to work here.

Jessie sighed dreamily, her gaze pinned on whoever it was. "I wouldn't mind bed-wrestling with him."

Curious, Echo turned around, and her stomach dropped as she watched Aethan survey the bar. A low growl vibrated in her chest at the images Jessie's words conjured in her mind. She shouldn't be jealous, knowing Jessie was all talk, even if there was a layer of lust in her voice. Besides, what right did she have to be jealous?

Aethan wasn't hers, would never be.

Dressed in his perpetual black, he carried off his patrolling gear with such masculine ease. But not a flicker of emotion showed on his handsome face as he glanced around. His gaze honed in on her, a determined light firing in his stone-cold stare.

Týr must have told him what happened. Humiliation, like a wave, engulfed her.

"Don't waste your time looking. He would never want a cold bitch like you!" Neal's malicious hiss slapped her across the face.

The pain expanding in her chest made it impossible to breathe. Because what Neal said was true—when it came down to it, Aethan didn't want her.

The glass rattled on the table where she dropped it. Slipping off her stool, she hightailed it out of there. She went to the staff restroom and locked herself in a cubicle, unable to control the hot tears spilling down her face. When she heard the door open several minutes later, she bit her lip to silence her sobs and prayed it was a staff member.

"Echo?"

The low cadence of his voice seeped into her, made her want to open the door and throw herself into his arms. Instead, she pulled her feet up onto the toilet and buried her face in her knees, hoping he wouldn't hear her and hating that the locked door would be no barrier for him.

She didn't want him to see her like this. Broken.

He rapped on her stall. "Echo, open the door. Please."

She didn't answer. A few more seconds passed, and she heard the click. The door opened. She didn't look up, keeping her face hidden. Leather rustled as he crouched in front of her. A hand brushing over her hair made the tears come faster.

"Don't hide from me, please. It kills me to see you like this."

Her head snapped up. "I'm not hiding. I need a moment to myself. Can't I even have that?"

His face darkened.

She didn't care that he was hurting, too. He'd brought them to this moment because he was too damn stubborn to listen. Releasing her knees, she stepped around him and left the cubicle. The cold water she splashed on her tear-ravaged cheeks did little to hide the damage. She tore paper towels off the dispenser, dried her face, and looked up to find him watching her in the mirror above the sink, his expression grim.

"Elytani is not my betrothed. You know this."

"It changes nothing. She is like you. *She* is what you need. Not me." She tossed the used paper towels into the overflowing trash can and walked out.

He followed her, his scent a torture of what could

have been. She had to get out of this place and away from him.

"Echo, wait." Kira stopped her. "Before you go—don't forget about Saturday. Uh, never mind. I'll text you." She glanced over Echo's shoulder. "Aethan, nice. Thanks for putting him in his place."

That caught Echo's attention. "Put who in his place?" she asked, but Kira merely smiled and danced off.

She turned to Aethan, her stomach knotting as she waited for him to answer.

A heartbeat passed.

"If you're prepared to talk to me"—his hard gaze pinned hers—"then it better be about something important. Like us."

"There is no 'us'."

***

No *us*?

Aethan refused to accept that as he followed her out. His jaw clamped down so tightly, it was a damn miracle his teeth didn't shatter. He saw her into the Range Rover and waited until she buckled up before slamming the door shut. He circled the hood to the driver's side and, moments later, tore through the street, ignoring the irate honking and squealing of tires.

If he didn't find a way out of this mess that was their life, the outcome was guaranteed. Michael's unspoken edict gnawed at his brain like a bloodthirsty parasite.

Mate with her to keep her safe, or she will ascend to the Celestial Realm.

There was no way, no way in hell Michael would

leave Echo on this cursed realm, unmated and a target for every evil out there.

Chapter 29

Andras stared at his reflection in the new, ornate mirror in his chambers and tugged at his long, brown dreadlocks. *Perfect*. It was uncanny, seeing his brother's reflection instead of his own, but as much as he hated the fucker's face, he had to put up with it, for now. Thankfully, the glamor remained longer this time, unlike in the bar when the damn thing wore off far too soon, and the binding hauled him back to the Dark Realm. If not for that, he would have had the prophesied one by now.

Still, nothing mattered but the victory he could almost taste.

Excitement stirred in him as he left his chambers and headed for the outer caverns. He wouldn't miss this shithole. He neared the place that marked his confinement to the Dark Realm and hesitated.

The binding barrier usually pulled him back to his chamber if he dared to cross it. An excruciating experience that he had continued to test, hoping to weaken the incantation.

Until he took Lazaar's blood.

Smiling, he passed the barrier and entered the dank cavern without a single stir in the spell. Secure in the knowledge all was well, he made his way through the tunnels.

Soon, it would all be over.

He took the potion from his pocket. *Three drops,* that sniveling little oracle had said. He didn't even care that someone had released her. As long as he had what he wanted. He took four, to keep the glamor bright and energized. Then he opened a portal and stepped through it, into the tunnels leading to a passageway near the surface of the mortal realm. He came to a solid wall. A touch and the concrete barrier moved.

The moment Andras sauntered into the crypt, he smelled the human. Mortal minions were far too irresistible, with the delicious light of their souls burning in them. However, he had to put temptation out of his mind, for now. Most important was getting the girl before someone else claimed her.

Bael followed orders well. Maybe he'd keep him when he ruled the realms.

The demon strode over to him. "He has news," Bael said and nodded to the minion.

The human's vacant brown eyes stared at Andras as he spoke. "The girl was in the bar. There was a clash over her between a blue-haired man and another—"

"Enough." Andras touched the human's mind, seeing the events for himself. "Are they still there?"

"Yes."

Andras shimmered and flashed from the crypt to the Peacock Lounge. Humans, he snorted, were such creatures of habit, making his job of hunting them so easy. First the alley in Chinatown and now the exact same bar.

Finding the warrior and the girl were no longer there was a disappointment, however, it didn't deter Andras.

Scanning, he found whom he wanted in the back. He strolled into the locker room. The human male was changing his clothes. His rage, a thick red haze, surrounded him. Inhaling, Andras let the negative energy fill his psyche and caught the scent of the male's embarrassment.

Oh, so perfect. A human failing that always worked to his advantage. "You aren't going to let them get away with that, are you?"

The human spun around, rapidly zipping up his jeans. "Who the fuck are you?"

Andras glanced around the poky little room with chipped lockers and mismatched chairs. "The warrior shoved you against the shelves, didn't he? Messed you up? No, not good at all." He could smell the alcohol and see the bits of glass still in the male's hair.

"I don't know what the hell you're talking about." The human brushed him off and pulled on a dry shirt.

Andras touched the male's thoughts with his mind and smiled. "Come now, Neal, I'm here to help you."

Neal scowled.

"You've wanted her for a long time, haven't you? You can have her, *if* you agree to a little proposition I have." Andras tugged at the annoying dark dreadlocks hanging in his face.

The human narrowed his eyes. "What's this got to do with you?"

Andras smiled. "You want the girl, and you want to avenge yourself against the warrior, correct?"

"So what if I do?" he snapped. "Why are you so

interested in them?"

Andras shrugged. "I have a score to settle. All you have to do is say *yes*."

He saw the male contemplate his words. The darkness of revenge, of hatred, filled the human's psyche.

"If I help you, then she is mine?"

"But of course," Andras lied. "I want the warrior dead. What better way than to use the girl to get him? Once it's over, she's yours. Agreed?"

Neal smiled, eyes bright with malice. "Count me in."

"Wonderful." Andras grabbed hold of Neal's mind and took over, so much easier when they forfeited free will for greed. His sire should be proud of him. The old bastard would see soon enough that he, Andras, was the better choice than that fuckhead loser, Lazaar, to inherit his Sin.

Chapter 30

Echo avoided the kitchen the next morning when she heard male voices there and wandered over to the library instead. She missed the solitude her apartment gave her. Even though Bob offered a small measure of comfort, it wasn't the same. The moment they took care of the demon who was after her, she'd move back—

She faltered to a halt, the reality of her situation hitting her hard.

She could never go back to her normal life, ever. She would have to be protected. Always. That meant she'd have to live here for the rest of her life and see Aethan every day, knowing he would never be hers.

Oh, God. She stumbled out through the French doors and into the freezing cold. Her arms wrapped around her waist, head lowered, she walked blindly into the garden, just wanting the pain to end. The vibrantly colored leaves beneath her feet soon gave way to damp ground. The smell of moss and decaying wood drifted to her, and Echo found herself in a dark canopy of trees.

She slowed down when she saw a tall figure heading toward her, a sword in his hand. Her flighty heart pounded like mad until she saw the wild black hair.

"Hello, Michael," she greeted the Archangel, as if coming out of a long sleep. She hadn't seen him since the day Aethan had introduced them in the study.

Michael sheathed his enormous sword in the scabbard strapped to his back. "Eshana." He drew closer. A light touch of his hand on her cheek and warmth seeped into her, banishing the cold.

A moment later, something warm settled across her shoulder. Her jacket. "Th-thank you."

He nodded, his gaze skimming over her face. Those shattered eyes probably saw everything, she'd bet her last dollar on it. She nervously stepped back. "I'm going for a walk."

"All right, I'll join you."

She didn't want company, but how did you say no to an archangel?

"Just say *no*."

An eerie shiver trickled down her spine. "Please don't read my thoughts."

"I won't if you promise to talk."

Right. Echo chewed on her lip, trying to figure out how to ask this man—archangel—what she wanted to know. *Speak to him like you do to any other*, she decided.

He spoke then, his voice soft, compelling. "There are many choices in life, Eshana. The ones you make at this moment will have the greatest impact on your future. You need to think carefully."

"Yeah? I chose, and it didn't turn out so well, did

it?" she said, unable to hide her bitterness.

Michael glanced at her, the wind whipping at the strands of his hair. Something shifted in his wild blue eyes. "Did Aethan tell you about the Celestial Realm?"

Why was he asking her about Heaven? "No. Should he?"

"There's something you should know."

God, what more can there be? Stopping, she slipped her hands into her jacket pockets and searched for her stones. She needed their warmth, their calming effect, only to discover she'd left them in her room. Her fingers clenched.

"As long as you're mortal and remain on this realm, demoniis will always come after you because of what they think you represent: Freedom for them. Your destiny is to journey to the land of the angels."

"You mean I need to die?" she asked, horrified. No matter how much her life sucked, and it did most of the times, she wasn't one to give up so easily.

You did with Aethan.

She pushed that thought aside. She didn't want to go there again.

"No," Michael said. "You are a descendant of an angel. Your heritage allows you entrance. It's the only place demoniis can't get to you."

"Why didn't Aethan tell me about this?"

"He refuses to let you go. Had you chosen to stay with him, you could have lived your human life here before journeying to the Celestial Realm. But you can't live here unprotected, and he won't tolerate another near you."

Shocked, she stared at him. "Are you kidding me? What kind of solution is that? Choose to live with Aethan or meet my maker early?" Her eyes shifted to the huge sword strapped to his back, her skin growing clammy despite the warmth of her jacket. "I just wanted normal. Instead, I got handed the crappiest deal ever."

"There's one advantage, or disadvantage to this," Michael said. "If you choose to go to the Celestial Realm, you won't retain your mortal memories."

He hung that incentive over her head like bait. It was no longer a choice of stay or go, but remember or forget. With anguish rolling through her like a living entity, his offer was exactly what she needed. But at the thought she'd never see or remember Aethan, her stomach hurt.

What was the alternative? Could she live here and see him with someone else?

No. She'd never accept him with another woman. God, she was tired of this. She only wanted a little peace.

***

Aethan walked out onto the terrace as night crept in accompanied by icy winds saturated with the salty scent of the sea. However, his mind wasn't on the weather.

Echo slept in the room next to his, but she might as well have been in another wing of the castle. He hadn't seen her in days, not even a glimpse, and it galled him that he'd had to ask Hedori for her whereabouts.

Now she'd gone to spend the day in the city because it was Kira's birthday. All he could think was that she'd use any excuse to avoid him. Frustrated, he lashed out, punching the stone balustrade bordering the terrace. The pain didn't register, but the cracks spidering through the concrete drew his attention as dust and bits of rubble rained to the ground.

The agony from his shattered knuckles finally made itself known. He flexed his fingers, warmth surrounding the broken bones as healing took place and the split skin knitted.

He sighed, lifting his eyes to the darkening skies. Gods, he was losing his mind. He needed to do something, keep himself occupied. Or else he'd go over to the Oracle's and haul Echo back—yeah, the way things stood between them, not a good idea right now.

"The cathedral on the East Side," Blaéz said from behind him.

He turned to the warrior. "What about it?"

"Found something there yesterday. You'll want to see this."

Blaéz dematerialized.

Perfect. This would give him the distraction he needed. Aethan followed. They took form behind the cathedral, near a small grove of trees. Aethan looked around the place, then finally at the stone angel, where he'd first seen Echo. Pain unhinged him. He fought to breathe again, forcing his mind back on the job.

Blaéz led the way farther into the copse of trees and through a small gate into a cemetery.

"Why the hell didn't I think of this?" Aethan looked around the cemetery shrouded by tall trees. It was the perfect hideout.

"Because it's too obvious," Blaéz said, leading him to a crypt. "And your head's not screwed on right."

"Asshole."

The Celt's mouth lifted in a parody of a smile as he willed the heavy door to the tomb open. The thing groaned loud enough to wake the dead. As they entered, the musty smell of decay, merged with the stench of sulfur, nailed Aethan full in the face. The crypt door creaked and slowly closed, sealing them in total darkness. It took Aethan only a second to adjust his sight.

Stairs led from the landing down into the bowel of the crypt. Fresh footprints marred the dusty floor. Cobwebs hung in tattered threads overhead.

"This has to be one of the fuckers' hideouts. We need to find out who's using this place. Where does it lead?" he asked Blaéz.

"Beneath the foundation of the cathedral. Through there." Blaéz nodded at a point on the wall that was now broken. "I've been keeping an eye on it, but nothing so far."

Aethan's mind raced. "Think it's him? The one after Echo?"

"Hard to say. Let's go." Blaéz turned back toward the door. "We don't want him picking up our scent here."

They materialized back at the castle. The winds howled around them as they stood on the portico.

"She can smell them," he told Blaéz. "She says each has an underlying scent that's different. That's how she knew the one at the bar the other night wasn't the same one who tried to take her through the portal, even though they looked the same. The one at the bar is who killed her friend."

If he took Echo back to the crypt, she'd know whether that hiding place belonged to the demonii they searched for.

But thoughts of her widened the chasm in his chest. He couldn't move. The weight of his despair crashed through his barriers. He sat on the balustrade, his head slumped to his chest, eyes squeezed shut. How the hell was he to go on without her?

"You could try," Blaéz said, sitting beside him. "If you don't claim her, you will lose her. And I don't mean that metaphorically."

Aethan's eyes snapped open.

"Ask her about tomorrow night."

Blaéz's words made little sense to him. What the hell was going on tomorrow night?

Aethan pinched the bridge of his nose and exhaled roughly. Fuck this. If the Fates had chosen Echo for him, then they'd better make damn sure nothing happened to her. Or there'd be hell to pay.

His cell rang. Retrieving it from his pocket, he answered.

"You'll want to head over to Anarchy," Dagan said, his tone clipped.

"Why?"

"There's something here that should interest you." He rang off.

***

Echo shivered, tucking her hands into the pockets of her cashmere coat, an extravagant present Damon had given her last winter. She still hadn't been able to reach him. Calls to his cell went unanswered, and now she was running out of time. She'd go to the loft tomorrow. She had to see him.

Uneasy, she glanced up then down the street. The sensation of being watched persisted but she couldn't

Georgia Lyn Hunter

see anything.

Please, just this one night, so Kira can enjoy her birthday. So she could say goodbye to her friend in her own way. She'd given Michael a letter to give to Kira after she left this realm and asked him not to say anything to Aethan about her decision, either, insisting on his promise.

Michael hadn't been happy about that. As an archangel, his promise, once given, bound him.

"This is so exciting!" Kira hooked her arm through Echo's, her hazel eyes glowing gold in anticipation.

Echo turned to her friend, an affectionate smile on her face. She didn't have the heart to remind Kira what else liked this place, too, especially on the prowl for human souls. These were her last moments with her friend, and she didn't want to take away her enjoyment of the evening.

Kira had changed her hair to a deep chestnut brown and had woven the length into multiple braids. A gleam of gold flickered through the strands at her excitement.

"So, how does it feel to be twenty-four?"

"Not a day older than sixteen." Kira laughed. "Gran thinks I'm still a kid. Good thing she didn't see the outfit."

"You mean you're lucky she was out for the night."

"Yep."

Smiling, Echo shook her head as Jessie walked up the street toward them, her spiked heels clicking on the concrete. The moment she reached them, she hooked her arm through Echo's other one.

"So spill. Who is he, and where can I get one? The

one who smashed up Neal yesterday."

"What are you talking about?" Echo asked.

Kira sighed. "Let it go, Jess."

Jess snorted. "Oh, sure. The most exciting thing to happen at the 'Cock and I'm supposed to let it go? Echo, you should've seen it. After you left the bar, that guy, the gorgeous one with blue hair, strode over to Neal, picked him up like an insect, and slammed him against the shelves. Bottles fell on top of him like an avalanche. Man, what a sight! He said something to Neal, and by the look on Neal's face, I was sure he'd piss himself." She laughed. "Can't know for sure since the broken liquor bottles wet him first."

The blood drained from Echo's face. So that was what Kira meant and what Aethan wouldn't talk about. The chagrined expression on Kira's face confirmed it.

"It was the most entertaining thing I've ever seen," Jess said. "Though Brian was pissed." She sighed, a dreamy expression on her face. "So, who is he?"

"Echo's b—"

"Let it go, please?" Echo squeezed Kira's hand.

Kira scowled then said, "He's a friend."

"Girls, you ready to go?" Jon asked, as he jogged across the street to join them.

Echo inhaled deeply, taking in the chilly air and stink of the alley as she followed the others to the entrance. While they waited to be carded and allowed admittance, she glanced around and smiled when she saw the bouncer. Tall, built like a linebacker, Tagg was a regular at the gym and moonlighted as a bouncer.

"Hey, Tagg."

"Echo. Good to see you." His crooked smile revealed lean masculine dimples in his bronze face. "You staying awhile tonight?"

It surprised her that he was aware she never stayed long. But, then, she'd been tailing demoniis. "Yeah. It's Kira's birthday."

"Echo?" Jon joined her. "The others are waiting."

She nodded to Tagg and moved back into line. And shut her eyes when she felt Jon's hand slide to her waist.

"You okay?" he asked.

She glanced at him and smiled, forcing herself not to step away from him. "Yeah, I'm fine."

Inside the club, the air was thick with musky perfume and liquor. The heavy beat of rock music pounded in Echo's head as multicolored laser beams and strobe lights assaulted her eyes, guaranteeing a headache by the end of the night.

Resting her elbows on the table, her hands around her Pepsi, Echo wished she was back outside in the cold air. She really didn't want to be here in the frenzied excitement of the club with unhappiness eating at her. She blinked rapidly and saw Jon pointing to the dance floor.

Why couldn't she have fallen for someone like him? Quiet, considerate, charming.

His gaze filled with admiration when she stood and he took in the short, black leather skirt, side-laced halter top, and icepick-heeled, knee-high boots she wore.

As she neared him, he leaned close so she could hear him above the heavy rock music. "You look amazing."

"Thanks."

He led her to the dance floor. And just her luck, a slow, dreamy song started. She inhaled a sharp breath, about to tell him she'd changed her mind when she met

Jon's hopeful blue eyes and hesitant smile. Then she remembered his broken pinkie.

What was one dance after the hurt she'd caused him?

A few seconds into the dance, she couldn't breathe with Jon's arms around her and the sea of bodies closing in on her, pushing her nearer to him. His spicy aftershave enfolded her. She had to clamp down on the urge to push him away.

She yearned for the scent of rainstorms. Her throat tightened—no! She had to be strong and shut down thoughts of Aethan, then Jon took her hand from his shirtfront, opened her palm, and pressed a gentle kiss in the center.

Her heart faltered in dismay.

***

Aethan surveyed the bodies moving around the VIP section of Anarchy. Their frenzied movement had little to do with the hard-core rap music splitting his eardrums from below.

He'd only been here a short while, and already he felt like smashing his fist into something again. The writhing couples in the closed booth next to them pushed his edginess up to dangerous levels. Then the music switched to a ballad of some kind. He hated that shit. Made him yearn for what had slipped out of his grasp.

Well, no longer.

Blaéz lifted a finger, and a waitress appeared. He ordered another shot of whiskey then leaned back in his seat. He studied the inch of amber liquid that remained in his glass, distorted by the whipping strobe lights.

"Still nothing?"

"No," Aethan growled. "The Sumerian is as tight-lipped as a damn vault. Said nothing, just to check out the club."

Whatever the hell it was, Blaéz and Týr could handle it. Though Týr would first have to detach himself from the female straddling him. The scent of sex and lust on this level battered at him, but Aethan ignored the blatant invitation from the females trolling the place.

"I'm outta here." He pivoted for the stairs, then staggered to a halt. Dagan's clipped message hit him square in the chest.

She wouldn't dare! He didn't care if it was Kira's birthday.

He strode back to the gallery overlooking the dance floor and scanned the place. The brittle hold on his sanity fractured. His vision blurred. Fury crashed through him like a huge wave. The lights in the place dimmed for a second.

Yo, man. Aethan, you okay? Týr's voice came to him from a distance.

He didn't answer. He walked out, death on his mind.

Chapter 31

Echo pulled away from Jon. She had to get out. "I'm sorry—I can't do this."

He grasped her hand. "Echo, wait."

She shook her head and bolted from the dance floor, only to stumble to a halt. Aethan stood several feet from her. Everything in her froze—except her foolish heart, which rushed around like mad in her chest.

He appeared as dangerous and wild as the storms that so often visited New York. *Oh, crap.* He had to have seen her with Jon, seen him kiss her hand. She had a moment of terrifying clarity. It didn't matter that she told Aethan it was over, she'd always be his mate, and that meant he could hurt Jon.

She cast a desperate glance at her friend. Jon smiled wryly, raised a hand, and headed for their table. Meeting Aethan's coldly furious gaze, she realized too late that she shouldn't have looked for Jon. Echo cut around Aethan and escaped down the corridor. She couldn't deal with this now.

***

Blood pounding in his veins, Aethan went after her. He grasped her wrist and hauled her down the dim passage to the back exit, ignoring the gaping patrons.

She yanked at his fingers. "Don't touch me."

He stopped and manacled both her hands with his. "So soon you forget. Two days—two fucking days and you're with someone else?"

"I'm not doing this ag—"

"Who is he?"

"That's none of your business."

"None of my business? You dress like this, let another put his hands—his fucking mouth on you? And it's none of my business?"

"At least Jon won't kill me when we become lovers, right?" she yelled, her eyes hot with anger.

Unadulterated rage cracked his control. His vision took on a white haze. "That will never happen. He comes near you again, I will kill him."

Aethan willed off the dim light above, clamped his arm around her waist and dematerialized. Taking form in his room back at the castle, he took her mouth in a hard, possessive kiss.

"No!" She broke free and pushed at his chest. "I'm not going through this again."

Aethan grabbed her hands, pinning them with his. The image of the human kissing her was a punch in his gut, knowing what could happen. But she was his. Every inch of her belonged to him.

"You think I don't want you?" he asked, tone harsh. "Every minute since you left me, I've died a little. Every breath hurts because you're not with me."

Tears filled her eyes. "Don't. Please don't say that. You know it can never be."

The broken note in her voice stabbed him in the heart. He remembered her crying in the bar restroom. He heard every anguished sob that tore through her and knew it wasn't the asshole in the bar, or the one she'd been with tonight who hurt her, but him.

"I can't live like this. You have to let me go."

"That's the one thing I cannot do." The agonized whisper left him, his fury dissipating. He lowered his head to hers and squeezed his eyelids tight. "I can't go on without you. I just can't."

***

"Aethan?"

He exhaled roughly and looked at her.

Echo sensed the change in him, but she couldn't read his expression. He'd reached some kind of decision about them, but with her luck, it could only go one way.

The embers sparked in the fireplace and flared to life. The soft crackle of wood broke the silence in the room.

"Whatever you want, *me'morae.*" A whisper.

Her breath caught in her throat. He agreed?

She wanted to smile as relief sung its way into her heart. But she wasn't foolish enough to let it distract her.

Echo watched him carefully, saw the fear in his gray eyes, and understood he hated being so helpless. Hated the thought of what could happen to her. But if they were to have a chance at a life together, he needed to trust her. She rested her hands on his chest and

Georgia Lyn Hunter

hesitated.

You can handle us, little one, remember that.

It struck her then. The man in the navy robe had said those words to her after he had healed her. Maybe this is what he meant. Christ, she hoped so.

"Echo? What is it?"

She blinked and shook her head. "Would you let me do this?"

A suspicious look entered his stormy-gray gaze.

She wanted to smile. God, she loved him. "Promise me you won't poof out of here, disappear when you think you're losing control."

His turbulent stare didn't waver, nor did he respond.

She didn't give up and pushed on instead. "If *I* think I'm not able to handle anything, I'll stop, okay? Think of it as..." A wicked smile curved her lips. "As domination and submission. Only I'll be the Dom and have a safe word, too."

A scowl appeared on his handsome face, then he gave a stilted nod.

"Oh, no, say the word, Aethan."

He squeezed his eyes shut, a muscle working his jaw. "Yes."

She slid her hands up the hard muscles of his chest and pushed his coat off his broad shoulders. His eyes snapped open. The leather fell to the floor in a rustle. He stood there like a statue. No matter. By the time she was done with him...well, she planned to have him begging for mercy.

She unfastened a button on his black shirt to reveal tawny-gold skin. She worked the rest of the buttons free, then glanced up. Not a flicker of emotion showed on his stone-like features.

"What do you think of *blue* as a safe word?" she asked, tracing a finger over his pecs. Lightly, she brushed his flat nipple, and it hardened. Unable to resist, she flicked her tongue over the tiny nub. And goosebumps dusted his skin.

Then she closed her teeth over his other nipple and tugged with just enough of a sting. His entire body shuddered. Well now. So her statue had life. She didn't let him see her smile as she licked the pain away.

"What was I saying? Yep, I think *blue* will do as a safe word." She leaned in close to whisper, "Because I like the color of your hair."

She tugged his shirt off, tossing it on top of his coat, and went down on her knees in front of him. He was already aroused. The prominent bulge in the front of his leathers beckoned her. She wanted badly to touch him, to feel the power of his erection as her fingers encircled his hardness.

Echo concentrated on his boots instead of the temptation of his sex. She tugged and got them off easier than she expected. But then he only moved when he wanted to.

Running a finger over the front edge of his waistband, she glanced up. His eyes burned with a hunger that made her blood heat up like she'd been dipped in lava. Her heart thudded, her fingers brushing his hard stomach, as she unbuttoned, then unzipped, his leathers. It took all her strength and determination not to touch him the moment his erection sprang free. She tugged his trousers down his legs. He shifted, letting her take them off.

She moved and her face brushed against his hardness. He jerked at the contact. Thick and rigid, his erection jutted out. Echo didn't think, she rubbed her

Georgia Lyn Hunter

cheek against his warm, silken flesh. Her fingers circled his thickness. A bead of moisture formed at the tip of his cock, she leaned in and licked it off. He stiffened, a guttural groan escaping him.

Then she ran her tongue from the base to the top of the blunt head. The heady taste of him filled her senses as she took him into her mouth. A hand brushed over her hair, his other braced on the wall. She'd never done this before but went with her instincts. While it was a little awkward, trying to find a rhythm, she felt his pleasure like it was her own. His fingers were in her hair, guiding her. Her lips tightened around him.

With a harsh groan, he hauled her up, his eyes a wild gray. Echo saw his rigid jaw and knew what he was doing. He was going to let her use him, while he remained in control.

Too bad for him.

She wanted it all. And she would have it.

Only his absolute surrender would do.

She pulled back. God, but he was beautiful naked. She had to bite down the urge not to go back on her knees and take another taste of him. His erection glistened from her mouth's exploration. Finally, she had him exactly how she'd imagined him so many times in her dreams. Naked, maybe not exactly defenseless, but all hers.

Her hands trailing over his hard abs, she moved behind him. The man had the most gorgeous butt ever. She traced the ropey muscles of his back with light fingers, then skimmed her lips over the old scars, kissing each new one she discovered. The goosebumps multiplied.

"You're cold." Taking his hand, she led him to the large rug in front of the fireplace and pushed him down flat on his back.

His gaze remained wary and pinned on her.

"I'm not going to do anything you won't like," she said, smiling. "Okay fine. We'll give you a safe word, too, if it will make you feel better. How about '*supercalifragilisticexpialidocious*'?"

Aethan's eyes narrowed at her teasing.

"No? Well, I'll have to think of another. In the meantime, let's try something else."

She straddled him, his erection fitting snugly between her thighs. He was so hot, so damn tempting. Playing with him was driving her insane with need.

***

Sensations overwhelmed him. Her touch. Her smell. Desire blazed. Gods, he burned for her. He could still feel her mouth wrapped around his sex, and his cock jerked, wanting to be sheathed in her. She leaned down and nipped his bottom lip. Then she licked away the sting, long and slow, like a godsdamn cat.

He growled.

She smiled. The warmth and love in her gaze melted away the hurt and anger like nothing else had in those unbearable hours away from her.

He became desperate.

His mouth fastened on hers. She pulled back and wagged a finger at him. "Nuh-uh. You don't get to do that. And keep your hands down."

He let his palms slide away from her hips.

Her gorgeous eyes glowing, she came back to torture his lips, grazing her teeth over the bottom one, but no damn kisses. He was close to tossing her on her back and ending this torment when she left his mouth

Georgia Lyn Hunter

and moved to his jaw, stringing kisses, then nipping and licking each bite as she explored her way down his neck. Her blunt nails scraped lightly across his chest, over his nipples, then she sat up. There was no teasing light in her eyes now.

Thank the gods! Maybe she'd end this madness.

"Kiss me," he demanded.

"Ah, now you're speaking to me?"

"Godsdammit, Echo. You're playing with fire."

"What a way to burn," she teased huskily and sucked his lower lip. "We're still doing this my way."

"Your way, and *I* may die," he growled.

Then she kissed him. Her lush lips fastened on his. So fucking torturous. He loved it. He tasted heaven, he tasted himself. He had to have her. He licked, bit, and tasted, then finally plundered her mouth, her gasp of pleasure pure nirvana.

Wanting more, he broke off their kiss. "Take your top off."

She eyed him like he was a predator waiting to pounce. She would be right. Then, with a deliberateness that drove him crazy, she undid the laces on the side of the leather halter. Slowly, she pulled it over her head, revealing pale, honey-toned breasts with tempting dusky peaks.

"Lean forward." He didn't recognize the guttural tone as his.

She braced her hands on either side of his head, her breasts just short of his mouth.

"Closer," he ordered.

The second she did, he clamped down on her nipple. She gasped. He licked and suckled the tight nub as his hand massaged the other.

Her moan filled the room. She rubbed her silk-covered center against his stomach. The scent of her arousal tormented his senses, his mind so hazy, he couldn't think straight.

"Take your skirt off."

Slumberous eyes gazed at him in confusion. "What?"

"Skirt. Off. All off. Now."

She straightened to move away from him.

"No. Stand over me and do it."

Her eyes widened, then she slowly pushed up and planted her booted-feet on either side of his head. She looked taller than normal in spike-heeled boots and the short leather skirt.

Her breasts were a perfect handful, her skin warmed to a rosy-toned honey by her passion and the glow from the fire. She was so mouthwateringly delicious, and he planned to lick every inch of her before the night was over.

He moved his arms and widened the space between her legs.

The light flush on her face deepened into a full blush. He wanted to see every bit of her, and he made damn sure she knew it.

"I'm waiting," he reminded her.

***

Echo swallowed her groan. She'd started this game, but he'd smoothly taken control without her even noticing. When he insisted she stand above him and undress, embarrassment gave way to searing lust. She was hot, aching for him to fill her and end this torment.

She unzipped her skirt and pulled it over her head, flinging it aside. The tiny, silky black panties she had

Georgia Lyn Hunter

on...well, she didn't see how she could remove *those* without stepping off him.

"Use the dagger."

"What?"

"Dagger. Cut them off."

Aethan might be thoroughly aroused, but his brain was still in gear. And she was plunging rapidly into full-blown lust. Breathing deeply, she reached into her boot for her dagger. She slowly brought out the obsidian, trailing it over her abdomen. Then she slipped the tip into the edge of her panties. His eyes followed her every move. With a deft twist, she slit the narrow strip over her right hip.

His gaze lingered on the dangling bit of silk then flickered up to meet hers.

"Now the other side." A hoarse demand.

Her hand trembling, she slashed through the left side with the obsidian tip. The tiny scrap of silk fell to his chest, leaving her exposed to his gaze.

Warmth flared across her face. She wasn't that adventurous after all, she realized, standing naked over Aethan's face where he could see her most intimate self. Dropping the dagger to the floor, she started to straddle him again when he tugged on her legs. She shrieked and went down fast. He grabbed her hips, guiding her core to his mouth.

The first lick of his tongue and she grabbed hold of the deep pile carpet as unbelievable sensations flooded her. She rocked her burning center against his mouth, heard him growl in satisfaction.

Her knees spread wider as he suckled her. One arm wrapped around her thigh, he ran a finger down her cleft and pushed it into her wet heat. She gasped at the invasion as he stroked her. He added another finger and worked it inside her.

Her thoughts scattered then gathered again, focusing on the sensations building between her legs. The lap of his tongue, the little nips on her clit then more licks. Her skin tightened, stretched, and she felt close to combustion. She tried to move away from the sensory overload, but his hand on her hips held her down, keeping her in place.

A blazing ripple started from deep within her womb. Her muscles clamped around the fingers he drove in and out of her. Her moans became louder. Her eyes squeezed shut as he worked her close to an orgasm. Her body grew too hot, too tight, craved his. If she didn't get him inside of her soon, she'd die. Then he dragged his tongue down her cleft and sucked on her clit. A mind-numbing explosion rocked her.

***

Aethan didn't give her time to recover. He reversed their positions and settled between her thighs, his cock sliding against her cleft. She arched up, rubbing her hot center against his erection. The pulse beating wildly in her neck drew him down. He sucked on it, and she moaned. Her eyes flashed open, glazed with passion as they met his.

"*Me'et'ah, me'morae,*" he whispered. He'd never seen passion this beautiful—so godsdamn tempting. The force of his need reverberated through his body and tightened his balls.

He positioned the head of his erection. In one swift move, he sheathed himself in her. Her silky warmth gripped him like a fist. His gaze turned hazy.

By the gods! *This* was heaven.

Her gasp, her nails biting into his arms, dragged him out of his sensual fog.

"Echo?" He started to pull out in alarm. What the hell was he thinking, taking her so fast?

"Don't you dare!"

Her threat was a husky caress and his cock pulsated violently with the urge to move. But he held on, letting her grow accustom to him.

Panting, she shifted a little then raised her hips. "Now, Aethan."

He drew back and pushed into her. She grabbed on to his arms, her fingers digging into his skin as he thrust in and out.

Then he shifted to his knees, reached for her and pulled her up, her heated body aligning against his. As his tongue penetrated her mouth, his cock impaled her again. Her arms circled his neck as he pulled out all the way before sinking his length back into her.

"Ride me, *me'morae*," he demanded huskily.

Her pert breasts in front of his face, he suckled on the hard nub, then let go when she started moving her hips. The friction of her feminine muscles dragging over his cock sent all rational thought out of his head as she rode him.

Gripping her hips with a fierce hold, he thrust into her as she came down on him. He was probably bruising her, but he couldn't slow down. Driven to possess, he had to make her his in the primordial way of his kind. He existed for this moment only.

She branded him with her very being, taking him out of his old skin and making him whole again, imprinting herself on his heart.

Mine. Only mine. The words drove through his head and settled in his soul. *My female. My mate. Mine.*

As he took her to the edge, her inner muscles tightened around his shaft, squeezing him with such force, it triggered a fiery response in him. With a harsh groan of surrender, he went over with her, spilling himself into her body.

A light flashed around them, brightening the room. He saw her eyes change before her lids closed. His roar of horror was lost in the blaze of energy. Her body jerked, convulsing beneath him.

Urias, no! He was killing her. He tried desperately to stop, to pull out of her, but he couldn't, held by an invisible force.

Oh, gods—don't take her from me!

Her body arched back. His erection was buried so deep inside her he swore he touched her soul. His mouth covered hers in desperation, breathing his love, his life into her. Her eyes flickered open, slumberous and passionate.

And they blazed with the power of his whitefire.

***

The force of their joining lit Echo from within, wrapping around her and holding Aethan in place. The beautiful sound of his surrender rang in her ears as their souls began to merge into a fiery iridescent ball of light. Deep within her, she could feel his power.

Her entire being glowed, sensitized, as if someone had plugged her in to a low-voltage outlet.

"Touch me, all over. Need you," she panted. "Don't—don't stop!"

He laid her back on the carpet and gave her what she wanted. He caressed her from hips to breasts. Lowered his head and suckled her nipple. She panted, trembled, and demanded more. Friction built, and her orgasm came hurtling, taking her over, and she fell once more.

But he was there to catch her.

Minutes later, the glow around them eased, as their soul bonding completed, before seeping back into them.

Echo clung to him, little jolts of pleasure still flowing through her body. She had no idea how much time had passed as she lay shuddering beneath him.

"I think you truly killed me," she said dreamily, glowing in contentment.

He lifted his head to look at her. And smiled. A smile of such unadulterated happiness, Echo knew she'd never forget it because it was so rare.

Now, she was finally joined to him, in body and soul.

Chapter 32

Aethan leaned over her, trailing a finger up her stomach to her breast, and circled her nipple. Her body trembled.

"Will it always be like that, making love with you?" She raised a hand and coiled his hair around her finger. "I mean, I expected to feel some of your powers because every time we were together I felt a jolt of it. But that?"

"It's the mating bond." He brushed her hair off her eyes. "I didn't expect it to be so..."

"Overwhelming? Amazing? Surreal?"

He laughed. "Yeah. All that." He ran a hand over the curve of her hips, stunned and grateful, she'd come out unscathed from his powers.

My powers were muted by the mating bond, he thought, as understanding dawned. "Gods, all this time wasted. My life, my mate." He removed her hand from his hair and pressed her fingers to his mouth. "Of course, you'd be compatible with me."

"You know, he said something similar, too."

"Who?"

Her brows furrowed into little creases. "That man in the navy robe. I'd always thought it a dream. That's why, when you told me where you're from, I got annoyed. I thought you were playing me—" She broke off and tried to squirm free.

"Where are you going?"

"I want to show you something. My backpack's in the other room."

He pressed her back onto the rug and kissed her. "Stay here. I'll get it."

Rolling to his feet, he flashed to the adjacent guestroom she'd been using. Locating her backpack on an armchair, he grabbed the thing and took form beside her again.

Aethan handed her the bag and sat next to her as she hunted through the pockets.

"When my foster brother hurt me—" Hearing his growl, she looked up and patted his thigh. "It's okay. All that's in the past. So let me say this, all right?"

It cost him to let it go, but for her, he did. He nodded.

"I'm telling you this so you'll understand, because all the pieces came together a little while ago. After Clyde hurt me that afternoon on my way back from school, I lay on the roadside, so sure I would die because of the pain. Then everything went dark..."

He stroked a hand over the curve of her spine, as much for his own comfort as hers.

"When I came to, I found myself in a ditch, close to my foster parents' home. How I got there, I have no idea, but I'd been healed. Until recently, I couldn't remember what happened." She set her backpack aside and turned to him, her beautiful, mismatched eyes serious. "But I do now—being in so much pain, I lost consciousness, until a healing warmth surrounded me. I awoke to find a man, the one I told you about, healing me. I was in a place that looked like a valley surrounded by high cliffs, with boulders scattered along the base. Everything there was beautiful. Magical. The thing is, the cliffs and the rocks were white—"

She broke off, grasped his hand, and put something hard and warm into his palm. "I loved being there in the valley surrounded by the tall white trees. It was so peaceful, I didn't want to leave. But he said my destiny had yet to unfold and I needed to go back home." She nodded at his hand. "He gave me the stones, said they would aid me in my time of need. When I awoke in that ditch, I had those stones in my hand but no memory of what happened... Aethan? You okay?"

"This man who healed you? Do you remember his name?" Aethan could barely get the words out. His throat felt like sandpaper.

"I'm not sure. I think it started with an A. Al... something."

"Allatus." He didn't have to look at the stones to know what they were. Already, he could feel the effects of them siphoning his powers. For over three thousand years he'd searched for something to help Ground him. Now Echo had given him what he'd once desperately needed—when he no longer did.

He opened his palm and stared at the two little pieces of Empyrea. One was a river-worn piece from the white boulder, and the other, an amber stone. Resin had settled over a white leaf from a Rean tree found only in that realm.

"What are they?" she asked.

"Empyrean Grounding Stones."

Her eyes widened at his words. "Are you sure?"

He nodded. "I can feel them drawing at my power," he said, dropping the stones on the carpet.

"Don't you want them?" she asked, concern flashing in her eyes.

"Not anymore. You are all I need. You Ground me completely."

A smile lit her face. "I'm glad." She touched his jaw with tender fingers and crawled into his lap. "I love you."

"You are my heart, my soul, Echo." He could barely contain the emotions rioting within him. "I love you so damn much."

Her eyes misted, and she leaned into him. He tightened his arms around her. Gods, he'd never expected to find his mate on this realm, and yet here she was in his arms, bonded to his soul for all eternity. It made his three thousand years of hell worth it.

***

Echo pulled back and stared at him. "What do you mean three thousand years of hell?"

"It's what life felt like until I met you." Then a stunned expression crossed his face. "You heard me?"

"What?"

"Echo, I didn't say that aloud."

"But—" She blinked. "I heard you. How is that possible?"

He smiled, looking pleased. "When we bonded, our souls joined and opened our telepathic pathways. Go on, open your mind and try it," he said. *Talk to me.*

"Okay." She relaxed as much as she could with that steely, naked wall of muscles surrounding her, his erection a tempting hardness pressing on her thigh. She'd far rather he made love to her, but— He shifted and bit her. "Ouch!" She glared at him, rubbing her sore nipple. "Why did you do that?"

You're supposed to speak to me and keep my mind off making love to you for now, Aethan said through their mind-link as he licked the tender nub, taking away the sting.

"Oh. You heard me." Heat streaked across her face. Then she tugged him to her as he continued his slow torment with his tongue. Her hands gripped his hair, keeping him in place. *So now, my love, what are you going to do about it?*

This. He set her aside, moved to his knees, and unzipped her boots. "Sometime soon, you're going to wear these for me again. The entire get-up." He pulled them off and tossed her footwear aside.

"I'll think about it."

He rose and carried her to the shower, but his gleaming gaze told her she would be wearing them again.

After their shower, Aethan carried her to bed and laid her down. As he rubbed the towel over her limp body, she gazed at the bank of windows. Darkness still shrouded the castle despite it being early morning. Her thoughts drifted to earlier that night—

"Kira!" She shot up. "Aethan, I left her behind at that club."

"No." He smoothed a reassuring hand over her damp hair. "She's here in the castle. I asked one of the others to bring her. I wouldn't leave someone you care about unprotected in that hellhole."

"Thank you." She sagged back against the pillows in relief. "Though, I can't imagine Kira going anywhere quietly."

"She's safe, and that's what matters," he said, sitting on the bed.

Her eyes tracked the droplets of water on his skin. They gleamed in the glow of the flickering fire. She picked up the discarded towel from the bed, the one he'd used on her, crawled behind him, and rubbed him dry.

"There. Now you won't catch a cold," she said, running her hand over his smooth, warm skin. Tossing the towel aside, she kissed his shoulder. "Let's go get some food. I'm hungry."

He glanced at her. Amusement flickered in his eyes. "All right. And just so you know, we don't—"

"Get sick, pick up any diseases. I know. Hedori told me." She moved to slide off the bed so she could get dressed. Thoughts of roast-beef sandwiches dripping with mayo made her stomach grumble.

"No." He stopped her. "Stay there. I'll go get us food."

She fell against the pillows and waited as Aethan disappeared into the dressing room. He came out a moment later wearing jeans, his feet bare, and the top button of his jeans left undone. God, the man was built for sex. Her mouth watered. She found herself getting damp again just gazing at that hard body, with its miles of rippling, golden skin.

Her gaze skated back to his face and she met his intense stare. Uttering a soft growl, he stalked out of the room.

***

Aethan headed downstairs, inhaling roughly. Finally, Echo belonged to him. And he still couldn't get enough of her. He'd just grab some food and get back to his mate.

Voices drifted to him as he neared the kitchen. The others must be back from patrol.

Aethan pushed open the kitchen door and all conversation died, as if a blast of wind had blown in and swept it away. He rubbed a hand on his chest—his bare chest. Okay, forgot the shirt. So he'd be the wind that snatched their vocal cords.

Assholes.

Ignoring them, he headed for the fridge and gathered up the makings for sandwiches.

"Er, sire. I have a tray prepared."

Thank the gods for Hedori. Somehow, the male always seemed to know just what he needed, even before he did. Now he could get out of here and back to his room. He set down his haul, but the stares coming from the dining area demanded attention.

He glared at them. "What?"

"Nope. Claiming his mate hasn't changed him at all. Still the same old grouch," Týr said, pushing aside his empty plate. He picked up his can of Red Bull and took a deep swallow.

Hell. Aethan couldn't ignore them any more than he could stop his smile.

"Now that shit's just plain creepy," Týr drawled, kicking back his chair to balance on two legs. "But I'm glad it worked out for you two."

Blaéz raised his squat whiskey glass in salute.

"Yeah, well..." Aethan raked a hand through his unbound hair. Words failed him. These males had stood by him when things with Echo fell apart.

"My lord? Shall I take the tray upstairs for my lady?"

"Yes, thank—*no!*" he snapped, startling Hedori. Shit, so not the way to start mated life by throwing his butler out of the house because the male walked in on his naked mate. "Er, that's okay, Hedori. I'll do that."

Laughter reached his ears. He'd forgotten Týr and Blaéz, who watched him with eyes like freakin' hawks.

"Bastards." But the word held no heat. He picked up the tray and headed back to his room.

* * *

At the sound of a knock on the bedroom door, Echo stirred awake. She opened her eyes to stare into smiling gray ones. "What time is it?"

Aethan leaned in to kiss her. "A little after seven."

"Hmm... There's someone at the door."

His busy fingers trailed a heated path down her belly. "Ignore them, maybe they'll go away."

The knock came again.

She grabbed his hand. "Aethan."

Growling, he rolled off the bed and headed for the door. Echo found the tee she was wearing earlier tangled in the covers and pulled it on.

Aethan returned moments later and grabbed his jeans off the floor. "Good, you're dressed. Michael wants to talk to you," he said, tugging on his pants.

"About what?" She got off the bed and smoothed her hand over the long t-shirt.

"He didn't say." Aethan went back and opened the bedroom door.

The Archangel strode inside, dressed in leathers

and a black crewneck tee. If she'd thought Aethan was intimidating and radiated menace when she first met him, Michael appeared ten times worse. But what did he want?

Oh, no. She was supposed to leave with him today.

"Eshana. Are you ready?"

"Ready for what?" Aethan's eyes narrowed. He pushed Echo behind him. Arms crossed over his bare chest, he stared at Michael, waiting for an answer.

Echo swallowed. If Michael said something before she could explain, Aethan would go Terminator on the Archangel. She moved to his side. "Michael? Can I have a word with Aethan, alone, please?"

Those fractured blue irises skimmed over her face, then he nodded and left the room, closing the door softly behind him.

Her stomach churning, she turned to Aethan.

"I'm waiting, Echo. What did Michael mean?"

Oh, hell. "You can't get angry—"

"You starting off like that is a sure way for me to do so."

Inhaling a deep breath, she said, "I met Michael out in the gardens yesterday morning. He told me about the Celestial Realm and that I'd be safe there."

Instantly, his gaze hardened. "So what? You asked Michael to take you there, away from me?"

"Aethan, please understand. I was out of options. I thought our relationship was over. Not being with you was tearing me apart. And as the Healer, I didn't have much choice. I couldn't live here unmated and unprotected—yes, Michael pointed out the dangers and gave me a choice to go back to you. Well, I couldn't live like that again." Her eyes pleaded with him, but not a muscle moved on his impassive face. "I made the only decision I could."

"What else? There must have been an incentive for you to agree. What was it?"

"Aethan, let it go. It's over now. Michael will understand that I changed my mind."

He simply stared at her with cold, gray eyes. She sighed. "He told me that if I went to the Celestial Realm, all my mortal memories would be gone."

"I see."

She winced at his flat tone. "Aethan—"

"Why did Michael not tell me any of this?"

"Because I asked him not to." She bit her lip when he walked away. He stopped by the windows and stared out into the night.

Please let him understand. She'd only wanted to spare them both pain.

***

Godsdammit! This was what Blaéz meant when he said to ask Echo about "tomorrow night." She'd planned to leave him. Forever. And he wouldn't have known.

He clenched his teeth, unable to even think about that. It was his own damn fault. He put her through this, forced her to make a choice, one she could live with. And with those demoniis after her, chances were one of them would have gotten to her, had she chosen to stay here.

Even *he* understood that it would be impossible for Echo to stay within the castle walls for the rest of her natural life. He hadn't left her with much of an option.

"Aethan, I'm sorry—"

"No, don't." He turned to her. "The fault's mine. If anyone should be apologizing, it's me. Just the thought that you wanted to forget me—"

"I didn't want to forget you." Her eyes misted. "But remembering what we had and having to live without you was destroying me. It was either forget and live to fulfill my destiny in the Celestial Realm, or die."

He hauled her to him. "Don't talk about dying. Gods, don't." His arms tightened around her.

Aethan, I need her answer.

At Michael's telepathic message, Aethan swallowed a curse. *You can come in.*

After a brief knock, Michael entered. His gaze skated over them to settle on Echo. "I guess that means you changed your mind?"

She didn't leave the shelter of Aethan's arms, just turned her head toward Michael. "I'm sorry for inconveniencing you."

"Do not be," Michael said. "It worked out and that is what's important. But, Eshana, you still need to be vigilant. This demonii won't give up."

Chapter 33

With Aethan closed in a meeting of the warriors, Echo headed for the kitchen and found Kira hovering around Hedori in the prep area. The aroma of something baking permeated the air. She sniffed appreciatively, but she needed coffee.

"Echo!" Kira dashed around the island, still wearing her sparkly, dark blue corset top and black leather pants. Her hazel eyes were troubled as she hugged Echo.

"I'm sorry about leaving you last night," Echo said, then she stared at Kira's hair, which was no longer brown but a brilliant shade of red.

"Don't be. You've been so unhappy the past few days. When Jon said your boyfriend showed up, I was hoping that meant you'd worked things out. You and Aethan are okay now?"

Happiness filled her when she thought of him. "Yeah, we're more than fine."

"Good." Kira pulled out a chair, sat down, and patted the seat next to her. "Now, I want all the deets."

Echo laughed and shook her head. Like she would sit there and talk about her sex life. "Let me get coffee, but I'm not telling you about *that*."

"Come on, I tell you everything," Kira protested, curving her body around the chair to watch Echo.

"Much to my dismay." Echo snorted and headed for the coffee pot. She poured a mugful of the hot, fragrant brew then took a sip.

"So, is it true? That thing about the size of a man's feet and his *you know what*?" Kira grinned wickedly, her dimples flashing.

Echo spurted out the coffee she'd just drunk. She set her mug down, grabbed a napkin off the table, and wiped her mouth and dripping hand. "You're evil! I'm still not talking."

Kira tugged her to the chair next to her.

Echo noticed then that Hedori had left the kitchen. But he'd set out a platter of vol-au-vents and a triple-layer carrot cake. Picking up a pastry, she bit into the flaky crust and tasted the chicken filling. The thing melted in her mouth.

"Argh. I knew you wouldn't spill. You never do."

"What happened to the brown hair?" Echo asked, changing the topic.

"I got bored. I had fun with Hedori, though. He showed me some really cool recipes."

Echo swallowed her groan and prayed Hedori hadn't let Kira cook anything. She'd hate to see immortal men cry when sampling her friend's offerings, though maybe not for long with Kira dressed in her dominatrix-style outfit.

"Who brought you to the castle?" Echo asked, finishing the rest of her pastry.

Kira looked up from eyeing the carrot cake. "That

stunning man with the short, dark hair. He drove me here. I think he said his name's Blaéz. But that's about all I could get out of him. Man's a tomb. Crap, Echo, when he looks at you with those pale-pale eyes, you feel the need to hide. It's like he can see into your soul or something."

Echo circled the rim of her mug with a finger. She didn't want to keep her friend in the dark any longer. "Ki, there's something I want to tell you."

"Okay," she said, her gaze back on the carrot cake. With a shrug, she caved and cut a slice.

"It's about Aethan and me..." By the time Echo finished telling Kira about everything that had happened over the last few weeks, her coffee had gone cold. Kira just stared at her wide-eyed, her cake forgotten.

Echo had left out the prophecy bit for now. Shocking her best friend into speechlessness wasn't her intention when she revealed the truth that Aethan was immortal and she was his destined-mate. Yeah, probably a good decision to leave the shockers of her ancestry for another time.

"Wow!" Kira blinked at her, then took the spoon from her coffee mug, scooped up a piece of cake from her plate, and ate it. "I can't believe what you just told me. The stuff about immortals and mates." She swallowed her cake and took another bite. Then, pointing her spoon at Echo, she said, "See, you should've listened to me. Didn't I tell you there was someone better out there for you than that loser, Philip?"

"Yes, you did." Echo smiled.

Kira licked her spoon. "This tastes super delish—" she broke off as the kitchen door opened and Týr sauntered into the kitchen, raking a hand through his pale hair.

He winked at Echo with his usual flirty smile. "Hey, gorgeous."

"Meeting's over?" Echo asked him.

"Yeah." His grin faded when he glanced at Kira. "I thought Blaéz took you back to the Oracle's."

"What?" she asked in horror. "And cut short my holiday in a fab place like this with the gorgeous Blaéz?"

He narrowed his eyes. Hell, if Echo didn't know Kira so well, she'd think her friend was serious. But Kira was leaving for the Village in a little while.

"You're wasting your time with him. And what is that thing with your hair?"

"You got something against cornrows now?" she asked. "And I'll waste my time exactly how I see fit."

Kira's belligerent attitude and feigned ignorance took Echo by surprise.

His jaw tight, Týr headed for the fridge. He grabbed a Red Bull and strode out of the kitchen.

Echo wheeled around to face Kira. "What did I miss? You know Týr?"

"I didn't realize arrogance had a name."

At Echo's astonished look, Kira snorted. "Last night, he ordered me—on my birthday, mind you—to get my butt moving if I didn't want to get into trouble. Made me want to punch him. All because I asked him who the hell they were and what they'd done to you. Then, that dark-haired one politely explained they were friends of Aethan's and you'd left with him. I only left the club because, well, I was worried about you."

"I'm sorry for ruining your birthday.

"Don't be, I'll have another one next year. So, are

Blaéz and Arrogance like Aethan?"

Echo blinked. *Arrogance?*

Kira sighed then, seeming to forget her question. "Echo, can I borrow some clothes? I can't stay like this. My boobs threaten to spill out with every breath I take." She glanced down at her corset-like top. "A t-shirt would do, because I can't let Hedori take me home looking like a slut. Gran would freak out."

"Come on. Clothes I can help you with."

***

"Bastards can never give me a break," Aethan snarled as his fist connected with the face of a demonii. The fucker had latched on to him like a blood-sucking parasite.

He'd gotten the call when Blaéz had come across a horde of them, trawling the backstreets on the Lower East Side, and found a portal in the alley close to Club Anarchy.

Týr's snort of laughter cut through the demoniis' guttural roars. "You're just pissed you had to leave your mate's bed this soon."

"'Cause I can't rely on you assholes to do a decent job—"

A fist landed in Aethan's midriff, and he cursed.

He'd had enough of this shit. He had no plans to go back to Echo with injuries that rendered him useless. Not when he planned to spend the latter part of the night and the next morning in bed with her.

Caught in a stranglehold, Aethan elbowed the bastard in the sternum, breaking his grip. A roundhouse kick had the demonii stumbling back. Streams of red shimmered in the asshole's hand.

"Fuck no, you don't!" Aethan summoned his sword and swung it, decapitating the demonii before he could attack with his annoying bolt.

"What the hell's wrong with the Celt?" Týr growled from behind him.

Aethan pivoted and found the demoniis circling Blaéz like damn coyotes, while two clung to him. And he just stood there, letting them get their punches in.

Týr drove into them like a bulldozer, slamming bodies out of the way. Dagan materialized in the melee, his sword swinging, as more of the fuckers spewed out of the portal.

Playtime was over. Aethan scanned the alley. Good thing the mortals had scurried out of the place. *Shield.*

The other warriors dematerialized. The next moment a white light, contained to just the decrepit alley, rolled out of Aethan like a wave, devouring demoniis and spewing out ash as it cleaned the area of evil filth.

It took him a moment to gather himself after expending so much of his power. He found the alley empty but for Blaéz and Týr, who reformed. Never one to linger, Dagan had already left.

About to take off for the castle, Aethan sensed another presence. He stared at the dark figure in the shadows. "As usual, you skulk about when there's a fight."

A'Damiel stepped forward. "Much more fun to watch you lot break a sweat. Besides, my ass isn't the one that's been sold into servitude."

Týr rushed him, like an exploding cannon, and slammed the male against the grimy walls. "You really want to shut the fuck up, right now."

Before Týr's fist could rearrange his face, A'Damiel flashed to the opposite side of the alley. "Entertaining as this is, we need to talk," he told Aethan. "Echo's in danger." That got the other warriors' attention, too. A'Damiel shoved back his hair, his expression grim. "The demonii Andras is on this realm. He's using a glamor to disguise himself as Lazaar, so he can go after Echo."

Aethan's blood turned cold. "What the hell are you talking about?"

A'Damiel pulled an old parchment from his coat pocket and tossed it at Aethan.

The aged paper crinkled as Aethan opened it and scanned the contents. "What is this?"

"It's a prophecy. Andras has gotten hold of an oracle and had the scroll translated. Now he wants Echo. Doesn't matter that it's too late and you've already bonded with her. He wants control of the realms and he's going to use her to get that. The shithead wants to prove himself to dear old Dad and reclaim his inheritance. His sire's the Sin of Greed."

"How do you know that's what it says?" Týr snapped.

"Unlike you *locos*, I can read. The humans have a great establishment called a school. You should try it."

Týr snarled. Blaéz grabbed him by the arm, keeping him back.

"What the hell are you?" Aethan asked staring hard at the male. Not many could understand the cryptic writings, but *he* could?

"Echo's guardian," A'Damiel said flatly.

Aethan narrowed his eyes. A'Damiel had been just as evasive centuries ago when Seth died. The detached asshole never got involved, except, apparently, where

Echo was concerned.

"This is no time to wonder at what has passed and the mysteries of all that is," A'Damiel said.

Aethan wanted to punch him just on principle.

"Keep Echo safe."

"You're just going to walk off and not see her?" Aethan demanded.

"She no longer needs me." A'Damiel leveled him an unreadable look as his form wavered, then he disappeared.

***

Andras paced the chambers deep in the labyrinth beneath the cemetery near the East River. He turned to the human in front of him. "You're sure about this?"

Neal nodded. "Yes. I heard her friend say she's staying on an island off Manhasset Bay."

"Excellent." Andras smiled, glad he hadn't taken over Neal's mind completely, as he usually did with his minions. He needed Neal to still mingle with other humans, to keep an eye on things for him. But once he got the girl, Andras would have to take control of this little idiot's mind to complete the last task. He was too focused on her. "You have done well."

Neal grinned at the compliment. "Once this is all over, I will *finally* have her."

Stupid mortal. Like he'd hand over the prophesied one to anyone. Andras hid his sneer and laughed. "Soon. Very, very soon. But here's what I want you to do..."

Chapter 34

The scroll of the prophecy lay on the desk, like a ticking bomb, dispelling any remaining doubts Echo had had about her destiny. To see tangible evidence of a prophecy relating to her wasn't a good feeling at all.

A hand on her churning stomach, she pivoted. The Guardians all stood crammed into Michael's small study, watching her. Any other time that would have made her feel like she couldn't breathe for the amount of space they took up, but the scroll took care of that—*and* learning the name of the demonii after her. Andras.

The warriors had come in just after midnight, and Aethan had called up this emergency meeting, summoning Michael, who'd been elsewhere. Dagan stayed at the back of the room, while Blaéz and Týr stood adjacent to her. Michael leaned against the desk and waited.

Aethan remained near the door. She could feel his gaze on her while she stood frozen near the fireplace.

"Echo?" he called out softly.

"I'm okay." She rubbed the healed scar on her

arm. "So Andras thinks he can take over the realms by capturing me?"

"Yes. We've already come across a shitload of them this evening, searching the streets for you," Týr explained. "Then we received that." He nodded to the scroll.

"Who gave it to you?" she asked.

Before Týr could answer, Aethan said, "My contact."

"I guess I can't go back to work?"

"Eshana, we are all concerned for your safety," Michael said. "But you are not our prisoner. Ultimately, the decision is yours. We will work around it."

Echo raked back her overlong bangs in frustration. She'd been stupid to think everything would get better once she'd soul-joined with Aethan.

"Echo." Aethan came over and took her hands in his. "About work—"

"It's okay. I've already handed in my notice. I was going to tell you. But my boss won't be happy with me leaving so suddenly."

"I'll take care of it."

***

Echo went looking for Aethan. Now that she was officially out of a job, she needed something to do. Aethan had altered Jimar's memories to make him believe she worked out her two-weeks' notice. It was the only way.

Maybe she could find out more about her job as the Healer. They should have something in that huge library downstairs. Hell, she had no idea if it would help her understand her job better, but it would give her something to do.

She took the stairs down to the basement level, walked past the elevator, and down the cool corridors until she reached the gym. Pushing open the door, the sound of something being brutally pounded filled her ears.

She stopped, forgetting what she wanted to talk to Aethan about as she watched him train.

He wore black Gi pants. His body, rippling with muscles, gleamed with sweat as he hammered at an enormous punching bag then leaped into the air and lashed out with a flying kick, landing agilely on the other side. He paused when he saw her, a smile tugging his mouth. "Bored already?"

She wrinkled her nose at his teasing. "Can I train with you?" That wasn't what she'd planned on asking, but it sounded like a good idea.

He grabbed the punching bag before it rammed him in the head. "I was going to wait, give you a day or two before I brought this up, but since you did—it's a good plan. We need to keep up your training now that you're no longer at the gym."

"I don't understand."

"You need to be strong, Echo. This will be nothing like what you know about fighting. You must strengthen not only your body but your mind, too. You need to be prepared for anything. What you experienced in Demon Alley was just a sliver of what can occur after a healing. After a day, your strength was renewed, but at other times it will take longer and your body needs to be strong." He picked up a towel from the floor and wiped his face, his expression serious. "You being mortal, I can't take chances with you. You're going to have to learn to fight with other weapons, too. So you're always prepared. A tear in any veil can be dangerous. You never know what lurks on the other side."

Like that would frighten her? Damon had taught her how to use a dagger. But fighting with swords was her dream. She smirked. "Bring it on."

Eyes narrowing, he tossed the towel down. "Always," he said, prowling closer, "be prepared for the unexpected." He lunged.

Startled, Echo didn't have a chance to evade when he grabbed her round the waist and brought her down. She gritted her teeth, anticipating a hard landing, except at the last minute he rolled, and she fell on top of him. Not that it was any softer than the darn floor.

Inhaling sharply, she scowled and pushed off him. "Again."

He took her through the steps in the way the warriors fought. Echo knew he was going easy on her. She didn't care for that but realized, being so much smaller, she needed to be cunning in her strategy. So, pretending he was a demonii, she came in fast, avoided his counterattack, and slid in low, her fist aimed for his crotch.

He froze. Then, in a move so quick it took her breath away, he seized her and dropped her on her back. Apparently, he hadn't cared for her surprise attack.

Winded, she laughed. "That was fun."

She stared at the ceiling. So she couldn't defeat him, but then she hadn't expected to. However, she'd learned a few things as she lay on the exercise mat. Her man was a bloody good fighter. Heck, she already knew that, but to work with him was exhilarating. He had a body so finely tuned, it was like a well-oiled fighting machine.

He crouched at her side, an eyebrow arching. "So that's your attack strategy?"

"Yup." She panted. "But it's usually my knee. And it works...every time."

He shook his head. "Want to go again?"

"In a moment. After I get my breath back."

Aethan held out a hand. She ignored it, continuing to gaze at the ceiling. When he straightened and moved away, she sprang agilely to her feet and tackled him, diving for his knees. He went down fast. Just as quick, he turned and made a grab for her. She fell on him, then straddled his chest, and grinned in victory.

"As long as I bring my opponent down, that's all that matters," she informed him in a breathless voice. "See, I don't always aim for the crotch."

Gray eyes locked on hers. The next minute, he tugged her head to his and captured her lips in a breathtaking kiss. His hands slid under her tank top to cup her breasts. He stilled, fingering the fabric of her bra. "You're wearing underwear?"

She rolled her eyes. "Of course."

He traced her nipple with a fingertip. "Take it off."

Her breath hitched. "No—"

With a shrug, he flipped her and had her bra off in seconds. Pinning her hands to the floor, he gazed down on her exposed chest.

She glowered at him. "That's not fair."

"So you don't want me doing this?" He lowered his head and sucked her nipple. A moan slipped out. Amusement lightened his eyes. "I guess that means you do." He rolled the bud in his mouth until it stiffened and bit down lightly.

She gasped, her body arching beneath him for more.

He smiled and sucked her again. "I could do this all day long—" Then he growled in displeasure. The sound reverberated against her sensitive nipple, causing her arousal to spike. He let go of her hands and yanked her top down. And just in time too, as the gym door opened and Blaéz entered.

Aethan rose to his feet and pulled her up before he crossed over to the warrior who waited at the entrance. Echo looked around for her bra. Finding it some distance from the mat, she squashed it into a small ball and headed for them.

She could read nothing off Blaéz's impassive stare as he spoke to Aethan. But she caught the tail end of Blaéz's words. "...not answering. She could be hurt."

"Who's hurt?" she asked, coming up beside Aethan.

He took her hand. "Blaéz had a vision. Lila's not answering her phone. We're heading there."

Fear spread through her. "I'm coming—no, you're not leaving me behind, Aethan," she warned before he could speak.

"Echo, Týr's already there. He would have called if it was bad."

"I don't care. I need to see for myself that she's okay," she said, her mood darkening with worry. "She's my family."

"We're dematerializing," he cautioned.

"Doesn't matter. I can put up with it."

***

Echo found Lila resting on the couch, looking frail.

Georgia Lyn Hunter

"Gran!" She rushed over to kneel near the older woman, searching for signs of injury. "What happened?"

A wry smile curved Lila's mouth. "Don't fret, child. I'm fine. The warrior, Týr, healed me, though I would've liked my battle bruises," she said, touching her forehead as if feeling for the lump. "But I don't want to upset Kira."

"Where is she?"

"I sent her on an errand. I'm glad she wasn't home, or she could have been hurt, too. A young man came to the door asking for directions, then attacked me instead."

Echo glanced around the lounge, but everything looked to be in its place.

"No. I don't think anything's stolen," Lila said.

Their recon of the surrounding area done, Aethan, Blaéz, and Týr came back into the room. Echo waited for their rundown.

"Everything's quiet," Týr reassured Lila. But his toffee-brown eyes blazed in fury. "No signs that a demon's been around—"

"Oh, no, he wasn't a demon, definitely human," Gran said. "I've never seen him before."

"What did he look like?" Týr asked.

"Fair-skinned. Red hair, cut very short. Average height."

Echo stiffened, a shiver darting down her spine. The only one she knew who remotely fit that description was that idiot, Neal. But even he wouldn't resort to assaulting old ladies. He was all threats and no action. All he wanted was to score with women.

"I need a favor, please," Gran said, drawing her attention back. "Don't tell Kira."

"You have our word," Týr reassured her.

Blaéz nodded, as did Aethan.

Echo sighed. She didn't like it, but she understood Gran's wish not to worry Kira. "All right. Let me make you some tea."

Gran shook her head and swung her feet to the floor. "No dear, you go on home. I'll be fine. If Kira sees you all here, she'll get worked up. I don't care to be treated as an invalid," she said with a wry smile.

Echo nodded. She knew far too well her friend could be an impossible nurse.

***

Aethan finished his shower and headed for the dressing room. It took everything in him not to check on Echo telepathically or call her cell as he dressed. So he rattled Týr instead, until the warrior snarled that he'd bring Echo back and Aethan could explain to her why she had to cut her stay short.

He understood Echo's need to visit Lila after her attack, but every time she was out of his sight, he felt like he couldn't breathe.

Groaning, he squeezed his eyes shut. She'd given up so much for him, her job, her entire life, and she'd lost that loser, her guardian, too. He had to ease up, which was the reason he didn't go with her in the first place, but it was damned hard to do.

He pulled out his cell and looked at the time. Still another hour to go. He refused to wait around any longer.

He dematerialized, took form by a grove of trees at the end of the narrow street, and headed for the Oracle's house. Týr had parked the Range Rover opposite the brownstone, but Aethan could sense him close by.

He hurried up the steps, willed the vines trailing over the trellised entrance out of his way, and knocked on the door. The moment it opened and he saw her, his heart settled into place once more.

She went up on her toes, grabbed a fistful of his shirt, and kissed him. "See? That wasn't so bad."

He caressed her jaw with the back of his knuckles. "Not from my point of view. Why didn't you call me?"

"I've only been gone for the afternoon. You worry too much, and that's why I asked Kira to spend a few days with us. There, better now?" she asked with a teasing look. Then she lowered her voice. "Since Gran's going to Seattle, which is good, Kira will be safer with us."

Thank the Heavens! At least Echo would be protected in the castle. But he knew better than to say *that* aloud.

***

"Echo, you have the candles, right?" Kira asked from the back of the Range Rover, as they left Greenwich Village.

"Uh-huh," Echo mumbled, trying to focus on what Kira said and not the erotic suggestions Aethan was making through their mind-link that had her cheeks heating up.

Candles—right. She rummaged through her backpack and found them. Check. "Aethan, can we make a detour to the cathedral?"

His expression tensed, the teasing light in his eyes flattened. "Echo, that place is out of bounds for now,

Absolute Surrender

405

you know that."

"Please? It will only take a few minutes." And it was a long time in coming, she realized. "It's taken me five years; I need to do this." Gran was right. She had to let Tamsyn go.

After a long moment, he nodded, even though he didn't look happy with the change in plans. He'd probably already sent out telepathic messages for the others to meet him at the cathedral. Aethan had told her they'd found a demonii's hidey-hole nearby, which they figured had to be Andras's.

Echo walked into the cathedral with Kira. Aethan followed. The fragrance of burning incense, candle wax, and wood polish scented the air. A tall, gleaming wooden crucifix stood to the left of the pulpit. The echoes of their footsteps were the only sounds in the silent place, and it added to the building's eeriness.

She inhaled a deep breath and tried to calm her unease, reminding herself that demoniis couldn't enter a place of worship. But if one of the suckers did, she'd just kill the fiend.

"Shan't be long," Kira told her and hurried off to the altar.

Echo turned and saw the hard set to Aethan's jaw. His gaze softened when he looked at her. He brushed the shallow dimple in her chin with his thumb. "Okay. It's safe enough. I'll wait outside."

Smiling, she watched him go and knew she'd never tire of looking at him. A tall, gorgeous man. A predator of the most dangerous kind. And he was all hers. Her mate.

The sooner she got all this out of the way, the sooner she could go home and drag him off for some alone time that he'd so graphically described earlier

Georgia Lyn Hunter

through their mind-link.

Echo turned back to the altar with the multitude of burning candles. The flames brightened the dim interior. A little unnerved, she decided to wait until Kira finished then she'd find out the ritual to lighting a candle. She wanted to do it right, so Tamsyn would have peace in her afterlife.

She sat down on a wooden pew and glanced around, her attention drawn to the elegant stained-glass window. She got up for a closer look, craning her neck to study the exquisite craftsmanship. The images made in glass depicted biblical scenes, and while they were beautiful, they couldn't compare to the ones at the castle. She preferred the warrior knights, angels, and ladies of the stained-glass windows at home.

Footsteps sounded. Kira nudged her in the back.

"That was quick," Echo said, turning. "Can you show me how—"

A hand clapped over her mouth. Shocked, Echo stared into bright green eyes glowing in triumph. "Told you I'd get you."

Pain exploded in her head, and all went dark.

Chapter 35

Aethan surveyed the back of the cathedral where the stone angel stood. With no hint of any demoniis around, his tattoo remained silent. He checked in with Blaéz, who was patrolling the cemetery. Nothing. He headed for Týr, and found him leaning against the wall near the entrance to the cathedral.

Týr pulled a pack of M&M's from his leather coat and dropped the sweets in his palm. "They're still inside," he said, frowning at the handful of brown ones left. Then, with a shrug, he tossed the lot into his mouth, shoving the empty wrapper back into his pocket.

"What exactly are they doing again?" Aethan asked, scanning the area around them.

"It's a human custom, to light candles for a departed loved one."

Rain started to fall, and a cold breeze blew in from the East River. The scent of the sea washed away the day's smog and exhaust fumes. Gulls flew overhead, squawking furiously.

"Ever been in one of them before?" Týr asked, ignoring, for once, the few females there who eyed them shamelessly as they sashayed into the cathedral.

"What? A cathedral? Other than the quick glimpse I just got now, no." Aethan paced along the top step in the misty rain. Stopping, he stared at the empty doorway. Edginess tightened like a noose around him.

Týr straightened from the wall and joined him. "Something doesn't feel right."

"I agree. I'm getting them now." He strode to the entrance just as Kira ran out.

"Echo," she panted. "Is she with you?"

Aethan flashed into the cathedral and scanned the interior, ignoring the females' gasp of surprise at his sudden appearance.

Echo, where are you?

When she didn't respond to his telepathic link, panic began to take hold. He couldn't sense any demoniis, so she had to be around somewhere.

Dammit, Echo, answer me!

He came back out to hear Kira snapping at Týr, "She was sitting in a pew while I was at the altar. When I looked for her, she'd disappeared. I thought she'd be with you. How is this my fault?"

A tick jumped in Týr's jaw. "She's your friend. You shouldn't have come here, knowing there's a damn demonii after her."

"You think I don't know that?" Her hands balled into fists. "You think I want some evil bastard getting hold of her? We only came to pay our respects to Tamsyn. We could do nothing less for a friend who gave her life to protect Echo!"

"Kira?" Aethan stepped between them, effectively stopping her furious outburst. "Tell me exactly what happened."

She inhaled deeply. "After you left us, Echo waited for me. She doesn't care for religious things, never has. She only comes to church—"

"Would you just answer the damn question?" Týr growled.

"I will, if you stop jumping down my throat every five seconds!" she hissed at him. She turned back to Aethan. "She sat down in the third pew... Wait, wait, she got up to look at the stained-glass windows, but when I looked again, she wasn't there. I thought she came back to you."

Fear seized Aethan. "She didn't come out this way."

He scanned the interior of the building and the surrounding areas again. Still nothing. He tried their telepathic link once more, but when only silence answered him, the vise on his gut tightened.

"I can't sense anything either," Týr said. "What about her obsidian? The dagger should summon you if she's in danger, right?"

Aethan shook his head. "It should, but the fact that it's not isn't a good sign. Can only mean one thing, we're not dealing with the supernatural here."

Blaéz, did you see Echo? he mind-linked with the warrior.

No. What happened?

Panic rolled through him. *She disappeared from inside the cathedral. What about the crypt?*

No activity here, Blaéz responded. *We'll find her.*

Aethan inhaled a ragged breath and found anxious hazel eyes pinned on him. "Týr, take Kira home—"

"No." Kira's hands shot out, stopping them. "I'm not leaving until we find her—"

Georgia Lyn Hunter

Aethan... Echo's pained voice was faint in his mind.

Echo, where are you?

Neal—cathedral...

Echo? Echo, talk to me!

Nothing. Just silence.

"Who's Neal?" he ground out.

Kira looked at him in confusion. "From the bar. The guy you tried to impale with whiskey bottles. Why?"

His vision turned hazy as anger spread through him like wildfire.

"Aethan?" Týr stepped in front of Kira, his hands on Aethan's shoulders. "Come on, man, breathe. We'll find her."

Aethan shook him off. "He has her! The bastard has her."

Kira's hazel eyes widened in alarm. "Oh, no. Aethan, he's bad news. He's still pissed at Echo for turning him down."

A chilling rage took hold of him. The fucker dared to touch his mate? For that, he would pay with his life.

Blaéz rounded the corner of the cathedral, his lean face set in its usual impassive lines. Dagan strode up the stairs to join them.

"Anything?" he asked, rubbing a hand down his unshaven jaw.

"A human has her," Týr told them.

Fury raged through Aethan, and he struggled for control. Rampaging the city wasn't going to help get Echo back. Jaw set, he said, "For him to disappear without us being aware of it, he must be traveling through the tunnels beneath the cathedral."

"Found something the other day," Dagan said.

"The crypt has a labyrinth of tunnels leading back to the understructure of the church. I explored some, but it branches out in several places, goes into the city and beyond."

Fuck! The bastard could just disappear with Echo. Aethan dematerialized to the crypt.

As he took form, he willed the tomb door open. Seconds later, a squeaking sound filled the quiet graveyard. He stormed into the cold, musty place, as Týr materialized behind him with a moaning Kira.

She shoved away from him. "What the hell did you do to me?"

Aethan approached the broken entrance and stepped inside the narrow, chilly passage. Then he moved with preternatural speed through the dark tunnel. Sensing a shift in the psychic planes, he pulled up short.

The strong stench of sulfur was a punch in his face. But beneath it, he picked up on a fading scent of his mate. *Shit.* The human was only a minion, used by the bastard demonii to get a hold of Echo.

By now, he'd have taken her to Hell.

Fury turned to ice-cold rage.

"I'll do this alone," he told Dagan and Týr, who'd followed him. Blaéz had stayed back with Kira. He couldn't risk any of them accompanying him to the Dark Realm. With their violent pasts of being held prisoner in Tartarus, the former gods would be a liability. And Echo was all that mattered right then.

But there was one other who probably knew the way in this cesspool. He pulled out his cell phone. Dammit. No service. He shot a mind-link message to Blaéz. Kira would do the rest.

Aethan hadn't opened a portal since he was

banished to this realm. But the old memories came back pixel-clear. He drew on his powers, picturing the shifting weaves of the psychic veils and a doorway into the Dark Realm to the level where Hell resided.

A moment later, a dark shimmering portal opened. His tattoo pulsed in agitation. Ignoring the sword's frantic bid for a summoning, Aethan stepped through the portal and into the suffocating stench of sulfur. His breathing shallow, he turned to find Dagan beside him. Sword in hand and jaw tight, his yellow eyes burned bright in the shadowy caverns.

"Echo is all that matters," Aethan warned him.

As usual, the Sumerian said nothing.

A'Damiel took form in front of them moments later and snarled, "I cannot believe you lost her. I should have killed that bastard, Neal, when he first crossed her path!"

Dagan's gaze narrowed. "You're the one who let Seth die."

"If you find comfort in that thought, so be it."

Aethan growled. He didn't have time for their face-off over a warrior who died centuries ago. He headed down the gloomy passages, his mind-link opened to Echo's. Despite the heavy silence from her, he took comfort in feeling her presence in his soul.

A'Damiel kept pace beside him. "This is not the place Andras is bound to. He created an alternate lair in the outer caverns, close to the demonii level," he told them. "So he can call on his demonii minions."

Soon enough, they arrived at a cave reeking of decaying flesh and heavy with the coppery odor of blood. Bits of moist entrails clung to rough walls gleaming with wet gunk. The screams of never-ending torture surrounded them.

"Dematerialize," A'Damiel snapped out. "It's better they don't see you in here."

Aethan let his molecules disperse, as did Dagan. As soon as they became one with the sulfuric air, a lizard-like demon appeared. Its scales oozing with black slime, the thing slithered toward A'Damiel. Its slitted red eyes glowed in the dark. "*Ssssire,*" it hissed. "Sssso good to ssssee you—"

"Stay out of my way, dung-heap." With a flick of his fingers, A'Damiel sent the demon-lizard reeling into the dark recesses of the cave, the scrape of its scales ringing in the burrows. "Stay away from those things. They'd crawl up anyone's arse to get back into Hell."

They traveled through more dank tunnels and bypassed several caves lit with flames erupting from the crevices in the rock face. The sounds of unbearable torture being carried out on the damned battered at them and thickened the air with suffering.

"What the fuck is this place?" Aethan asked. The increasingly rancid air made his stomach churn.

"The Lower Levels," A'Damiel said. "Between Hell and Tartarus in the outer strata. One might call it 'no man's land.'"

What felt like hours later, Damon paused at a dimly lit recess. Jagged rocks made up the entranceway. "This is Andras's new lair. I need to take care of Lazaar first and break the spell. Give me ten minutes. If you kill Andras while he wears his brother's glamor, Lazaar dies and Andras escapes," A'Damiel warned before dematerializing.

Aethan took form among the bile-inducing smells and scanned the humid place. Ten minutes was too fucking long. He needed to find Echo now. Then he stilled. Catching a whiff of sun-ripened berries in this hellhole of depravity, he tore through the underground tunnels with only one thought on his mind; Get Echo out and flatten this godforsaken place.

Aethan followed the scent to a door camouflaged to resemble the surrounding rocky wall. With his mind, he willed the heavy rock face apart. It slid open silently to reveal another dark chamber. The odor of pain, of death, stole his breath. Aethan let his sword shimmer into his hand.

The lifeless bodies of human females lay haphazardly in various corners, their clothes ripped, necks torn out. Some were naked, violently used...

Gods. Sick to his stomach, Aethan continued down the tunnel.

Chapter 36

Echo slowly regained consciousness. Her head ached. Sulfur burned her nostrils as she struggled to breathe. She found herself lying like a sacrificial lamb on some kind of stone slab in a dark cave. Amber fire, burning behind the cracks in the rock walls lit the place with a creepy glow.

She tried to sit up, but her body felt sluggish. And her mouth tasted vile. Nausea rose up and she vomited over the side of the stone slab.

"You're finally awake?" Neal grabbed her face. Pinching her nose, he forced some sort of potion down her throat.

Echo choked and shoved at him. She spat the revolting sludge on him. His face twisted in fury, and he slapped her. Pain spread through her jaw and into her throbbing skull.

"You thought you were too good for me," he snarled. "I'm going to kill that blue-haired bastard of yours, then I will take you."

"Enough." With a flick of his hand, Andras sent

Neal scurrying off. The demonii strolled to her, his eerie red eyes skimming over her prone body.

He reached out and ran his fingers over her stomach to her breasts. She batted his hand away, but her blow lacked strength. He laughed then trailed a finger down between her legs. Echo kicked at him, fear constricting her chest. She reached for the obsidian dagger tucked in her boot, glad now she'd hidden the blade in her footwear.

But Andras snatched her weapon and smiled. Grasping her flaying arm as she tried to grab it, he shoved the blade into his pocket.

"Dear girl, you're going to be mine. Yes, you've joined with the warrior, but you see, once *I* claim you, your mating bond will be broken—Neal, you fool," he snarled. His eyes flamed red. "Be careful with that."

Neal stood near the wall, watching her with an avaricious look, edged with hatred. In his hands was some kind of gun, his finger nervously playing with the trigger.

"It's my little surprise for the warrior," Andras said, turning back to her. "A lovely spelled bullet made especially for him."

"No!" Echo cried. Twisting, she broke free of the clamp Andras had on her arm. She lashed out and nailed Andras across the face. A snarl filled the cave, a fist crashed into her temple, and darkness closed around her.

***

Damon stepped out of Andras's chambers and found Belphegore leaning against the rough wall of the passageway, studying the glowing crevice that spurted out flames on the opposite side of the corridor.

Bel turned, and a smirk rode his face. "Another visit? I'm honored. Or does the delectable ward of yours need guarding again?"

Damon narrowed his eyes at the demon he'd left guarding Andras's chambers. "I need to find Lazaar now," he snapped. "Echo's life depends on it."

Instantly, Bel lost his banter and straightened. "What happened?'

"Andras tied himself to his brother," Damon growled. "Makes killing the bastard impossible as long as he wears Lazaar's glamor."

He dematerialized, heading deep into the Lower Strata of the Dark Realm. Bel followed him. The immense heat was so thick, Damon thought he would need an axe to cleave a path through it. Nostrils flaring, he closed his eyes and scanned psychically for Lazaar. In a place filled with hissing flames and scaly demons slithering about, he found one still figure.

"He's close." Ignoring the broken cries coming from behind the walls, he headed into a narrow passage. The searing heat and shooting flames filling the tunnel would have incinerated him, had he not been immune to it.

Bel shot up beside him, scowling as steam rose from his body. "I hate this place," he muttered. "I'm a mist demon, not fire. The things I do for a pretty face— Echo's—not yours."

Damon ignored him and stopped at the dead end of the tunnel. Two seven-foot-tall demoniis in their lizard-like forms snarled.

"Take care of them," he ordered Bel.

The demoniis attacked.

"Oh, shit!" Bel vanished. Seconds later, a heavy

fog surrounded the demoniis.

Damon left Bel to his games and scanned the area again, finding the entrance he wanted. With his mind, he willed the walls to open. Creaking loudly, the granite rock face to his left shuddered apart.

Lazaar lay in a tangle of limbs on the ground in an obscure, dugout cavern. As he set to work, Damon prayed to the Heavens—fuck that, he prayed to no one—he just hoped he had enough time to break the spell.

***

When Echo came to, she was still lying on the stone slab. She squinted, trying to focus but everything remained hazy and dark.

Torches burned in the distance now and added an eerie glow to the huge space. The serrated rock face gleamed with what she hoped was water. The thick stench of sulfur made breathing hard. A cough racked her lungs.

She turned her head to the side. Neal watched her with a zeal that didn't bode well for her. Yeah, she'd have to hurt the snake, make him wish he'd never crossed her path for threatening to kill Aethan. She'd slice the traitor up into pieces and toss his useless carcass to the hellhounds.

She rolled to her side to sit up. Only she fell off the slab and landed on her ass. Echo bit down on her lip as pain rushed up her spine. The cavern spun, or was it her head? Scooting on her bottom, she backed up until she hit the stone block behind her.

Hastily, she took stock of her condition and found she was able to move all her limbs, which was good.

The grogginess had faded a bit, but her jaw ached from when that bastard Neal had slapped her. But her head pounded like spikes were being drilled into it, and she recalled Andras planting a fist to her temple. She fumbled in her boot for her dagger. Empty.

Please, please work. She willed her dagger back—and breathed a sigh of relief when she felt the reassuring carved hilt moments later in her footwear.

Andras flashed in. Echo pulled back her hand as he sauntered over to her. "You're up again. Good. It's time, precious. Bring her."

Terror raced through her. *No—no!*

Neal grabbed her by the arm, hauling her to her feet.

The barricaded entrance exploded, showering the cavern with rubble. The stone ground beneath her feet vibrated violently. She stumbled and braced herself against the slab. Dust flew in the air as Aethan and Dagan burst inside.

His expression cold and lethal, Aethan's gaze zeroed in on her. Relief crossed his face.

Hold on, me'morae. *I'll get you out.*

"Keep her away from him," Andras ordered Neal. "And shoot him."

Neal seized her arm and held the gun with his other hand, aiming the weapon at Aethan.

No! Echo clawed at Neal's hand, unable to break free, her strength still feeble. It had to be the crap Neal pushed down her throat that had weakened her.

Demoniis rushed in from the shadows, filling the cavern. The horde attacked. A white light lassoed out of Aethan's sword, filled with his power, decapitating several demoniis at once as he worked his way to her. More came at his back, crawling like ants over him. A

Georgia Lyn Hunter

white flare of his powers seeped out of his body to incinerate the fiends on him. Their bodies, turning to ash, rained to the ground.

Dagan dropped demonii bodies as he waded through them with his sword, his long hair flying around him like another weapon.

Echo let her body go lax. No way would she let a vermin like Neal hurt Aethan. A demonii crashed into them. Neal's grip loosened. She broke away. Too close to plant a good fist in his belly, she gathered whatever strength she had and kneed the snake in the balls, dropping him to his knees. His howl became lost in the fracas of guttural grunts filling the cavern. She slid her hand into her boot and grasped the hilt of her dagger.

Echo, get out of here! Aethan yelled through their telepathic link.

A brutal hand grabbed her arm, almost crushing her bones. The odor of coppery vanilla taunted her nostrils. She didn't think, just reacted. She turned and plunged her dagger into the bastard's sternum. Andras reeled back in surprise, staring in disbelief at the obsidian blade in his chest, just as his appearance transformed. An almost skeletal form of the demon she'd seen five years ago in the alley shape. The brown dreads gave way to hacked-off blond hair. He staggered to the other end of the cavern. His form shimmered, but the glowing obsidian in his chest kept him from flashing out.

But dammit, she'd missed his heart. Echo shook her groggy head just as a hand hauled her against a rock-hard chest. Breathing hard, she took in the scent of rainstorms. Aethan.

Through their mind-link, he said, *Go with Dagan. He'll get you out of this place.* Aethan handed her over to the warrior and then decapitated his way to Andras.

Dagan grabbed her wrist, causing Echo to stumble as he hauled her to the cavern entrance. He swung his sword with one hand, clearing a path as he lopped off heads. One landed by her feet. Echo jerked back.

A flash of white light filled the dark cave. She looked over her shoulder, and her heart seized.

Aethan's fist punched through bone and flesh, straight into Andras's chest. White light flowed down his arm and into Andras, incinerating the demonii's body.

Echo's jaw fell open.

The moment Andras's body disintegrated into dust, the remaining demoniis scattered, leaving the cavern empty. Dagan let her go. She looked around, unable to believe it was truly over.

Andras was dead.

"Don't you listen?" Aethan growled as he came toward her, a scowl on his handsome face.

She smiled, not caring he was annoyed. All she wanted was to feel his arms around her—for him just to hold her.

A metallic click resonated in the silent cavern. Echo turned. Neal rose from behind a rock, where he hid in the shadows, the gun in his hands aimed at Aethan.

"*No—*" Her scream caught in her throat. She darted toward Aethan, who leaped for her.

A loud explosion filled the chamber.

Chapter 37

Kira paced the dusty concrete floor, stopping to pick off the ash-colored, spidery threads clinging to her clothes and hair. She turned to the two men standing at the other end of the crypt.

"Why haven't they come back yet?" she asked again. Not like she expected *him* to answer. He was as silent as this horrible place.

Týr barely spared her a look, just stared at the steps leading up to the outside entrance. Almost as if he wished he was out there instead. She certainly rubbed him the wrong way but he made her feel like a frivolous airhead every time he looked at her. Jerk!

Well, she didn't care. He could go jump into the Hudson. Better yet, dive off Niagara Falls.

At his sharp glance, she pivoted away from him, tugging at her loose braid. All that mattered was finding Echo. Another turn, she stomped back to them. Týr lowered to the stone ledge of the monument.

"You're sitting on someone—a *dead* someone," she pointed out. "Have a little respect."

Toffee-brown eyes flared in irritation. "Would you keep quiet for one damn second? I can't hear a damn thing."

"Of course you can't. We're underground. Everything's damn quiet." Scowling, she continued her walk-a-thon across the corrugated stone floor.

All she could think about was Echo. What if the demonii—no, no! She wasn't going to scare herself with crappy thoughts. Tugging at her hair, she stopped in front of Blaéz. "Please, tell me what's happening. Tell me something," she begged.

"He'll get her out." His gaze traveled over her face then settled on her hair. "Your hair is blue."

"What?" Oh. She inhaled deeply, forced her mind to relax, and changed it back to red. "What about the demonii?"

Blaéz shrugged.

Dammit. Kira marched back to the hole in the wall and peered into the gloomy tunnel. But the dark, shimmering portal several feet ahead had her rooted to the spot. The acrid scent of sulfur drifted to her. She so badly wanted to jump through and go find her friend but it meant going into Hell.

A blast reverberated from deep inside the portal, distorting it. The air shimmered. Dread iced her blood.

"Stay here," Týr barked, appearing at her side.

"No, I'm coming, too!"

Without a word, he grabbed her arm, and they jumped through the gateway into Hell.

***

"No!" Aethan's terrified roar resonated through the cavern, his heart shuddering in pain. He grabbed Echo as she staggered into his arms, a red stain spreading over the chest of her light blue sweater. "What did you do?"

"The b-bullet," she struggled to answer, "made to k-kill you. Couldn't let him..."

Aethan laid her on the ground and tore open her sweater. Blood gushed out of the hole in her chest saturating her bra. Frantically, he clamped a hand on the streaming wound and tried to stem the flow. Scanning her injury, he found where the bullet had pierced her lung. It rapidly filled with blood. Her heart stuttered as it struggled to beat.

"Damn you, Echo. Stay with me."

The blue healing light from him traveled through her body and coalesced at the puncture in her lung, but still it continued to bleed.

She coughed. Blood trickled down the side of her mouth. "I'm so c-cold," she whispered. Her body jerked, going into shock. Her eyes glazed over as the glow in them dimmed.

Dammit, Michael, he shot through their telepathic link. *Where the fuck are you?*

No answer.

"Hang on. You have to hang on." Aethan shrugged off his coat and covered her. "You are not leaving me. You hear me?"

So bossy, she said through their weakening mind-link. *Love you...always.*

The anguish in him grew. "Gods, *Echo*!" he cried, as the vibrant light in his soul that was all her started to fade. Her eyelids closed.

Michael appeared in a shower of silver sparks. He knelt beside Echo and took over the healing. A pure white light radiated from him and entered her.

Echo lay motionless as he worked. The seconds turned to minutes. Then Michael dropped his hands. A sheen of perspiration covered his tan face.

Aethan stared in disbelief at Michael's pained expression, his rage growing. Fuck him, if he gave up so easily. He sent his psychic energy back into her body, but her heart lay quiet.

"*No!*" His pained cry thundered through the grotto, sending rocks crashing to the ground.

Aethan wrapped her heart with his energy, his hand over her left breast. Using all the power in him, he shocked her. Her body convulsed off the floor then lay still.

He tried again.

And again.

A female screamed, calling Echo's name.

Someone touched his shoulder and muttered meaningless shit to him.

He shrugged him off. Violence tore through him, his mind fracturing. The cave glowed brightly, his powers ricocheting against the walls. Rocks broke off and rained around them. Nothing registered but the pain ravaging him, like being cleaved in two while his guts were ripped out.

Through a haze of tears, he swept Echo's body into his arms.

"Dammit—what the hell are you doing?" Týr bellowed, grabbing his arm.

Aethan shoved him aside. "If she has to die, then I'll die with her!" The next minute, a blinding flash lit the cave, and he disappeared with his mate.

Chapter 38

Kira broke free of the horror that held her in its grip.

No—no! Her friend couldn't be dead—

Her gaze fixed on a smirking Neal, she lunged for him, but strong hands held her back.

"Will you stop fighting me?" Týr snarled in her ear.

"He killed her! He killed my best friend," Kira cried, inhaling a choppy breath.

Neal watched them with a grin on his face, despite Dagan twisting his arms behind him. "I didn't want her to die, but still she got what she deserved. Bitch thought she was too good for me," he sneered. Then a sly look crossed his features. "By the way, how's your grandma? Did the bump I give her heal yet?"

At the thought of him hurting Gran, too, Kira's screamed, her rage filling the cavern. She tore free of Týr, grabbing the dagger off his belt. Like a whirlwind, she lunged for Neal. And plunged the obsidian into his belly. "Rot in Hell, you bastard!"

Neal stumbled back as Dagan released him. He

glanced down at the dagger in his gut.

"*No*—" a shocked cry left him. Pulling out the blade, he clutched his bleeding stomach and staggered toward her. "I'll kill you."

"Touch her," Týr snapped, shoving Kira out of harm's way, "and I'll make you wish for death."

Dagan grabbed Neal's arms again. "Stupid human."

"What do you want done with him?" Týr asked Kira, removing his obsidian from Neal. He wiped it on his tee and slid it back into the sheath on his belt.

"He wants to play with demoniis? Then leave him here to rot."

***

Aethan took form at the foot of the Catskill Mountains. A dark, velvety sky surrounded them. He sat on a rock, Echo cradled in his arms, his coat covering her. He wanted to hold her for one last time before he joined her. He pressed his lips to hers. But at the feel of her cool, unresponsive mouth, his tears fell faster.

"We never did have a chance, did we, *me'morae*? I can't feel you anymore. It's empty inside me. I'd give my life to look into your eyes again, but that's not going to happen. I'm never going to see your smile...see you."

Brushing her hair off her face, he stared absently at his glowing hands. He just wanted a life with her. But the time he'd had with her came down to a heartbeat in his life span—

Michael appeared opposite him. "Don't do it."

Aethan ignored him as the glow in him brightened. "I lived for three millennia in darkness and pain. Then I found Echo. My peace. My happiness. I refuse to live without her. Thank the Heavens, Michael, you never have to suffer the agony of having the one you love taken from you. Now, if you don't mind, I'd like these last moments alone with my mate—"

"Listen." Michael's eyes swirled with power so intense, Aethan stopped. "Listen," he said softly again. Then the Archangel shimmered and vanished.

Listen to what? All he cared to hear was the sound of Echo's laughter, her voice. He brushed his hand over her hair, then brought her cold fingers to his lips, and stiffened.

His eyes narrowed, his hearing honing in... A faint sound tugged at him. He looked at Echo lying so still in his arms as hope fluttered back in his chest again.

Urias, please.

***

Echo awoke to unbelievable serenity embracing her. She had to be dreaming. She breathed in slowly, relieved to find the severe pain in her chest had disappeared, just intense warmth remained. This must be what peace felt like. Soft and tender, like a hug, it wrapped around her.

She tried to swallow, but her tongue stuck to the roof of her mouth. Water. She needed water. Pushing off the bed, she wobbled as her legs gave way, and she abruptly sat again. A sense of déjà vu flooded her.

She glanced around, confused. Where was she? An enormous window dominated one wall, framing a picturesque view of several trees shrouded in pale yellow blossoms.

The rather spartan room she'd slept in contained just a bed, flanked by a bedside table, on which stood a drinking glass and a single candle.

The rays of warm sunlight poured over her from the window, making the walls in the room glimmer, as if millions of tiny little stars were embedded in them.

She smoothed the material of the white t-shirt that hung down to her thighs but stopped when she saw her hands. She was transparent. She could see right through her body.

Her heart jolted. *What the hell—*

Wait, if she could sit on a bed, she shouldn't resemble an apparition, right? Jeez. She needed a pin. Surely, that would wake her from this dream—or nightmare.

She snatched the candleholder from the bedside table. Next to it was a tall glass with pale green liquid inside it. She eyed it suspiciously. *Definitely, not drinking that.*

Pulling the candle off the stand revealed the tiny stabilizing spike. She stabbed her finger with it.

"Oww!" *Crap! That hurt.* She stuck her finger in her mouth. So why did she resemble a specter if she could still feel pain? Where the heck was she?

"Ah, so you're up?" an amused voice said.

Her head snapped up. She barely noticed the loose black pants or the tunic the man wore. The glow surrounding him was so intense, she turned away to give her eyes a chance to recover. But the image of him remained.

Tall, so tall. Incredibly stunning. As if a master artist had finely tuned the sculptured lines of his striking face. Black hair fell in a shimmer down his back, merging with black wings that looked as if their tips were dipped in fallen snow.

His silver-specked amethyst eyes blazed so brightly, they made the white walls around her look dull. "Go ahead, have your drink. It will nourish and heal you, then we can talk."

"Where am I?"

"You should be resting until the healing is complete."

"I'm fine, nothing hurts." She turned to him and squinted again. "Hey, can you dial yourself down? You're damaging my retinas."

Instantly, the glow dimmed, but his amusement rippled in her like a warm caress. Echo put mental brakes on that sensation. For some reason, it didn't feel right being turned on by this angel.

I see why he fights for you.

She caught his passing thought and stared at him. "What? Who fights for me?" she demanded.

He studied her for a long, silent moment, then said, "My name is Marmaroth."

She sighed. Why were men always so evasive? "Look, Roth, this is all very nice." She waved her hand around the serene room. "But I want to go…home."

"Ah. We are back to that, are we?" A glimmer of a smile touched his eyes, but his expression remained smooth and calm.

"Is there something funny about me wanting to go home?"

"No. I simply find the way mortals adhere to nicknames rather interesting."

She rolled her eyes. "What, no one's called you 'Roth' before?"

"Just one…he's lived too long in the mortal world."

Echo shook her head. "Wait, what do you mean 'back to that'?"

"As badly hurt as you were by the spelled bullet in you, you created quite a stir, insisting on going home to—" He stopped. Something dangerous flickered in his cool gaze. She was suddenly glad *that* wasn't directed at her. "You weren't meant to die. You were supposed to ascend to the Celestial Realm at the appropriate time. But the Fates messed up badly."

"I don't believe in fate." The words felt familiar. Like she'd said them before. Echo struggled to hold on to her memories, but they dispersed like wisps of mist. "Why can't I remember anything? I feel like I'm in a void, just floating. I don't like it. Look at me." She stuck out her hand. "I look like a ghost."

"Ah. That's because you hover between both realms. This is your astral form, while your corporeal self remains in the mortal world."

"Then send me back."

Roth waved his hand, and an image appeared before her. "This should help with your homesickness."

She peered at it and smiled. "I know this place... I think."

Streetlights winked. The night was hot, steamy. She could almost feel the heat rising off the asphalt to wrap around her. People hustled by, and a cacophony of sounds filled the streets. Greedily, she absorbed it all.

Then she stilled, a lone figure snagging her attention. A man walked down the street, his head bent, his dark blue hair tied at his nape. Silver earrings glinted in the streetlights. The short sleeves of his tee revealed an intricate tattoo on his biceps.

"Ah, a bad boy—" Frowning, she leaned forward.

The man looked up, revealing one of the most compelling faces she'd ever seen. She sensed the raw grief beneath his icy façade.

Her chest suddenly hurt, and she rubbed it, her other hand reaching out to him. Instead, she distorted the image, and it dissipated.

"So much sorrow," she whispered. "What happened to him?"

Roth manifested a tall stool and sat down, tucking his wings close to his body, but still they swept the floor. He leaned forward and braced his arms on his knees. Shrugged. "What happens to most people when they lose loved ones? It's the circle of life."

Her mouth opened then closed at such callousness from an angel, when all she wanted to do was comfort the man. How could anyone witness such pain and do nothing?

"I am an angel," he answered her unspoken question. "I don't do emotions."

She looked at him with pity. "I feel sorry for you then."

He eyed her contemplatively then shifted on his seat. "All right. If I do this for you, if I speak to him and give him peace, will you do something for me?"

"Why is there always a price for a favor?" she asked, setting the candlestand back on the table.

"You are selfless, little one, but nothing in life is ever free," he told her. "Especially for those of us who live forever. As you now do."

She did? Then she pushed that thought aside for now. "Okay, what do you want?"

"First, finish the nectar in the glass. Second, remain what you were meant to be."

"The Healer of the Veils," she murmured. "How

come I know that, but I can't remember anything else?"

"Because you now dwell in the Celestial Realm. Human memories fade here," he explained. "You were born to be the *Curantii*. Only the descendant of Zarias can take that role. Your ancestor saw to that." His expression changed ever so slightly, as though he disliked talking about it.

"Why would Zarias do that?"

"Seems like I have my work cut out for me, to teach you about your stubborn ancestors. First, I need your answer. Eshana?"

"Why do you call me that?" she asked, frowning again.

"It's the name you were given at birth."

"Oh..."

"Your answer?"

"Okay."

"Just like that?"

She thought for a second about the man in the image she'd just seen. Why he tugged at her heart, she had no idea. Besides, if she was born to be this Healer, how bad could it be? "Yes."

Roth nodded. "All right then. Rest now. As the *Curantii* you will need your strength."

"Who are you?"

The hint of amusement was back in his eyes. "Now you ask."

"Yes, because I'm curious why one like you would bribe me."

He was silent for a long moment before he said, "You mortals are unique. To answer your question, I am *the* one with the power to thwart the Fates. I am the Ultimate Fate. Your fate, Eshana, has been, as Michael would say, 'screwed over once too often.' He asked me to rescind your destiny as the Healer."

"Who?"

"The Archangel."

"Right." She rolled her eyes. "Why would *Michael* ask you to change *my* fate?"

His amethyst eyes burned fiercely. "Because when an injustice is done, it screws with the natural order of things. That's when I step in." He flowed to his feet, and the stool vanished. "Remember our deal."

"So, did Michael have to do you a favor, too, for asking you to do this?"

"But, of course."

***

Aethan laced his fingers through Echo's. Three weeks had passed since she'd been shot. Three weeks of sheer hell. He'd been prepared to end his life with hers on that fateful day. But Michael had intervened, telling him to listen.

And then he heard it. A heartbeat, so faint, only his exceptional hearing could pick it up. But his happiness was short-lived. Since that day, Echo had remained in a coma, her wound showing no signs of healing. Dark, thread-like veins leading from the lesion on her chest had crept over her breast and into her neck.

"Come back to me, Echo, wherever you are. Gods, I miss you." He pressed a kiss to her cool palm. "Sometimes...I hear the sound of your laughter...your voice, I turn around, but it's all a shadow of you, you're not there." His eyes burned with tears. "Echo, do you hear me? Squeeze my hand so I know you're still in there. Please."

Nothing.

Just unending silence in his soul, where she once blazed, an iridescent light, full of life.

The door opened, and Michael strode in, dressed in patrolling gear. "How are you holding up?"

Resentment churned to a vicious rage in him. Aethan placed Echo's hand back under the covers and faced the Archangel. "Do I look like I give a rat's ass about pleasantries? It's been three weeks. Three fuck—" He gritted his teeth. He didn't want to lose his temper in front of his comatose mate. "Her wound shows no sign of healing. It deteriorates. You were supposed to find out where she is and bring her back. You came back with nothing."

"She lives. That is what matters."

Bastard! His fucking prophecies were all that he cared about!

Aethan stalked out of the room. He had to get away from Michael before he did something regrettable.

Chapter 39

Aethan jerked upright, uneasy now. He'd fallen asleep in his chair. Something he'd never done while sitting with Echo. The passing months had left him raw with suppressed emotions, edgy enough to go back into the gym and pound the heavy bag until his knuckles were raw.

He dragged a hand over his face and stopped, his eyes narrowing on the strange male sprawled in an armchair on the opposite side of the bed. The fact he could bypass the protection wards of the castle meant he was on the "approved list", but Aethan trusted no one.

"Who the hell are you?" he growled, his tone deadly voice as he pushed to his feet.

Undeterred by Aethan's behavior, the stranger remained slouched in his seat. "That's not important. I wanted to see the female in the flesh. The one you fight so hard to keep, even though she remains in another world."

He rose, unfolding his gleaming black wings edged

with ice as he strolled over to Echo's side, the movements creating a light breeze around them, stirring the ends of Echo's hair.

His amethyst gaze lingered on her for a moment then came back to Aethan. "Let her leave this realm, and I will grant you anything you desire."

In a flash, Aethan stepped between male and the bed, his fingers fisted, power rioting beneath his skin, his every word etched in ice. "Get. The. Fuck. Away. From. Her."

The angel clasped his hands and watched him carefully, undeterred by his anger. "You sure there's nothing you want?"

Childish laughter filled the room. *'A'than!'* The voice caught at his heart.

Bastard.

"If you mean Ariana, I loved my sister. It took me three thousand years, and the love of my mate, to realize it was an accident. Now, get out."

"Very well. But first, I have a little story for you. So why don't you reel in that 'bad boy' attitude and sit?" The angel sat again, his wings spread over the armrests.

"I am Roth—" He paused for a moment, amusement crossing his face. "My name is Marmaroth. I will keep it brief. Eons ago, a male was born with a unique ability. While all immortals have their powers, he was special, born in the fury of whitefire."

Aethan stiffened, but he remained, didn't at the side of the bed. "You want to spout that bullshit, find someone else to listen to you."

"Sit down, Empyrean. I made a promise and I will keep it." Roth waved his hand back to the armchair Aethan had vacated. "The boy, despite his powers,

Georgia Lyn Hunter

didn't know his capabilities. None did, until the day a tragic event occurred. But you see, herein things take on a different context."

Aethan's teeth ground down, didn't move.

"He wasn't allowed near his sister, for one important reason. Had he done so, he would have allowed a cataclysmic prophecy to unfold. He had to leave Empyrea, Allatus had to make sure you were banished."

Aethan felt as if his knees would cave under the weight of his anger, a chill icing him to the marrow of his bones. "You're telling me my sister had to die, so I could be banished?"

"When Ariana died, had you used your powers, you would have given her life again, and *you* would have stayed, never to leave Empyrea."

Aethan shook his head, nothing computing through the shock seeping through him. "What the hell are you talking about?"

"You were born in the flames of God's Wrath. Not only do you take life, but you can give it, too. Only you must want it."

Fuck! This wasn't happening. He paced to the window, dragging his fingers through his untethered hair as the angel continued. "When a person dies, if in that split second you intervene with your powers, you can give them life again. And that is a gift none have, save you—"

"Then why couldn't I save my mate, if I have this amazing gift?" He slammed a palm against the wall near the window and spun back to the angel. "She hovers between here and wherever the hell the other place is."

"You, alone, keep her chained to this realm. She

needs time for the transition to complete."

Aethan's brow furrowed as he strode back. "What transition?"

"When her heart stopped beating, you brought her back. Your touch is one of immortality. Had she not died, she would have lived a very long but *mortal* life."

Felled by the angels words, Aethan dropped into his vacated armchair.

She would be immortal. She wouldn't die. Wouldn't leave him.

He reached for Echo's hand and pressed her palm to his lips. Gods, how much longer must he endure living without her? Truth was, he'd wait eternity if it meant she'd come back to him.

He heard Roth say something else, but he didn't care. He just wanted him gone.

The angel stood.

"Wait," Aethan said, stopping him. "Ariana?" He had to know about his sister.

"You had to leave to fulfill your destiny, and Ariana's fate lay elsewhere." But the room was filled with a sense of sublimity. "There is always a price to be paid. Your mother knew that when she *fell*."

Roth set something on the bed covers, a pearlescent feather that had streaks of silver running through it. A feather exactly like the one his father had in remembrance of his mother's wings.

"My mother's feather. Where did you get this?"

"Didn't say it was hers, did I?" The angel shimmered and disappeared.

Aethan picked up the feather and the scent of wildflowers swept through him in a gentle caress to his soul, as if his sister knew he'd get the feather. "Ariana," he whispered in a choked voice, a little smile starting, his pain, his guilt for his sister's death finally healing.

Ariana had taken his mother's place in the Celestial Realm.

***

Five months later...

It was the darkest hour before dawn. The coolness of the morning would soon vanish as the summer sun rose.

Exhausted, Aethan declined joining the others for their after-patrol meal. He trudged up the stairs and walked into his bedroom. Shrugging off his coat, he tossed it over a chair and willed the candles in the room to flare to life. He preferred their soft, healing light to the artificial ones these days.

Lila brought the candles over when she visited Echo. She and Kira came by daily to check on her progress. He had hoped, with them around, she'd respond somehow, but nothing so far. Even her guardian had come, except it was always when they were out on patrol.

Aethan glanced at the bed as he headed to the dressing room, and his heart stopped.

The bed was empty.

He wheeled around, scanning the dimly lit room. "Echo?"

Terror filling him, he rushed to the dressing room. She wasn't there. He sped back to the bedroom, scanned for her, then stilled. The bathroom door was shut and locked. He strode over, slowly, he laid a trembling hand on the door, and willed it to unlock and open.

There, in the center of the bathroom she stood, wrapping a bath towel around her slender form, water dripping down her face. Her hair had lost its choppy style. Longer now, it brushed her shoulders.

She turned, and her eyes widened in alarm when she saw him.

"I'm sorry—I'm sorry," she said quickly. "I wanted a shower, but I didn't know whose room this was and—hey-*hey*! What are you doing? You can't come in here!"

He stopped then. The sight of her brought him to his knees. He shook his head, barely able to see her at the tears in his eyes.

She stepped back warily, keeping a safe distance from him, despite the fact he was on his knees. "Er, who are you?"

Her words slammed into him as if someone had taken a tire iron to his gut, shattering his joy.

Slowly, Aethan rose to his feet, his jaw hardening. He'd waited long, agonizing months for her, only to have her return with no memory of him?

No way in hell would he wait another second.

"I am your mate. If you think for one moment I'm going to go through the whole fucking dance to claim you again, you are mistaken."

"I don't know what you're talking about." She glared at him with her unforgettable, bicolored eyes, her fist clasping the ends of the towel. "You'd better leave, or…or..."

"Or what?" His smile grew grim. "You'll yell?"

She looked around frantically. Her gaze settled on the obsidian dagger lying on the marble counter. For some insane reason, he had left the thing at her bedside while she'd been in a comatose sleep.

"Go ahead, take it. Stab me if you want. Anything from you is better than the months of silent hell I've had to live through."

Her brow furrowed in confusion. Aethan grasped her gently by her arms, didn't want to frighten her, but unable to not hold her.

"Let me go." She struggled, her small fists beating at him. He picked her up and set her on the counter. "Who are you?" She shoved at his chest, keeping him back. "Why are you doing this?"

"Here." He put the obsidian in her hand. "Your dagger, if you think I'll hurt you."

She stared blankly at the weapon. Then he spread her legs and moved in between them. She grabbed the towel at the bottom, preventing it from opening.

Her confusion made his pain more acute. He shouldn't be angry, but how could she forget him? "Gods, Echo, how can you not remember me?" The words were wrenched from deep form his soul.

"Echo? My name's Eshana."

She didn't remember her—

Fuck it. He wanted it all back, every smile, every look. The sparkle and light that had once filled his soul—they belonged to him. He went for broke and captured her mouth with his.

She struggled, pushing at him. The dagger dropped from her hand and fell to the floor with a dull clang. He gave her no quarter, determined to destroy the barriers surrounding her mind with a soul-searing kiss.

She went dead still.

And then that luscious mouth moved beneath his, seeking his, driving him out of his mind. Her hands went from pushing to sliding around his neck. She scooted closer, wrapping her legs around him. Her heart beat hard against his chest. All those anguished, lonely months fell away as the iridescent sparks of the mating bond slipped back into place, and he reveled at her warm presence in his soul again.

"Aethan?" she whispered, breaking their kiss. Tears shimmered in her eyes as she touched his face in reverence.

He nodded. His breathing jagged and raw, his vision blurred, he struggled to speak. "Saying 'I missed you' feels like the understatement of my life. But I missed so damn much," he rasped.

She blinked her teary eyes. "I missed you, too." Her smile wobbled. "Only, I didn't know why. There was this hole, this emptiness in me. But now—" Her arms tightened around his neck. "Now, I feel you again."

He pressed his face into her nape and inhaled her unforgettable scent.

She stroked his hair. "Aethan?"

He could hardly get the words out from a throat gone tight. "Yeah?"

"What happened to me?"

He pulled back, his expression fierce, wanting to resurrect then kill the bastard. "You were shot. You died in my arms. Never again place yourself in danger like that. Understand?"

"I couldn't let you die, but *you* brought me back," she whispered, pressing her wet face against his.

A deep sigh left him. "Shh, *me'morae.* What matters now is you're here."

"All this time of not knowing why I felt so empty."

"I'll never let you feel that way again," he promised.

She looked up at him, her face streaked with tears. "You said I died. What happened?"

He wiped her wet cheeks with his thumb. "Your heart stopped beating. I refused to let you go. I used my powers and jolted you back. You fell into a deep sleep. Seems you were in another realm."

"I remember." She told him what she recalled about being in the Celestial Realm and about the angel who had changed her fate. Aethan scowled, when she mentioned Roth. The bastard had tried to take her from him.

"He's not all bad," she said as if sensing his ire with the angel. "Anyway, he told me my history, about Zarias being the leader of the Watchers…seems I have a big, bad angel as an ancestor. No wonder I can't keep away from scary, badass immortals," she teased.

Snorting, Aethan picked her up, and carried her to the turret living room. He sat down in the leather recliner and settled her on his lap, absorbing the solid feel of her slight weight against him.

Echo curled into him, and through the windows, they watched the sun rise above the trees on the estate as a new day began.

Just like our life, he thought.

"Aethan?"

"Yeah?"

"Roth mentioned something about Michael asking him to change my fate—" She met his gaze. "Then Roth showed me a vision of you. I didn't know it was you, but I couldn't let it go. I saw the sadness in your eyes, could feel your grief, and I wanted to help you. He agreed, but in return for his help, I had to remain the Healer."

He went motionless. Shock surging through him at what she'd done. What she'd given up.

"You gave up your chance to be normal to help me—why? You didn't know me then."

"My heart did," she whispered. "I couldn't bear your pain. I wanted you to have peace."

Aethan simply stared at her. Roth, the damn, manipulating bastard knew what he was doing when he showed her the vision. But it completely floored Aethan that Echo was still drawn to him even then.

"Ah, *me'morae. Me'et'ah.* My love. My life." He rubbed his face against hers. "I just want to hold you until I'm convinced you'll never leave me again."

"I'm not going anywhere. As I understand it, we have eternity together." She pulled back and gave him a seductive smile.

Gods, he missed this so much. Missed her smile.

He couldn't stop the answering one from tugging at his mouth. "Yes, we do."

Then he took her mouth in a slow, heated kiss...

Epilogue

"So this is the earthly realm? Not very appealing, is it?" The droll tone broke the quietness of early morning.

Michael glanced at the angel standing next to him. To humans, Roth appeared mortal, albeit a very tall one with his wings concealed and his immense power leashed. "We're standing in an alley, Roth, and you think this is it? This is Earth?"

The reek of decaying trash and piss layered the dingy place with its looming buildings. What did he expect? A fragrant garden? A slight smile tipped up the angel's mouth, but he said nothing, his gaze on the lewd graffiti sprawled across the grimy wall opposite. He angled his head, studying the crudely illustrated scene. "Why am I here, Old One?"

Michael snorted at the name. Roth probably existed way before Michael did, not that the angel would confirm it. "How exactly did you get Eshana to remain the *Curantii*?"

"She wanted something. We made a deal."

"Right, you did." Michael's tone filled with sarcasm. He folded his arms over his chest, his attention on a scrawny dog sniffing along the dirt-encrusted wall opposite him and finally asked what he wanted to know. "Anything on her siblings?"

Roth pulled his gaze from the artwork and frowned. "They both died in the mugging along with her parents, you know this."

Michael bit back his irritation. Talking to Roth was a damn pain in the ass at times. "I know her parents died, but there is no markers for the dead kids at the cemetery. Why?"

"Really Archangel, you've lived too long on this plane, and have become too suspicious. You see things that are not there. They are no more."

Michael knew Roth was only stating what was found at the crime scene at the time of Eshana's parents and siblings' death.

"So *you* have no idea who's taken them either?" When Roth said nothing, Michael shook his head.

A dull gleam on the asphalt snagged his attention. Pushing away from the wall, Michael picked up the tarnished coin and absently scratched the grime. A glint of silver sparkled in the moonlight. *Life did thrive even in the bleakest of times...*

"The boy, Roth, where is he?"

"Dead."

"Her twin?"

"Alive," he finally conceded.

"Dammit, Roth! They should have stayed together—"

"Destiny decreed otherwise. Her sister would have died from her injuries, I made use of the situation and put her safely elsewhere. The Healer had to survive alone."

Michael swore silently. "This was your plan all along? You separated her from her sibling, made sure she had no one, then when it was time to go to the Celestial Realm, she'd do so without protesting and free will takes a back seat, because you knew who Eshana was!"

Roth shrugged. "It wasn't clear then, but when I saw her eyes, I had an inkling."

"You're one cold damn bastard—"

"We do not do emotions, Archangel. She gave me what I wanted of her own free will."

Anger rolled through Michael. He shoved his clenched fists into his jeans pocket as his Guardian oath surged to right an injustice. But it was in the past and he could do nothing now. Eshana was safe. At least she had no memories of her siblings.

A vagrant shuffled past, dragging a huge garbage bag behind him. He eyed them warily then hobbled away, leaving behind the ripe odor of unwashed body.

Roth grimaced, watching the vagrant settle for the night in a recessed doorway farther down the alley. "Do they not take a bathe?"

"Yes, they all have hot water waiting at home for them."

"You've become a little…temperamental, Michael," Roth drawled, Michael's caustic comment sliding off him. "Just let it be. All will work out as it should."

Yeah, right. Michael only hoped when Eshana found out the truth, she was still in the same charitable mind. As for her mate—no, Aethan would doubtless use that deadly power of his to exact vengeance on his mate's behalf, considering what she'd suffered in her young life because of a damn game.

"And no, you cannot negotiate another deal. I have the one favor I need from you." Roth stepped away from the wall. "So, old friend, show me a little of this world you now call home."

"Whatever the hell game you're playing, Roth, I hope it doesn't bite you in the ass," Michael muttered and walked past him. "C'mon then. Remember, games can be controlled up there, but down here? Things don't always follow the plan. This is a mortal world. And free will prevails…"

THE END…

Also by Georgia Lyn Hunter

FALLEN GUARDIANS

Absolute Surrender #1
Echo, Mine #1.5
Breaking Fate #2
Tangled Sin (Standalone)
Guardian Unraveled #3
For You, I Will #3.5
Heart's Inferno #4
Shattered Dawn #5

WARLORDS OF Empyrea

Darkness Undone #1
Winter's Awakening #2
Warlord's Storm #3

CONTEMPORARY: PLAYERS TO MEN

Breathless #1
Impossible You #2

About the Author

Georgia Lyn Hunter loves to create characters who'll take you to the far and beyond to unforgettable adventures, steamy encounters and heart-stopping love stories...

She grew up in the sultry climate of South Africa and currently lives in the Middle East with her family. An avid reader from a young age, she devoured every book she got her hands on. When she's not writing or plotting her next novel, she loves trolling flea markets and buying things she'd never use (because they're so pretty,) traveling, painting, and being with her wonderfully supportive family.

And there you have it, all the boring stuff.

Want more? Then subscribe to her new release:

Newsletter: http://eepurl.com/bpHvET

Website: www.georgialynhunter.com

FB: https://www.facebook.com/GeorgiaLynHunter

Twitter: https://twitter.com/GeorgialynH

Made in the USA
Las Vegas, NV
27 December 2021

39438802R10267